MUSIC UNDER THE SOVIETS

This book is No. 11 of the *Studies* of the
Research Program of the U.S.S.R. and
No. 32 of Praeger Publications
in Russian History and World Communism.

The preparation of this study was
made possible by a grant from the
Research Program on the U.S.S.R.
(East European Fund, Inc.)

MUSIC UNDER THE SOVIETS

The Agony of an Art

by

ANDREY OLKHOVSKY

GREENWOOD PRESS, PUBLISHERS

WESTPORT, CONNECTICUT

Library of Congress Cataloging in Publication Data

Olkhovsky, Andrey Vasilyevich, 1900-
Music under the Soviets.

Reprint of the ed. published for the Research Program on the U.S.S.R. by Praeger, New York, which was issued as no. 11 in series: Studies of the Research Program of the U.S.S.R. and no. 32 in series: Praeger publications in Russian history and world Communism.
Bibliography: p.
Includes indexes.
1. Music--Russia--1917- 2. Composers, Russian. I. Title. II. Series: East European Fund. Research Program on the U.S.S.R. Studies, no. 11.
ML300.5.04 1974 780'.947 74-20341
ISBN 0-8371-7856-8

A Greenwood Archival Edition—reprint editions of classic works in their respective fields, printed in extremely limited quantities, and manufactured to the most stringent specifications.

Originally published in 1955 by Frederick A. Praeger, New York for the Research Program on the U.S.S.R.

Reprinted in 1975 by Greenwood Press
A division of Congressional Information Service, Inc.
88 Post Road West, Westport, Connecticut 06881

Library of Congress Catalog Card Number 74-20341

ISBN 0-8371-7856-8

Printed in the United States of America

10 9 8 7 6 5 4 3 2

Dedicated
to my constant companions
on the roads of life--
my wife and son

A Note on the Author

Andrey Vasilyevich Olkhovsky, born 1900; musicologist, composer and pedagogue. Received his musical education in Kharkov and Leningrad (composer's diploma and degree of Candidate of Art Historical Science).

For sixteen years taught history and theory of music in Leningrad, Kharkov and (from 1934 to 1942) in the Kiev Conservatory, where he was head of the Department of History and Theory of Music. Confirmed in the rank of professor in 1934.

Author of a number of books and articles on musical subjects, and composer of various musical works, including three symphonies.

Left the Soviet Union in 1942; has lived in the United States of America since 1949, studying and teaching. Member of the Association of American Musicologists.

ACKNOWLEDGMENTS

The writing of a book on a subject so complex and widely ramified as Soviet music, it need hardly be said, is a task requiring the active help and sympathy of many persons. The author takes this opportunity of expressing his gratitude to a number of people whose assistance contributed in some degree to the composition of the book.

The author is conscious first of all of a profound debt to his teacher and unforgotten friend, Academician Boris V. Asaf'yev (Igor' Glebov), whose work, counsel and assistance have guided him up to the present time.

To his former students at the Kiev Conservatory and his close association with them the author is indebted for an insight into the nature of the new generation of Soviet musicians. It is his sincere wish that the time may come when some of these former students may read his book in a world of freedom and peace and comprehend the tragic fate of art under a totalitarian system.

The realization of the volume is the result of the manifold assistance rendered to the author by the Research Program on the U.S.S.R. In addition to his gratitude to the Research Program as a whole, the author wishes to express his thanks to Dr. Alexander Dallin, first Associate Director of the Research Program, whose help made possible the writing of the book. Miss Marina Salvin (Mrs. Lawrence Finkelstein), formerly Assistant Director of the Research Program, helped the author by obtaining material for his work, and in other ways.

The original translation of the text was made by Mr. Aaron Avshalomoff. Mr. Louis Jay Herman translated the foreword and some supplementary passages. To them the author expresses his thanks.

To the present Associate Director of the Research Program on the U.S.S.R., Mr. Robert Slusser, the author is deeply indebted for the editing of his book. Other members of the Research Program staff who contributed to the volume are Mr. Peter Dornan, who checked all the references and compiled the bibliography; Miss Barbara Chapman and Miss Anna Vakar, who compiled the index of composers and their works; and Miss Margaret Moore, Executive Secretary of the Research Program, who read the entire text, with beneficial results, before publication.

For permission to use copyrighted material the author and publishers are grateful to Professor George S. Counts and Houghton Mifflin Co., for the translation of the Central Committee decree on music of 1948, which was originally published in *The Country of the Blind: The Soviet System of Mind Control,* by Professor Counts and Nucia Lodge; the Columbia University Press for the translation of the Central Committee decree of 1932, which appeared originally in *The Proletarian Episode in Soviet Literature,* by Edward J. Brown; Harvard University Press for a short quotation from Igor Stravinsky's *Poetics of Music*; and *The Saturday Review* for the statement by Mr. Stravinsky on music which is included in the foreword, and which was first printed in the article "The Composer Tells How" by J. Douglas Cook in the June 26, 1954 number of *The Saturday Review.*

Special thanks are due to Mr. Leo Gruliow, Editor of the *Current Digest of the Soviet Press,* for permission to make use, in Annex D, of a number of translations of Soviet articles which first appeared in that publication. For providing advance copies of texts and translations on Soviet music the author and publishers are grateful to Mr. Fred Holling, Associate Editor of the *Current Digest.*

The author wishes to thank Mr. Peter Odarchenko of the Library of Congress, who provided material and checked references, Mr. and Mrs. Andrew Fessenko, of the same library, for their help, and Mr. Robert E. Hoag of the St. Paul library for his assistance in locating material.

A. O.

FOREWORD

Not so long ago, not only in the West but in the Soviet Union itself, no one had any idea of just what "Soviet music" was, what its special characteristics were, and what claim it had to a history of its own. But now, since approximately the mid-1930's, not only has the concept of Soviet music begun to be firmly established in musical journalism, even in the West, but the practice of Soviet music has also gradually emerged.

It is natural that the question of what Soviet music really is, what its qualities and historical role are, should increasingly attract the attention of all who are concerned with the development of musical creation and man's artistic culture as a whole.

Superficially, Soviet music can be defined as the musical practice of the territorial expanse controlled by the Soviet regime, that is, by the totalitarian dictatorship of the Communist Party of the Soviet Union. In essence, however, it is nothing less than the musical policy of that regime, a policy which aims at the "reconstruction" of not only the historically developed musical forms but the essence of music itself as artistic creation. In reality that policy is an attempt to utilize the vast, rich tradition of Russian music, and of world musical culture as well, for purposes which have nothing in common with music as artistic creation.

The concept of Soviet music, like its theory and practice, took shape during the period of Soviet historical development which is linked with the name of Stalin, beginning with his final crushing of the intra-Party opposition in the 1930's and ending with his death in March 1953. It was during those years that Soviet music acquired its peculiar features, developed its most characteristic distinguishing marks, and determined the paths of its evolution. In those years, too—a particularly important fact—it acquired that rigidity which has kept it unchanged to the present time, as well as its single creative method, that of "socialist realism," which actually meant its complete loss of creative freedom and total subordination to the aims and tasks of Bolshevik political propaganda. And however much some students of contemporary Soviet developments may try to detect in the "new course" of the period of post-Stalinist "collective leadership" a movement toward democratization of Soviet life in general and Soviet artistic creation in particular, their efforts will lead to nothing. A change in the state of Soviet music can come about only through the complete and unconditional divorcement of music from politics, and that in turn is inconceivable without the profound regeneration, or more probably the complete transformation, of the regime, which does not recognize artistic freedom as the indispensable prerequisite of artistic creation.

The best proof of the immutability of Soviet music policy is provided by a recent article by one of the leading Soviet composers, Aram Khachaturian.[1] Unquestionably inspired by the authorities with a view of creating an illusion of democratization, this article broaches with some temerity the question of the necessity of creative freedom for the development of Soviet music. It was understood in just that way in the West and was therefore immediately followed by a "refutation" by the author himself, who hastened to publish a second article in the English-language Moscow magazine *News*, which is especially designed for foreign consumption.[2] In the latter article Khachaturian sought to convince the reader that the first article had been misunderstood and that Soviet music was not at all in need of freedom, since it enjoyed independence in the achievement of its unchanging goals. Thus illusions about the perfect

1. "*O tvorcheskoi smelosti i vdokhnovenii*" [On Creative Boldness and Inspiration], *Sovetskaya muzyka* [Soviet Music], November, 1953, No. 11, pp. 7-13. (Translation in *Current Digest of the Soviet Press*, Dec. 30, 1953, Vol. V, No. 46, pp. 3-5).

2. "The Truth About Soviet Music and Soviet Composers," *News*, No. 5 (64), March 1, 1954, pp. 17-19.

creative system of Soviet music are propagated for the benefit of the outside world, whereas, in reality, it remains as before, merely a means for the political expansion of the Soviet regime.

To expose, so far as possible, the true nature of Soviet music is the task of this study. It is a complex task, not only because of its novelty and many-sidedness, but also because of the complexity which Soviet music reveals in its relation to Soviet life as a whole. However, it is a task which should not be deferred and one which, in the author's opinion, is a cardinal and decisive one in contemporary musicology.

Proponents of the view that the source of life lies only on the other side of the Iron Curtain will, of course, cast doubt upon the honesty of the author's intention. For them, the boundaries of good and evil are wholly determined by criteria of political collaboration. The book, therefore, is addressed to the reader for whom the distinction between true art and political intrigue, between passionate concern with the fate of artistic creation and "the logic of the knout," has not yet been obliterated. The author will be content if his book serves to deepen such a reader's anxiety for the preservation of life's essential values.

The finest gift of life, after all, is the ability to dream of something better. To us it seems that Igor Stravinsky was right when he said, "I love music, therefore I create music,"[3] rather than the Central Committee of the Communist Party of the Soviet Union, in its conviction that a truly Communist policy requires the Soviet composer to write music only for the purpose of helping to enslave the minds, the will and the feelings of the peoples under its sway.

It is about these things that this book is concerned.

St. Paul
July 1954

Andrey Olkhovsky

---

3. As quoted in Cook, J. Douglas, "The Composer Tells How," *Saturday Review*, Vol. XXXVII, No. 26, June 26, 1954, p. 43.

ERRATA

page	line	reads	should read
25	6 from top	sole	role
41	note 18	*Ibid.*	Asaf'yev, *op. cit.*
67	7 from bottom	*Outlines*	*Essays*
78	11 " "	of possible.	of the possible.
158	1 " top	of Russian	of the Russian
166	1 " "	Sveshnikov	Svechnikov
209	12 " "	provide	provides
250	7-8 " bottom	*Thoughts of the Black Sea*	*Black Sea Ballad*
265	11 " top	style."	style";
265	12 " "	influence	influences
267	note 1	ideologist	ideologists
280	5 from bottom	"O opere	"Ob opere
281	7 " top	Ingushi and Chechen	Ingush and Chechens
288	11 " bottom	youths	youths.
404	13 " top	Ukraïnskaya	Ukraïns'ka
410	9 " bottom	*Tenth Symphony*, 263,	*Tenth Symphony*, 236,
413	13 " "	*Thoughts of the Black Sea*	*Black Sea Ballad*
418	3 " top	Communist Part	Communist Party
424	1 " bottom	*Rad'yanska Muzyka*	*Radyans'ka muzyka*
425	6 " top	Revuts'kyi, Dmitri	Revuts'kyi, Dmytro

TABLE OF CONTENTS

TABLE OF CONTENTS

MUSIC UNDER THE SOVIETS

PART I

Introduction

ART AND LIFE

The historical destinies of the arts are not accidental. Like life itself, they are subject to definite laws. Notwithstanding the differences among them they all preserve a unity which connects them with one another and with life. It is this mutual interconnection between art and life which determines the essential nature of art and enables the artist to create an integral and generalized image of existence from the heterogeneous impressions of life.

But human experience transferred to the sphere of art is inevitably recreated. Preserving the fundamental content of life, art gives it that exalted and refined coloring which makes it not a mere reflection of drab reality but a kind of incarnate vision, a realization of man's hopes and aspirations. In the ability of the artist to give to the media of art a sense and meaning other than that which belongs to them in ordinary life lies the essence of artistic creation. With his creative instinct a genuine artist seizes the truly progressive tendency of the aspirations of his times, separating it from the manifestations of daily life. The ability to create effective artistic imagery, to present one's personal experience, the most subtle movement of the spirit, and to convey the typical characteristics of this hardly perceptible reality—such an ability is the very essence of art, particularly of music, the art which, more than any other, is capable of deep and subtle generalizations and which is called upon, as is perhaps no other art, to express the turbulent power of human passions freely and without external constraint.

It is in music especially that there lies an opportunity for the direct development of the forces of life, unimpeded by intermediary stages, visual or tangible. In music the human will finds its characteristic expression; in the fluid succession of its sonorities the fullness of feeling is embodied, and the uttermost profundities of the mind are reflected in the beauty of the blending and alteration of its consonances.

Joy and sorrow—these are the poles between which stretches the shoreless ocean of music; its waves are tinged with various shades of joy or sorrow and no matter how much he might want to, the artist who is called upon to create music cannot hide in his creation that which he has experienced and felt deeply in his life—he cannot completely achieve concealment. He lived, therefore his life contained both sorrow and joy; and the more intensely he lived, the more glowing his music will be, for the expressive power of music is its vital essence. That is why musical compositions —whether they are a confession of the soul, the thoughtful aspirations of the intelligence, or the picturesque fancy of the imagination—captivate us by their power and compel us to relive that which the composer himself experienced when he arranged his thoughts and feelings in musical images.

Throughout the history of its development art has been frequently confronted with the question whether it should represent everything just as it exists in life, and in answer to this question art has always given one and the same reply: truth in art in this sense would be mere vulgarity. The only truth in art is that which corresponds to the ideal image created by the artist's imagination. It is for this reason alone that art is capable of translating life into the controlled world of poetry.

Artistic creation is convincing only when it serves as the medium by which the artist tells of what he has seen and felt, of his experiences, thoughts and feelings—in short, when he speaks to us of life. But the life, the reality observed by the artist is an entirely new reality which had simply not existed previously. Genuine art is remarkable for its ability to express a nonexistent world, a world, however, which is not only better than that which does exist but which also has a closer resemblance to truth.

In appearance these nonexistent creative worlds often closely resemble something ordinary, something unembellished by the creative imagination, something which can be observed and experienced in "real life." Then the listener is enraptured, as for example by the "realism" of Tchaikovsky. Who has not experienced at some time the impact of his *Fourth* or *Sixth Symphonies?* Yet the "realism" of such works is a special, artistic, realism which fixes its gaze not on the "substance of things seen" but on what lies behind and beyond. Such realism has little resemblance to ordinary everyday reality; it is related to some other reality which does not coincide at all with the first.

The wisdom of genuine art lies in its knowledge that our visible world is scanty and dull and that it is necessary to revive and enrich it with new worlds. It is only the artist who is *free* in his vision, however, who can build these new and imaginary worlds from the depths of existence.

To create genuine art, a sincere and unconquerable faith in the life-affirming force of man is necessary, a faith in the possibility of a harmonious solution of life's contradictions. Was it not due to this fact that art has always wisely maintained the position of imitating nothing and inheriting nothing except artistic truth? And was it not due to this fact that it has always striven towards the liberation of man from whatever restrained his powers, his progress towards the triumph of reason and freedom, towards light? Was it not due to this fact that the best artists have always been courageous experimentalists who elicited from nature, one by one, the secrets of its action on man; that they were ardent thinkers who understood the meaning of philosophy and its majestic concept of the regularity of existence?

"Knowledge and virtue": Socrates' double formula impregnates not only every active philosophy but also the art of modern times and thus ascribes to art the power of boundlessly elevating man, assimilating him to God. It is thanks to this that the marvellous, humanizing transformation of life into art and of art into life is possible. The ability of art to incorporate the most complex and profound emotional states is unique. That the habitual discords between the human will and reality can be reconciled; that imagination can meet reason, with thought illuminating the play of imagination and the forms of imagination coming to the assistance of thought—ethically real and esthetically justified; and that thought and imagination can finally merge into a single beauty—for all of this we are indebted to art. That is why man is and always will be drawn to it.

"For man to know and to believe at every moment," wrote Dostoyevsky in *The Possessed,* "that somewhere there already exists a quiet and fulfilled happiness, for each one and for everyone, is more necessary to him than his personal happiness. . . . The whole law of human existence is that man should always bow down before the infinitely great. If the people were to be deprived of the infinitely great, they would not live but would die in despair. Immensity and infinity are just as necessary for man as is that tiny planet on which he dwells."

MUSIC AND PROGRESS

Progress in music is the result of the accumulation of creative experience and knowledge handed down from generation to generation. Thus the evolution of music is a logical process resulting from the aggregate of the preceding experience of composers, performers and listeners. The consolidation of this heritage gives rise to new creative problems, to solve which musicians of various countries contribute their strength and their mastery of existing creative experience.

It is for this reason that the obvious attraction towards Western modernism in music manifested by a leading group of Soviet-dominated composers[1] (Prokof'yev, Shostakovich, Myaskovski, *et al.*) is not a matter of chance. There is nothing surprising and certainly nothing unnatural or irregular in the fact that the formation of a common creative style should have led to a common creative search. Such a coincidence of experience, artistic methods, ideas, means of expression, and musical thinking in general is a more or less natural consequence of the silent collaboration of musicians preoccupied with common creative problems. Artistic truth, like ethical truth, is one.

The progress of art, however, is not an immanent law of history. From time to time art, like mankind as a whole, falls below the level of civilized history. Then democracies suffer shipwreck, civilizations perish, humanitarian regimes fall, and savagery and barbarism revive; then it appears as though art is moving backwards. The history of mankind and the history of music, its component part, are subordinated not only to their own historical logic; their course is determined not only by the logic of causality but also by chance. It is to "chance"—not as the negation of causality but as the conjunction of two disconnected historical lines—that is due not only the appearance of creative personalities of genius or talent but also the retardation of creative development or the "reorientation" of the aims of art.

From the point of view of causality or historical logic a musical crisis like that experienced in the present age—one of the most severe in the entire history of music—represents an epoch when for the new circles of composers, performers and listeners not only the individual works of the past but also the accumulated vocabulary of sounds which underlie the musical experience of the preceding epoch, and with them the demands made upon music, have grown old and artificial. At such times, in the name of the "new truth in sounds," music casts aside everything superfluous, abstract and nonmusical, and a struggle begins for new sound combinations, new means of expression.

In those cases where the interference of extraneous forces, of "chance," paralyzes creative progress, however, as is particularly the case in the Soviet Union, the stimulus of creative ideas determined by the inner logic of the development of art and its accumulated historical experience becomes impossible. That is why Soviet policy in the field of music, which openly testifies to its hostility towards all courageous innovations, progress and elementary creative freedom in general, poses an urgent question not only to every contemporary musician but to everyone concerned with the destiny of music: has any evolution taken place in Russian music during recent years, the years which fall within the boundaries of the Soviet period? Has the creative level, the curve of its development, risen or fallen, and why?

SOVIET REALITY AND MUSIC

What is now generally called the "musical culture of the peoples of the U.S.S.R." or simply "Soviet music" is so intertwined with the policies of the Soviet state that to separate music from policy is simply impossible. When Soviet official sources speak of music they have in mind nothing but the art policy of the Soviet state; even highly specialized questions of musical form are often considered from the point of view of their political significance. It could hardly be otherwise in a country where "all branches of culture serve a sole purpose, the construction of communism," and where "music, like every other realm of ideology, is a matter of great socio-political significance."[2]

Yet music in the Soviet Union, to the extent that it has not ceased to function as an expression of the creative spirit and has not been transformed into a tool of political propaganda, is primarily determined by its own laws of formation and development. Besides, "Soviet music" as such is not the product of some extra-historical system of life but is nothing but a stage—possibly an artificially created stage—in the historical development of Russian music. Would it not be more correct, therefore, when speaking of Soviet music to have in mind the contemporary stage of Russian music, conditioned by those demands for life and creation which were shaped not by historical logic but by conditions imposed by the Soviet political system? The basic question here is the degree of freedom and independence which music enjoys from extraneous influences, especially political power controlled by the state apparatus. Herein lies the basic difference between "Soviet music" and the musical culture of free nations. Soviet musical life not only depends completely and manifoldly upon the state authority but in reality functions as a part of the government apparatus.

Nevertheless, Soviet experience shows that the totalitarian state has not discovered the secret of altering the irrational nature of man and art and that the very objects of planning, the Soviet people, can never be transformed into mere robots forever deprived of their personal creative aspirations and desires, which refuse to fit into any schemes. Hence the history of Soviet music is one of unceasing struggle between two irreconcilable principles, force and protest; a protest which may be silent and scarcely noticeable but which is nevertheless still not entirely subdued.

The development of Russian music thus outwardly appears to have been violently interrupted. Yet the art policy of the Soviet authorities, which has overturned the traditional concepts of the historical laws of the development of art and has replaced them by its own will, carries in itself the seeds of its own doom. Therefore the present attempt to liquidate Russian music constitutes only a crisis in its development and by no means its death.

There are times and circumstances when indulgence or an exaggerated tendency towards impartiality become dangerous and even pernicious "virtues." In our times they have become equivalent to complicity and negligence. When the existence of human culture is at stake there can be no indifference towards good and evil. To restrain one's anger and to lock oneself in a guarded and calculated egocentrism means to push art into a yawning abyss beyond which lies chaos; it means the loss of everything for which the best minds of the past and present wrote, thought, spoke and fought.

It might be supposed that the fact that Soviet-dominated music boasts such names as Prokof'yev, Myaskovski, Shostakovich, and Khachaturian—and many other excellent musicians who only by chance are little known in the West—could be considered a sufficient reason for being calm and awaiting with confidence the future of Soviet music. Such an attitude, however, would be extremely naive. What is taking place in the Soviet Union, in every phase of life and creative work, is a ruthless life-and-death struggle. Often it is hidden in the secret recesses of the soul but it is merciless and uncompromising.

That which is called "Soviet music" in the proper sense of this term is not a fiction created by Soviet propaganda; it is a real fact, which must be taken into consideration by everyone who is not indifferent to the future destiny of music. The ominous significance of this "music," which forms an important and influential part of Soviet-dominated musical culture, is steadily growing. And no matter how much resistance Soviet-dominated composers may put up against the regime which is trying to transform music into a means for its own political ends and into an aspect of the "socialist way of life," the "new Soviet composer" and his "creations" are a threatening danger.

The Soviet press presents this "new music" as endowed with all kinds of virtue: high ideals, ethical force and perfect mastery. In the opinion of Soviet propaganda it represents the highest level of contemporary musical culture towards which all progressive music must inevitably gravitate. But in reality, unlike genuine art which is not limited in its creative freedom, "Soviet music" is based on a monochrome life invented by Soviet propaganda. A Soviet composer who willingly or unwillingly becomes a political tool is deprived of the opportunity for a creative vision of life in its totality, variety and animation and loses the possibility of choosing from this totality and variety the essence which constitutes its artistic meaning. In "Soviet art" there are neither the spark of illumination nor the infusion of courageous resolution which are the hallmarks of genuine style, the qualities without which the artist himself is nonexistent. Deprived of elementary creative freedom, the "new Soviet composers" have been transformed into craftsmen shamelessly indifferent to good and evil. "Soviet music," hailed by the Soviet government as a "new type of Soviet socialist music," is an emblem of the most dangerous impoverishment of humanity.

The gradual drying up of traditions, complete isolation from contemporary Western art, cultivation of the forms of "mass-art," intuition as the basis for creation with its dependence on folk music, the deterioration and eventually the complete atrophy of the sense for profound musical satisfaction—these are the consequences of the triumph of Soviet art policy in the field of music.

There is only one means of salvation from this creative and moral twilight: a warm heart, humanity and determination. Those who see where the Soviet music policy is leading cannot remain indifferent. True musicians must not take refuge in indifference and in prudent and calculating selfishness; they must be capable of anger in the service of mankind and art, firm in the conviction that genuine artistic values are an individual, not a collective achievement, and that true art is the product of the ability to study human nature and recreate its multiformity.

THE TECHNIQUE OF ENSLAVING SOVIET MUSIC

The first direct encounter between Soviet man and the Western world after more than twenty years of isolation, during the Second World War, showed the Communists that it was still as easy as ever for the Soviet citizen to adopt the advanced ideas of the West in preference to his faith in the "golden age of communism." The Party recognized the urgency of a policy previously followed to a lesser degree: the policy of walling off the Soviet Union from the temptations of the West at any price. In the West man is at least relatively free. Could such a situation be allowed in the Soviet Union? In the West the individual can and does change his lot by any means available to him. In the Soviet Union it is dangerous even to think of such freedom.

It is this policy which has caused the present devastation of Soviet culture, particularly of art as being most susceptible to progressive influences. The essence of the policy is the counterbalancing of the Soviet Union against the West in every field and the ceaseless repetition of the idea that absolutely no elements of Western culture are usable or acceptable in the Soviet Union. Even relative freedom of thought and of the revolutionary potential of man's creative consciousness are outlawed.

The principal role in this crusade, ostensibly against the West but in reality against spiritual freedom, was played by one of the pillars of the Politburo, Andrei A. Zhdanov.[3] To Zhdanov belongs the "honor" of having led the attack on literature (the "discussion" of the journals *Zvezda* and *Leningrad* and the works of Zoshchenko and Anna Akhmatova); on philosophy (the "discussion" of Aleksandrov's *History of Western European Philosophy*); and finally on music (the Party Central Committee's resolution on the opera *The Great Friendship* by V. Muradeli,[4] and the "First All-Union Congress of Soviet Composers" in 1948).

The methodology of the attack was presented by Zhdanov in an article in *Pravda* which said in part:

> If the inner content of the process of development as taught by dialectics is the struggle between opposites, the struggle between the old and the new, between that which is decaying and that which is developing, then our Soviet

philosophy should show how this law of dialectics functions under the condition of a socialist society and what constitutes the nature of its application. We know that in a society divided into classes this law functions otherwise than in our Soviet society. This is the widest field for scientific investigation, yet none of our philosophers have cultivated this field. Nevertheless our party long ago discovered and placed at the service of socialism that special form of disclosing and overcoming the contradictions of a socialist society (these contraditions exist but our philosophers are afraid to write about them), that special form of combat between that which has outlived its usefulness and that which is coming into being in our Soviet society, which is called *criticism and self-criticism.* [Italics in the original.]

In our Soviet society where antagonistic classes have been liquidated, the struggle between the old and the new and, consequently, the development from lower to higher is accomplished not in the form of a struggle of antagonistic classes and cataclysms, as is the case in capitalist society, *but in the form of criticism which is the real strength of our development and a powerful tool in the hands of the Party. Without doubt this is a new kind of movement, a new kind of development, a new dialectical regularity.*[5]

It is not hard to see that in essence this "new dialectical regularity" boils down to the fact that it was necessary for Zhdanov to discover a new "law," the "law of criticism," as the motive power for Soviet society and Soviet culture, since if, as he claimed, there are no classes in the Soviet Union and consequently no basis for "cataclysms," i.e., revolutions, then there is no motive power for social development and, consequently, Soviet society ought to achieve a condition of immobility.

The meaning of "criticism" in the Soviet Union is well known: it is the authority which the Party possesses to assert that white is black and black is white. The meaning of "self-criticism" is also known: it is the repetition and confirmation of what the Party has said. It follows that the real purpose of Zhdanov's campaign was to train the Soviet people to believe once and for all that the historical development of the Soviet Union, its social, cultural and artistic life, are due entirely to the Party and the government and that the masses and man in general as a subject for history are categorically excluded from creative life. In other words there is not only no possibility of a revolution in the Soviet Union but there is no room for elementary freedom of thought and of the creative consciousness in general nor even for any partial opposition to the orders of the Party and the government. For art and for music this means complete servitude to the criticism and self-criticism of the Party, i.e., to the will, whims, aims, tastes, and arbitrary administration of a small group of Party bureaucrats.

In its book *The Ways of Development of Soviet Music* the Musicology Commission of the Union of Soviet Composers states that "the year 1948 is a year of historical change in the history of Soviet and of world musical culture,"[6] that "the international significance of the events which have taken place in Soviet music during the year cannot be doubted,"[7] and that

> the Central Committee resolution of February 10, 1948 on the opera *The Great Friendship* by V. Muradeli, condemning sternly the anti-popular, formalistic tendency in Soviet music, has broken the shackles that fettered the creative work of Soviet composers for many years; it has defined for many years to come the only proper paths for development of musical art in the U.S.S.R. . . . The International Congress of Progressive Composers and Musicologists of the World which took place in Prague in May 1948 has shown that the censure of formalism in music as stated in the resolution. . . has acquired a tremendous international significance.[8]

If the meaning of "formalism" attributed to it by the Soviet politicians corresponded to the generally accepted meaning of this term, one could only shrug one's shoulders in astonishment. What is there historic in the condemnation of formalism, which as a form of creative impotence has always been overcome by genuine art?

For the Central Committee of the Communist Party, however, formalism means something quite unlike its ordinarily accepted meaning; it means "non-Partyism in art," and "to censure sternly the antipopular formalist tendency in music" means to confirm Lenin's thesis on "the Partyism of the arts."[9]

Confirmation of this view is provided by the pamphlet in its comment on Lenin's words "down with non-Party men of letters":

> These remarkable Leninist thoughts, which constitute the foundation of the teaching of the Partyism of literature, resounded with new force in 1946 in the report by Comrade Zhdanov on the journals *Zvezda* and *Leningrad*. . . . These appeals are addressed in full measure to musicians also. *Soviet composers, like Soviet men of letters, have no right to be nonpolitical, hiding themselves away from the present in their personal little worlds. We do not need composer supermen separated from the common cause which constitutes the life of the whole Soviet people.*[10]

Thus it is clear that the historical and international significance of the events which occurred in Soviet music during 1948 is that Soviet composers no longer have any right to be nonpolitical, i.e., to be independent of the will of the Communist Party Central Committee, and that the Soviet authority considers absolutely useless those composers who "isolate themselves from the cause which constitutes the life of the whole Soviet people," i.e., from the cause forced on the people by the Communist Party.

There is little doubt, of course, that these developments are of historical and international significance; but there is equally little doubt that they are a chapter in the decline of morals rather than in the history of music. The Soviet attack on "formalism" is actually part of the complete enslavement of creative music for political aims.

FOOTNOTES TO PART I

1. The Russian adjective *podsovetskyi*, literally "sub-Soviet," here translated as "Soviet-dominated," is used here and elsewhere to characterize the individuals and events of the Soviet period. —Tr.

2. Shaverdyan, A.I., ed., *Puti razvitiya sovetskoi muzyki: kratkii obzor* [The Ways of Development of Soviet Music: A Brief Survey], Moscow, 1948, p. 7. Hereafter cited as *Puti*.

3. Politburo member Andrei A. Zhdanov (1896-1948) until his death was one of the most prominent Party theorists in the field of cultural policy. —Tr.

4. For the full text of this resolution, see Annex B, pp. 280-285.

5. *Pravda*, July 30, 1947. My italics. —A.O.

6. *Puti*, p. 5.

7. *Ibid.*, p. 119.

8. *Ibid.*, pp. 5-6.

9. There is no exact equivalent in English for the Soviet term "*partiinost'*," literally "partyness" or "partyism," meaning "devotion to the service of the [Communist] Party." —Tr.

10. *Puti*, p. 10. My italics. —A.O.

PART II

The Historical Development of Russian Music

A. CLASSICAL TRADITION[1]

1. *DEVELOPMENT*

One of the principal theses of Soviet music policy is that Soviet music is the lawful heir of the Russian classical composers. For example, in a report presented at the First All-Union Congress of Soviet Composers in Moscow in April 1948, it was claimed that

> ...the traditions of Russian folk art, as well as the arts of all the peoples of our land, have served as the basis, the foundation, for the development of Soviet music. That is why the resolution of the Party Central Committee concerning the opera *The Great Friendship* clearly indicates to Soviet composers the need to inherit and develop the best traditions of classical realistic art.[2]

It is necessary not only to test the validity of this thesis but also to understand the characteristics of Soviet music in general first to consider briefly the intellectual and creative content of Russian music of the past. Without first reviewing in at least condensed form this prologue to Soviet music one could not understand clearly the features which are characteristic of the Soviet-dominated period of Russian music.

The first contact between Russian music and the West took place in the Ukraine in the late seventeenth and early eighteenth centuries. The materials contained in the libraries of the Razumovskys and the Repnins, which have become available for research only during recent years, are an eloquent testimony to this fact. These two collections, which were stored in the library of the Ukrainian Academy of Sciences in Kiev before World War II, proved to be of much earlier origin than the libraries of the Yusupovs and Naryshkins which until recently had been the only basic sources available for studying the initial period of the development of Russian music.

A considerable number of musical compositions of the most diverse genres are contained in the Razumovsky and Repnin libraries; particularly extensively represented are German, Italian and French composers of the eighteenth century. The analysis of these compositions shows that they were fairly widely known in the Ukraine, and that, even more important, those West European composers, mainly Italians, who were at work in Russia at that time,[3] creatively combined the Western European style with elements from Ukrainian folk music. A curious example of this interaction is Astaritta's opera *Sbitenshchik* [a vendor of spiced drinks] in which the Western European style of that period is quaintly interwoven with Ukrainian folk songs.

Beginning with Glinka (1804-1857) the folk song exerted an increasingly powerful influence on the musical texture and technique of the works of Russian composers. The compositions of The Five[4] and Tchaikovsky reflect the nature of Russian folk music with its multiformity of modes, its characteristic technique of subordinate voices and its free and supple interweaving of vocal variants derived from the basic melody.

It would be completely unjustifiable, however, to limit the significance of popular art in the development of Russian music to the part played by Russian folk music. An equally important factor, observable even as early as the end of the seventeenth century, was the influence of the ancient musical cultures of the Caucasian peoples—Armenians and Georgians—and of Ukrainian folk music, as well as of the folk songs of the other peoples of Russia. Without the influence of the music of the Caucasian peoples it would be difficult to account for the role played by "oriental" elements in Russian music; without this influence it would be impossible to explain either Glinka's *Ruslan and Lyudmila* or the "eastern" tinge in the music of The Five.

Even at the beginning of the nineteenth century Russian music, having assimilated and organically recreated the most fruitful influences of Western European culture, achieved a position of significance in world art. Russian composers were particularly attracted by the romantic art of the West which was struggling, in the final analysis, for the enrichment of artistic content, for truth and vitality of feeling, for humanism and optimism. In Russian music these qualities were developed particularly broadly.

Although Russian music was wholeheartedly absorbed in the movement of Western art, however, it did not become derivative or imitative. However much it was indebted to the West, Russian music nevertheless remained deeply original, not by opposing itself to the West but by developing its own characteristic nature. While learning from the West, Russian musicians with even greater attention listened to and looked at the life surrounding them and studied their own native, national art. It is mainly due to this fact that Russian music, notwithstanding the profound influence exerted on it by other cultures, always preserved—more, perhaps, than the music of any other people—its own spiritual "strangeness" and distinctiveness from the general trend of European music. This distinctiveness was expressed in Russian music's predilection for everything nationally characteristic or unusual, in its tendency to exaggerate national peculiarities, in its affinity with folk music, and most of all perhaps, in its emphasis on the social function of music and its resolute rejection of "pure art." Russian music, like Russian literature, was always concentrated to a considerable extent on social themes and problems. Nineteenth century Russian composers demanded from their art an answer to the complicated and painful questions of existence. Through their art they wanted to understand themselves and their times. The idea of art as the expression of the pure essence of the human spirit they considered a fallacy; art as the direct spiritual acceptance of life was for them something almost heretical.

As the result of the predominance of such didactic and moralizing aesthetics Russian music had ceased by the 1860's to be confined to an expression of moods, feelings and sensations in general, and had become a "narrative in sound" concerning that service to society with which its creators were concerned. Carried away by the spirit of the times Russian composers were transformed into educators and reformers.

Aesthetic values as such hardly attracted the attention of Russian composers; the isolated, purely aesthetic approach to life was for them often tantamount to a denial of life's metaphysical essence. Hence that external peculiarity which became characteristic of the work of Russian nineteenth century composers, particularly the deep bond between their music and folk music, both vocal and instrumental, and their clearly expressed tendency to join music to words, to poetry, to literary images, and to the theater.

Editor's Note: In the next section of his work (pp. 61-119 of the original manuscript) the author presents a historical sketch of the development of Russian music during the nineteenth century, based mainly on the standard Soviet textbook *A History of Russian Music* edited by Professor Pekelis.[5]

Although considerations of space prevent the presentation of this material *in extenso*, a brief summary of the subject is essential as a background to the subsequent discussion of music under the Soviets. The main features of the development of music in Russia before 1917 can be presented most conveniently in terms of individual composers, of whom the following are of particular importance:

Mikhail I. Glinka (1804-1857) is generally regarded as the founder of the Russian school in music and as its first composer of major significance. In his operas *A Life for the Tsar* (also known as *Ivan Susanin*) and *Ruslan and Lyudmila* he succeeded in combining the European operatic tradition with characteristically Russian subjects and thematic material.

Sharing with Glinka a keen interest in folk music, Alexander Dargomyzhsky (1813-1869) contributed by his works to the development of a national Russian school. His best known composition, the opera *The Stone Guest* [*Kamennyi gost'*], is a forerunner of the psychological realism of much Russian music of the later nineteenth century.

Aleksandr Serov (1820-1870) served Russian music in a triple capacity: as a composer, as a pioneer in the scientific study of Russian folk music and as an influential critic. As a critic Serov consistently advocated the thesis that for its highest realization music requires not only beauty but relevance to contemporary life. Serov's most important work is his opera *The Power of Evil* [*Vrazh'ya Sila,* literally "The Power of the Enemy"], in which he achieved an effective synthesis of psychological realism and folk music.

Anton Rubinstein (1829-1894), once well known as a piano virtuoso and as the composer of a large number of works in various forms, is of historical importance chiefly because it was as a result of his determined efforts that the first Russian conservatory, that of St. Petersburg, was founded in 1862. With the establishment of this institution Russian music was provided for the first time with a solid professional basis.

Basing themselves on the creative heritage of Glinka and Dargomyzhsky, the group of composers known as The Five[6] formulated and put into practice during the 1860's an aesthetic program of which the principal features were artistic realism, the use of Russian national subject matter as the basis for their compositions, and the acceptance of folk music as an inspiration and model. The leader of the group, Mily Balakirev (1837-1910), was not only a prolific composer but an effective protagonist of the artistic program of the group. In his publication of folk music Balakirev set a standard for subsequent students of the subject and provided a rich source on which later composers have drawn for inspiration.

Probably the most gifted composer among The Five was Modeste Petrovich Musorgsky (1839-1881) whose fame rests securely on his operas *Boris Godunov, Khovantshchina* and *The Wedding.* More perhaps than any other member of the group, Musorgsky succeeded in fusing creative inspiration with an organic understanding and re-creation of the principles of popular art.

Aleksandr P. Borodin (1833-1877), somewhat more of a classicist and symphonist than Musorgsky, shared with him a devotion to the ideal of the creation of a national Russian school incorporating elements both of professional Western European music and Russian folk music. Another vital component of Borodin's style, recognizable particularly in his opera *Prince Igor,* is the influence of the music of the non-Russian peoples of Central Asia.

Nikolai Andreyevich Rimsky-Korsakov (1844-1908), originally destined for a naval career, turned instead to music under the influence of Balakirev. His extensive work as a composer covers many genres—opera, symphony, chamber music, song, etc. It is characterized by the strong influence of Russian and oriental folk music and by the choice of subjects derived from Russia's past, especially the pre-Christian past of pagan Russia. As a teacher Rimsky-Korsakov exerted a profound influence on the subsequent development of Russian music. Appointed professor of composition at the St. Petersburg Conservatory in 1871, Rimsky-Korsakov played a major role in training a generation of Russian composers. Among his pupils were such later masters of Russian music as Stravinsky, Lyadov and Glazunov. By his teaching Rimsky-Korsakov also helped to establish national schools of music among a number of the minority peoples of the Russian Empire, particularly the Armenians, Georgians and Ukrainians. Outside Russia his influence has been most profound among the French composers of the early twentieth century.

César Cui (1834-1918), of French descent, was perhaps the least nationalist in his music of The Five. By profession a military engineer, Cui turned to music during the 1860's. He served The Five not only as a composer of operas, songs, chamber music, and symphonic compositions but also as a critic through his contributions to the *St. Petersburg Gazette*, of which he was a regular contributor from 1864 to 1917.

Perhaps the most eminent Russian composer of the nineteenth century was Peter Ilyich Tchaikovsky (1840-1893), the founder and chief representative of a tendency in Russian music which has been called the Moscow School. Standing apart from The Five in both his music and his aesthetics, Tchaikovsky nevertheless shared with them a number of basic characteristics: a tendency towards realism in music, the use of Russian folk music as a source of harmonic and thematic material, a predilection for subjects drawn from the Russian past, and a pronounced idealism in aesthetics. In addition Tchaikovsky's music is characterized by great psychological power and a tendency to philosophic speculation. Generally regarded during his lifetime as a "westerner", especially by The Five and their followers, Tchaikovsky actually stood at the center of the development of Russian music, and its subsequent course represents a combination in varying proportions of the traditions and influence of Tchaikovsky's music with that of The Five.

2. THE HERITAGE OF RUSSIAN MUSIC AND SOVIET ART POLICY

Theoretically Soviet music ideologists are in favor of the broad cultivation of national traits in art. At the Conference of Workers of Soviet Music which preceded the First All-Union Congress of Soviet Composers (1948) Zhdanov said:

> Internationalism in art develops not on the basis of the depreciation and impoverishment of national art. On the contrary, internationalism develops where national art is flourishing. To forget this truth means to lose the leading line, to lose one's own features, to become a homeless cosmopolitan.[7]

In its real attitude towards the Russian classics, however, Soviet art policy intentionally reduces the complicated and many-sided nature of their creative work to the role of forerunner of Soviet policies. In truth, of course, each of the great Russian composers of the nineteenth century was a complex psychological figure; each of them was subject to manifold influences which complicated and enriched both his work and his personality.

Soviet orthodox critics, however, have no wish to recognize the complexity and diversity of these composers—they prefer to dress them up as "national heroes" and as victims of the political conditions of their times.

The patriotic civic-mindedness ascribed to the Russian classics by Soviet propaganda, however, has nothing in common with the "Soviet patriotism" with which it is officially identified. In the same way the concreteness and realism which are inherent in Russian music of the past are far from the "socialist realism" with which they are equated.

Possibly there is no other national musical culture of recent times in which the organic contact with literature was as close as as the case in Russian nineteenth century music. Russian classical music was fed by the same intellectual sources as Russian literature. Russian writers and thinkers—Pushkin, Gogol, Lermontov, Turgenev, Dostoyevsky, Tolstoy—were not only the spiritual fathers of Russian culture as a whole but also of the leading Russian composers of the nineteenth century. The aesthetic views of Russian democratic journalists of the mid-nineteenth century—Chernyshevsky, Dobrolyubov and Belinsky—were close to many Russian composers of that period. Musorgsky's aesthetic credo that "the artistic representation of mere beauty in its material significance is crude childishness, the infantile age of art," or that "art is the means of intercourse with people, not an aim in itself" was shared by many contemporary Russian composers. But what has this credo in common with that "socialist realism" which acknowledges only a single "reality"—the political interest of the Party, and which recognizes only the man whose views and actions are acceptable to it?

The creative ideology of the classical Russian composers was based on the recognition of the people, in contrast to the state, as the most important factor in the historical development of mankind. From this followed their stand in defense of human rights and personal freedom, as well as the right of the people for self-determination. To serve the people as a whole, with none of its components laying claim to hegemony over the others, was for them the means to achieve truth in life and art. Such is the artistic and social meaning of their work, standing in sharp contrast to the Soviet art policy which denies the role of the individual in history.

The Soviet cultural politicians like to talk about their alleged youth; they make frequent use of the word "new"—"new Russia," "new literature," "new music," etc. In reality, however, they fear progress. They stand neither for the past nor for the future; their claims to art are outside of history and amoral, for they are the results of a political lie. It is to serve this lie that they proclaim their inheritance of Russian classical music.

That this is so is attested to not only by the theory and

practice of Soviet music itself but by the very logic of the historical development of Russian music which has already sharply changed the aspect of the Russian musical classics under Soviet conditions.

B. SENIOR CONTEMPORARIES (MODERNISM)

1. *THE CRISIS IN THE DEVELOPMENT OF THE CLASSICAL TRADITION*

The opposition between the two basic creative trends in Russian music of the nineteenth century, i.e., between The Five and Tchaikovsky, resulted not from any fundamental difference in creative ideas but only from certain differences in methods. Tchaikovsky differed from The Five by the use of more restrained and moderate innovations, by a certain "classicism" in his thinking, and by his inclination towards a generalized emotional rather than a concretely descriptive interpretation of life. But when Rimsky-Korsakov entered the St. Petersburg Conservatory as a professor in 1871 he reconsidered many of the ideas of The Five and produced a broader and more objective point of view on several aspects of music.

By the 1880's Rimsky-Korsakov and Tchaikovsky had become the leading Russian composers, around whom were grouped the younger generation of Russian musicians. The combination of the advanced traditions of The Five with the solid academic basis of Tchaikovsky's music served as a foundation for the systematic and well-planned dissemination and transmission to the next generation of the heritage of creative experience. This synthesis of two influences which had seemed so opposed and irreconcilable in the fighting days of the 1860's determined the subsequent development of Russian music.

At the beginning of the eighties there was formed the "Belyayev circle" as the result of Rimsky-Korsakov's friendship with M.P. Belyayev, an outstanding patron of music in whose home young musicians met regularly. Rimsky-Korsakov, the recognized head of the group, not only took an active part in the Russian Music Publishing House which Belyayev established to publish works by Russian composers but also became the conductor of the "Russian symphonic concerts" which Belyayev organized to disseminate such works.

It was at the Paris World's Fair of 1889, where Belyayev organized a series of concerts under the baton of Rimsky-Korsakov, that the new Russian school of symphonic music was first demonstrated in the musical capital of the world. The "Belyayev circle" solidified the new creative forces of Russian music, uniting them through the idea of professionalism regardless of the stylistic path followed by each of the members of this extremely heterogeneous group, most of whom were pupils of Rimsky-Korsakov (Glazunov, Lyadov, Arensky, Ippolitov-Ivanov, Grechaninov, Cherepnin, Stravinsky, Spendiarov, Gnesin, and Shteinberg.)[8] Taking an equal part in this new movement in Russian music were a number of students of the Moscow Conservatory—Taneyev, Scriabin, Rachmaninov, Catoire, Conus, and Kalinnikov—whose work was strongly influenced by Tchaikovsky.

The revolt against tradition in Russian music at the beginning of the twentieth century was manifested in a variety of forms: in the work of some composers it was acutely evident, almost grating on the listener's ears with its unusual images, while in the work of others it was less noticeable, being hidden under a surface of external self-restraint. But its essence in every case was the same: the search for creative freedom.

The most prominent Russian symphonic composer after Tchaikovsky was A.N. Scriabin (1872-1915) whose work, incorporating the new modernist trend, was at once a continuation of and a revolt against the Tchaikovsky tradition. Scriabin's works were based fundamentally on the same philosophic and psychological problems as those of Tchaikovsky: man and his struggle against the forces which restrain his aspiration towards happiness (or ecstasy, as Scriabin would have said.) In the solution of these problems, however, Scriabin departed from the psychologism on which Tchaikovsky's works were firmly based.

In the process of developing modernism in music Scriabin played a major sole, not merely in Russian music. Since the aesthetic basis of his work was not new, however, being only the result of carrying the basic principles of romanticism to the limit, rather than a new type of musical thinking, his work has exerted a relatively slight influence on contemporary music. Nevertheless, Scriabin, with his dynamic means of expression, undoubtedly played an important part in the subsequent process of the activation of musical form.

Even more pronounced was the role of Sergei Rachmaninov (1873-1943) in the formation of the new music. There is a widespread impression that Rachmaninov was an eclectic. However, here also, as was the case with Scriabin, there has been a misunderstanding in our time. When evaluating creative phenomena a composer's contemporaries are inclined to exaggerate the significance of certain elements of his music while ignoring others. In music as a temporal art the scale of development has always been one of the central creative problems. And it is precisely here that Rachmaninov, in contradistinction to a certain conservativeness in other aspects of his work, achieved unprecedented results.

Like Scriabin a consistent romantic, i.e., concerned primarily with music of lyrical self-expression, Rachmaninov with his refined creative instinct not only perceived the tendencies of the new development in music but by extending the scope of music assisted in further overcoming the traditions of his predecessors.

Entirely by-passed by his contemporaries was the creative heritage of S.I. Taneyev (1856-1915) who is little known in the West and by no means sufficiently appreciated in Russia. Yet Taneyev's "polyphonism" was a forecast of the considerable trend in contemporary music towards linear thinking.

Thus Scriabin, Taneyev and Rachmaninov assisted in overcoming and transforming the traditions of Russian classical music.

Nevertheless, it was only Scriabin's romanticism, developed towards philosophical abstractions and subjective willfulness, which became a determining factor in overcoming the musical traditions of the past. As a reaction against his "romantic arrogance" there developed the skepticism and irony of Stravinsky and Prokof'yev.

The beginning of the present century marks the sharpest turning point in the history of Russian music. One can point with certainty to the exact dividing line in the process: it lies between 1908, the year when Scriabin's *Poem of Ecstasy* appeared, and 1911, the year of the first appearance of Stravinsky's *Petrushka.*

Of course, Scriabin and Stravinsky are not alike in their pursuits. It is true that both composers strove to overcome the "populist traditions" of Russian music, its "descriptive ethnography" and "psychological realism" and its dependence on feeling. But whereas Scriabin's disciples have continued to follow in the footsteps of the past, attempting to express delicate, barely perceptible, vacillating and refined moods that push the aesthetic principles of romanticism to the limit, Stravinsky and his followers began a general assault on the tradition of music as lyrical self-expression, calling instead for objectivity in music. The spirit which underlay this movement has been well expressed by Igor Stravinsky in these words: "Do we not, in truth, ask the impossible of music when we expect it to express feelings, to translate dramatic situations, even to imitate nature?"[9]

2. *MODERNISM AS SEEN BY SOVIET-DOMINATED COMPOSERS*

The best expression of Soviet musicians' views on contemporary modernist music (those, that is, who live by their own ideas and not according to those imposed upon them by the Party or the government) is still *The Book About Stravinsky* by B.V. Asaf'yev (Igor' Glebov),[10] even though the book appeared as long ago as 1929.

In this book Asaf'yev gives a most convincing characterization of Stravinsky's work and its significance in relation to both Western and Russian music. Furthermore he discloses on the basis of Stravinsky's work the fundamental characteristics of modernism in general and its historical logic as a new phase in the development of music. In drawing the reader's attention to this remarkable work we have in mind not only the fact that it remains almost inaccessible to the non-Russian reader but also that it represents a conception of modernism in music which is directly opposed to the Soviet art policy's dogmatic denial of the existence of any positive values in modernism. Since it still remains the ablest and most spirited defense of modernism in music which has appeared under the Soviet regime it will be useful to present a number of characteristic extracts from it. "Stravinsky," writes Asaf'yev,

> is a representative of European urban musical culture, a daring constructor and a master strong in the knowledge of his craft. In his work there is not a trace of emotionalizing dilettantism, abstract scholastic academicism or philosophizing erotic individualism... With all the depths of his soul Stravinsky is attached to Great Russian melodics, to the folk and peasant song art, both vocal and instrumental.[11]
>
> . . . .
>
> [He] has mastered Russian popular art not as a clever stylist who knows how to hide the quotations nor as an ethnographist who does not know how to assimilate the material and re-create it on the artistic plane but as a master of his own musical speech.[12]
>
> . . . .
>
> The contemporary composer's attitude towards his material has also changed radically. Raw undigested material, not reworked in the constructive sense, has been banished. What is now valued is the intelligent, deliberate choice of material

and expressive means in accordance with the aim and the task. Moreover the principle of utmost economy and rigorous use of rhythmic material has begun to be particularly observed. The material which has been selected is so organized as to unfold everything characteristic and substantial which it contains, so that every detail corresponds to the whole without deviations, however good they may be in themselves.

The constructive rhythmic basis has been reinforced as an organizing principle and as a dynamic factor, disciplining the attention. Deductive, rationalized form-schemes are subjected to the test of their viability. Thinking becomes important, rather than the forms into which it is poured. One cannot write music imitating the experience of the "great," but in reality dead, schemes.[13]

. . . .

If anyone does not wish to learn from Stravinsky's mastery and thinks he can get by in music with the technique of the pre-aviation, the pre-automobile (and for some the pre-railroad) epoch; if the virile rhythms of his music say nothing to some and if his intonations appear demoralizing—then there is no use quarrelling; the final word must be left to the future. Every work of a great artist is always to a certain extent a protest and reaction against the philistinism of his epoch. And such is Stravinsky's creative work.[14]

. . . .

There are two techniques—the imitative technique of the epigones and the evolutionary. The former consists of knowing how to carry on what has been invented by others and at best how to vary it. But the evolutionary technique is always a conquest of new methods, new expressions. ...

All controversy about the "rights of new music" comes down to this: It is impossible to understand why at present one should speak musically in the language of "classicism," for instance in Beethoven's language, when he in his time went ahead of everyone and talked in a language new to his epoch, even though he was reproved for it. It is one thing to appreciate the heroic tone of Beethoven's music and quite another to translate into contemporary life the language in which he expressed his ideas. The first procedure is natural but the second is useless. Each epoch has its own language and its own means of expression. ...[15]

. . . .

Musical forn. is the summation of a complicated process of crystallization in our consciousness of the combined sound elements. The material by its own characteristics determines the form but the choice and arrangement of the component elements of the composition is the task of the composer's organizing intelligence. In the final analysis form is the concrete expression of the composer's conception. Contemporary music gravitates ever more unmistakably towards investigation of the *process* of formation of musical form and at the same time towards an analysis of the role of the intellectual factor in musical creation.

. . . .

Thus the formal aspect of contemporary music is by no means a narrow technical sphere or a sterile aesthetic superstructure. Progress in this realm is always a result of the progress of musical thinking which makes possible new possibilities of expression that follow in its footsteps. One may object to the predominance of intellectualism in musical creation in certain epochs, but to reduce the manifestation of intellect—form and the process of formation—to a technical refinement, in my opinion, means to be completely unaware of musical evolution and to debase music as a phenomenon.[16]

. . . .

[With *Petrushka*] Stravinsky definitely became himself. The whole contemporary generation of musicians followed after him. Everyone who wished to avoid becoming a "living corpse" understood that a great event had taken place, that Russian music had really made a new and unheard-of conquest. ... [In *Petrushka*] Stravinsky felt for the first time, as nowhere previously, the elements of festivity, of the street and of mass movement; he revealed the peculiarities, the ringing qualities and the brilliance of the native instrumental intonations;[17] he disclosed the energy of the diatonic Russian melodies to its full extent and completeness. He established the supremacy of mode as a free original principle, not as something undeveloped and subordinate to major and minor, brought in merely for purposes of stylization or archaic coloring. ... [Stravinsky] was not afraid to give artistic form to tunes which are familiar to everyone and to preserve in them everything characteristic and vitally concrete. *He demonstrated that reality should not be dressed up for the sake of rules which have outlived their usefulness but that on the contrary one should proceed from living musical practice, from the every-day musical language of the city and the village, from those intonations and rhythms which are produced through experience, created by a way of life, and consolidated over a period of generations. It is the direct and constant choice created by life which should enrich the composer's consciousness.*[18]

. . . .

The turning point in Stravinsky's conception was expressed, first of all, in the fact that for him form definitely ceased to be a self-contained pattern weighing on his thought. On the contrary, the musical conception creates the form ... There are no patterns established once and for all; there is the free choice of means for the embodiment and development of ideas. The regularity of choice is determined by the composer's organic conception and not by school instructions which block the path of inner necessity.[19]

. . . .

The former school technique was for the weak; it helped them to arrange one note after another without thinking. The new, organic technique is only for the strong. It knows no "eternal" rules. It is dependent on the character and peculiarities of the composer's conception. ... Of course it is more difficult to think in "free forms" than it is to embroider on a ready-made canvas, merely varying what one has been taught by one's seniors. But the life and development of music lie in the progress of thinking and not in the imitation of handicraft skill.[20]

. . . .

To give music the power and ability to express the new vital content, to give back to it its essential energy, it was necessary first of all to destroy at the root the withered dogmas of academicism.[21]

. . . .

Common to Stravinsky and Tchaikovsky is their attitude towards popular art. For them it is organic and vital material rather than archaic language suitable only for stylization and elaboration. Neither of them reached this view at once; both began with the adaptation and incrustation of popular songs. Both began to use folk music material, not as prescribed by the generally accepted rules of arrangement but on the basis of the general principles of formation peculiar to the material itself, both archaic and contemporary.[22]

. . . .

It goes without saying that Russian composers have always ardently loved popular art, but they did not trust it as a powerful, original culture and system of tonal conceptions, regarding the principles of its formation, which had been created through centuries of peasant art, as something accidental in comparison with the aesthetic principles of the strict style based on harmonic polyphony, etc. Laboring under this delusion they did not trust the people's music and often plundered it for themes for variations, symphonies and other forms, presenting it to the public in settings not always appropriate to it rather than learning from it examples of using melodic materials which are far more durable, ancient, natural, and regular than anything they could learn from elementary courses of theory and harmony. ... This difference in relation to folk music then and now must be understood. It is one thing to imitate archaic intonations and rhythms and quite another thing to forge one's own language, to deepen one's own world outlook on art and one's own creative work on the basis of sociomusical experience by way of organic mastery of those rich intonations and rhythmic formulas of popular art which are almost excluded from use in rationalized European music.[23]

. . . .

From the purely musical point of view *Les Noces* discloses the mastery of a great artist in sound, the outstanding composer of modern times. Our musical epoch is the epoch of Stravinsky. It is so and it will remain so in all future histories, no matter how much people of ill-will and envy try to deprecate his significance. They deprive themselves of great joy. But the younger generation will find in the score of *Les Noces* an inexhaustible source of images and of new examples of musical forms—a school of the most exalted mastery.[24]

. . . .

Stravinsky led Russian music out of the blind alley of the "school of composition technique" and transferred music into the sphere of thinking. ... Setting itself some specific creative task, the conception henceforward defines both the structure of the music and its expressive means. It ceases to concern itself with ready-made patterns which merely serve to increase the number of persons writing music "correctly" by stuffing into moribund schemes musical ideas which have long been done to death and which are mechanically retained in the memory.... Stravinsky's contribution lay in once more increasing the demands made upon the composer; he emphasized the role of the intellect and of creative invention in place of the passive observance of school precepts. In other words, he returned music to the fundamental base inherent in every higher human intellectual activity.[25]

. . . .

That Stravinsky's enemies maintain that his work is decadent, an imitation in accordance with Parisian taste, a caprice of fashion, etc.—all of this, I repeat, is a lie and a slander invented by those whose hopes Stravinsky has not justified. It is not Stravinsky who imitates; he himself is imitated. He dictates his own tastes. He is the first to take new material and work it over in his own way as no one did before him.[26]

. . . .

It would be strange if, in our businesslike age, the age of organization and discipline, among the mighty buildings, the rhythm of machines and the dynamics of noise, the posters and the electric signs of the street at night, the hustle and bustle of automobiles, trucks and passers-by, emerging from the mist into the glare of electric lights and disappearing again into the mist, the colossal influence of the cinema on all our perceptions—it would be strange indeed if music were not to reflect the full reality of our life and were to lock itself in a room with drawn curtains and wander about in the realm of poetic fantasy of the romantic past. Is the sphere of music the contemplative sphere only? Or is it only the sphere of personal feeling? Is it true that music does not dare to penetrate into every corner of everyday life and absorb all of life? This is not to say that music should not live by the emotions. I am merely defending music's right to take its material from wherever it likes. ... Why should music not be as characteristic and pungent as a poster? Why should it not dare to show actions and figures with uninterrupted rhythmic beat just as the motion pictures do (as was frequently done, for instance, by Prokof'yev in his opera *The Love for Three Oranges*)? Why should it not break up rhythms and intonations as they are broken up in the babel of the street? Why should it not have the right to interpret the noise and hubbub of the contemporary city? ... Some say music reflects in sound the inner world only—this is her sphere, her aim. My belief is that it is not so—not only this.[27]

. . . .

The opera-oratorio *Oedipus Rex* (1926-1927) is undoubtedly the synthesis of the composer's persistent search for a new "working" style and a neutral language in the sense of one not contaminated by nationalist elements and acutely emotionally subjective intonations -- a kind of musical Esperanto.[28]

. . . .

The music of *Oedipus* sounds appropriate to its time, as a powerful word in the defense of that humanity and humanism which modern European civilization has violated. Abandoning the subjective emotionalism of the nineteenth century and deliberately selecting intonations which are devoid of "subjective nervous associations" (with few exceptions), intonations which are well-known and even commonplace, long since retained in the memory and consequently tested as to their effect, Stravinsky achieves a classical, well-proportioned style and a majestic, supra-individual expression of tragic conflict. In *Oedipus* there is not yet, of course, a new musical culture and aesthetics. It stands at the threshhold of such a development. ...[29]

. . . .

[In *Oedipus Rex*] Stravinsky made the transition from the stage of creation in general to the stage of an appeal to "plain words". His music aspires to become accessible, oratorical speech.[30]

. . . .

With *Oedipus* Stravinsky confidently enters a phase of post-individualist creation, striving to express the content of universally significant ancient tragedy through the simplest sound formulas, through broadly socialized lines and rhythms, through intonations which constitute new selections and new combinations from the classical and popular phrases of the European operatic language, outside the framework of the national and the romantic, mainly from the experience of the musical oratorio forms of the eighteenth century. ...

On the social artistic plane [*Oedipus*] is an experiment in entering the region of supra-individualist aesthetics and a step towards the exit from the blind alley of subjective searchings, no matter how beautiful and profound they may be, no matter how valuable as a conquest of intonations that might influence the further evolution of music.[31]

3. SOVIET ORTHODOXY AND MODERNISM

Such is the conception which Soviet-dominated musicians have of the regular development of musical tradition in general and of Russian music in particular. The fact that Asaf'yev in his *Book About Stravinsky* restricts himself to an examination of Stravinsky's creative evolution and with it the evolution of modernism as a whole to the period up to the beginning of the 1930's (it will be recalled that the work appeared in 1929) in no way indicates that Soviet musicians' knowledge of Stravinsky's music and of contemporary Western modernist music as a whole came to an end at that point.

Indeed, the fact that the Soviet power has not ceased its struggle against "formalism" in the work of Soviet-dominated composers (in reality its struggle against the contact of Soviet music with modernism) is convincing proof that this contact not only has no tendency to wither away but in fact affects the creative thoughts of Soviet-dominated composers ever more deeply, although it now takes latent forms and is kept in the dark.

In this connection there arises a question of particular significance: how does the Soviet art policy interpret the present evolution of Russian music? Does Soviet music really constitute, as the propagandists claim, the "only rightful heir" of the artistic treasures created during the century and a half of Russian music development?

No, by no means! Branding everything associated with the progress of Russian music towards modernism—its faithfulness to creative freedom and to independent seeking, its consistent humanism and democracy—as "formalism" and "cosmopolitanism," Soviet art policy has waged a bitter campaign against that tradition, particularly against its contemporary manifestations. "Formalism" as a self-contained goal of the technical progress of music and "cosmopolitanism" as the alienation of musical content from "real Soviet life" (in reality, however, from the "life" invented by Party propaganda) became the conceptions under cover of which Soviet art policy tried to eradicate everything that was and is most significant and valuable in this tradition: the love of creative freedom, imaginative inventiveness and hostility to everything that blocks the path of progress. The antitotalitarian animus of this tradition was and is too obvious.

It is no wonder that in the Soviet Union, where the authorities fear personal creative initiative more than anything else, Stravinsky has been used as a scarecrow to frighten the already intimidated Soviet composers. The Soviet ideologists of music are not accustomed to think of music and, confusing their personal taste and whims with critical evaluation, identify the aims of their political propaganda with an evaluation of music. Everything which can be suspected of originality becomes subject to public defamation. The Party ideologists judge creative work by comparison with the derivative music which they can understand in which everything is smooth, familiar, obvious, and "entirely explainable." What could be better? They do not understand that this is not creative work but only a lesson in orthography or in copying from a textbook.

The real reason for the Soviet art policy's struggle against modernism in music was well expressed by Asaf'yev in his *Book About Stravinsky:*

> As long as the fresh forces which have entered the world of music have not yet assimilated the latest conquests, the backward will take the opportunity to attack everything contemporary and will continue to live in complacency, accustomed to think about music by inertia, to compose according to tradition and to judge everything with condescension and malice.[32]

In 1951 the American National Institute of Arts presented a gold medal to Stravinsky for his "great services in the realm of musical culture" and particularly for such of his works as *Petrushka, Les Noces* and *The Rites of Spring.*[33] At nearly the same time, in Stravinsky's fatherland, there appeared an article in the government organ *Izvestiya* by the Party critic Nest'yev entitled "The Dollar Cacophony," an article obviously inspired by the formulators of Soviet music policy, in which an attempt was made to prove that Stravinsky's works are evidence of the "complete spiritual emptiness" of "this homeless cosmopolitan."[34]

Nest'yev's article was part of the general campaign of Soviet ideologists against modernism in music which was launched by the Central Committee resolution on the opera *The Great Friendship*. The Party musicologists were trying hard to make up for lost time and in accordance with the Party directives were not only attacking "formalists" with particular bitterness but were striving to "overthrow" the very foundations of modernism in music.

A characteristic specimen of the literature of this campaign is V. Gorodinski's book *The Music of Spiritual Poverty* which was published in 1950.[35] In this production the propagandistic passion of this "court musicologist," who has long been distinguished by his journalistic hooliganism, reaches a new low. The basic thesis of the work is that "contemporary bourgeois music is the music of spiritual poverty, of catastrophic mental impoverishment and of the most profound moral decline."[36]

Basing his work on Lenin's statement that "the dominating bourgeoisie in its fear of the growing and strengthened proletariat supports everything backward, rotten and medieval,"[37] Gorodinski exerts himself to the utmost to convince his readers that everything outside the Soviet sphere is of the devil. Here, for instance, is his characterization of contemporary European and American musicology:

> Just as in other fields of bourgeois science, the "learned" decadents provide the dead philosophic-aesthetic systems with new artificial argumentation, restoring Pythagorean conceptions, renovating the musical aesthetics of Kant and Schopenhauer with Freudian mystical means, providing a base for the formalist speculations of modernist composers, implanting the loathsome amoralism of a Jean-Paul Sartre or an André Gide, or that English troubadour of mud and swinishness Aldous Huxley (who, by the way, has for long manifested special and specific interest in music) proclaiming

> betrayal as valor and preaching an infamous homeless cosmopolitanism. Such is the shameless "ideology" of international rascals and black treason.[38]

Gorodinski's characterization of the creative work of contemporary European and American composers is saturated with similar propaganda of open hatred, interwoven with hysterical spite against Russian émigré musicians for whom the author can find only the terminology used by the MVD—"white guard scoundrels," "liars," etc.

A particular object of Gorodinski's wrath is atonality which he describes as

> ....the most reactionary formalist musical system which characterizes all the most important schools and trends of bourgeois decadence in music .... Atonality categorically denies to musical creation any factor whatsoever except pure form and refuses to express human feeling and experience, substituting the self-contained search for unheard-of combinations of cacophony for ideal content. The deeply reactionary character of atonality is especially manifested in its open hatred of national art and its conspicuous expression of cosmopolitanism. Thus atonality is the typical phenomenon of bourgeois decadence in music and the catastrophic decline of bourgeois aesthetics, and is the living and audible embodiment of the antinational, anticultural character of capitalism in its final, imperialist stage of development.[39]

It is not necessary to dwell any longer on this typical product of Soviet musical propaganda. Indeed the words of Romain Rolland concerning Théophile Gautier which Gorodinski quotes in order to slander contemporary foreign criticism of Soviet music could be applied to him with the greatest aptness: "He does not understand and does not like music, but this does not prevent him from talking about it."

It is refreshing to turn from Gorodinski's political demagogy to Asaf'yev, who wrote:

> No one would think of saying that Goethe or Kant was obliged to stand on the level of Philistines. But music is supposed to be accessible to everyone; the predominance of intellectual factors in its content is considered reprehensible, and the right to independent musical thinking is regarded as dubious. Bach's ***Inventions,*** one may say, are

> "trifles," yet the power of their influence is irresistible just because they are controlled by thought rather than by evanescent feeling.[40]

Has the creative work of contemporary modernists weakened the tie between music and all mankind? Is not the essential spirit which contemporary composers have added to the treasure-house of art a point of departure, a center for the permanent, infinite expansion of the human soul; is it not the foundation on which the contemporary artist stands in order to serve the single general cause of culture?

A belief in the absolute truth of art and in its singleness of creative aim, however, is by no means the faith which inspires the Soviet musical politicians in their attempt to combine art with political aims and requirements in the interests of "proletarian music." And this at a time when the direction of contemporary progress is completely clear: not the dismemberment of mankind into sections—nations, classes and groups—but the unification of nations, classes and groups into mankind as a whole. From this movement follows the meaning of contemporary art in its aspiration towards integration, towards the synthesis of aesthetic views, styles, systems, and schools.

Art has never been divisive; on the contrary, it has always had the task of unifying, of overcoming divisions of all kinds. It is this tendency particularly which characterizes contemporary art, with its aspiration towards the spiritual identity which is inherent in the infinite variety of human nature, its aspiration towards objective artistic truth.

Soviet ideologists believe that underlying the relationship among peoples is the principle of human diversity. In their view the national, political, spiritual, and class differences that subdivide mankind rest on the diverse aspects of human nature, and when they encounter a work of art they ask first of all to which of these divisions it belongs; then they file it under the appropriate label, willfully ignoring its similarity to other art forms which forces upon us the recognition of the true unity of man and art. They forget the elementary truth that the artist who lives according to his own law may have a moral value even in terms of the law common to all mankind; instead of appreciating him for his personal creative qualities, they hold him "responsible" for the mass qualities of the group to which he belongs.

Modern art, however, with its movement towards universalism and the integration of culture, has taken its place in the history of mankind's development alongside those movements which serve as indicators of the intellectual and moral creative currents of universal life; it is a collective force in which the separate ways of human life jointly manifest themselves, disclosing the identity of their basic principles. The movement of contemporary music represents the equinox of forces which mankind obeys all over the world; this movement proclaims to all future generations that it is not something forced or invented but that it exists in the very essence of human nature and is thus one of the forces that guide the paths of history.

There is no need, of course, for contemporary Russian composers to follow blindly the methods of Western modernism—methods are subject to change and what is represented as a genuine style today may be considered false, spurious and artificial tomorrow. It is a matter of the spiritual kinship and psychic solidarity with the progressive tendencies of the contemporary world which are denied to contemporary Russian composers by the Soviet authority. The movement of contemporary music proves that art rejects not him who extends the boundaries of human love but him who forcibly contracts its confines.

FOOTNOTES TO PART II

1. "Classical composers" in the present context and as used throughout this section means the major Russian composers of the nineteenth century.—Tr.

2. "Doklad B.V. Asaf'yeva" [Report by B.V. Asaf'yev], *Sovetskoye iskusstvo* [Soviet Art], No. 17 (1105), April 24, 1948.

3. Gennaro Astaritta, c. 1749- ?, Domenico Cimarosa, 1749-1801, Baldassare Galuppi, 1706-1785, Giovanni Paesiello, 1741-1816, and Giuseppe Sarti, 1729-1802.

4. A group of composers known in Russia as the *Moguchaya Kuchka* (literally "mighty little heap") from a combination of two references to the group, one by the hostile critic A.N. Serov, the other by the ideologist of the group, V.V. Stasov. The members of the group were M.A. Balakirev (1837-1910), A.P. Borodin (1833-1887), C.A. Cui (1835-1918), M.P. Musorgsky (1839-1881), and N.A. Rimsky-Korsakov (1844-1908)—Tr.

5. For full title see the bibliography.

6. See footnote 4, above.

7. "Doklad B.V. Asaf'yeva", *op. cit.*

8. Later on Prokof'yev and Myaskovski were also pupils of Rimsky-Korsakov.

9. Stravinsky, Igor, *Poetics of Music*, Cambridge, Mass., 1947, p. 77.

10. Asaf'yev, B.V., *Kniga o Stravinskom*, Leningrad, 1929.

11. *Ibid.*, p. 6.

12. *Ibid.*, p. 7-8.

13. *Ibid.*, p. 9.

14. *Ibid.*, p. 12.

15. *Ibid.*, p. 13.

16. *Ibid.*, pp. 17-18.

17. The word "intonation" (*intonatsiya*) in Russian, thanks largely to Asaf'yev's use, has acquired the special sense of "the shortest melodic construction possessing a definite expressive and connotative significance," to quote the definition in K. Sezhenski, *Kratkii Slovar' muzykal'nykh terminov* [Short Dictionary of Musical Terms], 2nd corrected and enlarged ed., Moscow-Leningrad, 1950, p. 34.

18. *Ibid.*, p. 32. My italics—A. O.

19. *Ibid.*, p. 34.

20. *Ibid.*, p. 35.

21. *Ibid.*

22. *Ibid.*, p. 99.

23. *Ibid.*, pp. 109-110.

24. *Ibid.*, p. 215.

25. *Ibid.*, p. 217.

26. *Ibid.*, p. 259.

27. *Ibid.*, pp. 351-352.

28. *Ibid.*, p. 365.

29. *Ibid.*, pp. 367-368.

30. *Ibid.*, p. 383.

31. *Ibid.*, pp. 385-386.

32. Asaf'yev, *Kniga o Stravinskom*, p. 16.

33. *New York Times*, March 1, 1951.

34. Nest'yev, I., "Dollarovaya kakofoniya", *Izvestiya,* January 7, 1951.

35. Gorodinski, V., *Muzyka dukhovnoi nishchety,* Moscow-Leningrad, 1950.

36. *Ibid.,* p. 3.

37. *Ibid.,* p. 4. For Lenin's statement, see his *Sochineniya* [Works], 4th ed., Vol. XIX, p. 77.

38. *Ibid.,* p. 4.

39. *Ibid.,* pp. 130-131.

40. Asaf'yev *Kniga o Stravinskom,* p. 222.

PART III

Soviet Music Policy in Theory and Practice

In his memoirs Lunacharski writes that once when he expressed anxiety about the mass destruction of valuable cultural monuments which was taking place during the early phases of the Revolution, Lenin replied, "How can you be concerned with some old building, no matter how fine it is, when it is a question of clearing the way for a social order which will be capable of creating a beauty infinitely superior to anything dreamed of in the past?"—Lunacharski, A.V., *Lenin o kulture i iskusstve* [Lenin on Culture and Art], Moscow, 1938, p. 165.

A. SOVIET MUSICAL AESTHETICS

1. HISTORICAL BACKGROUND

The October Revolution of 1917 constitutes a watershed in the history of Russian art and culture. It marks the point at which the inner laws of development of Russian art were replaced as causative factors by external historical processes having no organic relation to art. Thereafter Russian culture, particularly music, developed in accordance not with the requirements of its own nature but with the demands and aims which were imposed upon it by the political power of the state.

During the February Revolution[1] the Russian artists who were members of the Union of Art Workers had issued the slogan "Long live Russian political life—and long live art free of politics!" In mid-November, however, when A.V. Lunacharski, People's Commissar of Education in the new Soviet government, called on the Union of Art Workers to join in the creation of a State Council of Arts, the executive organ of the Union of Art Workers on November 17/30 voted not only against the establishment of a State Council of Arts but against any contact whatsoever with the new Soviet authority. According to a contemporary account, "the Union of Persons Active in Art [Soyuz Deyatelei Iskusstva] opposed in principle cooperation with the representative of the new government in charge of art matters, Commissar A. Lunacharski."[2] Even in those years, however, the new Soviet power could not agree to leave art alone but claimed to be the sole custodian of the cultural heritage as well as a producer of new art values.

During the first decade of the Soviet regime, it is true, music as an art and a creative activity was hardly touched by the Soviet state. The material bases of the art, on the other hand—the state musical schools, the concert and theatrical organizations, the musical press and publishing industry, etc.—were all nationalized at an early date.[3]

The end of this period during which the state left creative musicians more or less to their own devices was marked by the First All-Russian Musical Conference which took place in the spring of 1929 under the auspices of the People's Commissariat of Education, headed by Lunacharski. Behind this conference lay a bitter struggle among various composers' unions. Some musicians honestly wished to establish closer contact with the developments of the "revolutionary epoch"; others were intent rather on exploiting the crisis for their own selfish ends. Maneuvering behind the scenes were the state authorities with their political aim of "inflaming the class struggle in the sector of art."

One will search in vain in the printed materials concerning this conference, however, for any clear statement defining the policy of the Soviet power with regard to music. The various competing groups merely obtained the right to seek what recognition they could from the authorities and from the public. The only point which was clearly established as the result of the conference was that henceforward each of these organizations was obliged to serve the interests of "class, proletarian art."

Several attempts were made, particularly during the first twenty years of the Soviet regime, to work out a general Marxist aesthetics, e.g., by Liya Ya. Zivel'chinskaya, Ivan L. Matsa and I.I. Ioffe.[4] In all cases, however, these efforts were shipwrecked by the Party's criticism with the resulting disgrace and even disappearance of their authors.

There is no doubt that this situation was due to the fact that the theoretical generalizations made or sanctioned by the Politburo were distinguished by their ambiguity and political motivation rather than by any concern for the right of positive artistic values to exist. Stalin's "dialectical materialism," which for nearly two decades has been the obligatory basis of the Soviet world outlook, denies spirituality, reducing it to a derivative of matter. The spiritual sterilization of art is the objective meaning of this philosophy and aesthetics.

Hence the essence of the Party's methodology of art is reduced to the teaching that art is a superstructure over the economic foundation and, as such, is always a class phenomenon, and that in the sphere of art there are not and cannot be values which are independent, neutral and nonpolitical.

To serve as reference works for Soviet art critics, textbooks are published from time to time giving statements by Marx, Engels, Lenin, and Stalin on the question of art. Yet even in these works one will find nothing directly relating to art, simply because there are no such concrete pronouncements, especially with reference to music.

2. CONTEMPORARY SOVIET MUSICAL AESTHETICS

A fairly complete program of the contemporary methodology of Soviet music can be found in a book entitled *The Ways of Development of Soviet Music* which was published in Moscow in 1948.[5] The work was published by the Musicological

Commission of the Union of Soviet Composers, an indication that it represents the official Party line.

According to this publication,

> The First All-Union Congress of Soviet Composers which took place in April 1948 demonstrated the indestructible unity and solidarity of ideas of composers and musicologists of all the sixteen Union republics and *their fervent aspiration to develop musical art in accordance with the realistic way* indicated by the Central Committee of the CPSU(b).[6]

The "realistic way" referred to is that indicated in the Central Committee resolution on the opera *The Great Friendship* by Muradeli.[7] It is this "fervent aspiration to develop musical art in accordance with the realistic way indicated by the Central Committee" that the authors of this book have in mind when they speak of the development of Soviet music.

What is the real meaning of this "realistic way" of development of Soviet music? What are its peculiarities and what are the bases of its aesthetic principles? Clarification of these questions is necessary, particularly because the official Soviet musical press attaches to it great revolutionary significance and sees in it a force capable of reconstructing the whole history of musical development and opening gigantic perspectives for the future of music.

First, it is clear that the general principles of "socialist aesthetics" exclude the theory of "art for art's sake" which, it is alleged, is "frankly proclaimed by bourgeois musicians ...to justify the alienation of musical art from the problems of practical vital struggle."[8] Citing Belinsky's contention that "freedom of creative work can easily be combined with service to the contemporary world. . .and that for this it is only necessary to be a citizen, a son of one's society and of one's epoch, to assimilate its interests and to fuse one's own aspirations with its aspirations,"[9] the authors of the "new socialist aesthetics" give their full approval to "Party instructions [which] invariably assert the principle of a highly ideological [*vysokoideinovo*] and popular realistic art."[10]

One would be mistaken, however, if one were to see in these words a repetition of the "applied aesthetics" of the 1860's. The Soviet methodologists of a "realistic art" go far beyond this, affirming the general relevance in art of Lenin's thesis of the "Party character [*partiinost'*] of art."

"Literature must be of the Party," Lenin said.

> In opposition to bourgeois morals and manners, in opposition to the bourgeois commercial press and to bourgeois literary careerism and individualism, to 'parlour anarchism' and the pursuit of gain, the socialist proletariat must advance the principle of *literature of the Party* and must develop this principle and realize it in life in its most complete and integral form.[11]

"These striking thoughts of Lenin," the authors comment,

> which lie at the foundation of the doctrine of the Party character of literature, resounded with new force in 1946 in Comrade Zhdanov's speech on the publications *Zvezda* and *Leningrad.* They apply with full force to musicians also. Soviet composers, like Soviet writers, have no right to be indifferent to politics or to hide away from the contemporary scene in an individual little world of their own. We do not need composer supermen who are detached from the common cause that constitutes the life of the whole Soviet people . . . .Music, like literature, should be tendentious and should be based on the principles of Partyism; it should play an actively transforming role in public life, in the Communist education of Soviet man and in the formation of his ethical character and the whole structure of his feelings and world outlook. These are the most important conclusions that follow from the Party instructions pertaining to questions of art.[12]

. . . .

On the basis of Lenin's thesis of the partyism [partiinost'] of art there arises a complete and orderly system of

> aesthetic principles [of musical realism]. Soviet musical art must be *realistic* and must truthfully and vividly embody reality in all its multiformity and complexity. Our times, which are times of decisive, deadly skirmishes between the expiring bourgeois order and the new, victorious, Communist order which is being created before our eyes, open for Soviet composers an exceptional wealth of ideas, images and subjects.[13]

This being the case it is a remarkable fact that one cannot find in the Soviet press any clear definition of what is really meant by "socialist realism" as a method of Soviet music. What are its characteristics and how does it differ from non-Socialist realism? In answer to such questions Soviet aestheticians usually limit themselves to vague and meaningless assertations, e.g., "the essence of [socialist realism] lies in the fact that a writer or artist truthfully presents reality in its revolutionary development as if looking at the present from the future."[14]

What does "looking at the present from the future" mean? One can understand this expression only if one remembers that the "future" in this case means the myth of "the golden age" which has been invented by Soviet propaganda; to look "from the future into the present," therefore, means to assist in implanting this myth, i.e., to be made use of by its fabricators.

In reality, however, when evaluating works of art from the point of view of their "socialist realism" Soviet critics are guided by simpler criteria. Certain compositions, often judged on the basis of their program or content, are declared to be absolutely realistic; others, judged on the same basis, are condemned as absolutely deficient in this essential quality. Questions of the composer's artistic conception or of his technical procedures are simply ignored. The meaning attached to "socialist realism" therefore is either a concentrated emotionalism or, more frequently, simply "This is what I like."

3. "REALISM" IN MUSIC

The question of realism in music is not a new one of course. Composers have always tended to base their creative conceptions on the conventional idioms, and then, after exhausting and becoming tired of the "conventional," have begun to be attracted by what is "natural" and "realistic."

But such a historically justified movement towards "realism" in art has nothing in common with the official approval of "socialist realism" in Soviet aesthetics. The "realism" demanded by Soviet aestheticians is not the usual kind but is "socialist," i.e., "realism" that does not assume any objective artistic truth but on the contrary imposes upon art the duty of carrying on political propaganda.

The question, of course, is not whether the Soviet artist should or should not draw his inspiration from the ideas of Bolshevism or from the political tasks of everyday life. Art is not obliged to limit itself to a single sphere of life at the expense of all others. The ideas of Bolshevism could also be such a sphere among others and could attract the artist. But the Soviet artist is *compelled* to be nothing but a "socialist realist." It is sufficient to observe the way in which the Communist Party and the Soviet government treat the two hundred million persons who are so contemptuously referred to as "the masses" to discover the real nature of this "realism." It is the duty of the Administration for Propaganda and Agitation of the Party Central Committee to use every means to tell "the masses" what they should believe and how they should think. All the means of mass communications, including art, are controlled by this Administration and the composer must therefore accept as "realistic" whatever his masters consider useful to themselves.

To Soviet cultural politicians the basic task of a "realistic musical art" is the employment by Soviet composers of "vital, actual, real subjects and themes" and the "organic transformation of the leading, progressive demands of ideology which are advanced by contemporary life."[15] Moreover, they consider that this problem

> should be solved not only in operatic works but also in all forms of music requiring a text (cantatas, choral works, romances, and songs). Instrumental textless music should also have a plot, a purposeful idea and a program—in the broad meaning of this word; ... [while] the vital, honest musical idiom which has been developed by the classics must be accepted creatively by Soviet composers and enriched with the newest intonations born from the elements of the contemporary song and the intensive development of the folk music of the various nationalities of the Soviet Union.[16]

Summing up the problem of "socialist realism in music" the authors conclude:

> The fundamental task of Soviet composers, basing their work on the principles of socialism realism, is to express the leading ideas of the present time in a simple, natural musical language understandable to the people but with all the power of aesthetic influence.[17]

The greater part of the activity of Soviet musicologists during recent years has consisted of nothing but the theoretical elaboration of this "fundamental task" of Soviet composers, while its practical realization takes all of the composers' time and energy. The whole organization of musical life in the Soviet Union, including composing, performance, musical education, music appreciation, folk music, and amateur activity, is mobilized for the discharge of this "fundamental task." The result has been a startling change in the musical life of the Soviet Union. In 1949, only a year after the publication of the Central Committee resolution on the opera *The Great Friendship*, the Secretary General of the Union of Soviet Composers, Tikhon Khrennikov, speaking at the second plenary session of the Union, referred to such composers as Prokof'yev, Myaskovski, Shostakovich, Shebalin, and

Popov as belonging to a stage which has passed long ago in a tone permitting no contradiction. Referring to the allegedly "complete failure" of Prokof'yev's opera *The Story of a Real Man* and its "extremely formalist music" Khrennikov said: "We hope that this experiment will serve as a lesson for Prokof'yev and for some other composers who still cannot overcome their inherent individualism."[18] Shostakovich did not escape a similar haughty reference: "Recognizing the full importance of this composer's work for motion pictures," Khrennikov said, "we must nevertheless remind [him] that the Soviet public expects from him compositions in other forms imbued with the spirit of realism and embodying the vital images of our actuality."[19]

"We want N.Ya. Myaskovski," he went on in the same categorical tone, "when solving problems of creative reconstruction to overcome consistently and resolutely the gloomy moods which have been characteristic of his creations. . . in the past . . . ."[20] This was said literally on the eve of the death of this remarkable composer.

"We have a right to turn to Khachaturian with the same reminder as to Shostakovich—the necessity for active work in other forms and for not retiring exclusively into the realm of cinema music," Khrennikov continued.[21] Speaking as the chief representative of the purity of Soviet music he stated that Shebalin's *Seventh Quartet*, which was performed at the plenary session, "did not leave [him with] the impression of an artistic whole."[22] Concerning the composer G. Popov he said, "To our regret, one cannot form any definite impression of [his] work for this period."[23]

But to make up for this the plenum, through the mouth of Khrennikov, was enthusiastic about the "creations" of a vast number of nameless composers who, in his words, are clearing the way "for the appearance of those beautiful works about our life which the Party has called on us to create."[24]

Let us consider in greater detail just what these Soviet

khrennikovs have in mind when they talk about such "beautiful works."[25]

"Our Soviet socialist aesthetics is different in principle from the old, including even the most advanced democratic [*sic*] aesthetics," it was claimed in one of the leading addresses delivered at the First All-Union Congress of Soviet Composers.

> Its basic distinction is defined by the new qualities of our socialist epoch and by the new world outlook of Soviet artists....
>
> Soviet art has no need to dress up its heroes in the garments of "romantic" epochs as is done by many bourgeois artists (even in their best periods). The romantic hero of our contemporary Soviet life is here, side by side with our artists. In search of the idea of the beautiful the artist does not need to idealize the past or paint a fantastic future in misty images. *The beautiful is around us, in our life.* Sensing the best qualities of Soviet man, realistically representing the development and enrichment of these features in the future, our art workers, the "engineers of men's souls," *are called upon actively to promote the process* of uprooting the remnants of the past from the consciousness of Soviet man and of creating images noble, truthful and beautiful.[26]

In thus affirming that "the beautiful is around us, in our life," the Soviet aesthetics of "socialist realism" plainly limits the role of the Soviet artist to the "creative affirmation" of the Soviet system of life. The "leading ideas" which the Soviet composer is called upon to embody in "simple musical language which can be understood by the masses," i.e., the idiom of folk music or the mass song—these ideas are in reality nothing but the political ideology of the Party. The composer's role is thus at best nothing but that of a literate official propagating Party directives.

4. *"NATIONALISM" IN MUSIC*

As important to art as "realism" in the opinion of orthodox

Soviet aestheticians is "nationalism" [*narodnost'*].[27] According to the authoritative publication *The Ways of Development of Soviet Music,*

> ....nationalism in art demands from the composer the most profound penetration into the spirit of the people and the most complete fusion of his interests and aspirations with the interests and aspirations of the people. Nationalism in art likewise demands strong ties between the composer and the people's art of his native land.[28]

However, here too the Soviet propagandists really have in mind nothing but service by composers for the political aims of the Party, since in Soviet terms "the people" is always directly identified with the Party.

Like the question of "realism," that of "nationalism" in art, including music, was a central theme in the ideological polemics of the nineteenth century. What was really at stake in these debates was the right of the artist to speak in the name of the people.

The theoretical question of nationality and of the ways and means of creating a national art was not entirely clear to The Five even though they were supplying an answer to it in their creative practice. Although they were far from uniform in the use they made of folk music they nevertheless manifested an extraordinary flair for understanding popular vocal music, displaying in their works a number of its characteristic features, particularly its singing quality, its variational development of the thematic material and its linear exposition.

However, their search for nationality was by no means exhausted by their appeal to folk music alone. Both Stasov and Balakirev were disposed to see in the works of their adherents a healthy reaction against "pure art" and considered as fundamental signs of nationality not only the use of national subjects drawn from the Russian past but also the positive tone of their work. This they considered to be a fundamental characteristic that established points of similarity between their music and the true "spirit of the Russian people," in opposition to the "tearful and elegiac" mood of their predecessors.

The appeals of Soviet orthodox aestheticians for an inheritance of the Five's conception of nationalism, however, sound completely false. The official canonization of the "Russian style" by the Soviet art policy has nothing in common with genuine nationalism in music and threatens to swamp every vital impulse born from inner necessity. The tradition of The Five which has been imposed upon Soviet composers by the heavy hand of Zhdanov cannot be separated from the creative work of these composers, which has only a superficial connection with Soviet artistic ideology. In reality that tradition is positively hostile to the one-sided, narrow Communist view of life.

The folk music garb which Soviet composers are obliged to wear to dress up their thoughts and feelings cannot be looked upon as genuine contact with the people. Everything written by Soviet composers is exposed to public dishonor and attacked as antinational if it does not meet the official demand for a return to folk music. The whole trend of recent Soviet music is nothing but an artificial resuscitation of folk music. This is the inevitable outcome of the process of determining musical forms and style not by historical factors of musical development but by orders of the Party and the government.

5. *"MUSIC FOR THE PEOPLE"*

At the conference of musicians which was held preceding the First All-Union Congress of Composers in April 1948, Zhdanov argued that the compositions of many leading Soviet composers were inaccessible to the masses and that these composers had broken away from the people. "Some Soviet composers," Zhdanov said, "also have a theory that they will be appreciated in fifty or a hundred years. That is a terrible attitude. It means a complete divorce from the people." And in the same context he went on to say that "music that is unintelligible to the people is unwanted by the people."[29]

Alexander Werth, citing these words in his book *Musical Uproar in Moscow,*[30] comes to the conclusion that the question discussed at the congress boils down essentially to the alternative "music for the few or music for the masses," and that Zhdanov and the Party as a whole recognize only one criterion: "the people like it," or "the people don't like it."[31] What a profound error! Is it really possible to imagine that Zhdanov and the Politburo were thinking only of how to be benefactors to the people? The real point of the discussion is something far different from this, a fact to which the Soviet press itself attests with all obviousness.

The Central Committee resolution on the opera *The Great Friendship*[32] repeatedly stresses the need for overcoming the lack of contact between Soviet music and the people and asserts that "during recent years the level of cultural interests and artistic tastes of the Soviet people has been raised to an unusual degree." However, the apparent radicalism of this phraseology will mislead only some naive people. In reality the appeals for "nationalism" in music and the whole concept of "music for the people" or "music for the masses" represent nothing but an attempt at levelling art in order to enhance its propaganda value, with no regard whatever to the artistic education of the consumer.

Poverty of musical material and the prevalence of debased standards are called upon to ensure the mass success of Soviet music. Soviet "music for the masses" is the music of spiritual enslavement rather than of the artistic education of the masses; it is music by propagandist-composers who know how to invent a tune but not how to develop it and who are frequently unable even to write it down satisfactorily.

The compulsory fusion of the aims of creative art with those of political propaganda has become the basic task of Soviet art policy. The Soviet press is filled with exhortations to the artists to undertake this task, and with assertions like the following:

> The masters of Soviet art, inspired by the great ideas of the Party of Lenin and Stalin, are devoting all their energies to their beloved motherland, creating works accessible to the people and loved by them, educating the mind and will of the working masses and encouraging the Soviet people to fight for the complete victory of communism. In this, and only in this, lies the meaning and significance of artistic creation, the holy, patriotic duty of Soviet artists, all of whose thoughts and hopes must be directed toward the people.[33]

Thus resolutely and unequivocally the Soviet power is transforming art into a tool for its political struggle and a subordinate addition to its propaganda resources.

Music, however, like other forms of art, has always followed its own path in conformity to its own nature, rejecting outside efforts to pervert its creative aims to other uses and throwing off clumsy experiments which lie outside its boundaries. The genuine composer has always been a searcher of human destiny, keeping aloof from the everyday pragmatic aims of political power. The basic and most important element in every genuine aesthetics was and remains the creative freedom of the artist and his rejection of any form of external control.

The spiritual development of Russian music, particularly since the end of the nineteenth century, was not something self-contained and detached from the general process of human culture; it followed more or less the same path as that of Western music, although sometimes at a later date. The Russian composers at the beginning of the present century could with entire justification call themselves Europeans. Both Slavophile regionalism and an attitude of hostile pride toward the West were alien to them. They were far from considering Western culture as being exhausted; on the contrary, they were deeply convinced of its creative Faustian spirit which had never ceased to serve as a source of spiritual nourishment for Russian music. It is precisely this factor which has caused the Soviet authorities to brand contemporary Russian composers of the senior generation as "homeless cosmopolitans."

The Soviet authorities accuse them of "servility towards the West" which, they claim, prevents them from fulfilling the tasks assigned to them by the Party. It is claimed, furthermore, that these composers are guided not by the interests of an uncompromising struggle against "manifestations of bourgeois ideology" but rather by considerations of their personal creative intentions. Thus, it is claimed, they bring incalculable harm to the State's effort to "educate the masses in the spirit of communism," fail to discharge their duty to the people and completely compromise the social function of their art.

It is because of this attitude towards the existing creative life of Russian music that the key positions in Soviet music during recent years have been occupied not by such men as Myaskovski, Prokof'yev and Shostakovich but by a host of unknown, nameless music officials whose only merit is their willingness to execute the task assigned to them by political propaganda.

The general disparity between Soviet works of art and Soviet reality is the result not of the Soviet artist's ignorance of reality but of the fear Soviet ideologists have that truthful images of Soviet reality might be disseminated through the channels of art. It is for this reason that they have invented their own "socialist aesthetics" to prevent the true thoughts and feelings of the Soviet-dominated people from finding their way into art. It is precisely this situation which creates in Soviet music the "impoverishment of soul" and the "distortion of images" about which Soviet art critics complain so bitterly.

The cynical atmosphere of slander, fabrication and abject repentance, with promises to "correct one's mistakes" and to be "more careful," the atmosphere in which humiliated musicians pretend to be happy and grateful to those who control them—this in reality is what constitutes the "creative conditions" under which Soviet composers work. A genuine artistic atmosphere, which is a prerequisite for normal artistic activities, has long since ceased to exist in the Soviet Union. In its place there are continual purges and the physical and moral annihilation of "homeless cosmopolitans," "bourgeois nationalists," "admirers of the bourgeois culture of the West," and "spiritual liberals." In this atmosphere Soviet music and Soviet art as a whole undergo creative depression, stagnation and general artistic degradation.

The revitalizing power of the idea of humanity, the great spirit of liberty and the flaming creative enthusiasm which existed in the hearts of Soviet composers during the first years of the Soviet regime are now only distant memories. In their place reigns the staggering monotony of political standardization.

The meaning of this suppression of creative freedom in the Soviet Union is obvious: it is part of the effort to crush the spark of conscious intellect, a clear manifestation of the materialist conception and philosophy of life as a terrible tool for the enslavement of man.

B. SOVIET MUSICOLOGY

1. ORGANIZATION AND DEVELOPMENT

The major Soviet institutions in which research and instruction are carried on in the history and theory of music are the State Institute of the History of Arts under the Soviet Academy of Sciences and the Institute of Theater and Music in Leningrad, until recently a subsidiary of the Committee for Art Affairs. The second-named institute was organized during the early years of the Soviet regime on the basis of the Institute of the History of Arts which was founded before the Revolution by a well-known art patron and connoisseur, Count Zubov. In addition, musicological studies are conducted in the pedagogical departments of the various conservatories, particularly those of Moscow, Leningrad, Kiev, Tbilisi, and Yerevan, and in the Musicology Commission of the Union of Soviet Composers.

As to the Institute of the History of Arts under the Soviet Academy of Sciences, its musicological activity has been very slight up to the present, with the exception of a short period of work by Boris Vladimirovich Asaf'yev (Igor Glebov), who until his death in 1949 was the only musicologist who held full membership in the Soviet Academy of Sciences. Mention should also be made of the contributions in this field made by a small number of corresponding members.

On the other hand the Musical Section of the Institute of Theater and Music has been a most productive institution in the realm of musicology. At the head of this section of the Institute from the day of its "reorganization" by the Soviets up to his death in 1949 was the leading contemporary Russian musicologist, B.V. Asaf'yev. In recent years the musical section has been under the supervision of A.V. Ossovski, the head of the Institute's scientific branch. The relatively few collaborators of the Musical Section were chiefly professors of the history and theory of music at the Leningrad Conservatory and postgraduate students from various other Soviet conservatories who had been sent to the Institute for scientific training.

Until the mid-thirties the central governmental organs manifested little interest in the Musical Section of the Institute. The work of the section was done independently of and frequently even in opposition to the directives of the government and Party. During this period the section was organized into a number of subsections and commissions, e.g., subsections for musical culture, life and literature, a methodological section, a commission for musical acoustics, and a commission for instrumentation. Each of these groups was headed by one of the section's senior collaborators who had shown his ability in a specific field of research and each worked in accordance with plans approved by the leaders of sections or groups. Members studied subjects corresponding to their own research interests and experience. Reports on work in progress were read and discussed at general meetings of a group or of the whole section.

During the twenties the Institute acquired some equipment for carrying out laboratory research which made possible the fairly extensive development of experimental work, particularly in such fields as acoustics (the first thereminvox experiments were carried out there) and instrumentation (particularly interesting work was done in the invention of electrical musical instruments and a quarter-tone keyboard). The Institute also had one of the most extensive musical and musicological libraries in the Soviet Union which was especially rich in material on contemporary art.

Up to the mid-thirties very few of the Institute's collaborators deemed it necessary to base their conclusions exclusively on the doctrines of Marxism-Leninism. It is true that there was a special "sociological seminar" attached to the Institute where the members of each branch, particularly postgraduate students, were required to present themes developing some question of music from the point of view of Marxist-Leninist philosophy and aesthetics. In the other subsections and groups, however, everyone was left to himself. Since most of the collaborators of the Musical Section were either pupils of Asaf'yev or completely shared his views, the activity of the section had the clearly expressed character of free idealistic investigation which was evident in the work of Asaf'yev himself.

One can say with confidence—and this is confirmed by the subject matter and methodology of research of the works published by the Musical Section prior to 1930—that the dominant interests of its members were on the one hand questions concerning the development of Russian music and on the other questions concerning contemporary Western music. Problems relating to Soviet music or to Soviet musical conditions in general lay entirely outside the orbit of the section's scientific work. This is understandable since those were years of an especially vigorous growth of modernism and the Musical Section, under its leader Asaf'yev, was not only a pioneer and inspirer of the movement of contemporary music but also carried out a number of practical measures for the diffusion of contemporary Western music. During those years it was still possible to write dissertations, for instance, on the creative work of the contemporary Viennese school (Schoenberg, Alban Berg, von Webern, etc.)[34] or books on Stravinsky (e.g., one by Asaf'yev himself); to organize within the section a group interested in quarter-tone music, as was done by G.M. Rimsky-Korsakov, the nephew of the composer; to work out Schillinger's "mathematical method of composition"; to be interested in Henry Cowell's theory of the "harmony of seconds" (Cowell himself read a paper on the subject at the Institute); and to elaborate the principles of electrical instrumentation.

Periodic concerts of modern Western music were organized by the Institute during that period as well as special seminars to provide an opportunity for making the acquaintance of contemporary music through piano transcriptions.

The Institute carried on a fairly extensive publishing program devoted to questions of contemporary music. It issued, for example, a collection of articles entitled *De Musica,* the collection *Music and Musical Life in Old Russia* and several monographs devoted to individual composers.[35] The subject matter and style of these publications testified to a wide range of interests, from philosophy, aesthetics and the psychology of musical creation to stylistics and special aspects of musical idiom.

The middle of the thirties saw the beginning of a "new course" in the activity of the Musical Section and in the Institute as a whole. The rout of "modernism" which followed the publication in 1932 of the Central Committee resolution "On the Reorganization of Art and Literary Organizations"[36] set back for a long time the progress of Soviet musicology or, to be more exact, rendered impossible henceforward its free development. A realistic consequence of this crushing of modernism in the Institute was the exile to a Siberian camp of the director of the Institute, Academician Fyodor Ivanovich Shmidt, an outstanding scholar in the field of art. This event was followed by the complete reorganization of all sections of the Institute "in order to bring its work closer to the problems and requirements of Soviet art policy." In actual fact the work of the Institute was paralyzed for a number of years, and it was not until 1937 or 1938 that the Musical Section somehow managed to pull itself together, only to find itself completely at the service of the political propagandistic aims of the Soviet power.

Since that time the exclusive concern of the Musical Section of the Institute of Theater and Music has been the preparation of publications for use in Soviet music schools and conservatories, incorporating the concepts of Marxism and the transformation of values in the spirit of the slogan "Soviet music, the most progressive in the world." The most important single part of this work has been the writing of a "History of the Musical Culture of the Peoples of the U.S.S.R." which was supposed to show the

> historical formation of the musical culture of the peoples of the U.S.S.R. as a unified process, conditioned in the past by the common struggle for liberation of the peoples inhabiting Russia against social and national enslavement by Tsarism and in the present by the Soviet policy of friendship among the peoples, inspired by the ideals of the Communist Party.[37]

This work, which enlisted the services of all the outstanding musicologists of the Soviet Union, did not, however, lead to the desired results. It was almost ready for publication in 1940, but it was then subjected to the usual revision and refinement and apparently has still not seen the light of day.

Along with the work on the History, which was planned as a general re-evaluation of the past, present and future of musical culture as a whole, the members of the Institute are diligently working on propagandistic articles for the current press and on articles for the *Large* and *Small* Soviet encyclopedias. These, too, must be reworked for each new edition, giving entirely opposite evaluations of the facts and phenomena of musical culture in accordance with the current political situation. The Institute members are also compiling a special "Musical Encyclopedia" on which they have been working for the past twenty years but which has made hardly any progress. They also prepare collections of source material for use in schools and monographs devoted to the life and work of outstanding composers, mainly of Russian music of the past.

The functions of the other Soviet musicological organizations can be summarized briefly. During the first years of the Soviet regime there existed in Moscow a special research institute called the State Institute of Musical Science which, unlike the State Institute of the History of Arts in Leningrad, specialized mainly in problems of the history of Russian music (under Ivanov-Boretski), the history of Western music (Kuznetsov), singing techniques (Dr. Levidov), piano playing (G. Prokof'yev), and musical acoustics (Garbusov). After five years of existence this Institute was reorganized as the "Scientific Office under the Moscow Conservatory," combining the activities of the scientific-pedagogical departments of the conservatory.

The Musical Section of the Institute of Theater and Music and the scientific-pedagogical departments of the Moscow Conservatory during recent years have become institutions of purely applied significance. The tasks assigned to these institutions are concerned mainly with narrow pedagogical problems, such as preparation of the program of school courses and of textbooks and pedagogical aids for students. Similarly the work of the Musicological Section of the Composers' Union is directed mainly towards answering the inquiries of Soviet musical journalists and critics. Since these bodies are now occupied exclusively with problems connected with the current objectives of Soviet art policy they cannot carry out any genuine research work inspired by freedom of research initiative. Both the Musical Section of the Institute of Theater and Music and the departments of the conservatory are directed by Party officials who guard the political purity of institutions whose sole reason for existence is to serve the Soviet art policy.

Since the publication in 1948 of the Central Committee's resolution on Muradeli's opera *The Great Friendship*, the range of activity of Soviet musicologists has been formulated with particular clarity. A clear picture of this range is given in a review by *Soviet Music* of the All-Union Scientific Session on Musicology which took place in March 1950.[38]

"The basic task of the session," according to this review,

> was the discussion of prospectuses for scientific research works on the history of Soviet music, on new textbooks and on projects of curricula for the history of Russian and foreign music, on the history of the music of the peoples of the U.S.S.R., on Russian folk music, and on certain theoretical disciplines (harmony, polyphony and Russian polyphony).
>
> This task arose from the necessity for a basic reorganization of the entire educational work in musical institutions in conformity with the Central Committee resolution of February 10, 1948 by the CC of the CPSU(b)[39] in which it was specifically stated that the vicious antipopular formalist tendency in music has exerted a pernicious influence on the training and education of young musicians.[40]

The general tasks of Soviet musicologists were formulated in the main report presented to the session by Professor A.V. Ossovski, Corresponding Member of the Soviet Academy of Sciences, entitled, "Basic Questions of the Study of Russian Musical Culture." "The task of the musicologists," said Ossovski in his speech, as summarized in *Soviet Music*, "is to advance that which exalts Russian music and ensures its foremost role in the development of the world's musical culture—its great ideas and the great perfection of their artistic and musical embodiment."[41] Ossovski's immodest formulation, to put it mildly, which elevates Russian music to the unprecedented role of being the sole bearer of "great ideas and the great perfection of their embodiment" and which raises the role of the Soviet musicologist to that of a prophet of the future universal harmony, is somewhat modified by a more sober commentator on Ossovski's report who writes:

> We must highly evaluate what is new and imbued with profound principles... [i.e.,] the aspiration to rebuild our musicological science on the basis of Marxist-Leninist methodology; the aspiration to draw the ultimate conclusions from the exhaustive instructions given in the decrees of the Central Committee of the CPSU(b) pertaining to ideological questions and in the addresses by Comrade Zhdanov at the conference of workers in the field of Soviet music: to destroy formalist and cosmopolitan tendencies and similar survivals of bourgeois ideological influences; to overcome the theory of a single current [of cultural development] and to re-examine the musical-historical process in the light of Lenin's thesis of two cultures; to show the development of musical culture as the process of struggle between two trends—the realistic trend and the antipopular, antirealistic trend; to expose the deep interconnections between Russian musical culture and the musical cultures of the fraternal peoples of the U.S.S.R.; and to emphasize the significance of Russian and Soviet musical culture.[42]

Of course, as was to be expected, the session once again reaffirmed Zhdanov's dictum that "healthy criticism by the Bolshevik Party is the genuine motive power of our development."[43]

Thus the complete and unconditional subjugation of Soviet musicology to the political aims of the Soviet power has become the essential factor determining the work of Soviet musicologists, rendering impossible any further progress in the investigation of the real problems of musical culture.

2. *HISTORICAL MUSICOLOGY*

The Conference of February 1949. Until fairly recently Soviet musicologists were to some extent able to ignore the strident clamor of Party propaganda and write books and articles on subjects of interest to themselves, although frequently they had no intention of publishing them.

The Party, however, was aware of this situation and took the necessary steps to bring musicology under its control. Its chief weapon for achieving this goal was the "re-education" of Soviet musicologists by means of periodic purges, one of the most significant of which was the "working over" to which a number of leading Soviet musicologists were subjected at a conference of the Union of Soviet Composers held on February 18, 21 and 22, 1949.[42]

The usual procedure in such cases is for a trusted Party member to deliver a report on some current problem, simultaneously subjecting to criticism certain "oppositionists" to whom the Party objects. Following this there is a discussion of the report which includes a statement of repentance by those who have been criticized and finally the appropriate organizational conclusions are drawn. On this occasion the subject of the main report was "Cosmopolitanism and Formalism in Music Criticism and Musicology," delivered by the Secretary General of the Union of Composers, Tikhon Khrennikov. The accused included practically everyone of any stature in the field of Soviet musicology–musicologists, critics and professors at the Moscow and Leningrad Conservatories. Incidentally the ostensible targets in such cases are always persons of secondary importance; in this case the main attack was levelled at the musicologists I. Bėlza and A. Ogolevets.

Khrennikov first spoke of the tasks which "the Party and the people" had assigned to Soviet musicologists and called for a "militant, principled, Party criticism and self-criticism." He went on to assert that "[Soviet] music criticism has not only not placed itself in the vanguard, but in many respects hampers, retards and impedes the development of Soviet music in the one true and realistic direction indicated by the Party and the people."[45] Turning his attention to individual critics, Khrennikov continued,

> Up until the present time many of our musicologists and critics, who until recently were advocates of formalism in Soviet music, still stand aside from musical creative work developing along the new path and remain concealed, sometimes even nourishing hopes of revenge.
>
> ....One of the most active cosmopolitans and fertile advocates of formalism in music criticism has been I. Belza....
>
> Supporting everything that is ugliest and most negative in the work of Soviet composers who have taken formalist positions, Bèlza simultaneously slandered the great Russian composers of the past. To the work of Glinka, Tchaikovsky, Musorgsky, Taneyev, and Rachmaninov he ascribed features of religious mysticism and idealism, effectively castrating their works of advanced ideological content and democratic orientation.
>
> ....While this group of musicologists and critics has been propagating their antipatriotic views in journalism and in action,... the musicologist A. Ogolevets has for many years been foisting his own doctrine on the musical community with all his strength. Exactly what is Ogolevets' doctrine? It is a frankly formalist theory, deeply alien to the Marxist-Leninist science of art.[46]

The "zealous apologists of formalism" who were attacked at the conference included almost all the most important Soviet musicologists, for example, M. Pekelis, a professor at the Moscow Conservatory, the director of its department of the history of Russian music and the author of what Khrennikov described as a "profoundly corrupt textbook on the history of Russian music which in every possible way belittles the originality of Russian national culture"; Professor T. Livanova, also of the Moscow Conservatory, the author of a book entitled *Outlines and Materials on the History of Russian Musical Culture* which allegedly expresses "cosmopolitan views"; and Professor L. Mazel', director of the department of musical theory at the Moscow Conservatory, whom Khrennikov condemned as a "carrier of reactionary theory." Also mentioned as "carriers of antipopular, anti-Party tendencies which block the paths of development of the Party science of musical art" were Professor R. Gruber, formerly of the Leningrad Conservatory, now of Moscow, where he is the director of the department of the history of Western European music, and Professor G. Kogan, director of the department of the history and theory of pianism at the Moscow Conservatory. Not forgotten were the most active Soviet musical critics and journalists, authors of numerous articles in *Soviet Music,* such as S. Shlifshtein, G. Shneyerson, D. Zhitomirski, I. Martynov, and Yu. Vainkop.

It is hardly necessary to comment on the real meaning of this "creative assembly." The very fact that it was held and that it included within the sphere of its "critical attention" the great majority of the leading Soviet musicologists and critics clearly demonstrates that the real purpose of the meeting was not to criticize the "mistakes" or "cosmopolitan delusions" of the theorists of Soviet music but rather to attack the openly expressed opposition of Soviet musicology and criticism to the official demands of Soviet art policy.

How sharp the conflict with this secret opposition became can be judged by the tone of the speaker who described the work of those who were criticized and by the organizational conclusions which the conference reached:

> The assembly has instructed the secretariat of the Union of Soviet Composers to examine the question of the desirability of retaining as members of the Union those major proponents of formalism and cosmopolitanism in music who have fully discredited themselves as bitter enemies of the progressive realistic trend in Soviet music and as spokesmen of a militant bourgeois ideology in musical art.[47]

To be expelled from the Union, however, meant to be simultaneously expelled from musicological institutions, i.e., to be compelled to move to some small provincial town which would be equivalent to exile.

Just how Soviet musicology as represented by its best minds had "compromised" itself can be seen quite clearly from the fairly detailed account of the speeches delivered at the meeting as reported in *Soviet Music.*

It appears, for example, that Professor L. Mazel' as early as 1940 "in the pages of *Soviet Music* openly declared the legitimacy and inevitability of the separation of science and pedagogy from militant journalism and the task of actively serving the contemporary building-up of music";[48] that Professor Zhitomirski in discussing the *Ninth Symphony* of Shostakovich raised objections to the view of the music critic Keldysh that the principal criterion for Soviet music should be "what the Soviet people want and expect" and had said, "all this is true; but great art is not created as the result of the social command, [and] this point of view is a resurrection of the theory of the social command";[49] that the musicologist Ogolevets had written that what is important is "the succession which we have demonstrated of the development of the phases of the tonal system throughout the world, independent of the national and racial character of its creators; what is important is the world-wide action of the laws of development of musical thought....";[50] that Professor Livanova in her works, and particularly in her *Essays and Materials on the History of Russian Musical Culture,* had defended the thesis that "it would hardly be too bold to assert that even up to the present time the conception of the historical process of Russian music to some extent approaches a kind of 'Slavophile' viewpoint";[51] that in the two-volume *History of Russian Music* edited by Professor Pekelis the predominant methodological basis of research was the "tracing of 'influences' and of the effect of Western music upon Russian music";[52] and that Professor Gruber's *History of Musical Culture* "suffers from defects of principle," in that "in attempting to draw a picture of universal musical culture, Gruber, in blindly retaining the conceptions of Western European bourgeois scholars, completely ignores the Slavic cultures and the cultures of the peoples of Transcaucasus and Central Asia."[53]

It is not difficult to understand the real meaning of these

objections to the ideas of Soviet musicologists, ideas which are not only not harmful but which on the contrary provide evidence that Soviet-dominated musicology is profoundly progressive. The real meaning was stated succinctly in the words of one of the musicologists at the conference: "In our country a sharp struggle is going on for Partyism in science." Where such a sharp struggle is under way, however, it is doubtful whether it is necessary to take science into consideration at all or even the elementary honesty of the scientific worker. Is this not confirmed by the pathetic declaration of V. Kukharski, one of the politically orthodox speakers at the conference who, on hearing the statement that "it is necessary to examine one's tastes and sympathies" from one of those who had been criticized, indignantly exclaimed, "after the resolution of the Central Committee, the man still needs to examine his tastes and sympathies!"[54]

One other curious and extremely significant detail proves that even after the Central Committee resolution Soviet musicologists sometimes find an opportunity to "examine their tastes and sympathies," even though these are strictly defined for them in the office of the Administration for Propaganda and Agitation. It happened that one of the critics could not refrain from stating in an article on contemporary American music that "creative musical work in America is on the ascent. Youth, creative enterprise and energy, belief in their own people and in their own powers and good professional training characterize the contemporary generation of American composers."[55] Of course, one can never tell: perhaps this extremely incautious declaration is to be ascribed to the tactical zigzags of the Propaganda Department which sometimes has to operate on two fronts.

More significant as an indication of the existence of a secret but dynamic protest by Soviet musicologists against the enslavement of their "tastes and sympathies" by resolutions of the Central Committee was the highly courageous declaration of Professor Zhitomirski of the Moscow Conservatory who, in discussing the *Ninth Symphony* of Shostakovich, said,

> Among us there exists a very superficial principle which requires that all Soviet artists must be nationalists, optimists, profound thinkers, etc.; otherwise they are not fulfilling their norm.[56]

It can be positively stated, however, that this principle is inescapable for Soviet musicology also, no matter how heroically it may try to throw off the yoke by which the Party and the government keep it in check.

The *History of Russian Music* edited by Professor Pekelis. In just what concrete form does the opposition of Soviet musicology to the Soviet art policy manifest itself? Part of the answer to this question is contained in the pages of the *History of Russian Music* edited by Professor Pekelis, to which Khrennikov referred in his report.[57] This textbook is particularly significant both because it is one of the most recent works giving a systematic account of the views of Soviet musicologists on the history and evaluation of Russian music and because it is the first and perhaps the only publication which has ever appeared in the Soviet Union carrying the approval of the Committee for Higher Education as a textbook for use in conservatories.

The first and second volumes of this work, which appeared in 1940, cover the history of Russian music to the end of the nineteenth century; the third volume, which has apparently not yet appeared, was supposed to deal with the music of the late nineteenth century and the early twentieth century, including the Soviet period. The aim of the work was defined by the editor as follows:

> In compiling this book the authors have set themselves the task of showing by concrete facts how *Russian national musical culture* was formed in the process of the interaction of various social, cultural and artistic factors.[58]

In actual fact this approach differs little from that of the numerous books on the history of Russian music which were written before the Soviet regime. Perhaps the only difference is that the *History* edited by Pekelis follows a more rigid line, at times almost schematic, in evaluating the past of Russian music, emphasizing on the one hand the organic connection of Russian music with native folk music and on the other its relation with Western European music. It is difficult to find an instance in the book where the authors have refrained from emphasizing both influences equally.

As to the connection of Russian music with native folk music the authors are so dogmatic that they frequently identify every manifestation of this relationship as evidence of the consistent nationalism and democracy of Russian composers. As soon as a connection with folk song, no matter how indirect, has been discovered in a composer's works, whether it is a question of Glinka, Dargomyzhsky, Musorgsky, Borodin, Rimsky-Korsakov, or Tchaikovsky, that composer is thereby confirmed as a conscious "realist" and "populist."

Of course such a one-sided conception of the history of the development of Russian music is the direct consequence of the role and significance ascribed to folk music by Soviet art policy. In this respect the textbook does not sin against communist orthodoxy.

Considerably more complex is the question of the authors' evaluation of the connection between Russian music and Western European music. They deserve credit for conscientiously tracing this relationship, elucidating it as fully and as objectively as is possible under Soviet conditions. But it is just this question in which is hidden the root of the evil. Theoretically Soviet aesthetics does not deny the interaction of cultures but in practice, particularly during the postwar anti-Western propaganda campaign, a statement of the fact that Western European music has influenced Russian music is considered to be evidence of "cosmopolitanism." It was this factor that called forth the undisguised anger of Khrennikov, and more particularly of those who stood behind him, against the authors of the textbook. How could its authors claim, for instance, that the Western European romantic composers, particularly Berlioz and Liszt, could have had any influence, even in the smallest degree, upon the development of The Five? Such a thing simply could not have happened and if nevertheless it did, "one should not talk about it." Such is the logic of Soviet propaganda.

The *History* makes an obvious attempt to base its statements on materialist philosophy, particularly on Chernyshevsky's "materialist aesthetics."[59]

On this basis the *History* lays particular emphasis on the connection of the Russian musical tradition with life and on the "populism" [*narodnost'*] of Russian music of the past; it portrays pre-Soviet Russian music as a civic agency sitting in judgment on society and as a "realistic" art. This effort to establish a direct relationship between life and art, although at times expressed with obvious sketchiness, could not but win the approval of the directors of Soviet art policy. Nevertheless the authors of the *History* sinned greatly against the demands of political propaganda by their objectivity in disclosing the connection and interrelationship of Russian music with Western European music. Moreover, simply by refraining throughout their book from attacking Western art of the past, the authors displayed an obvious sympathy toward it. What is worse, in fact a downright crime, is that they said nothing at all in criticism of contemporary modernism. For this omission they were accused of insinuating into the minds of music students the "harmful ideas of cosmopolitanism."

There is one extremely interesting detail illustrating the secret sympathies of the authors of the textbook with modernism. Having casually mentioned, at the end of the second volume, the "reaction against Scriabin's romantic arrogance" in the "skepticism of the most recent modernist art," the authors inserted on page 13 of Volume Two a portrait of F.I.

Stravinsky, the father of the composer, although there was nothing in the text to require the inclusion of his picture. There is no doubt that the authors betrayed their sympathy with the composer when, having mentioned his name, they not only passed over in silence any reference to the "destructive role" which he played in Russian music according to official Soviet propaganda but also inserted a portrait of his father. For no matter how strong the official hatred of Stravinsky may be, it cannot overcome the inner creative affinity of Soviet musicologists and musicians for the composer of *Petrushka, The Rites of Spring* and *Les Noces.*

Other Historical Studies. An important role in Russian musical criticism and musicology during the first years of the Soviet regime was played by several musicologists and writers of the senior generation, particularly Vyacheslav G. Karatygin, the author of numerous works dealing with contemporary Western European music and Nikolai F. Findeizen, whose *Outlines of the History of Music in Russia,* on which he worked for many years, enriched Russian musical historiography.

Among the works of the younger musicologists, of particular importance are those by Tamara N. Livanova on the history of Russian music and by Roman I. Gruber and Ferman on the history of Western European music.[60] Incidentally, the latter works seem to have disappeared recently from the horizon of Soviet music. Can this be the result of the "German" origin of the authors?

These writers, like Soviet musicologists in general to the extent that they still attempt to withstand Party pressure, manifest a common characteristic: the desire to reconcile things which cannot be reconciled—freedom of research and the decrees of Soviet musical orthodoxy. Hence their compromises and contradictions, their inconsistencies and their concessions to the demands of Soviet art policy.

Special mention should be made of the immense work done

by P.A. Lamm (1882-1951) in the study, editing and restoration to their original form of the works of such Russian classical composers as Musorgsky, Borodin, Tchaikovsky, Taneyev, and Rachmaninov. Lamm also edited and published a number of compositions by Western European composers including Schubert, Schumann and Grieg.

Among other studies by active Soviet musicologists, i.e., those who prefer to work rather than to chew the cud of the latest Central Committee resolution about "realism" in music, fairly important work has been done by a number of writers on problems of Russian music of the eighteenth century, e.g., Professor Livanova's *Essays and Materials on the History of Russian Musical Culture*, A.S. Rabinovich's *Russian Opera Before Glinka*, and articles by B.V. Asaf'yev on Bortnyansky and Russian music of the eighteenth century.

Perhaps the heightened interest in eighteenth century music among many Soviet musicologists can be explained by the fact that Russian music before Glinka is still a comparatively virgin field for the researcher and also, of course, by the fact that this subject until recently was remote from the everyday concerns of Soviet musical policy and thus offered an opportunity for Soviet musicologists to enjoy a much-needed respite from propaganda.

During recent years, however, Russian eighteenth century music too has begun to engage the attention of the Party musicologists. For example, an article by Academician A. Ossovski entitled "Fundamental Questions of Russian Music Culture of the Seventeenth and Eighteenth Centuries"[61] indicates that the Soviet power's boundless appetite for hegemony has begun to manifest itself in musicology as well. Ossovski writes,

> Soviet historians of music have the task of revising, deepening, expanding, and refining our knowledge of these most ancient sources of Russian musical culture.
>
> It may be asked whether it is worth-while to disturb the dust of such remote ages. Yes, it is worth-while.

> First of all from the scientific point of view, in order to create an orderly, scientifically established conception of the historical process of Russian music and to reveal the antiquity and continuity of existence of Russian musical culture. It is worth-while for political considerations, in order to be able to refute the absurd fables and malicious calumny by fascists and fascist science about the Russian people, whom they consider an inferior race, and about Russian national culture.[62]

Ossovski goes on to reiterate the "Slavophile" claims of Soviet musicology:

> And behind the ancient Russian culture there stands the still more ancient, original Slavic, pan-Slavic culture. Let us simply remember the colossal territorial expanse of Slavdom—on the east to the Oka and the Volga, on the west to the Baltic and Lake Ladoga, on the south from the Balkan peninsula [to] the north shore of the Black Sea and the Sea of Azov. Let us remember further that the Slavs in their whole tenor of life were a single people, merely divided into separate tribes.[63]

When Soviet music was searching for its ancestors in the epoch of the French Revolution, Soviet musicology was engaged in the intensive republication of French music of the eighteenth century. Now a new problem has been advanced: the search for "ancestors from the times of the original Slavic, pan-Slavic culture." Thus we see that here, as elsewhere, there is a strict, consistent regularity. To be tied to this "regularity" which is motivated by the current political situation of the Party and the government—that, and only that, is the real meaning of the current tasks of Soviet orthodox musicology.

3. *THEORETICAL MUSICOLOGY*

Soviet theoretical musicology suffers from similar defects, although during recent years it has given numerous proofs of its initiative in research. In this connection attention must be drawn first of all to the works of Professor L. Mazel' of the Moscow Conservatory, such as his study *Chopin's Fantasy in F Minor: An Essay in Analysis* (1937) and his "Special Course in the Analysis of Musical Compositions" (unpublished).

In these works Mazel' deviates sharply from the methods of musical analysis advocated in such books as Ernst Kurt's *Linear Counterpoint* and *Romantic Harmony* or Ernst Toch's *The Study of Melody* which were translated and published in the Soviet Union and which were especially popular among Soviet composers and teachers of music theory during the thirties.[64] Mazel' attempts to go further, extending and broadening the technique of analyzing musical form (this is not, of course, to say that his analysis is "formalist" in the Party sense.) Limiting himself exclusively to what can be seen and heard in the composition under analysis and without resorting to the oversimplified generalizations of which Soviet musicology makes such extensive use, Mazel' isolates the basic elements which determine the form of each composition and shows how the music's particular traits of expressiveness are derived from these elements.

Other theoretical works marked by originality of conception are those by a number of older Soviet musicologists, e.g., Georgi L. Catoire, Georgi E. Conus, Boleslav L. Yavorski, and Nikolai A. Garbuzov.

In Soviet theoretical musicology there is a tendency towards "rationalized" interpretions of the means of expression which frequently lead to curious oddities. In their pursuit of that objectivity which guarantees not only the "scientific" character of their conclusions but also the authors' peace of mind, Soviet musicologists sometimes make simply ridiculous statements. A characteristic example occurs in an evaluation of the Soviet march in an essay by V. Tsukkerman entitled "Compositions for the Brass Band," which forms part of the book *Essays on Soviet Musical Creation.*[65]

According to Tsukkerman the basic requirements of the Soviet march are

> . . . simplicity, clarity, connection with the musical art of the people, originality and innovation, and a lofty artistic taste. But to these criteria which define the general evaluation of the march there are added other specific criteria. Since the march should raise the fighting spirit of the troops, its emotional basis should be active and clear. Since it synchronizes the steps of the soldiers according to the principle "all as one," the demands put on its rhythm are extremely exacting.[66]

But even this, it seems, is not enough for the Soviet march. The author continues,

> The most important tasks assigned to the march by the Great Patriotic War [i.e., World War II] lay in the planes of ideas and of practical application. It was impossible for the march of that period not to reflect the heroism of our time. Of course we are not talking about symphonic dimensions and profundities which lie beyond the reach of this art form. Nevertheless the march has possibilities favorable to its interpretation on a heroic plane: compactness, rhythmic and phonetic power and expression of the principle of will which is quite within its scope. If all this is combined with significant melodic and harmonic expressiveness, the application of dynamic form and the artistic tactical utilization of the picturesquely descriptive principle, then it is clear that the march allows a degree of dramatization which includes heroic images within the limits of possible.[67]

At this point, it seems, one should take pity on the composers of marches and stop, but for the zealous analyst of the Soviet march this is still not enough. He continues,

> Furthermore, the march should bear the imprint of the national aspect of the peoples of the Soviet Union who fought so selflessly against fascism and who destroyed it. . . . The radius of action of the march has been somewhat expanded; therefore, the demands [made on it] for simplicity, clarity and accessibility have increased.
>
> In time of war the march is, first of all, military music:

> to many Soviet citizens to whom the country had entrusted its weapons the march was their service-drill music. Hence it is clear that in the music of a drill march the element of what specialists call "militarization" of the march should predominate. The augmented role of strict military discipline also had to be reflected in march music.[68]

We can only express our sympathy for the Soviet composer who might try to compose a military march according to this recipe.

The numerous attempts by Soviet musicologists to revise traditional textooks on harmony deserve more serious attention, for example, the *Study of Harmony* by Yu. N. Tyulin, the *Manual of Harmony* by a group of teachers at the Moscow Conservatory (3rd edition 1947) and the *Essays on the History of Theoretical Musicology* by I. Ryzkhin and L. Mazel'.[69]

Just as the *History of Russian Music* edited by Pekelis was to a certain degree a summation of a definite stage in the development of Soviet historical musicology, so the *Manual of Harmony*, which was accepted as a textbook for students specializing in performance in Soviet conservatories, filled an analogous role in the field of theoretical musicology.

Basically this textbook is simply a more concise treatment of the *Practical Course in Harmony* published by the same authors some time earlier.[70] It represents the foundation on which until recently the theoretical knowledge of Soviet conservatory students was based. In order to establish "contact with living artistic practice"[71] the illustrative material is presented directly rather than according to the principle of systematic exposition of a course divided into self-contained sections. Based as much as possible on examples from musical literature and avoiding the use of schematic conceptions the *Manual* introduces the elements of form in their simplest manifestation, presenting a study of methods of various developments of musical material and focussing the student's attention on questions of analytical technique.

Such planned contact with musical literature, promoting a closer approach by the student to the composer's musical text and a more conscientious execution or study of what the text contains, clearly has a great attraction for Soviet musicology. Cautious with respect to traditional harmonic theory and avoiding any vulgarization or oversimplification, the authors of the *Manual* satisfy to a great extent the demand for a rational presentation of the elements of musical expression.

A characteristic feature of this textbook is that in general it remains within the bounds of the classical tradition of harmony, with periodic excursions into the field of Russian or other Soviet national folk music in order to clarify idiomatic and modal peculiarities.

It would be a great mistake, however, to think that the more or less successful attempts by Soviet musicologists to develop and deepen theoretical musicology have found any support from the Party. It is not only curious but extremely significant that in 1950, after thirty years of Soviet musicological "progress," *Soviet Music* enthusiastically announced the publication of the seventeenth edition of Rimsky-Korsakov's fifty-year-old *Practical Manual of Harmony*, a textbook of unquestionable merit but one which is hopelessly out of date.[72] *Soviet Music* asserts that

> the new edition of N.A. Rimsky-Korsakov's textbook on harmony should satisfy the urgent need for musical-theoretical training of the students of our musical colleges and academies.[73]

What is there to be enthusiastic about, however, when the standard not only of teaching of Soviet students but also of composing in general has declined to a level where even Rimsky-Korsakov's textbook, with its revelations of harmony within the limits of the first and fifth relationships of the scale, will soon represent the limit of the dreams of Soviet composers?

4. THE POSITION OF B. V. ASAF'YEV

Of great significance as an expression of Soviet musicology's views on modernism, as well as in regard to the general role of contemporary Russian musicology are the works of B.V. Asaf'yev (Igor' Glebov). An unusually versatile and prolific musician, the author of a large number of historical and theoretical works, Asaf'yev was also an outstanding teacher who trained a brilliant group of young composers and musicologists and who exerted a tremendous influence upon the whole musical life of the Soviet Union. Asaf'yev's incontestable importance is based on such works as *Russian Music from the Beginning of the Nineteenth Century*, which laid the foundation for a new period of development of Russian musical historiography, and *Musical Form As Process* which exerted a major influence upon Soviet-dominated musical theory. His monographs on Glinka, Tchaikovsky and Stravinsky mark the highest point reached by Russian musicology on the appreciation of the works of these composers.[74]

But it is not merely in his works that Asaf'yev gave an example of the genuine vitality and progressiveness of Russian musicological thought; the life of this truly outstanding man was also an example of fortitude and of an unyielding struggle for the right of creative independence against Bolshevik pressure.

During the twenties Asaf'yev as a leading adherent, inspirer and director of contemporary music was subjected to such fierce attacks from the leaders of RAPM that it is hard to understand how this extremely sensitive man could have endured it. To anyone who was connected in any way with Asaf'yev or who had carefully read his works it was unmistakably clear that his world outlook and his musical aesthetic conceptions, those which he professed himself and which he persistently implanted in his pupils, did not change one iota during his entire career of almost half a century, half of it under the harsh conditions of Soviet reality. But the tactics of the Soviet politicans are sometimes hard to understand. After the rude and unscrupulous baiting to which Asaf'yev was subjected during the RAPM period there suddenly appeared in *Soviet Music* an article by Zhitomirski,[75] a teacher of the history of music at the Moscow Conservatory, which was undoubtedly inspired by Party circles and which referred to Asaf'yev in superlatives such as the Soviet press almost never uses in connection with a "non-Party intellectual." Zhitomirski's article spoke of the "great pleasure" of knowing that "Igor' Glebov... is living among us and together with us is building the great musical culture of our country."[76]

Following the publication of Zhitomirski's article an exceptionally persistent campaign began for the purpose of drawing Asaf'yev into the role of ideological leader of Soviet music. Titles, decorations, Stalin Prizes, and benefits of all sorts were rained on him, up to and including the chairmanship of the Union of Soviet Composers.

Nevertheless Asaf'yev's real role in Soviet music was just the opposite of that which is ascribed to him by official Soviet journalism. Far from becoming the "patriarch" of Soviet music, whose works were models of orthodoxy, Asaf'yev was one of the few who kindled and kept alight the smouldering spark of creative opposition, who stood steadfastly on guard to protect its free creative expression and who, notwithstanding the spiritual and physical toll exacted by the hardships of his life, considered it his privilege to remain true to the end of his life to the lofty ideals of contemporary creative thought. How otherwise can one explain the fact that almost on the eve of his death Asaf'yev wrote,

> What is new in the 'material' given us by the great masters is seldom subjectively arbitrary and seldom fails to meet the demands posed by the whole ideational structure of the epoch.[77]

In defense of creative freedom and the right to creative inventiveness he wrote,

> It is not only the first magnitude stars [among composers] but also the lesser and smaller stars who, flickering with their light and color, reflect amidst the cruelty of the age that which is beautiful in man and in the reality he perceives. Of course their music is psychological and generally makes no attempt not to be the music of the human heart: Berlioz, Chopin, Liszt, Schumann, Mendelssohn, Weber, Glinka, Schubert, Wagner, Tchaikovsky, Verdi, Bizet, Grieg, Brahms (this is but a small list!)—no matter how varied their talent, power of imagination, intellect, tastes, characteristics, tendencies, and creative methods, they all observed the human soul and sympathized with the unfathomable questions about the meaning of life which arise in the human consciousness.[78]

It may be asked how it is that what Asaf'yev wrote in his report to the First All-Union Congress of Composers (1948) is altogether different from what he wrote in his *Book About Stravinsky* and other critical works. Not everything written and signed in the Soviet Union, however, expresses the writer's real thought, a fact which is graphically demonstrated by the numerous "confessions" extorted from those who have been imprisoned. Even Alexander Werth noted that much of Asaf'yev's report to the congress had undoubtedly been "subedited" by the Party.[79] This explanation is supported by the fact that Asaf'yev did not read his paper personally, excusing his absence on the ground of illness.

In all his works Asaf'yev consistently carried forward the best traditions of Russian writing on music of the past century. He resolutely fought for the primacy of content in music. To Asaf'yev music was an intellectual labor that constituted the joy of creation.

> [It is commonly assumed] that thought can be expressed only through words and...that content and other elements constituting music are independent of one another....Such an absurd "division of labor" and of the meaning associations in music influences the approach of people who are ignorant of music and who do not understand its significance in human culture.[80]

Does this not sound like an accusation against the Soviet ideologists who confuse music with collective farm property? To Asaf'yev the content of music meant free creative thought, seeking embodiment through original means of expression, and not the political propaganda imposed upon it by Soviet orthodoxy. Asaf'yev's struggle against all types of vulgarization in musicology will go down in the history of Russian music as a bright page in the defense of the rights of the composer's creative freedom and the right of music to creative progress in general.

5. THE STUDY OF FOLK MUSIC

Collection and Publication. In one of the reports presented at the First All-Union Congress of Soviet Composers (1948) it was stated that "an important task"

> directly connected with the new socialist aesthetics is the problem of the idiom of our Soviet music. In the profound and direct study of folk song there lies the life-giving source for the development of a creative taste for melody and priceless material for cantilena and recitatives. Let us recall how Musorgsky bowed down before this source.
>
> To love, to collect, to study popular art, to learn from the people, from the great masters of Russian classical music, from Glinka, Musorgsky, Borodin, Rimsky-Korsakov, Tchaikovsky—this is the sacred duty of every Soviet composer. Without this we cannot create Soviet musical classics.[81]

As its part in carrying out this "important task" Soviet musicology has been forced to devote increased attention to the study of folk music. The official emphasis on "Soviet patriotism" and "nationalism" [*narodnost'*] in music has led to detailed work on the characteristics of Russian folk song and its connection with the idiom of Russian professional music. It must be said that in this respect Soviet musical theorists have achieved a great deal, not so much in discovering these characteristics—this was done, to a great extent, long before their time—as in systematizing and putting into order information which had previously been scattered. A noteworthy example is the section on "The Natural Minor Scale in Russian Song" in the *Manual of Harmony* by a group of professors at the Moscow Conservatory.

Possessing fairly extensive physical facilities and having been left for some time more to its own devices than other branches of Soviet musicology, the study of folk music achieved quite considerable results during the Second World War, particularly in collecting and writing down folk songs.

The organization of Soviet folklore studies is concentrated chiefly in the Institutes of Folklore attached to the All-Union and Republic Academies of Sciences and in the folklore departments of a number of conservatories (e.g., those of Moscow, Kiev, Kharkov, and Minsk). The most important work in the study of the theoretical problems of folk music has been done by a group of collaborators of the folklore department of the All-Union Academy of Sciences in Leningrad, particularly Ye. Gippius and Z. Ewald; by K. Kvitka, a member of the folklore department of the Moscow Conservatory who specialized in the study of Ukrainian folklore; by the Kiev Institute of Folklore (especially Professor Hrinchenko); by the Kiev Conservatory (Beregovski); and by the Kharkov Conservatory (Steblyanko).

In its study of folk music, however, Soviet musicology attempts to identify the folk song with the "people's social consciousness" and to assign to folklore a class function and a role in "the struggle for building communist society," thus reducing popular song to a form of political propaganda. In this lies the real meaning of the Soviet theoretical study of folk music and its practical application under the conditions of Soviet reality.

"Soviet Folk Music." If Soviet folk music study has achieved much in the field of writing down and arranging folk songs of the past there is no reason to speak of any achievements in the field of folk music of Soviet origin. On the contrary, the alleged revival of oral musical creation in the Soviet Union is an outright invention by Soviet propaganda. Whatever has been "created" in this field has nothing in common with popular art but is the handiwork of Soviet propagandists from start to finish. The authors of the *History of Russian Music* edited by Professor Pekelis are therefore guilty of a flagrant lie when they write,

> Along with the intensive dissemination and tremendous popularity of the urban mass-song, many characteristic features of ancient Russian song creation have received new development in the models of Soviet folklore. Heroic Soviet epic songs have been created on the basis of the epic traditions of the most distant past—the *byliny* [epic narratives], legends and poems about Lenin and Stalin, about Chapayev and Shchors and about the *Chelyuskin* and Papanin.[82] There is a genuine epic spirit in the lament for Lenin "All stone-built Moscow was weeping" by the White Sea folk tale narrator M.S. Kryukova and in the profoundly expressive lament for Kirov "When I learned of the death of Sergei Mironych" by the Mordvinian narrator Ye. P. Krivosheyeva.[83]

All of this is an invention, from beginning to end. The technique of such "popular creation," like that of the "creations" of the Kazakh *akyn* [poet and musician] Dzhambul and of the Daghestan "national bard" Suleiman Stal'ski, is extremely simple. The secret lies in the resourcefulness of the government and Party administration, the Composers' and Writers' Unions and the Central Houses of Amateur Activity, all of which are generous in providing material encouragement and "consultation help" for the purpose of obtaining the desired results from the "popular narrators." It is entirely a matter of sleight-of-hand on the part of Soviet propaganda and in no way an expression of the creative initiative of the author-performer, to say nothing of the people. During the first years of the Soviet regime, it is true, there was a broadly developed anti-Soviet and genuinely popular art, but this was gradually strangled by harsh repression, like everything else in the Soviet Union which failed to conform to the Party line.

Thus the Soviet study of folk music, like other fields of Soviet art, has been transformed into a subordinate medium of political propaganda. The extensive utilization of folk music by Soviet composers has led to typical dilettantism in the place of high professional standards and to the replacement of genuine creation by pseudo-folk music. It has led to the triumph of the aesthetics of "mass art," "art for everyone" and what the Soviets call *samodeyatel'nost'*.[84]

C. MUSIC JOURNALISM AND PUBLISHING

1. *PERIODICALS*

Soviet musical journalism, which degenerated into a form of political propaganda before other branches of musical life in the Soviet Union, is in general limited to occasional articles in the general press and in *Soviet Art.*

It is true that during the mid-thirties a special music newspaper was published in Moscow, but it naturally did not meet with support from governmental circles and soon ceased publication since the Soviet press is not interested in music as such. For the Soviet leaders music is only a means for political propaganda and a special music paper would hardly be suitable for this purpose.

In the regular provincial press, articles on music are extremely rare. In the majority of cases such articles, when they do appear, concern anniversaries of various kinds, particularly the dates of the birth and death of outstanding composers of the part—mainly Russian—or reviews of Soviet musical events such as festivals and competitions which provide a convenient opportunity for defaming the pre-Soviet system and praising existing conditions. Such articles are generally written according to a more or less standard pattern. If they concern a composer of the past they present him as a zealous champion of "popular democratic ideals" and almost as a champion of Soviet policies.

Occasionally contemporary Soviet composers are favored by a special article, but in the majority of cases such articles are not a toast to the composer's health but a requiem. Such articles ordinarily serve to settle accounts with big and little "formalists" and "cosmopolitans" after the metropolitan newspapers have published one of the Party or government decrees on the "current tasks of Soviet music." A curious tradition has been established: if the guilty person is Shostakovich or Muradeli (or some other composer), it is considered essential to discover in one's own town or collective farm a local Shostakovich or Muradeli and hit him hard, in order to teach all Shostakovichs and Muradelis to mend their ways.

It would be a task beyond the power of a Soviet critic to write an article on a living composer concerning whom an authoritative opinion had not yet been handed down by the Party. Such a critic would be taking a great risk: what if some influential person should not like what he had written? Still fresh in everyone's mind is the case of the opera *With All One's Heart,* when even the committee for awarding the Stalin Prizes was forced to beat a hasty retreat.

Unlike the articles on music which appear in the provincial papers, which are not obliged to have their own opinion, the articles in *Pravda* and *Izvestiya* are noteworthy for expressing the opinion of the Party and the government more or less at firsthand. These papers print extensive articles by music critics, musicologists and composers who may be in close contact with Party circles, articles either inspired by the Party and which express the views of "authoritative comrades" or simply articles written on special assignment.

One should give credit to Soviet journalists—they have learned Aesop's language well. At times it is difficult to doubt the naturalness of their temperament. With true virtuosity they can write about the "sincerity" and "humanity" of the Soviet music trade. And with what hatred and malevolence they write about everything which is beyond their comprehension! Has the history of musical criticism ever known such a malignant style and such virtuosity of lying, for example, as are found in Nest'yev's article on Western composers entitled "The Dollar Cacophony?"[85] Yet in his articles in *Soviet Music* Nest'yev is restrained in his language and is even capable of subtlety, refinement and thoughtful generalizations. When he is ordered to do so, however, he finds strength to overcome his musical tastes and sympathies and his refined language.

But whereas Nest'yev's *Izvestiya* article, which was undoubtedly inspired by high Party circles and which belongs to the category of anti-American propaganda, nevertheless refrained from denying Stravinsky's mastery, the articles in *Soviet Art* make no pretense of ceremony. With rare exceptions these articles, prior to Stalin's death, were concerned less with music than with the shameless glorification of Stalin, using music merely as the pretext for this purpose.

Here, for instance, is a sample of such "criticism":

> The *Cantata about Stalin,* with text by the Lithuanian poetess Salomei Neris, was completed by the composer I.A. Tallat-Kelpsha to commemorate the thirtieth anniversary of the Great October Socialist Revolution. Good technical schooling, which the composer received from Lyadov (Tallat-Kelpsha graduated from the St. Petersburg Conservatory) made it possible for him to create a cantata on a strict academic basis with well-developed contrapuntal texture. The cantata is rich in Lithuanian folk song motifs, on which Tallat-Kelpsha is an expert. Its four movements are devoted to the struggle of the Lithuanian people for socialism. Its bright, joyful finale resounds with glory to the people, glory to the great Stalin.[86]

If one suspects that the reference here to Stalin is due merely to the fact that the article concerns a cantata about him, it will be instructive to look at an article in the same issue describing a cantata on Soviet Kazakhstan:

> The cantata *Soviet Kazakhstan* by Ye. Brusilovski is written for narrator, soloists, chorus, and symphonic orchestra and is devoted to the historic path traversed by the Kazakh people from the times of their semi-enslavement by tsarist Russia to their powerful rise during our times. Every episode of the cantata corresponds to a definite historical stage for which the composer has attempted to find special means of expression. For example, the music of the first episode which is connected with the gloomy prerevolutionary past is built on themes of the Kazakh *zara*—the people's wailing and lamentation. In the final, sixth, episode, devoted to the contemporary postwar upsurge of the people, the composer brings in two choruses, one of which sings the hymn of the Kazakh Republic while the other sings a toast to Comrade Stalin.[87]

Soviet critics evaluate the phenomena of artistic life not in accordance with their own judgment but in conformity to commands from above. In the Soviet Union those who take up music criticism as an occupation are people having no personal relation to art and creative work. Their criticism is based on the servile fear of that totalitarian power which dominates the people's will and feelings.

This characteristic of Soviet music criticism has imposed its own gray and uninspired tone upon Soviet music journalism—although it is doubtful whether Soviet musical periodical literature, as such, can be said to exist at all. During recent years it has been represented by the sole music magazine published in the Soviet Union, a monthly entitled *Soviet Music* which is the organ of the Union of Soviet Composers. It is true that before the war almost every "national" union of Soviet composers published its own *Soviet Music* (e.g., the Ukrainian *Radyans'ka Muzyka*, the Georgian *Gruzinskaya Muzyka*, etc.), but these journals were distinguished from one another only by being published in the native language and by being more provincial than *Soviet Music*. None of these periodicals could really be called music periodicals for they were organs of political propaganda using musical facts for purposes having nothing to do with music.

Earlier, during the twenties, musical journalism in the U.S.S.R. was represented by a considerable number of periodical publications: *New Music, Music, Musical Culture, Music and Revolution, Proletarian Musician, Musical Virgin Soil,* etc.[88] which reflected the complicated and intense struggle among various creative groups and which were full of pregnant and wide-ranging thoughts and discussions. But after the Central Committee resolution "On the Reorganization of Art and Literary Organizations" (1932) the field of musical journalism was narrowed down to a single magazine, *Soviet Music*, which represents the policy of the authorities in the sphere of music.

Before the war one could still find in *Soviet Music* interesting articles by authors who seemed still to be living in the past or in the distant future; articles which contained some not yet extinguished gleams of free creative initiative and living thought. It was still possible to find interesting material about the work of Prokof'yev, Myaskovski, Shostakovich, and other Soviet composers; discursive investigations of questions of style and form; original and highly technical analyses of musical compositions; valuable biographical material—but all this is now only a memory. The spark of living thought becomes ever dimmer and in its place there triumphs cold bureaucratic propaganda and the political slogans of Party and government.

The best proof that *Soviet Music* has ceased to be a journal of musicology is that during recent years it has simply ignored music as a subject for research. It would be futile to look in recent numbers of *Soviet Music* for even a single article devoted to specifically musicological problems (style, mode, harmony, counterpoint, form, means of expression, etc.). In its analysis of musical compositions it not only avoids special musical terminology but limits itself to formulations and generalizations which mean nothing to a specialist.

Undoubtedly this style of analysis reflects not only an

attempt to become a publication for the "masses," accessible to the nonprofessional reader, but a desire to saturate this "accessible" style as much as possible with literary images which emphasize the political-propagandistic significance of the subject matter. This trend in itself cannot be considered reprehensible, for after all it is a question of taste and of the aim pursued by the journal; but the question arises whether *Soviet Music* is a musicological journal at all or merely one of the many varieties of Soviet mass-propaganda. As an organ of the Composers' Union, i.e., as the organ of a professional music organization, *Soviet Music* does not exist; instead there now exists under its mask a journal for mass propaganda which aims not at the professional musical guidance of its readers but at their political "education."

2. MUSIC PUBLISHING HOUSES

The situation in regard to book publishing was somewhat better, at least before the war. Even a partial bibliography of published Soviet works on music would testify to the industry of Soviet musicologists and the variety of their subjects, even though it is true that the emphasis is primarily on Russian music of the past. Most of the material is documentary but it nevertheless represents an important contribution to the history of Russian music.

All pre-Soviet private publishing houses were taken over by the Soviet regime when it came to power and replaced by a single centralized publishing organization called Muzgiz [*Muzykal'noye Gosudarstvennoye Izdatel'stvo,* Music State Publishing House].[89] If one takes into consideration the fact that Muzgiz is the only music publishing house for the entire Soviet Union[90] it is obvious that its output falls far short of normal requirements. The need for elementary music literature in the Soviet Union is so acute that many educational institutions and even the Union of Soviet Composers frequently resort to various kinds of mimeographed publications in order to satisfy their needs.[91] This situation is connected first of all, no doubt, with problems of financing Muzgiz. The decisive considerations in this matter are clearly the aims of political propaganda and not the development of art. The result is that the output of music literature is limited chiefly to mass agitational propaganda and the mass-song. From the music of the past Muzgiz prints mainly the Russian classics, although usually only in connection with various anniversaries. The publication of scores by contemporary composers is extremely restricted; such works often have to wait as long as five years for their turn. As for contemporary Western music it is not published at all.

From time to time the Soviet press finds it necessary to criticize Muzgiz for its obvious shortcomings. For example, in a recent article entitled "On the Work of the Music Publishing House" it was stated:

> The entire tendency of the activity of Muzgiz during the years 1948-1950 has been defined by the resolutions of the Central Committee of the CPSU(b) pertaining to ideological questions, particularly the resolution on the opera *The Great Friendship.*
>
> . . . .
>
> In the plan of Muzgiz publications for 1948 the number of titles of compositions by Soviet composers was approximately 74 per cent of the total, in 1949, 64 per cent and in 1950 somewhat higher. Among these must be mentioned in the first place the compositions dedicated to our great socialist country and to the struggle for peace.... More than seventy new works, among them fifty-two mass-songs, were published in celebration of the seventieth birthday of Comrade Stalin.... During 1948-1950 a *Songbook* containing seventy compositions was published twice, in an edition of 200,000 copies; two large collections of war songs and a collection of revolutionary songs are in preparation.[92]

It must be said to the credit of the author of this report that he has not toned down his none too favorable characterization of these publications. For instance, he reports that

> sometimes a composer responds to a present-day political theme (e.g., the elections or Korea) with mediocre music and sometimes a poet claims that his rhymed conglomeration of words is a valuable creation. It is regrettable that it is not only Muzgiz that is littered with poetical waste paper and with "texts" instead of poetry but also the section on mass-forms of the Composers' Union, Mosėstrad,[93] the Radio Committee, and other organizations dealing with songs.[94]

One could end this review of Soviet music publishing with this eloquent comment on the activities of Muzgiz, which strives to fulfill the tasks assigned to it by the Central Committee by earnestly propagating "musical waste paper," if it were not necessary to say a few words about the technical defects of Soviet music publications. The appearance of such works is frequently impaired by bad printing, even though the paper used is often excellent.

FOOTNOTES TO PART III

1. The liberal democratic revolution which preceded the Bolshevik Revolution–Tr.

2. Rostislavov, A., "Oktyabr'skiye sobytiye" [Events of October], *Apollon* [Apollo], No. 6-7, 1917, p. 84.

3. This was accomplished by the two following decrees: (a) "O perekhode Petrogradskoi i Moskovskoi Konservatorii v vedeniye Narodnovo Komissariata Prosveshcheniya" [Concerning the Transfer of the Petrograd and Moscow Conservatories to the Jurisdiction of the People's Commissariat of Education], July 12, 1918, Article 581 in *Sobraniye uzakonenii i rasporyazhenii rabochevo i krest'yanskovo pravitel'stva* [Collection of Decrees and Orders of the Workers' and Peasants' Government], p. 597, also in *Izvestiya* [News], No. 150, July 18, 1918 and (b) "O natsionalizatsii notnykh, muzykal'nykh magazinov, skladov, notopechaten i notoizdatel'stv" [Concerning the Nationalization of Music Stores, Warehouses, Printing Houses and Publishing Houses], December 19, 1918, Article 1020 in *Sobraniye...*, p. 1279, also in *Izvestiya*, No. 288, December 31, 1918.

4. For the titles of these works see the bibliography.

5. Shaverdyan, A.I., ed., *Puti razvitiya sovetskoi muzyki: kratkii obzor* [The Ways of Development of Soviet Music: A Brief Survey], Moscow, 1948. Hereafter cited as *Puti.*

6. *Ibid.*, p. 5. My italics.–A.O.

7. For the text of this document see Annex B, pp. 280-285.

8. *Puti,* p. 8.

9. *Ibid.*

10. *Ibid.*, p. 9.

11. Cited in *ibid.*, p. 10; Lenin, V.I., "Partiinaya organizatsiya i partiinaya literatura" [Party Organization and Party Literature], *Sochineniya* [Works], 4th ed., Moscow, 1947, Vol. X, p. 27. Originally published in *Novaya Zhizn'* [New Life], Nov. 13, 1905, No. 12. Italics in the original.

12. *Puti*, p. 9

13. *Ibid.*, p. 11.

14. Pertsov, V., *Mayakovski: zhizn' i tvorchestvo (do velikoi oktyabr'skoi sotsialisticheskoi revolyutsii)* [Mayakovski: Life and Work (Before the Great October Socialist Revolution)], Moscow-Leningrad, 1950, p. 19.

15. *Puti*, p. 12.

16. *Ibid.*, pp. 12-13.

17. *Ibid.*, p. 14.

18. Khrennikov, T., "Tvorchestvo kompozitorov i muzykovedov posle postanovleniya TsK VKP(b) ob opere 'Velikaya Druzhba' " [The Work of Composers and Musicologists Following the Decree of the Central Committee of the All-Union Communist Party (Bolsheviks) Concerning the Opera *The Great Friendship*], *Sovetskaya muzyka* [Soviet Music], January 1949, No. 1, p. 25.

19. *Ibid.*, p. 30

20. *Ibid.*

21. *Ibid.*

22. *Ibid.*

23. *Ibid.*, p. 31.

24. "Vystupleniya na plenume: T. Khrennikov (zaklyuchitel'noye slovo)" [Speeches at the plenum: T. Khrennikov (Concluding Word)], *ibid.*, p. 55.

25. One of the participants at the meeting carelessly let the cat out of the bag by remarking, "Before the plenum all of us had a feeling of anxiety and tenseness like that which any experienced soldier might have before executing a battle order entrusted to him." Address by K. Dan'kevych, *ibid.*, p. 45.

26. "Doklad B.V. Asaf'yeva" [Report by B.V. Asaf'yev], *Sovetskoye iskusstvo* [Soviet Art], No. 17 (1105) April 24, 1948. My italics.—A.O.

27. The Russian term *narodnost'*, derived from *narod*, "people," has no exact equivalent in English but can be rendered as "populism," "democracy" or "nationalism." It must be understood, however, that the use of "nationalism" in this sense refers to the people rather than to the state.—Tr.

28. *Puti*, p. 14.

29. "Vystupleniye tov. A.A. Zhdanova na soveshchanii deyatelei sovetskoi muzyki v TsK VKP (b)" [Speech by Comrade A.A. Zhdanov at the Meeting of Soviet Musicians in the Central Committee of the All-Union Communist Party (Bolsheviks)], *Sovetskaya muzyka*, January-February 1948, No. 1, p. 18.

30. Alexander Werth, *Musical Uproar in Moscow*, London, Turnstile Press, 1949.

31. *Ibid.*, p. 31.

32. For full text of this resolution see Annex B, pp. 280-285.

33. "Velikaya sila sovetskovo iskusstva" [The Great Power of Soviet Art], *Sovetskoye iskusstvo*, No. 17 (1105), April 24, 1948.

34. Mr. Olkhovsky's own doctoral thesis, written for the Musical Section, dealt with the works of this group of composers. Despite the fact that the thesis was characterized by Asaf'yev as "unique in the breadth of its grasp of the material and in the profundity of its elaboration, not merely among us [i.e., in the Soviet Union] but abroad," the thesis was withdrawn from publication as a "formalist" work.—Ed.

35. For titles, see the bibliography.

36. For the text of this resolution, see Annex A, pp. 278-279.

37. From the methodological prospectus for the "History of the Musical Culture of the Peoples of the U.S.S.R."

38. Blok, M., "Vazhnyi etap v razvitii sovetskovo muzykoznaniya (Vsesoyuznaya nauchnaya sessiya po muzykoznaniyu)" [An Important Stage in the Development of Soviet Musicology (The All-Union Scientific Session on Musicology)], *Sovetskaya muzyka*, April 1950, No. 4, pp. 48-54.

39. The resolution on the opera *The Great Friendship*.—Tr.

40. *Op. cit.*, p. 48.

41. *Ibid.*, p. 49

42. *Ibid.*, p. 54.

43. *Ibid.*

44. For an account of this meeting see "Vystupleniya na otkrytom partiinom sobranii v Soyuze Sovetskikh Kompozitorov SSSR, posvyashchonnom obsuzhdeniyu zadach muzykal'noi kritiki i nauki (18, 21 i 22 fevralya 1949 g.)" [Addresses at the Open Party Meeting in the Union of Soviet Composers of the U.S.S.R. Devoted to a Discussion of the Problems of Music Criticism and Science (February 18, 21 and 22, 1949)], *Sovetskaya muzyka*, February 1949, No. 2, pp. 16-36.

45. *Ibid.*, p. 7.

46. Khrennikov, Tikhon, "O neterpimom otstavanii muzykal'noi kritiki i muzykovedeniya" [On the Intolerable Lag of Music Criticism and Musicology], *Sovetskaya muzyka*, February 1949, No. 2, pp. 8-12.

47. *Sovetskaya muzyka*, February 1949, No. 2, p. 36.

48. Speech by Khrennikov, *ibid.*, p. 8.

49. *Ibid.*, p. 9.

50. *Ibid.*, p. 13.

51. *Ibid.*, p. 14.

52. *Ibid.*

53. *Ibid.* p. 15.

54. "Vystupleniya na otkrytom partiinom sobranii...," *ibid.*, p. 29.

55. *Ibid.*, p. 30

56. *Ibid.*, p. 31.

57. Pekelis, M.S., ed., *Istoriya russkoi muzyki* [History of Russian Music], 2 vols., Moscow, 1940. The book is a collective work prepared by a group of teachers of the history of music at the Moscow Conservatory.

58. *Ibid.*, p. 3. Italics in the original.

59. *Ibid.*, Vol. II, pp. 4-5. N.G. Chernyshevsky (1828-1889) constructed a system of "realistic aesthetics" based on the principles of Feuerbach's materialism. Disputing the theory which deduces art from the idea of the beautiful and considering the degree of the artist's knowledge of real life as the basic criterion of the value and significance of every work of art, Chernyshevsky maintained that "the general characteristic mark of art, that which constitutes its essence, is the reproduction of life. Often works of art have another significance also: ...as a judgment on the phenomena of life." Chernyshevsky, "Esteticheskiya otnosheniya iskusstva k deyatel'nosti"[The Aesthetical Relationship of Art to Reality], in *Estetika i poeziya* [Aesthetics and Poetry], St. Petersburg, 1893, p. 108.

60. For full titles of these and other works mentioned in this section, see the bibliography.

61. Ossovski, A., "Osnovnye voprosy russkoi muzykal'noi kul'tury XVII i XVIII vekov," *Sovetskaya muzyka*, May 1950, No. 5, pp. 53-57. (The article is substantially the same as Ossovski's report delivered March 1, 1950 at an all-Union meeting on musicology in Moscow.)

62. *Ibid.*, pp. 53-54.

63. *Ibid.*, p. 54.

64. For full titles, see the bibliography.

65. Tsukkerman, V., "Proizvédeniya dlya dukhovovo orkestra," in *Ocherki sovetskovo muzykal'novo tvorchestva*, ed. by B.V. Asaf'yev, A.A. Al'shvang, *et al.*, Moscow, 1947, Vol. I, pp. 277-319.

66. *Ibid.*, p. 277.

67. *Ibid.*, p. 291.

68. *Ibid.*

69. For full titles, see the bibliography.

70. *Prakticheskiĭ kurs garmonii*, 2 vols., Moscow, 1936.

71. From the introduction to the 1936 edition.

72. Ryzhkin, I., "Novoye izdaniye uchebnika garmonii" [A New Edition of a Textbook of Harmony], *Sovetskaya muzyka*, February 1950, No. 2, pp. 108-110.

73. *Ibid.*, p. 108.

74. For extracts from Asaf'yev's monograph on Stravinsky, see Part II, above, pp. 27-33. For full titles of works cited see the bibliography.

75. Zhitomirski, D., "Igor' Glebov kak publitsist" [Igor' Glebov as a Publicist], *Sovetskaya muzyka*, December 1940, No. 12, p. 14.

76. *Ibid.*

77. Asaf'yev, Boris, *Muzykal'naya forma kak protsess* [Musical Form as Process], Vol. II, *Intonatsiya* [Intonation], Moscow, 1947, p. 136.

78. *Ibid.*

79. Werth, Alexander, *Musical Uproar in Moscow*, p. 97.

80. Asaf'yev, *Intonatsiya*, p. 67.

81. "Doklad B.V. Asaf'yeva" [Report by B.V. Asaf'yev], *Sovetskoye iskusstvo*, No. 17 (1105), April 24, 1948.

82. The *Chelyuskin* was a vessel engaged in the exploration of the Arctic; Papanin is a polar explorer. See Armstrong, Terence, *The Northern Sea Route*, Cambridge, England, 1952, pp. 41, 63.—Tr.

83. Pekelis, *op. cit.*, Vol. I, p. 60.

84. The expression *samodeyatel'nost'*, literally "self-activity," is used to designate the music-making of politically organized amateur musical groups. On this phenomenon of Soviet musical life, see Part IV, below.

85. Nest'yev, I., "Dollarovaya kakofoniya," *Izvestiya*, January 7, 1951; English text in *Current Digest of the Soviet Press*, No. 1, 1951, p. 16.

86. "Prekrasnye traditsii" [Excellent Traditions], *Sovetskoye iskusstvo*, No. 17 (1105), April 24, 1948.

87. *Ibid.*

88. For the full titles of these periodicals, see the bibliography.

89. Incidentally Muzgiz "inherited" one of the largest pre-Soviet music publishing houses, that of Yurgenson.

90. The volume of music publishing by the "national" publishing houses in the various Soviet republics is so limited that it is hardly worth mentioning. Everything connected with the publication of music and books on music is concentrated in Muzgiz which has its headquarters in Moscow, with a branch in Leningrad.

91. One of the most difficult problems for the Soviet composer is the acute shortage of music manuscript paper.

92. Bol'shemennikov, A., "O rabote muzykal'novo izdatel'stva," *Sovetskaya muzyka*, January 1951, No. 1, pp. 58-59.

93. "Mosėstrad" is a contraction for *Moskovskaya ėstrada* [Moscow Stage], the designation of a special organization serving the concert and entertainment life of Moscow. Unlike the Philharmonic Organizations, which are organized on an all-Union scale, Mosėstrad is concerned mainly--but not exclusively--with the organization of concerts only in Moscow.

94. *Ibid.*, p. 59.

PART IV

Soviet Musical Life

A. MUSIC EDUCATION

1. THE MUSIC TRAINING OF CHILDREN

Before they enter school Soviet children as a rule are deprived of any contact with music except the musical life of the street where the decisive formative influence is that of the propaganda mass-song.

The earliest musical impressions of childhood are usually those received at home in the family circle. In a typically Soviet family, however, music has no place. The living folk songs which before the Revolution were so widely and richly cultivated in the family, particularly by the women—the holiday song-cycles, the wedding cycles which would frequently go on for weeks, the songs sung by women at their gatherings during the spinning season, the songs sung at evening parties of all sorts, and the labor and funeral songs—all this has lost its meaning completely in the Soviet way of life, both in the city and in the village. During the late nineteenth century native instruments were widely used and even the piano had become fairly common in urban Russian homes. Now, however, the only thing that represents music in the average Soviet home is a radio set which brings in the government broadcasts. Even the fairly numerous radio programs designed especially for children are distinguished not by their artistic quality but by an obvious political bias.

In the same way the special children's concerts in the larger cities also serve the aims of political propaganda more frequently than those of art. Moreover, even children of medium income families are often deprived of the opportunity to attend these concerts for various reasons—because they cannot afford the small extra expense for transportation (the concerts are given free of charge), because they lack decent clothing or because the parents are tired and prefer to stay home and rest rather than accompany their children to a concert. Another significant factor in the inadequate musical education of Soviet children is the almost complete absence of record players in Soviet homes.

When Soviet young people go to school they are subjected to a strictly organized system in which music serves either as an aid for physical training in combination with gymnastics or lends its powers of expression to the formation of the political views desired by the regime.

In the planned curriculum of Soviet schools of general education one lesson per week is the time allotted to the study of music. This is entirely insufficient for the students to develop any significant interest in music, to acquire technical familiarity with a musical instrument or to learn to sing. The aim of the program, like that of the state radio broadcasts, is to impress upon the students the concept of "the class nature of music" and to instil in them a belief in the superiority of the Soviet system of life, in accordance with the slogan "We thank Comrade Stalin for our happy childhood." It is noteworthy that the faculties of the conservatories where the specialist teachers of the "musical discipline" are trained were known until 1940 as "Departments of Social Education" (*Sotsvos*),[1] a designation which emphasized the fact that their real subject was not musical education but rather "social," that is, political, education.

The program of this course is based on the system of periodization used in Soviet courses of general history in which each epoch is characterized not by musical but by socio-political and economic factors. Subjects include sight-reading and writing (notation, basic musical forms and means of expression) and performance of typical works of the musical literature of the past and of Soviet music, using piano or vocal presentation. The program is so much overburdened, however, by interspersed lectures accompanying each theme, in which the emphasis is on politics rather than on music, that the educational effect of the course in a musical sense is negligible. At best the students are able to remember a few names of some of the outstanding composers of the past and some facts of their biographies. On the other hand they will have learned a large number of mass-songs about Stalin, "class hatred towards the bourgeois culture of the West," "the Soviet motherland," "Soviet patriotism," etc.

Nor is this gloomy picture in any way compensated for by the general development of musical activity in the schools. Only rarely do Soviet schools of general education have their own chorus and even more rarely do they include an orchestra or a musical group offering students the opportunity to learn to play an instrument after school. As a rule parents who wish to give their children at least a nonprofessional music education or appreciation of music are obliged to send them after school to a special music school or studio, of which there are very few even in the larger cities.

It is extremely probable that this clearly expressed neglect of musical education in the general schools betrays a tendency towards the deliberate, conscious suppression of the musical-aesthetic interests of the child in order to deprive him of those human traits without which the emotional perception of life is impossible. Such an educational system achieves its inevitable result in Soviet life, with its unmistakable neglect of man's individual, subjective and spiritual nature.

2. *SPECIALIZED MUSIC TRAINING*

The Soviet system of professional music education is organizationally part of the general system of Soviet education. Depending on the level concerned, music education comes under either the Committee for Higher Education or the Ministry of Education which deals with all questions relating to secondary and elementary schools.[2]

Before World War II the music schools of the Soviet Union were organized as follows: (a) schools to train professional musicians offering courses of four and ten years which were in effect high schools giving either a complete secondary education or preparatory training for higher schools; (b) various kinds of music courses, e.g., evening courses, "popular conservatories" and elementary music schools which usually offered a four-year course for non-professional musicians; and (c) institutions of higher music education, the conservatories. Prior to the war there were nine conservatories, those of Moscow, Leningrad, Kiev, Odessa, Kharkov, Sverdlovsk, Tbilisi, Baku, and Yerevan.

The normal course of study in the conservatories is from four to five years depending on the subject chosen. Some of the conservatories have adopted the system of a ten-year course in which the curriculum of a secondary music school is combined with that of the general secondary school. This system, which was first introduced in the conservatories of Moscow, Leningrad and Kiev and later in those of other cities, is designed to prepare the student for professional study at one of the conservatories. A complete professional music education under this plan takes fourteen or fifteen years.

The reason for organizing the ten-year courses was to overcome the critical condition of music education in the Soviet Union during the mid-thirties when the decline of general musical culture had reached such proportions that it was impossible for the conservatories to rely any longer on the recruitment of students from the secondary schools of general education. In prerevolutionary Russia the ranks of conservatory students had constantly been replenished from the excellent secondary music schools or from the schools of general education. Under Soviet conditions, however, training of this caliber is to be had neither in the secondary schools nor in the home. In this connection it is significant that there has been a marked change in the type of students at the higher music schools. By the 1930's the students in Soviet schools were being drawn in the main from social groups, particularly the peasantry and the urban middle class, which had previously lacked any well-established musical tradition.

It thus became necessary to provide the trained students to enter the conservatories from among the students of the conservatories themselves and it was to meet this need that the ten-year music courses were organized. There is no reason to assume, however, that the crisis has been overcome during recent years; the discrepancy between the level of musical culture of the masses and a professional standard of music training is too great.

Even in the case of the ten-year course, however, an insoluble problem arose: how can ten years of study in a music school provide the student with the preschool training of which he has been deprived by the conditions of Soviet life, give him a thorough general education and at the same time fit him for professional work? Since the problem was insoluble, the authorities began to select for these courses only highly gifted children, for which reason these schools are often called "schools for gifted children."

The ten-year courses, however, were not open to all gifted children but only to those who were "selected." As a rule, such schools accept only children who are specially selected from the provinces and who have been brought up in special boarding schools or who are the children of Soviet officials.

With all their deficiencies, nevertheless, the ten-year courses from the very beginning of their existence became the basic source from which the conservatories obtained their students. The percentage of students entering the conservatories from other institutions, such as the numerous music schools and studios, is negligible.

Only the three largest conservatories, those of Leningrad, Moscow and Kiev, offer all the specialized music courses represented in the Soviet Union. These conservatories include the following departments: composition; orchestral conducting; music history and theory for prospective teachers of these subjects in professional music and musicological schools; solo instruments; voice; pedagogy, for teachers in schools of general education (in the department known until recently as *Sotsvos*);[3] and teacher training for choral directors, leaders for orchestras of folk instruments and instructors for amateur musicians. The six other conservatories have fewer departments.

Each of the three largest conservatories also offers a three-year postgraduate course for the training of conservatory teachers. Students for this course are primarily those who have graduated from the conservatory with distinction but also include composers, musicologists and performers of outstanding merit.

The curriculum in the conservatories is broken down into four main subject matter divisions: (a) political-philosophical subjects, including political economy, dialectical and historical materialism, history of the Communist Party, and Marxism-Leninism; (b) humanities, including the history of art and aesthetics (although this is seldom taught as a special course, having recently been transformed into a seminar on Marxism); (c) the special musical disciplines (theory of music, harmony, counterpoint, form, and instrumentation, together with "popular art" and "popular polyphony" which were introduced recently); and (d) the history of Russian music (or the music of the peoples of the U.S.S.R.) and of Western music. In addition the students prepare individual work on special subjects.

The number of school hours allotted to each discipline depends on the curriculum for each category of student. For example, students of solo instruments receive from forty to sixty hours in music theory during the ten-month school year, whereas in the special classes for composers and for history and theory students, almost twice as many hours are allotted for this subject. The method of teaching also varies in accordance with the subject of study. Composers and musicologists are taught mainly by ear while singers and instrumentalists are trained by actual performance. For prospective teachers various courses in teaching methods and practice are added.

One of the indisputable achievements of Soviet music pedagogy has been the rationalization of school hours. Deliberately limiting themselves to music of the classic and romantic traditions and during recent years more specifically to Russian music of the nineteenth century, Soviet music teachers have established a number of curricula, particularly for theoretical courses in which the stress laid upon direct contact with the music provides a sound basis for strict and consistent generalization of the laws of creative evolution. Particularly during the years just before the war it was possible to eliminate from the program the formerly compulsory popularized sociological excursuses which served only political ends and thereby to bring music theory to some extent back to its proper subject, music itself. Of course the scope of material for study in the main was limited to music of the eighteenth and nineteenth centuries, but nevertheless the students came into contact not only with old masters such as the contrapuntal composers of the sixteenth century but also with contemporary Western music under the guise of "false examples." Until the end of the 1930's the conservatory students, especially those who were studying composition or historical and theoretical subjects, were acquainted with everything important that was being written by the outstanding composers of the contemporary West.

It is only in recent years that the curriculum has been brought completely under political control. At present the choice of musical examples is limited in the main to Russian nineteenth century music and contemporary Soviet compositions. In courses in the history of music Marxist-Leninist dogmas now tend to crowd out the living historical material, not only imposing on the student false conceptions of historical phenomena but distorting the historical development of music as a whole.

It should be noted that the programs of Soviet music schools are standardized for all educational institutions. These programs, which are examined yearly at special conferences and which must be approved by the Committee for Higher Education, are obligatory for all teachers in the Soviet Union. Thus the teacher's role is limited to that of transmitting the principles and methods set by the Committee for Higher Education.

The conservatory curricula serve two entirely distinct aims: the training on the one hand of highly qualified specialists in some field of music, equipped with professional knowledge and technical efficiency, and on the other of obedient proponents of the Soviet art policy and the general policy of the Party. The second aim is accomplished by means of political-philosophical courses, particularly the course on the "History of the Party." Most of the teachers of these courses are open or secret collaborators (*seksoty*)[4] of the MVD, who have the duty of "forming the political consciousness" of the students and keeping both students and teachers under surveillance from the point of view of their political reliability.

These MVD collaborators, who in the majority of cases are persons of exceptional ignorance, have the right to attend lectures and lessons given by the teachers of special musical subjects. If they find that any of the teachers or students are permitting themselves to "take liberties" endangering the aims of political orthodoxy, a general meeting of teachers and students is called immediately and a process of "re-education" begins. For example, in one case a venerable and respected professor in summarizing the lectures prepared for the use of his students (the general lack of textbooks often necessitates the use of summaries prepared by the teachers) emphasized too clearly the national character of certain compositions by Ukrainian composers. This was interpreted by the *seksot* as evidence of "bourgeois nationalism" and since the professor did not know how to repent, he was dismissed from the conservatory. Another case is even more curious: one of these "inspectors" attended a lecture at the beginning of the school year and found the teacher and students discussing their summer vacations. As a result the teacher was accused of "unnecessary personal contact with students with the aim of distracting them from study and consequently from the active upbuilding of the country..."!

In addition to the *seksoty* and the *"diamatchiky,"* as the teachers of dialectic materialism are nicknamed, other guardians of "Party purity" in the schools include the *partorg* (the secretary of the Party organization), the secretary of the Komsomol group, and, as a rule, the assistant director of the administrative department. During recent years there has been a tendency for even conservatory directors themselves to be Party members. Since the war the number of Party members on the school staffs has greatly increased. These representatives of the Party, although many of them have little or nothing in common with music, constitute the "social entity" of the conservatories, and it is their activity which is the decisive factor in determining whether a conservatory is to receive an honorary award or some other material blessing.

Quite different are the teachers of the purely musical subjects in the conservatories. Most of them received their musical education in the old schools under the earlier system; many of them were teachers in conservatories in pre-Soviet times. All of them without exception interpret their loyalty to the new order as an obligation to fulfill conscientiously the artistic tasks entrusted to them, and they often strive to obtain from their students a maximum of professional competence even at the expense of the students' "political training." This tendency is facilitated by the fact that all special lessons are given individually. The intimate relationship thus established between teacher and student frequently develops into friendship on the basis of a common determination to master the material and common professional interests. Naturally such relationship is conducive to productive school work.

Thanks to this dissociation of professional interests from political training, students who graduate from the conservatories often achieve a high level of technical competence.

Since 1940 tuition in the conservatories, as in other higher educational institutions, has been paid for by the students.[5] The number of students has not been significantly diminished, however, by this circumstance. Used to the hard conditions of Soviet life the students are satisfied to get along on extremely little. Although they can hardly make both ends meet by their casual earnings or by very modest scholarships (a considerable number of conservatory students are sponsored by industrial organizations which pay their tuition) and although they frequently lack the bare necessities of life, they nevertheless heroically avail themselves of the right to study.

In general the students of Soviet conservatories are genuine "virgin soil." They are either children of the "new Soviet intelligentsia" which has not yet had sufficient time to overcome its predominantly peasant tradition or they are the children of workers or collective farm peasants. Inevitably they lack both knowledge of life and the culture which is acquired only by generations of effort. Moreover, they are wanting in that refinement of musical perception, an essential prerequisite for music education which must be acquired very early in life. In its place, however, they possess a direct living contact with the traditions of peasant folk music and, most important of all, a passion for learning and the cultivation of feeling.

Dedicating themselves to their music education, the overwhelming majority of these students regard it as a blessing sent to them by fate. Their contact with the world of music opens unknown horizons and takes them away from the hard and unattractive work of a collective farm or Soviet life in general. Hence with few exceptions they throw themselves uncompromisingly into the task of learning and punctiliously execute the tasks entrusted to them. All the more bitter, therefore, is their disillusionment when they encounter the harsh realities of Soviet life after graduation from the conservatories. While he is at school a Soviet student is in contact with some form of creative incentive, implanted, it is true, sometimes by contraband during individual lessons, and he is tempted by what he can sample of contemporary Western art. After graduation, however, he is compelled to become an artisan and a propagandist.

The Soviet press itself bears eloquent witness to this situation. A number of recent articles in *Soviet Music* are concerned with the problem of a fundamental reorganization of music education. As is customary the authors of these articles begin by making claims of an exceptional improvement in Soviet music education. At the same time, however, they cite numerous facts that indicate the existence of a catastrophic decline in the level of training of professional musicians.

For example, in an editorial in *Soviet Music* for August 1950 entitled "Towards a New Improvement in Music Education" it is stated:

> The Soviet Union is a country of the most advanced mass music education. The Bolshevik Party and the Soviet government attach great importance to the training of Soviet music cadres. A major role in the fundamental improvement in this field has been played by the resolution of the Party Central Committee on the opera *The Great Friendship*.
>
> In the two-and-a-half years since the publication of this historic document an important work has been accomplished. In conservatories and other institutions of music education the adherents of formalism have been exposed and school programs which were filled with depraved ideas and which were methodologically useless have been withdrawn and replaced by new, more perfect programs. The repertoire of student performers has been purged of formalist compositions alien to our people. The subject matter of student works presented for a higher degree has been changed; they no longer manifest one-sided enthusiasm for themes of the remote past; the unworthy servility of the Soviet people towards the bourgeois culture of the West is a thing of the

past. The leading place in the works presented for the diploma by our students of theory and history is taken by the study of the Russian classics and contemporary Soviet music.

The educational process of many important subjects has been reconstructed to a considerable degree. For example, the teaching of the course on "popular art" has markedly improved; contemporary choral works which reflect our heroic socialist reality occupy a significant place in this important course. Also improved is the course of musical analysis, and more attention is now given to democratic forms of music. The selection of students for vocal classes is more painstaking. The operatic departments of many conservatories have broadened their activity, thereby ensuring the successful training of opera singers. In many respects the classes for composers have been reorganized—one-sided enthusiasm for textless forms of instrumental music has been overcome and the attention of young composers is now turned towards Soviet subjects, towards forms which are close to the people. Ideological and political mass-work is now much better organized. The quality of the work in the departments of Marxism-Leninism has risen and their contact with the specialist departments has become closer.[6]

It is obvious that all these "successes" are in reality directed towards a single aim, the transformation of the schools of music into institutions for training Soviet propagandists. The time devoted to music is intentionally reduced to the bare minimum so that it becomes a secondary study limited to the status of an applied trade. Such a system of education is bound to produce failures in the professional training of Soviet musicians like those to which the Soviet press itself calls attention. Thus the editorial in *Soviet Music* continues,

Some teachers of composition still think that their task is merely to teach the future composer certain professional technical skills, and that education in ideas should be left to teachers of the social sciences.[7]

This, of course, is a deeply mistaken point of view!

A teacher of composition must educate his pupil as a future Soviet artist—"an engineer of human souls"—and must instil into him clear-cut, lofty ideological and artistic principles; the whole complex of technical means to be mastered by the future composer should be considered as a way towards the most powerful and honest unfolding of new artistic content, born of socialist reality....

A most important and urgent problem is to improve fundamentally the training of singers.... No less important is the problem of training good orchestra players, especially those of the wood-wind and brass sections.... The problem of the curricula and textbooks for theoretical and historical subjects is also not solved.... The correct methodological organization of teaching specialties (performance, composition and musicology) is the most important condition for training musical cadres. However, what we need is not musicians in general but good Soviet musicians. That is why it is necessary to improve still further the teaching of the leading subject in higher educational institutions, the fundamentals of Marxism-Leninism.[8]

It is difficult to understand how even a "good Soviet musician" can be trained under conditions where the leading subject is a course in the fundamentals of Marxism-Leninism. Evidently this is also not quite clear to the author of this article, for he writes,

A serious obstacle to the further improvement of [music] education is the great number of subjects. Twenty-four or twenty-five required subjects plus six or seven specialized subjects constitute the average full-time program for a conservatory student during the school year. The average for students of singing is as high as forty subjects.... With such a load, the conservatory student actually has no free time to concentrate on his chosen subject (the same is true even in the preparatory schools). One must not forget that the preparation of lessons by the student in his special field -- piano, violin, trumpet, etc. -- requires many hours of intensive practice daily. But where can the student find so much time, if most of it is already scheduled for lectures, seminars and individual class lessons?[9]

Of great interest in this connection is another article in *Soviet Music* entitled "On the Problem of Training Music Cadres."[10] The article is signed by the Komsomol secretary of the Gnesin State Musical-Pedagogical Institute in Moscow, an indication that it has the approval of the Party or the Komsomol. It reads in part as follows:

The colossal overloading of the students' program by collective and individual tasks and, consequently, the lack of time for any independent work whatever, the endless repetition of subject matter, the complete alienation from work and individual musical performance—such is the list, though far from complete, of the basic defects of our system of music education.

This is true particularly with reference to our higher music institutions, the top levels of the excessively long process of music education.

On our desk there is a schedule of students' work in one of the music colleges of the capital.

Here is a list of the required lectures for a theory student of the second year: Monday, from 1 to 3 P.M., popular art; 3 to 5 P.M., methods of teaching the theory of music; 5 to 7 P.M., seminar on the fundamentals of Marxism-Leninism; 7 to 9 P.M., practice teaching. Tuesday, 9 to 11 A.M., fundamentals of Marxism-Leninism; 11 A.M. to 1 P.M., analysis of musical forms; 1 to 3 P.M., history of Western European music. Wednesday, noon to 1 P.M., polyphony; 1 to 3 P.M., foreign languages; 3 to 6 P.M., history of music. Thursday, 11 A.M. to 1 P.M., physical culture; 1 to 3 P.M., score reading; 3 to 5 P.M., methodology of teaching the history of music. Friday, 9 to 11 A.M., practical lesson in Russian music; noon to 2 P.M., foreign languages; 2 to 3 P.M., political hour; 4 to 5 P.M., piano lessons. Saturday, 9 to 11 A.M., fundamentals of Marxism-Leninism; 1 to 3 P.M., history of Western European music; 3 to 5 P.M., polyphony. Total 38 hours....

In addition, in order to ensure his normal development, a student in one of the instrumental faculties must practice on his instrument not less than four hours per day, making 24 hours per week.

Moreover students are required to prepare systematically the lessons for seminars of socio-political subjects and the history of music, besides working on foreign languages, harmony, score reading, and general piano studies.

Even this, however, does not complete the training of a student of musical culture.

Can one imagine a future worker in the field of art and ideology without any understanding of painting, architecture,

> drama and cinema, and literature? Nor can we forget social work, a powerful factor in the students' ideological and political education. Correctly organized social work develops a sense of responsibility toward the assigned task and forces the individual to live the collective life in full measure. Under the existing school curriculum, however, the students are allotted so little free time that social work has to be done at the expense either of the student's rest time or school hours. Frequently the leaders of the Komsomol or social organizations are confronted with a difficult situation in distributing social assignments, realizing on the one hand the necessity for the work and on the other the impossibility of correctly coordinating it with the educational process.
>
> Social work also requires time. This is a serious question.[11]

It would be difficult to add anything to the author's conclusion:

> We request the comrades of the Committee for Art Affairs to add up the number of hours and answer this question: What should be the admissible load for the student, considering that he, like any other human being, simply must have some time for relaxation?
>
> It is obvious that under such a heavy schedule there can be no place for that independent creative work without which the teaching and education of a professional musician is unthinkable.
>
> The student is compelled to cut lectures and have recourse to deceiving his teachers. The knowledge acquired under such conditions is superficial and flimsy; the students hear little and are poorly acquainted with music.[12]

But is a knowledge of music really necessary for the Soviet musician who has been so consistently converted by Soviet art policy into a political agitator and propagandist and whose activities are limited to the "realistic," "popular" pseudoculture so energetically propagated by the Party Central Committee in its numerous decrees defining the path of development of Soviet music?

The Soviet music school is degenerating not merely into a school for propagandists but into a school for political propagandists rather than music propagandists. Such is the natural course of its development in a country where music itself has been converted into a medium of political propaganda for the "masses" and where every tie joining it to its true character as a free art has been severed.

B. THE ORGANIZATION OF CONTROL: THE UNION OF SOVIET COMPOSERS

All musical composition in the Soviet Union is controlled by the Union of Soviet Composers. Even nonprofessional composers are subject to its supervision, in the form of a special section for "consultative help for beginners in composition." The "national" unions of composers, such as those in the Ukraine, Georgia, Byelorussia, Armenia, and Azerbaidzhan, are in reality only subsidiaries of the all-Union body and have no independent power.

The Union's membership includes not only composers but music theorists, musicologists, journalists, and critics. The decisive criterion for membership is not ability or experience but "social purity," i.e., devotion to the Party's policies. The leading role in the local bodies of the Union, as in all Soviet organizations and institutions, belongs to the Party cell and its secretary the *partorg*, regardless of whether the cell is made up of composers and musicologists or (as is usually the case) of persons having little knowledge of music but who are in possession of Party membership cards and who occupy posts in some music institution. This situation has come about for the simple reason that among genuine composers, performers, musicologists, and teachers, only a very limited number are Party members, and even among these only a few are politically active. Before World War II, as a general rule, no outstanding composers belonged to the Party. During the postwar years, however, the situation in this respect has apparently altered radically. To belong to the Party, even if only as a formality, has become a prerequisite not only for a healthy life but also for the opportunity to engage in active work, even among persons well advanced in years.

The work of the Union is concentrated mainly on the allocation of the "creative tasks" which are assigned each year for compositions on subjects connected with the current political line. It is of course understood that these compositions must be written in accordance with all the rules of "socialist realism," that they must have a descriptive program and that they must be adjusted to the level of perception of the masses. The commissions include not only operas, symphonies, quartets, and sonatas, but also popular songs for mass consumption, based preferably on political themes associated with historical events or current Soviet developments.

The Union's board of directors is responsible for the care of the personal needs of members, such as living accomodations, vacations and medical care, and most important, for the supervision of their political education by means of assemblies, conferences, reviews, lectures, etc. The Union makes extensive use of "creative conferences" at which finished or projected works by composer-members are discussed. These meetings are one of the forms of "creative control," and although their atmosphere is familiar to members of the Union, to an outside observer they would seem to be entirely unconnected with a normal act of composition. At such meetings the members discuss the sketches of the first draft of a new composition or the separate stages of its realization, if larger musical forms are under consideration. The composer is forced to answer detailed questions concerning his compositional plans and to expose his innermost creative thoughts.

The most characteristic feature of such meetings is the deadly critical method employed which frequently results either in the complete destruction of a composer's original plan or in its transformation into its opposite. Sometimes it happens that a composer whose work has been criticized at one of these meetings loses his self-control and makes unwise statements which are later brought to the attention of the MVD. As a result, the offender may be given the opportunity to apply his creative efforts to the "production of material values" in some forced labor camp. The fate of the Ukrainian choral composer Lebedynets' is instructive in this connection. Following a critical session of this type he was sentenced to spend nearly ten years in labor camps. After he had served his sentence he returned to Kiev just before the war, where he composed the new Ukrainian national anthem. Such a case of successful "re-education" is truly remarkable; not many composers are as lucky as Lebedynets'.

Only an extremely small number of composers, men of the caliber of Prokof'yev, Myaskovski or Shostakovich, can permit themselves to avoid such "creative criticism." In the case of such composers the Union so far has not ventured to employ the same methods it uses with the rank and file. In general, however, "critical discussions" of the work of outstanding composers does take place fairly frequently, in the composers' presence or in their absence—the difference is immaterial. Often such criticism, which carries the sanction of the Party, provides an opportunity for a real "class struggle" by the "composers' proletariat" against the privileged "masters." Not only among mediocrities of all sorts but also among the overwhelming majority of representatives of that grey mass of Soviet composer-propagandists who are compelled to earn their living by the thankless labor of musical hack-workers, there exists a real hatred of outstanding composers, as much for their creative ability as for their better material position.

There is also a deep mutual dislike between composers and musicologists in the Soviet Union, particularly those active as critics. The composers have nicknamed the musicologists "music eaters," i.e., persons who earn their living by "devouring" music.

Even among the masters a feeling of external indifference

toward one another predominates. Many leading composers, for example the late Myaskovski and Prokof'yev, prefer to lead a secluded life, avoiding direct contact with their environment. Some of these composers have made it clear that their contact with the Union and the Party is to be exclusively by means of letters. Whenever their presence is required at congresses, conferences, anniversaries or "ceremonial meetings," they write letters or reports explaining their inability to be present personally on account of ill health. In this respect B.V. Asaf'yev's attitude was characteristic. He was a man who disliked the crowd and who contrived to limit himself to letters in reply to inquiries, even those from persons in responsible Party offices. For example, his report to the First All-Union Congress of Composers in 1948 was read in his absence.

Prokof'yev managed to maintain a similar purely epistolary contact with the musical world. It was useless to expect to meet him at conferences or gatherings; he was even absent from the celebration of his own sixtieth birthday held in the hall of the Moscow Conservatory on April 24, 1952 with typical Soviet pomp. Such obvious disregard of the Soviet cultural politicians' hospitality, however, turns out well only for a few people.

The dependence of the Soviet composer's creative existence upon the arbitrary rule of Party officials creates an atmosphere of ill will, jealousy and sycophantism, more or less openly expressed. Instead of exercising his talents as a creative artist the composer becomes more and more a mere functionary.

Another adverse factor is the overdeveloped system of bureaucratic rewards–the honorary titles, the orders and the monetary prizes. Under such circumstances genuine creative work becomes more and more difficult and the composer's activities, to the extent that he resists Party control, take on semilegal or altogether illegal forms.

C. LIVING CONDITIONS OF SOVIET COMPOSERS

Soviet composers live under the same conditions as ordinary inhabitants of the Soviet Union. With rare exceptions they have only a single room for their family, often composing to the accompaniment of a baby's cries and the smell of burning food. There are literally no more than ten Soviet composers whose royalties and whose knowledge of "the ropes" have secured for them comparative comfort. For example, in 1938 and 1939 gossip among Soviet composers concerned the almost oriental splendour of the country house of Dunayevski, the writer of patriotic propaganda songs such as "Broad Is My Native Land."

Far more typical are the reverse instances such as the case of the talented Ukrainian composer V. Kosenko which received wide publicity in 1936. From the day of his arrival in Kiev in 1929 up to his death in 1938, Kosenko, the author of a considerable number of genuinely interesting piano compositions and larger orchestral works (e.g., his *Heroic Overture, Piano Concerto* and *Cello Sonata*), and a professor at the Kiev Conservatory, lived with his wife and daughter under truly impossible conditions, in a single damp room which was hardly large enough to contain a piano and a couch which doubled as a bed. In addition the composer was ill, and the dampness of his small room was a direct contributing cause of his death. What concern this situation caused to "musical society," not only in Kiev but also in Moscow! Nearly everyone tried to help improve Kosenko's situation, but all efforts were in vain. Kosenko's case even reached the Central Committee's "viceroy" in the Ukraine, at that time Khrushchov, who came personally (an unheard-of case) to the composer's home approximately a month before Kosenko's death and, handing him with great solemnity a medal for his "self-denying work in the education of musical cadres," promised "to concern himself immediately about a home for Kosenko." But the composer died... with the medal but without a decent home.

How many such cases there are. Most terrible, perhaps, are the housing problems of the Moscow musicians. The great majority of even outstanding musicians there live with their families in single rooms where in order to sleep one must first move the table. For example, one of the leading professors and department heads at the Moscow Conservatory lived with his wife and small child under such conditions.

The problem of living conditions is also connected with the composer's earnings. The situation is better for those composers who in addition to their income from creative work can derive a more or less steady income from teaching or administrative work. Teaching in particular is paid more satisfactorily than other types of work. Since 1938 a professor at one of the conservatories whose position has been approved by the Committee for Higher Education earns from 800 to 1,500 rubles per month depending on the length of his active service, his academic degree and rank and the amount of teaching he does. An assistant professor or an instructor receives correspondingly less. But of course even such a salary suffices at best to make ends meet providing one's family does not exceed two or three persons. Otherwise one has to use one's wits and get outside jobs composing, writing articles or doing some other work.

Considerably worse is the position of those who attempt to live exclusively on what they earn by their creative work. A few composers of the caliber of Prokof'yev or Shostakovich, or such propagandists as Dunayevski, can count on some income from the "authors' fund," in which a certain percentage from the proceeds of performances of their works accumulates. The great mass of composers, however, are compelled to exist by executing government commissions for which they receive payments ranging from 50 to 1,500 rubles depending on the type and length of the work. Such commissions, however, can be obtained at best only once or twice a year. Even if one adds to this the possibility of commissioned work from some other organizations (the philharmonic organizations, the Houses of Amateur Activity, etc.) and advances from the Union of Composers on account for future work, it is clear that the average composer lives a miserable existence.

The most reliable and sizeable earnings for Soviet composers come from journalistic work. Authors of newspaper or magazine articles and books are remunerated quite handsomely, thus substantially easing their material situation.[13] It is not by accident that during recent years all Soviet composers, from great to small, have been writing more books and articles than music.

Like other Soviet citizens the Soviet composer lives within the intellectual boundaries which the government considers appropriate for him. In the evenings, as a rule, composers instead of attending concerts have to sit through dull meetings at the Composer's Union, studying the history of the Communist Party and the current directives about "reconstruction on the music front," or performing "self-criticism" and listening to the "creative help" of some Party hack.

It is not the instability of personal life that most oppresses the Soviet composer, however, but the system of Soviet life itself, which has declared war against those moral values that are the foundations of every genuine culture.

D. MUSIC IN PERFORMANCE

1. *RESULTS OF THE SOVIET CONCERT POLICY*

Because of the complexity of much contemporary music it is unusually difficult for the listener to grasp and retain its form. In general, music, because of its temporal character, requires repeated impressions and a special effort of the attention. This effort, unlike that required for perception of the visual arts which are always before our eyes, acts as an obstacle to the inclusion of new sound complexes within the circle of those generally accepted. It is mainly for this reason that the social memory of music is so conservative. By way of recompense, music which speaks to the intellect and heart becomes firmly lodged in the creative and perceptive consciousness and is retained there for generations.

The social conservativeness of musical perception is well known to performers who, in general, are little inclined to novelty in the choice of their repertoire. The public likes to hear what is familiar, and that is only natural, since what is familiar requires the least effort of comprehension and gives the most pleasure.

In the Soviet Union those composers who prefer to break new paths in music encounter nearly insurmountable obstacles in the dissemination of their music, not so much, however, because of the public's lack of preparation as because of the Party's "repertoire policy" which establishes fixed norms for performers. These obstacles leave their mark on all musical life in the Soviet Union.

Throughout the entire history of music the lack of contact between composer and listener has been steadily increasing with every new style. Ever since spontaneous vocal improvisation ceased, this terrible process of the separation of composers from listeners, of creation from perception, has been under way. It constitutes one of the inner crises that corrode music.

Nevertheless, the people to whom art is vital and necessary are never lacking in receptivity to what is new. The assertion that the social consciousness of the Soviet public is opposed to the vital creative work of our contemporaries, as represented by those composers who are stigmatized by Soviet critics as "formalists," is a lie invented by Zhdanov. There can be no doubt that the natural conservativeness of the mass audience could be easily overcome by repeated performances of new works. This, of course, would require a wise and attentive attitude on the part of Soviet politicians instead of the existing unrestrained arrogance towards contemporary composers and music.

There is no question that the classics ought always to be heard, but unfortunately very few works of this priceless heritage are performed in the Soviet Union, and it almost seems that performers vie with one another in this deficiency. In relation to the musical heritage the Soviet repertoire policy has established insurmountable barriers, accepting only that music which is connected with epochs of political upheaval within "bourgeois culture," particularly Beethoven, The Five and the early Romantics.

The level of performance in the Soviet Union is far from satisfactory. Particularly bad is the situation with regard to orchestral conducting. Nearly all those artists who during the first years of the Soviet regime were outstanding in the field of conducting have long since left the Soviet Union, while the situation among the younger generation of Soviet conductors is truly deplorable. Even the best among them, such as Mravinski and Ivanov, do not recreate the music but simply reproduce it mechanically, frequently forgetting that metrical divisions are not traffic signals.

The question of musical performance in the Soviet Union has other aspects as well. A vital musical work, one that stimulates its listeners' minds and feelings, arouses controversy and creates a demand for its performance, particularly by small circles of musical amateurs, either as a whole or in various transcriptions or arrangements. In this way such a composition grows into the consciousness of its listeners who retain in their memory its separate fragments which they sing and at times even whistle unconsciously or play on any available instrument. This is true popularity. The characteristic melodic lines and harmonic progressions of the composition are caught up and become a kind of stylistic standard, the obligatory expressive formulas of their time. Thus the enlightened listener plays an important role in the comprehension and dissemination of what is new and vital.

All this constitutes that "natural selection" of music which is characteristic of normal conditions of development. In the Soviet Union, however, the obstacles to such "natural selection" resulting from the Party's art policy create an artificial selection of music that has absolutely nothing in common with the historical logic of development.

Only that music receives wide dissemination which can be used for political propaganda. This applies first of all, of course, to the most orthodox forms of Soviet music: the mass-song, instrumental works with a clearly expressed political program, operas with Soviet subjects, symphonic compositions written for special occasions and, most of all, compositions in praise of Stalin and other leaders. Even in the selection of musical literature from the past the right of performance is given only to those compositions which can be used for political aims.

Thus the existence of a musical composition in the Soviet Union is extremely insecure and depends on numerous chances having nothing to do with questions of music. This is especially true of the work of those composers who have not yet lost contact with contemporary Western art; for them life is extremely difficult.

In regard to the technique of performance Soviet critics speak of the "individuality of the performer style," a concept associated with vague ideas of "socialist realism." For example, during the mid-thirties, in connection with the first concert appearance of the pianist Emil Gilel's (he was then sixteen or seventeen years of age, one of a group of Odessa infant prodigies), much was written about the "style of Soviet performance," and there were even attempts by various critics to create a special "theory of Soviet performance." These critics considered it necessary for the Soviet performer to base his performance on Marxism-Leninism, with its theory of the "objectivity" of art and its rejection of everything which in any way deviates from the "mass standard," i.e., everything that is individually original, lyrical and human. The "objectivity of the machine" was thus postulated as the performer's ideal.[14]

Later, however, these attempts to replace living performance by machine-like objectivity were censured, and outstanding performers were left to themselves. Another theory had triumphed, that of the presence in the musical language of Soviet composers of stirring and meaningful elements which are accessible to everyone. The task of the performer was defined as conveying these "stirring and meaningful elements" to the audience. The critics' reasoning was simple: aesthetics, they said, in no way excludes the vital reality and socializing properties of art. Music becomes vulgar only among people who consciously listen for trivialities or among composers and performers with a naive faith in inspiration. It is only necessary, therefore, for the Soviet composers and performers to get rid of sentimentalism for the problem to be solved.

The theory sounds simple and even convincing. But the whole horror of Soviet musical experience is contained in the fact that sentimentality and naive reliance on inspiration not only did not cease to be significant but became the basis for creative and performing practice, particularly among composers of the orthodox group. This, of course, is the natural result of Zhdanov's demand for "music for the common man."

The Soviet listener, deprived of variety in musical literature and obliged to be satisfied with the orthodox music offered him by Soviet performers, naturally manifests a greater interest in the performer's technique than in the artistic content of the work being performed. To the Soviet performer the words of Arthur Honegger are particularly applicable: "A virtuoso...uses music as a dancer does his rope, ...anxious to win the applause of the spectators.... Virtuosos are actors who do not penetrate into the secret of music as an art."[15]

During recent years, Soviet journalism has been filled with

declarations about the necessity of creating "normal conditions for the work of philharmonic societies" and for "greater attention to performances by guest artists." Yet the level of Soviet performing culture remains, as heretofore, far from what it should be.

2. CONCERTS AND THEATERS

With regard to concert and theater life Soviet propaganda, with its usual irresponsibility, proclaims that "in our country thousands of musical professional collective bodies have been established, palatial new theaters have been erected and immense concert halls have been built"[16] and that "the power of Soviet art lies in its indisoluble bond with the people."[17]

The truth, however, is far different. The real bond between music and the people is maintained not merely by supporting the traditions of vocal music and cultivating professional composing and performance but by drawing into the creative life of music ever new groups of listeners, giving them music education and knowledge and communicating to them the cultural values of the music of the past and present by means of an extensive network of concert halls and theaters, radio, record-players, and other means of disseminating music. It would be highly inaccurate to think that the construction during the Soviet period of two or three theaters and a few concert halls or the formation of five or six new groups of performers were achievements meriting any specially favorable comment.

In the Soviet Union with its two hundred million inhabitants there are certainly not too many symphony orchestras, opera houses or musical professional associations, and those which are functioning, with few exceptions, date from the prerevolutionary period and owe their continued existence merely to Soviet indulgence. As to Soviet concert life, its development is not such that one can consider it as being of importance to the masses on a genuinely popular scale.

There are only about fifteen major symphony orchestras in the Soviet Union. The most important of these are the Symphony Orchestra of the U.S.S.R. and the Radio Symphony Orchestra in Moscow, the Leningrad Philharmonic Orchestra and the symphony orchestras of Kiev, Odessa, Sverdlovsk, Baku, Tbilisi, and Yerevan. Even if one adds the so-called philharmonic organizations with their permanent and touring concert and operatic ensembles the number is still far too small to provide for any extensive degree of concert activity.

The official line which guides the activities of those in charge of concert life in the Soviet Union -- mostly Party members having little in common with music -- is "the development and perfection of Soviet art and its safeguarding against contamination by elements of bourgeois decay."[18] In plain language this means the inculcation of political propaganda and the eradication of every surviving tie to music as a manifestation of human culture, i.e., the complete subjugation of Soviet concert life to the political aims of communism.

As the result of this policy, programs of symphonic concerts in the Soviet Union are usually overloaded with works by Soviet composers, especially those which conform in content to the requirements of the Party's political line -- all sorts of "cantatas about Stalin," overtures and symphonies on Soviet themes, etc. Such works appear with special frequency on the programs of the annual concerts called "Decades of Soviet Music" which run sometimes for months during the concert season.

One finds Soviet critics already referring to a "gold reserve" of Soviet music which includes such works as Glière's *Concerto for Voice and Orchestra,* Shostakovich's *Fifth Symphony, Quintet* and *Song of the Forests,* Shaporin's *On the Field of Kulikovo* and *The Tale of the Battle for the Russian Land,* Khachaturian's *Violin Concerto,* Tallat-Kelpsha's *Cantata About Stalin,* Karayev's symphonic poem *Leili and Medzhnun,* Arutunyan's *Cantata About the Fatherland,* Svechnikov's symphonic poem *Shchors,* Zhukovs' kyi's *Glory to Thee, My Country,* and Muravlyov's *Azov Mountain.*[19] As works of art these compositions are of unequal value and significance but for the Soviet concert policy their importance lies either in the fact that, regardless of their importance as works of art, they glorify Stalin or the Soviet regime, or, as in the case of the works by Shostakovich and Khachaturian which are outstanding by reason of their musical significance, that they can be used to demonstrate the alleged advantages of the Soviet system under which they were created.

Besides works by Soviet composers the programs of symphonic concerts regularly include compositions by Russian classical composers, particularly Tchaikovsky, Borodin, Musorgsky, Glinka, and Rimsky-Korsakov, and a very small percentage of works by Western European classic and early Romantic composers such as Bach, Mozart, Beethoven, Schubert, Schumann, and Berlioz. Completely absent from these concerts are works by contemporary Western composers which "reflect the decay of bourgeois culture" and which consequently the Soviet public cannot be permitted to hear.

The technical level of performances by the major Soviet orchestras is generally above criticism, but there is much to be desired in regard to their interpretation. Their deficiency in this respect is due, in part, to the catastrophic decline in the art of conducting in the Soviet Union (Mravinski of the Leningrad Philharmonic and Ivanov of the Symphony Orchestra of the U.S.S.R. in Moscow are the only important conductors among the younger generation). In part, however, it is due to the extreme restriction of the repertoire which leads to an inevitable decline in the art of performance.

3. *OPERAS AND OPERETTAS*

A closely parallel situation exists in the operatic repertoire. The number of opera houses in the Soviet Union is only slightly larger than the number of symphony orchestras. They are concentrated mainly in the big cities: Moscow has the Bol'shoi Theater and its subsidiary the Moscow State Art

Theater named after Stanislavski and Nemirovich-Danchenko; in Leningrad there is the Kirov Theater of Opera and Ballet; and there are opera houses in Kiev, Odessa, Kharkov, Sverdlovsk, Dnepropetrovsk, Tbilisi, and Baku. These do not play a significant role so far as the masses are concerned; they exist for the entertainment of the Party bureaucracy rather than for that of the average listener.

Nevertheless there is no doubt that the general public in the Soviet Union is more interested in opera than in instrumental music. This is not only because the tradition of vocal music is more fully developed in Russia but also, evidently, because the operatic repertoire is further removed from Soviet reality than the standard repertoire of instrumental music, with its predominance of compositions written on political themes. The opera is perhaps the only place in the Soviet Union where one can be free of political propaganda, which is at least one reason why people go to hear *Traviata, Carmen, The Queen of Spades,* or some other grand opera.

In the field of opera, too, however, there is a basic "repertoire policy" aimed at the production of a maximum number of operas of Soviet origin, including the inevitable political propaganda. To strengthen this repertoire the authorities take extraordinary measures including direct commissions for operas on Soviet themes from the Committee of Art Affairs, the directors of the various opera houses and the Union of Composers. The results of this policy, however, have been meager. Sometimes these attempts at encouragement end in catastrophe such as befell the opera *With All One's Heart* for which the composer received a Stalin Prize but which had to be taken off the boards when it displeased Stalin himself.[20] Frequently such operas quietly disappear after the first performance, having been found unacceptable both to the public and to the singers.

It is evidently not easy to adapt opera to the aims of propaganda. The reason for this lies, of course, not in any lack of musical ability of the part of Soviet composers to cope with such tasks, for even such composers as Prokof'yev have tried their hand at creating Soviet operas, nor in any inability to guarantee the "Party purity" of such works; the decisive factor in the case is that the public does not want to hear operas which merely repeat the Party line which has been presented at countless gatherings and political meetings. Going to the opera is not an easy undertaking for the average Soviet citizen. It entails considerable material difficulties, and a person who permits himself this luxury wants to hear *Carmen* or *Aida* or some other similar work which will carry him away into a world far removed from reality, into a world of illusion.

Almost the only Soviet operas which have secured a place in the repertoire of the Bol'shoi Theater in Moscow (and consequently in the repertoires of other theaters, since the Bol'shoi is the acknowledged leader in matters of operatic orthodoxy) are *The Quiet Don* by Dzerzhinski, *Mother* by Zhelobinski and *The Battleship Potyomkin* by Chishko. More or less secure in the operatic repertoire is *Abesolom and Eteri* by the classic Georgian composer Paliashvili, a work composed long before the Soviet era. The basic repertoire of Soviet opera houses, however, still consists of operas by Verdi, especially *Traviata, Rigoletto, Aida,* and *Otello;* Puccini's *Madame Butterfly* and *Tosca;* Bizet's *Carmen;* Tchaikovsky's *Yevgeni Onegin* and *The Queen of Spades;* Borodin's *Prince Igor;* Musorgsky's *Boris* and *Khovanshchina;* Rimsky-Korsakov's *Snow Maid* and *The Golden Cockerel (Le Coq d'Or);* and a few others.

Whereas in Moscow and Leningrad the classical operatic repertoire is presented on a fairly generous scale, the same thing cannot be said of the other Soviet opera houses, the repertoire of which is limited to perhaps a dozen works repeated each year. The main reason for this limitation is the lack of competent operatic singers. The best singers, of course, are concentrated in the Bol'shoi Theater in Moscow. The majority of them are artists of pre-Soviet schooling and experience, for example, the tenors Kozlovski and Khanayev, the basses Pirogov, Mikhailov and Reisen, the coloratura-soprano Barsova, and the sopranos Davidova, Obukhova, Maksimova, and Kruglikova. The best operatic conductors are also employed by the Bol'shoi Theater, including Golovanov and Melik-Pashayev, both members of the older generation, and Nebol'sin and Kondrashin among the younger conductors. (The Bol'shoi also has the best Soviet ballerinas–Semyonova, Ulanova and Lepeshinskaya.)

Another unfavorable factor is the circumstance that the operatic stage is still occupied by numerous "Honored Art Workers" and singers who have received some honorary order but who have long since lost their voice; on the other hand, members of the new generation of singers, lacking preliminary music training, general culture and experience, owing to the lack of vacancies in the opera houses, frequently cannot make the grade and have to retire from the stage prematurely.

It is a significant fact that during recent years a prominent place in Soviet musical life has been taken by the operetta. Soviet critics frequently attack the operetta as an empty form of amusement, one which by its very nature carries the stamp of its "bourgeois" origin and which consequently is not proper entertainment for a "proletariat engaged in the building of socialism." The critics suggest, therefore, either that the operetta theaters should be liquidated as being unnecessary under Soviet conditions or that their repertoire should be entirely changed. A critic in *Soviet Art* declares:

> In the Soviet operetta laughter must be raised to the level of genuine social satire; it must become a weapon in unmasking the enemies and betrayers of the people–the aggressors. At the same time laughter in the operetta must become a means of educating the people, a weapon of criticism and self-criticism, scourging the survivals of the past in the people's consciousness and in human relationships... So far operetta composers have failed to produce bitter social satire...[21]

Nevertheless, from the material point of view operettas

are flourishing in the Soviet Union. Just as before, the theaters stubbornly retain in their repertoires operettas by Strauss, Kalman and Lehar, with only slight changes in the texts to eliminate *doubles entendres.* The numerous attempts which have been made to create a Soviet operetta repertoire have led to no results. At best the plots of comedies are based on episodes from Soviet life, but musically they are still imitations of the pre-Revolution operettas. Evidently the Soviet authorities tolerate operetta as a source of income, for after all money is as necessary as propaganda.

4. THE PHILHARMONIC ORGANIZATIONS

The standard organizations by means of which the Soviet government provides symphonic, ensemble and solo concerts, both instrumental and vocal, are the "philharmonic organizations" (*filarmonii*). As a rule these organizations exist in all more or less important towns and include performers of all kinds: vocalists, instrumentalists, ensembles, orchestras, and operatic troupes.

Philharmonic concerts are a fairly frequent phenomenon in the life of the larger cities. The philharmonic organizations also serve the most remote working and *kolkhoz* centers. This is quite natural because these bodies, more perhaps than any other musical organizations in the Soviet Union, are first and foremost organs of agitation and propaganda. The artistic quality of their performances is significant only to the extent that they must attain a certain technical level in order to make the desired propaganda effect on their audiences.

The injection of political propaganda into their programs is a simple and straightforward operation. The Composers' Union supplies the musical literature, a repertoire suitable for performance on any occasion, whether it be a slow-down in some branch of industry, a harvest campaign, the reorganization of a *kolkhoz,* anti-American propaganda, or the "struggle for peace" (which in reality means rearmament). Thus performers always have at their disposal a repertoire corresponding to the occasion, ready for presentation at a concert in a "critical" area, including not only an appropriate text but also a corresponding "artistic" interpretation of the work to be performed.

A characteristic feature of Soviet concert life which deserves mention is the "introductory talk" without which no concert in the Soviet Union, large or small, would be considered complete. The ostensible purpose of these lectures, which are frequently of an hour's duration, is to explain to the audience the program to be performed. Actually, however, they are political propaganda pure and simple, imposing upon the audience a definite political line by means of the musical program. Each of the philharmonic organizations has a staff of lecturers who more or less effectively drill into the listeners' heads the current propaganda line. The public, however, being aware of these introductory talks, has adopted the habit of arriving at concerts just at the end of the talk. This stratagem has its dangers, of course—the audience is always likely to have to listen to a lecture on its "irresponsibility."

In the metropolitan cities the philharmonic organizations maintain special "Universities of Musical Culture," groups headed by a lecturer whose talks are in theory designed to educate and broaden the musical horizon of listeners but which in reality are dissertations of "Party history." Since the lectures are often followed by good soloists and even symphonic orchestras, however, they draw good-sized audiences.

For example, a list of lectures given at the University of Musical Culture of the M.V. Frunze Central House of the Soviet Army in Moscow during 1949 included the following topics: "The formation of the Russian school of music and its sources," "M.I. Glinka," "A.S. Dargomyzhsky," "Musical life in Russia during the 1860's," "M.P. Musorgsky," "A.P. Borodin," "N.A. Rimsky-

Korsakov," "P.I. Tchaikovsky," etc.[22] The content of another series of lectures is described as follows:

> Recent lectures were devoted to Soviet music. The history of the development of Soviet musical culture was set forth in the light of the struggle against formalism and for a realistic art. The themes of these lectures were "The basic stages in the development of Soviet music," "The culture of musical performance in the Soviet Union," "The new stage of Soviet music," and "Soviet military music."[23]

If one takes into consideration the fact that these lectures comprise the plan of yearly work at the University of Musical Culture it is quite clear that the listeners are kept in almost complete ignorance of music outside the Soviet Union. Such exclusion of everything which does not belong directly to Russian classical music or to Soviet music has become during recent years the standard basis for the concert and theater life not only in the Soviet Union but also in the "People's Democracies." In this connection *Soviet Music* reports the following characteristic development:

> In accordance with the decision of the Committee for Matters of Science, the Arts and Culture under the Council of Ministers of the Bulgarian People's Republic, the Board of Directors of Musical Creation and Performing Art has organized 120 concerts for workers and youths in honour of J.V. Stalin.[24]

One hundred and twenty concerts! Probably they filled the entire yearly quota of the concert organization in Bulgaria!

5. CONCERTS BY PRIZE-WINNING SOLOISTS

Special consideration must be given to the concerts of those soloists who have earned the designation "laureate." These are musicians who have received Stalin Prizes or who have won prizes at the competitions organized by the Committee for Art Affairs for conservatory graduates or in the all-Union and international competitions, particularly those of Warsaw and Brussels.

The reason for the participation of Soviet musicians in the international competitions is not so much the encouragement of pure art as the satisfaction of nonmusical, political aims. Soviet participation is intended to serve as a demonstration, particularly for foreign public opinion, of the "abundance" of the Soviet Union's "prosperous life" and of the "advantages of the Soviet system over capitalism." Then too, the competitions are one of the methods used to educate loyal and obedient cadres of propagandists. Finally they are a means for glorifying the leaders' "kindness" and "solicitude for art." It is not for nothing that these competitions usually end with a reception at the Kremlin which is designed to spread among the broad masses the myth of the Party leaders' humanity.

The prize winners include some excellent musicians, such as the pianists Mikhnovski, Gilel's, Oborin, Fliyer, Zak, and Ginzburg, the violinist Oistrakh and the coloratura soprano Pantofel'–Nesnetskaya.

It may be asked how it is possible that, notwithstanding the catastrophic general decline of musical culture in the Soviet Union, Soviet performers at international competitions frequently turn out to be the victors. This problem appears particularly difficult to solve to non-Soviet musicians who, unfortunately, often accept the evidence of the competitions as proof of the alleged advantages of the system of organization of Soviet musical life.

There are two factors to be considered in reaching a correct solution of this problem. First, it is a fact that not every child prodigy develops into a great artist. The majority of Soviet performers who have taken part in international competitions have been too young to make it possible for anyone to guarantee that their future will be brilliant.

Second, the secret of the "mass talent" of youthful performers in the Soviet Union is not the alleged superiority of Soviet art policy but the careful selection and training of promising students by Soviet teachers. As in every large country, there are in the Soviet Union inexhaustible resources of gifted children, and the whole secret lies in their selection and training. This selection and training is greatly facilitated by the Soviet system of values, which leads to an exaggerated passion to "be better than others," an aspiration which is encouraged by the government and by enthusiastic teachers (whose enthusiasm, incidentally, is not quite disinterested, since a teacher of talented pupils may expect material and other rewards). The government has established special groups of gifted children in almost every large conservatory and has guaranteed their material security. The teachers often donate their time to finding and training such children, while the parents are not only proud that so much care and attention should be given their children but also derive a monetary profit from the situation.

Particularly wide acclaim as one of the most zealous enthusiasts in discovering talented children was won by a certain Stolyarski, formerly an obscure violin teacher in Odessa, but a man who has taught almost all the contemporary Moscow violinists, including the famous David Oistrakh. Many curious and even malicious stories are told about Stolyarski, all of which, however, no matter how fantastic, reflect his exceptional ability to discover talented children and the unusual care he took with their training. It is rumored, for example that he used to walk through Odessa, in particular all formerly Jewish settlements, in search of talented youngsters. When he found what he was looking for, he would devote himself completely to the training of his protégé. Whatever his training methods may have been—and there are reports that they involved great severity—the results spoke for themselves. Under his care were trained the best of the contemporary Soviet violinists. In recompense for his achievements he not only received various orders but even had built for him a school in Odessa bearing his name.

The music schools for gifted children which were organized in Moscow, Leningrad and Kiev during the thirties, and in which talented children from all over the Soviet Union were gradually concentrated, became in reality "workshops" for turning out prize winners. In any case, there is no reason to exaggerate the results attained by these schools. Endowed as they are with almost unlimited material support, having the opportunity and ability to search and select the best from the whole country, their output of soloists is still so inadequate that the Soviet press regularly complains of the absence of an adequate number of performers and of the mediocre quality of those who are available.

Subjectively, each of the more important Soviet soloists undoubtedly possesses all the qualifications for attaining the level of mastery, but objectively the system of Soviet life under which they live, with its repressive control of all aspects of art in the interests of Party propaganda, hardly assists their development. Cut off as they are from a genuine standard of mastery which requires the contact with international culture for its development, Soviet soloists inevitably lower their artistic level. There is no doubt that among them there are still some who maintain genuine mastery and who are inspired by the spiritual beauty of the music they perform. But this is not enough to make up for the lack of a vital cultural tradition.

In the Soviet Union everything from the past, the culture and heritage of centuries which was passed on from generation to generation, has lost its meaning, and the new generation of Soviet performers who come mainly from the classes which previously had little connection with this historic succession of musical perception is now faced by the problem of making up for what has been lost.

6. *MUSIC ON THE RADIO, IN THE FACTORIES AND ON THE COLLECTIVE FARMS*

Everyone is familiar with the importance of radio broadcasts in contemporary life. Perhaps the Communists understand this better than anyone else. That is why radio broadcasting in the Soviet Union allots to music such an important place in its programs.

The overwhelming majority of Soviet subscribers to radio sets use the "radio-points" which are capable of receiving only transmissions from the state broadcasting centers. Foreign broadcasts can be heard only by that very limited number of Soviet citizens who have short-wave sets. Moreover, those who possess such radio sets risk exposing themselves to great danger since listening to foreign broadcasts is regarded as politically suspect. In any case there exists a well organized system of jamming foreign broadcasts.

Soviet music broadcasts are divided into those intended for the foreign listener and those for internal consumption. In the case of the former the broadcasts aim at impressing the listener with the "high level of Soviet musical culture," its "progressiveness" and its "independence." The listener is expected to admire the breadth and variety and even the taste of the programs broadcast. He hears classical works, romantic music by such composers as Richard Strauss and Mahler, music by the older composers and even by the Netherlands polyphonists, and, of course, works by Shostakovich, Prokof'yev and Khachaturian. Hearing these programs, one would never suspect that Soviet art policy has any political bias or any tendency to interfere in the free development of musical life. One hears excellent performers; one can even admire the recording technique unless, of course, one realizes that most of the records were made in America.

Quite different is the impression made by transmissions broadcast for internal Soviet consumption. From children's programs to the "academic concerts," there is not a single broadcast without propaganda, not one that does not suggest to the listener "confidence in the world triumph of Communism," not one which does not call for "vigilance." Every broadcast defames whatever does not come from the Soviet

Union and ceaselessly repeats that "the golden age is here, all around us, achieved for the good of all mankind by the will and care of our great Leader." Marches, mass-songs, choral works, oratorios, cantatas, overtures, symphonies—all proclaim the "joy" and "power" of the Soviet Union. Before the concert, before and after each piece and at the conclusion of the concert there are words and yet more words—oceans of words, in the midst of which is lost not only the music of Dunayevski but that of Beethoven as well!

Even more terrible in its one-sidedness and political tendentiousness is the organized amateur musical activity of the Soviet industrial and collective farm workers. In the democratic countries of the West every genuine music-lover in his spare time enjoys listening to musical radio programs or to a record-player, going to a theater or visiting his friends for an evening of music at home. In the Soviet Union, however, such amateur music-making, the most intimate of man's musical necessities, is made to serve political ends.

For this purpose the social and cultural "organizations for enlightenment" (which like everything else in the Soviet Union are controlled by the Party and government) arrange various musical groups and choruses in which the people's love for music is used as the means by which Soviet music with its political texts is drummed into the heads of the members. Thus are created the countless amateur groups among collective farm and industrial workers, students and army men. Their activity, however, has nothing in common with musical self-expression but is a purely political activity directed by Party functionaries. Many of these groups have fairly good orchestras, choruses and even operatic studios. While the members are working out some problem of instrumental technique, however, their minds are being filled with communist phraseology, accustoming them to life outside the family and instilling in them the fundamentals of communist morals and ethics. The political importance attached by the Party to such musical activity is indicated by the fact that there exists a widely developed network of "Houses of Amateur Activity," extending from the villages up through the regions, provinces and republics, to the "Central House of Amateur Activity." It is the function of these bodies to organize and direct all "amateur activity."

Numerous contests, parades, theatrical productions, and concerts by amateur performers throughout the Soviet Union draw the great mass of young people into this system for political indoctrination.

In connection with Soviet amateur musical life, an important question of principle in regard to musical culture has arisen which has been widely debated in the Soviet press during recent years: the question of the elimination of the boundary line between professional music and the people's amateur musical activity.

Without going into an examination of this question, and particularly without considering its "solution" by Soviet musicologists, it can be affirmed that in actual practice the boundary line between professional and amateur musical activity in the Soviet Union is really becoming obliterated. Soviet composers now strive to write like those who are musically uneducated but who are the creators of "oral" music. Whether this is a worthy attainment, as many Soviet theorists would argue, we will permit them to judge. For our part we are inclined to think that "professional" and "oral" music are two different fields and that the question of obliterating the distinction between them could only be raised where music has been transformed into a means for aims not its own.

7. PRODUCTION OF MUSICAL INSTRUMENTS

The situation with regard to the production of musical instruments in the Soviet Union is truly catastrophic. There are so few Soviet factories which produce musical instruments that their role in replenishing the shortage in this field is insignificant. As to the quality of the Soviet-manufactured instruments one can only say that it is below any standard. No good musician can use these instruments. It is significant that not one of the conservatories uses them, preferring to acquire instruments which may be older but on which it is at least possible to play. Instruments for concert use, particularly in the major music centers, as a rule are of foreign make acquired recently.

To purchase even old instruments, however, is a difficult problem. It frequently happens that not only music students but teachers at the conservatories as well, especially those of the younger generation, are compelled to get along without instruments. Consequently conservatory students have to use instruments either belonging to the conservatory or to the student hostels, arranging among themselves the hours for practicing.

Even the Soviet press clamours for an improvement in the musical industry but the situation remains as bad as ever. In the July 1949 issue of *Soviet Music,* for example, a report was published concerning a conference of active workers of the musical industry in the R.S.F.S.R. which stated:

> In absolute figures, production during 1948 was as follows: small pianos, 4,738; plucked instruments, 478,982; harmonicas, bayans [a kind of accordion] and accordions, 52,782; string instruments, 11,011; Young Pioneer bugles, 24,116....
>
> Unfortunately our keyboard instruments industry still lags behind in the production of grand pianos, for which there is an acute need among institutions of music education and qualified specialists. The manufacture of twelve grand pianos per year is an absolutely insignificant figure and cannot satisfy the need even to a small degree.[25]

Such is the truth about "music for the people." It is frequently impossible for a pianist to play in a workers' club, even in large cities; either there is no instrument at all or if there is one it is in such poor condition that it is simply impossible to play on it. In such cases the singers use an accordion for their accompaniment or bring a piano with them.

The shortage of instruments in the Soviet Union has given rise to a widespread practice of using special "concert trucks" in which a piano has been installed so that the artist can travel with it to the most remote parts of the country, thereby avoiding the danger of finding himself without the piano needed for his recital or concert. In the Soviet Union this is called "disseminating music among the broad masses of the people." And with justice, for without such "dissemination" it is doubtful whether the collective farms situated at a distance from the cities would ever have an opportunity to see a piano.

It is true that from time to time one finds statements in the Soviet press such as the following:

> A special commission of musicians and musicologists has examined a concert grand piano manufactured by the Tallin factory "Estonia"; this instrument, in the opinion of the experts, is of a quality equal to that of a Stradivarius violin.[26]

Perhaps one piano of this quality was produced, but it is far more likely that this report is simply part of the standard propaganda about the "achievements" of the Soviet musical industry. The proof of this contention is the fact that up to the present in the concert halls of Moscow, Leningrad and Kiev, the instruments used are either of foreign make, mainly American, or are relics of the past.

FOOTNOTES TO PART IV

1. A contraction of *sotsial'noye vospitaniye*—Tr.

2. The organization of Soviet education described here has been somewhat modified since Stalin's death.—Tr.

3. See footnote 1, above.

4. *Seksot* is an abbreviation for *sekretnyi sotrudnik* (secret collaborator.)—Tr.

5. For an English translation of the relevant decree see Meisel, James H., and Edward S. Kozera, eds., *Materials for the Study of the Soviet System,* Ann Arbor, 1950, pp. 360-361.

6. "K novomu pod"yomu muzykal'novo obrazovaniya," *Sovetskaya Muzyka* [Soviet Music], August 1950, No. 8, p. 3.

7. *Ibid.*, p. 4.

8. *Ibid.*, pp. 4-6.

9. *Ibid.*

10. Karp, S., "K voprosu o podgotovke muzykal'nykh kadrov," *Sovetskaya Muzyka,* April 1949, No. 4, pp. 51-53.

11. *Ibid.*, p. 51.

12. *Ibid.*

13. Before the war a single folio [*pechatnyi list*] running to 40,000 letters was paid for by the publishing houses at the rate of 600 to 1,000 rubles and occasionally even higher.

14. It might be said that in the performances Gilel's gave at that time there was something of this ideal.

15. Honegger, Arthur, "Old Ears for New Music: Our Listening Habits Are Outdated," *Musical Digest,* March 1947, p. 16.

16. "Doklad B.V. Asaf'yeva" [Report by B.V. Asaf'yev], *Sovetskoye iskusstvo* [Soviet Art], No. 17 (1105), April 24, 1948.

17. "Velikaya sila sovetskovo iskusstva" [The Great Power of Soviet Art], *ibid.*

18. *Ibid.*

19. Vartanyan, Z., "Navesti poryadok v rabote Moskovskoi filarmonii" [Introduce Order into the Work of the Moscow Philharmonic Organization], *Kul'tura i zhizn'* [Culture and Life], No. 6 (170), February 28, 1951.

20. See below, p. 175.

21. "Puti sovetskoi operetty" [The Paths of Soviet Operetta], *Sovetskoye iskusstvo,* No. 11 (1399), February 6, 1952.

22. B., "God raboty Universiteta muzykal'noi kul'tury TsDKA im. M.V. Frunze" [A Year of Work by the University of Musical Culture of the M.V. Frunze Central House of the Soviet Army], *Sovetskaya muzyka,* July 1949, No. 7, p. 89.

23. *Ibid.* On the work of the philharmonic organizations, see further Annex C, pp. 286-291.

24. "Sto dvadtsat' kontsertov v chest' I.V. Stalina" [One Hundred and Twenty Concerts in Honor of J.V. Stalin], *Sovetskaya muzyka,* March 1950, No. 3, p. 100.

25. Zimin, P., "O muzykal'noi promyshlennosti RSFSR" [About the Musical Industry of the R.S.F.S.R.], *Sovetskaya muzyka,* July 1949, No. 7, p. 86.

26. *Izvestiya,* July 12, 1951.

PART V

Creative Work and Performance

A. HISTORICAL DEVELOPMENT

1. THE DEVELOPMENT OF PARTY CONTROLS

During the 1920's a bitter struggle was going on between Russian creative thought, which was then reviving after many years of quiescence (the years of the First World War, of the Revolution and of the period of "war communism") and the art policy of the Soviet power which was attempting to impose on art the aims and methods of a "proletarian" culture which was gradually coming into existence.

The major protagonists in this struggle were first, the Association of Contemporary Music (ASM)[1] in which all active composers were united and which aimed at the preservation of the national artistic heritage and at the inclusion of Russian music in the sphere of contemporary European creative aims and problems; and second, the Russian Association of Proletarian Musicians (RAPM),[2] an organization directly inspired by the Propaganda Section of the Central Committee of the Communist Party with the aim of disrupting the activity of ASM, "kindling the class struggle on the music front," and disseminating the concept of "proletarian music." RAPM'S membership consisted chiefly of Komsomol members at the Moscow Conservatory.

A minor role in the struggle was played by the Association of Revolutionary Composers and Musical Performers (ORKIMD),[3] which had originated as the result of attempts by several musicians to find a basis for compromise between the two major antagonists, ASM and RAPM.

Each of these associations had its own magazine. ASM originally published *Contemporary Music*, later *Towards New*

Shores and *Musical Culture.* RAPM published *Musical Virgin Soil* and later *The Proletarian Musician.* ORKIMD published *Music and Revolution.*[4]

Those were years, particularly for ASM, of seeking new ways, years of an unceasing effort to make up for lost time. Every activity of ASM was directed towards creating an opportunity to establish points of contact with the contemporary Western European musical public, towards educating new national creative forces that would be able to carry on the further development of music which had been interrupted by the war and revolution, and towards achieving the goal of a world culture. It was the time of Lenin's New Economic Policy, a tactical retreat along certain sectors by the Soviet Power; years when Stalin's terror with its purges and concentration camps was still unknown; years when people could breathe a little more easily, cherishing illusions of the improvement of the Soviet regime.

There was an unusually keen interest in everything new which was thought or felt throughout the world. The new books, articles, motion pictures, and musical works that were brought into Soviet Russia at that time were accepted as prophetic revelations. Concert and theater activities were particularly stimulated and there were entire series of concerts by outstanding foreign composers, conductors and soloists. This activity was promoted by the Soviet authorities since the New Economic Policy aimed among other things at obtaining material resources for maintaining the existence of the Soviet regime as well as moral support from abroad.

During those years the musical circles of Petrograd (renamed Leningrad in 1924) had the opportunity of hearing more new music than ever before. Everything written by Stravinsky up to that time was performed: *Petrushka, The Rites of Spring, Les Noces, Symphony for Wind Instruments,* and *Oedipus Rex.* Performances were given by Béla Bartók of his own works; by Hindemith (there were repeated performances by the Amar-Hindemith quartet with the composer's participation); and by contemporary French composers, particularly "The Six."[5] The Leningrad public had an opportunity to form the acquaintance of Bruckner, Mahler and Strauss (*Der Rosenkavalier* and *Salome* were performed during several seasons at the former Maryinski Theater); of Schreker, whose *Distant Sound* was performed at the same theater; of Schoenberg (the *Gurre-Lieder, Five Orchestral Pieces,* the *Chamber Symphony,* and *Pelleas*); and of Křenek (*Jonny spielt auf* and *The Jump* were both performed at the former Mikhailovski Theater.) The Leningrad public was deeply shaken by Alban Berg's opera *Wozzek* which became one of the most popular presentations at the former Maryinski Theater. It is simply not possible to enumerate here all the works which were presented during those years. It was truly an invasion by contemporary music.

Russian musicians at that time stood at the crossroads. In their search for new ideals, foreign musical theories and authorities were unhesitatingly placed above the native ones; the Russian composers' disappointment in the Revolution led them to look abroad in search for a force to unify the world's culture and reconcile East and West.

Those years of comparative freedom made an indelible impression upon many Soviet composers, particularly on Shostakovich and his generation, whose later years only served to develop and perfect the inner experience acquired during the twenties.

The comparatively free development of Soviet music during the first phase of the Soviet regime was brought to an abrupt halt in 1932, with the publication of the Communist Party Central Committee's decree "On the Reorganization of Art and Literary Associations." Although the primary emphasis of this decree was on literature and art, the policy of increased Party control of the arts which it represented was applied to music as well. Both ASM and RAPM were abolished and their place was taken by a new body, the Union of Soviet Composers, which was completely under Party control. The earlier profusion of music journals gave way to a single publication, *Soviet Music*, the organ of the Union. Extensive personnel changes took place throughout the Soviet Union in the conservatories and musicological institutions.

· It took some time, however, for Soviet composers to realize that they were no longer free to write music as they wished, without regard to the Party line. This was particularly true of such a composer as Shostakovich, who found it hard to forget the relative freedom of the twenties and whose style was closely related to that of contemporary Western composers. It was necessary for the Party bureaucrats to discipline Shostakovich not once but repeatedly and through him the Soviet composers who followed his example. In 1936 *Pravda* censured the "formalist" trend of his ballets *The Golden Age* and *The Limpid Stream* and his extremely interesting opera *Lady Macbeth of Mtsensk*, in which he had yielded to the desire to follow out a development influenced by the German expressionists.

During World War II the Soviet power had its hands full with problems directly related to the war, and Soviet composers were granted a temporary respite from the more extreme forms of political control. As soon as the war was over, however, and the Party had had time to put its house in order, controls were tightened once more.

The process of re-establishing Party control of the arts after the war began in 1946 in the field of literature. The musicians' turn came in 1948 with the publication of the Central Committee's decree on Muradeli's opera *The Great Friendship*.[6]

2. *THE ATTACK ON "FORMALISM" AND "COSMOPOLITANISM"*

At the First All-Union Congress of Soviet Composers which took place in 1948, the Secretary General of the Union of Soviet Composers, Tikhon Khrennikov, stated that

> the entire thirty year history of Soviet musical art represents an intense and contradictory [sic] process, the leading tendency

> of which is the establishment of popular and realistic bases and the struggle against the pernicious, poisonous influences of formalism.[7]

By the "pernicious influences of formalism" Soviet music critics mean the contact of Soviet music with Western musical culture, i.e., its contact with free creative initiative, while by "popular and realistic bases" they have in mind the forms of "socialist realism" approved and dictated by the Party.

Even a cursory examination of the creative work of Soviet composers will show that the creative development of Soviet music has indeed been "intense and contradictory." Careful study of the situation, however, fails to disclose any basis for speaking of a uniform tendency toward the establishment of "popular and realistic bases." It is easier to observe the opposite tendency, i.e., an inherent aspiration for freedom of creative development and for the establishment of contact with contemporary Western composers.

It is mainly due to this fact that in the Soviet Union there exist two directly opposite creative purposes. This situation was acknowledged by all the speakers at the First All-Union Congress of Soviet Composers, particularly by Zhdanov himself who at the conference of musicians held prior to the Congress said,

> One trend represents the healthy progressive principle in Soviet music based on the recognition of the enormous role played by our classical heritage and particularly by the traditions of the Russian musical school; [the principle based] on a combination of high ideals [*ideinost'*] with rich content—its truthfulness and realism, its deep, organic link with the people, with their instrumental and vocal creative work, combined with high professional mastery. The other trend represents a formalism which is alien to Soviet art, the rejection of classical tradition under the banner of dubious innovations, the rejection of the popular character [*narodnost'*] of music and of service to the people, in order to satisfy the especially individualistic theories of a small clique of select aesthetes.[8]

One could not but agree with this classification if the Soviet orthodox critics, and particularly Zhdanov, did not operate on the principle that black is white and white is black. How otherwise can it be explained that under the category of the "healthy, progressive principle" were included chiefly mediocre orthodox composers who flood the Soviet musical world with propaganda mass-songs, while under the category of "formalists" who are allegedly alien to Soviet art were included such outstanding masters as Myaskovski, Prokof'yev, Shostakovich, and Khachaturian? Is it not clear that the creative works of the latter group, works which always leave an impression of independent, inexhaustible inventiveness, represent the genuine progressive principle of contemporary Soviet music? Are the works of these men not based on the "recognition of the classical heritage and particularly of the traditions of the Russian musical school?" Are "high ideals and rich content" not combined with "professional mastery" in their works and, consequently, is their music not "genuine," not realistic, not of the people? But, on the other hand, those plodding, nameless journeymen of musical orthodoxy who have become mere functionaries of political propaganda—are they not in reality "formalists" in the true meaning of the term who base their work on a fabricated myth about the "golden age?" Is it not rather they who have refused to "serve the people" "in order to satisfy the individualist theories of a small clique"—not, it is true, of "select aesthetes"—but of Kremlin politicians?

Besides these two sharply contradictory and hostile trends of Soviet music there exists a third trend characteristic of a fairly numerous and influential group of composers, the eclectics, whose work is characterized by a clearly expressed tendency towards traditionalism.

In short, when we attempt to classify the work of Soviet composers we come to the conclusion that in the Soviet Union, as elsewhere, there are composers who are ahead of their times, composers who lag behind and composers who stand "outside of time," i.e., the eclectics. Despite all the efforts by Soviet ideologists to impose uniformity upon musical creative work at all costs, they have not been successful and cannot be, so long as music remains a creative activity and not a means to an end which has nothing in common with art.

Nevertheless, the process of smothering creative freedom in the Soviet Union has gone so far that there is now reason to assume the presence of certain general characteristics in Soviet music which result from the efforts of the Party and the government to "reconstruct" the nature of music.

In this connection it is a question first of all of the contact of Soviet music with the traditions of Russian music and its interaction with the contemporary musical culture of the West.

There is absolutely no reason to suppose that as the result of the modernist revolt against the classical-romantic tradition, the music of the past, even of the fairly remote past, has lost its role as a vital source of influence on the musical public generally as well as on contemporary creative work. Especially under the conditions of Soviet life, with its artificial propagandistic call for a return to the "psychological realism" of The Five, the music of the classical-romantic tradition is still very much alive, forming the basis of much of contemporary Soviet musical thought and fertilizing the composer's creative concepts with its life-sustaining current.

As to the contact of Soviet music with that of the West, the Party aestheticians, who consider music only in relation to their political aims, regard all contemporary Western music and the entire history of modernism since the end of the nineteenth century as nothing but "dark reaction," "extreme subjectivism," "obscurantism," "insanity," etc. In Soviet aesthetics "decadence" and "modernism" are identical concepts, the reason being that a scapegoat is needed for the struggle against every manifestation of creative freedom.

It is a curious fact that Soviet music critics in their efforts to discredit contemporary Western music fall back on antiquated arguments which they were using thirty years ago.

For instance in a report presented at the First All-Union Congress of Soviet Composers it is claimed that

> the philosophy and aesthetics of contemporary bourgeois society are permeated with the most gloomy pessimism. The ideologists of that society appeal in mortal fear to moribund doctrines and to Hartmann, Oswald Spengler, Bergson, and Nietzsche. They search for peace of mind in the dusk of the Freudian theory of the subconscious, in the senseless mysticism of Swedenborg, etc.[9]

Making no attempt whatsoever to differentiate the phenomena of contemporary western music nor to define the essence of their own music, the Soviet propagandists lump everything together in a breathless attempt to convince (whom?—perhaps themselves) that

> the musical activity of West European and American modernists has resulted in the disintegration of harmony and the logic of tonality and in the death of melody. The creative work of all these composers [Messiaën, Menotti, Britten, etc.] is imbued with the spirit of extreme subjectivism, mysticism, obscurantism and revolting insanity.[10]

But what has all this in common with the real state of affairs? Not that the Soviet propagandists have any real interest in the actual state of Western music. To them the important thing is to defame, with the aid of such phraseology, the social and political system of the democracies and their inner spiritual resources that provide opportunities for the full freedom of creative manifestation to every artistic tendency, no matter how extreme. Hence the Soviet propagandists' consistency in smothering every manifestation of even relative creative freedom. Such persecution could not but set its mark upon Soviet music.

Each year the boundaries of Soviet music's freedom of creative expression are being still further narrowed. Even the work of such remarkable composers as Prokof'yev, Shostakovich and Khachaturian tends to become more colorless and uninspired, while the younger generation of Soviet composers frequently cannot even imagine the possibility of other conditions for composition.

The themes and subjects of creative work are becoming increasingly standardized in conformity with current propaganda slogans; the limits of form are being narrowed with an emphasis on the vocal genres—operas, cantatas and songs—and on program music; and the means of expression are becoming more inflexible, repeating outworn formulas.[11]

The struggle of Soviet art policy against "formalism," however, is only one aspect of the enslavement of Soviet music in the name of "socialist realism." A closely related phenomenon is the struggle against "cosmopolitanism." In this connection the fundamental characteristic of Soviet orthodoxy is the absurdity of its claim to nationalism. If there were really a sound basis for the struggle against "cosmopolitanism" in creative art, could it be in reality anything but an effort by the artist to experience and express life in all its aspects? The system of Soviet life, however, does not permit such an effort. The totalitarian law-givers dare not allow the artist to touch on any subject other than those prescribed by the state. It is precisely here that one finds the tragic delusion of the Soviet ideologists (although perhaps it should be called not a delusion but a categorical imperative, one which has produced the agonizing crisis of Russian music). Forced to accept a synthetic myth about the "golden age of communism," having become in all literalness "homeless cosmopolitans," Soviet composers have lost, as have the Soviet people as a whole, their sense of psychological stability. Soviet composers, like Soviet citizens in general, are trained to ignore the present day in order to project their thought into the "communist future." Hence the characteristic "futurism" of Soviet art, the symptomatic phenomenon which accompanies the basic disease of Soviet life and art, the doctrine of materialism.

Thus the development of Soviet music has been determined not by those factors which directly affect music as a creative activity but by the "current tasks" imposed by Soviet propaganda policies. The development of Soviet music is not an expression of the creative interests of Soviet composers but is the unambiguous manifestation of a policy of oppression of the individual will which underlies the whole program of "building communism in the Soviet Union." It is therefore only natural that there should exist a hidden opposition to this oppression which is manifested both in the creative work of certain Soviet composers and in the "creative neutrality" characteristic of the traditionalists. The same factors are responsible for the servility with which the mass of orthodox Soviet composers defend the "progressiveness" of Party policy in the field of music.

It is not the attack on "formalism," and "cosmopolitanism" in the name of "socialist realism" which has become the central problem of Soviet art, but rather the question whether it is possible to create art without experiencing any satisfaction from life, whether it is possible to create out of despair, out of hopelessness, out of self-hatred. For it is dissatisfaction and despair and self-hatred which are taking possession of the Soviet composer's creative power, forcing him towards the complete repudiation of music as an intellectual creative activity.

3. *DEVELOPMENT AND INFLUENCE OF THE MASS-SONG*

In 1947, shortly before the publication of the Central Committee's resolution on the opera *The Great Friendship,* there appeared in Moscow a volume of articles entitled *Essays on Soviet Musical Creation.*[12] The authors of this publication give a fairly accurate picture of the development of Soviet music, divided according to the various forms of musical composition. Nevertheless, although they selected the most significant phenomena and facts of Soviet music, the authors of the *Essays,* imprisoned by the orthodox methodology, avoided drawing conclusions.

Thus in his article "The Paths of Development of Soviet Music,"[13] B.V. Asaf'yev writes,

> The paths of development of Soviet music are determined

> by three basic stimuli: the natural influence of Russian musical past and its reconsideration, the attention to the music of the West and the selection [from it] of what is most essential and valuable, and the study of the music of the peoples of the U.S.S.R.[14]

"The influence of these stimuli," Asaf'yev continues, "is closely related to the course of historical events, to the economic and political life of the country, to ideological improvements and the mighty growth of cultural construction.."[15] All of this, of course, is fairly obvious, and the author of the article fully realizes that fact. The problem with which he is faced is to define in neutral terms those factors which led to the formation of the Soviet art policy. He therefore continues,

> ...from the very outset [of Soviet music], there began a movement for the 'mass-song'.... Subordinating to itself the personal and individual vocal lyric poetry, this movement became the operative basis which influences all types and forms of musical creative work: the Soviet symphony, the opera especially, and the fields of the cantata-oratorio and the song are influenced by the atmosphere of the mass-song, as is every [Soviet] composer in every branch of his work.[16]

Even though he has thus discovered the essential factor in the development of Soviet music Asaf'yev nonetheless can only trace the "beneficial" influence of this "movement towards the mass-song." This is not at all surprising since it is exactly this movement which constitutes the real meaning of the numerous Party and government declarations about the "realistic path of development of Soviet music." This movement is officially defined as the only correct, incontestable, absolute guiding principle for the Soviet composer. Thus it would be foolish to expect from the authors of the *Essays on Musical Creation* any statement of the disastrous results of the mass-song movement upon the development of Soviet-dominated music and upon Soviet musical culture as a whole.

There can be no doubt that this movement has established a firm hold on the creative work of all Soviet composers without exception. The "struggle" for the mass-song is regarded as an indication of the active participation of the Soviet composer in "building up Soviet culture" and of his loyalty to the official aesthetics of "socialist realism." It defines his role in the propaganda apparatus of the Soviet system and consequently his place in Soviet life itself. To estimate to what extent the mass-song movement is something natural and regular, however, it is necessary to consider not only the generalizations imposed by the Party, generalizations which the authors of the articles in the *Essays* were forced to employ in self-defense, but also those facts about musical creation in the Soviet Union which they cite. We shall make use of these facts in order to determine whether the mass-song movement has really enriched Russian music.[17]

First of all our attention is attracted by the fact that the origins of the mass-song movement had absolutely nothing in common with the natural creative initiative of Soviet composers. The movement was implanted and supported from above, by the organs of the Party and the government. As early as 1921 there was established in the office of the "music sector" of the State Publishing House a special section for agitation and enlightenment which had the task of creating a "new musical repertoire for the masses." The first models of this repertoire, which were associated with the names of the composers Mikhail Ivanovich Krasev and Grigori Grigor'yevich Lobachov, were known as "agit-music" (agitational music). (It is incidentally noteworthy that *Pravda,* in its issue of October 2, 1926, wrote apropos of this agit-music that it was "an impoverishment of the agitational program, a lisping imitation of the little *muzhik* [prerevolutionary peasant] and a display of bad taste." *Pravda* went on to state, however, that "in the contemporary situation there is a need for the cultivation of this form."

Pravda's recognition of the "need to cultivate this form" may have served as the basis for the organization in 1925 of the "Composers' Productive Association" (Prokol),[18] the aim of which was to create a political repertoire for the masses. Whereas the majority of composers who were attacked by *Pravda* for their "lisping imitation of the little *muzhik,*" however, were people who had had no musical training prior to their first experience with the mass-song, Prokol was to a certain degree an organization of professional musicians. Most of its members were, if not mature composers, at least students at the Moscow Conservatory and at the same time members of the Komsomol. It is only natural, therefore, that it was in Prokol that there was formulated for the first time the meaning of the mass-song, as well as those "new and collective methods of musical composition," as they were called by the members of Prokol, which were designed to serve as a definite guarantee of the "mass" character of the song. Especially popular among the Prokol composers was A. Davidenko whose works were not without sincerity and spontaneity. Wide popularity was attained by such songs of his as "The First Cavalry" and "My Little Rifle," with their popular melodic progressions of intervals of the sixth and seventh, and their primitive melodic harmonization; "Mother," built on intonations of sentimental petit-bourgeois melodies; and "The Sea Was Moaning Furiously," a song of the "dashing" march type. Up until very recently these songs have maintained their popularity, particularly among Soviet Army circles and in collective farm organizations. Not only did they serve as a model for similar songs which during recent years have engulfed the whole creative activity of Soviet composers, but they set the pattern for those melodic devices which are typical of Soviet music as a whole and which chiefly constitute its expressive means.

The members of Prokol composed large numbers of songs of this type, most of them artificial, lifeless and oversimplified. In addition they propagated the songs widely among the army men and young workers, devoting exceptional efforts to rehearsing them with amateur choral groups and drumming into the consciousness of singers and listeners their agitational-propagandistic texts and mawkish melodies.

In 1928 the basic group of Prokol members—A. Davidenko, V. Belyi, Marian Koval', N. Chemberdzhi, B. Shekhter and others—formed the composers' section of RAPM. This organization demanded that music reflect all the current political campaigns and urgent questions of international problems. It considered the mass-song the only legitimate form of music, a policy which is reflected in the orthodox line up to the present time.

The movement for the mass-song led to the decline of instrumental music, the triumph of vocal music and the cultivation of small musical forms. It has resulted in an impoverishment of the means of expression and has helped to obliterate the boundaries between professional musicianship and amateur musical folklore. Most significant, the mass-song movement has forced Soviet music back to the times when music was closely bound to explicit texts and was an adjunct of magic.

A significant role in consolidating this retrograde movement of Russian music was played by the "Red Army Ensemble of Songs and Dances" which was organized in 1928 at the Central House of the Red Army in Moscow under the direction of A.V. Aleksandrov. This group, later reorganized as the "Ensemble of Songs and Dances of the U.S.S.R.," became the model for other similar groups and a center for the development of "Soviet musical culture for the masses."

Sporadic attempts were later made to diversify the Soviet musical world for the benefit of the mass auditor (for example, the first Soviet jazz band was organized in 1929 by Leonid Utesov in Leningrad)[19] but none of these efforts led to any significant results. The mass-song became the leading art form of Soviet music and exerted a powerful influence on all other forms of music. Even such composers as Prokof'yev, Myaskovski, Shostakovich, Khachaturian, Shebalin and Kabalevski have not only devoted their creative experience and knowledge to the mass-song as such, but have been influenced in their work by its melodic and structural characteristics.

The songs of A.V. Aleksandrov, Dmitri and Daniil Pokrass, Blanter, Zakharov, and other "composers for the masses," which have become widely popular even beyond the borders of the Soviet Union, make use of urban melodies and the romantic-sentimental idiom of the music hall. Such songs have completely inundated Soviet music, squeezing out whatever still survives of a healthy taste for genuine style. Such songs as Dunayevski's "The Song of My Country," which became the signal call of the central radio station of the U.S.S.R. or the same composer's "March of the Joyful Lads," Listov's "Song about the Cart," Knipper's "Little Field," Dzerzhinski's "From End to End" from *The Quiet Don,* and "The Cossack Song," from *Virgin Soil Upturned,* Novikov's "March of International Youth" and innumerable other similar compositions have become the models of Soviet music and the embodiment of its creative ideals.

In the Soviet Union the mass-song resounds from early morning until late at night. Soviet citizens work and rest–insofar as it is possible to rest at all–with its insistent melody in their ears. And when they sleep the mass-song takes to the ether, filling the air waves with communist propaganda.

Even the directors of Soviet music themselves cannot refrain from occasionally criticizing the irresponsibility with which orthodox composers try to "outsing" one another, and their frequent disregard of technical requirements. Thus at the First All-Union Congress of Composers in 1948, Tikhon Khrennikov in his report made a not particularly flattering comment on the mass-song. Having noted the achievements, from the Party point of view, of such postwar songs as "The March of Democratic Youth" and "The Roads" by Novikov and certain songs by Blanter, Mokrousov and Solov'yov-Sedoi, Khrennikov pointed to the "prevalence of the lyric form which is being interpreted superficially," the "echoes of the vulgar gypsy style," and "the lack of patriotic songs... praising the labor and heroism of Soviet man."

"We have not sufficiently developed," Khrennikov complained, "the excellent traditions of Russian revolutionary songs of the past. In the music of our songs we frequently [sic] feel a poverty of intonation, the use of clichés, the lack of professional mastery, and uninspired workmanship."[1]

This seems to be one of the few true statements made by Khrennikov in his verbose report to the congress. Moreover, these truths demonstrate that Khrennikov himself evidently understands very well the destructive role which this "uninspired workmanship" has played in Soviet music.

In pursuit of a pseudo-"mass character," the Soviet song is losing to an ever greater extent its choral basis and is being transformed into a single-part monody comparable to works from the early period of musical culture. This is particularly true of the songs of Dunayevski, Blanter and the Pokrass brothers. An interest in polyphony is preserved to a certain degree by Aleksandrov who is generally more inclined towards the arrangement of folk songs. (This tendency was particularly noticeable in his "Hymn of the Bolshevik Party," on the basis of which he composed the new "State Hymn of the U.S.S.R." which was officially endorsed in 1944.) The same tendency is manifested by Zakharov, the leader of the Pyatnitski chorus, whose compositions are like stylizations of peasant songs, (In this respect his song about Stalin and Lenin, "The Two Falcons," is typical).

Let us pause briefly to describe the musical means employed in these songs: their melody, rhythm and harmony.

The banal melody of the mass-song is a terrible force which cripples the ear, memory and taste of its mass audience (for it is always within the hearing of millions of people). The prevalence of this sentimental melody catastrophically reduces the ethical stimuli and aesthetic content of genuinely creative work. It is precisely this primitive, sentimental, oversweet melody—what Soviet critics call the "gypsy style"—that saturates the Soviet mass-song and along with it the musical life of the Soviet masses. It will suffice to listen to such extremely popular songs as Dunayevski's "Broad is My Native Land" or K. Listov's "Songs," to be convinced of the truth of this assertion.

But the impression of musical banality created by such mass-songs is no less promoted by their rhythm and harmony. The normal ear apprehends the texture of music as the sum total of its elements, as a complex movement given form by the leading voice and disciplined by rhythm. The elements constituting musical texture are not normally differentiated in the listener's consciousness unless one of them has been deliberately stressed by the composer. It is because of this fact that the representatives of the most advanced and vital trends in contemporary music make extensive use of accentuated beats, metrical dance or march rhythms, and pre-established progressions of the bass.

"The practice of chord accompaniment (*basso continuo,* general bass, figured bass)," writes Asaf'yev in *Intonation,*

> i.e., the practice of performance, produced corresponding forms of harmony—a harmony of the performer's practice rather than a *creative,* composer's, practice....
>
> What then were the contributions made by the practice of accompaniment (*continuo*) to composition? 1. It produced—and this is important—the rapid adaptation of compositional technique to the harmonic potentials contained in a given melody, in the melodic voice, but at the same time it led directly to homophony, with all its positive and negative characteristics—(the negative characteristics include the subordination of the melody to the tonic-dominant bass). 2. It facilitated the rapid evolution of dance music:—from the suite, with its polyphonic texture, to the homophonic dance of the theater and of public and domestic music making. 3. It contributed to the permeation of the musical texture by various kinds of chordal, "clavier"-like figurations and thus aided in the liberation of pianism from the ponderous organ intonations; but it retarded the development of pianoforte timbre polyphony and purely pianistic instrumentation, leading to a generalized "neutral" style of pianism: the pianism of the clavier and of transpositions. 4. It strengthened the mechanical formula of the full cadence, [and]

> overdeveloped its application with regard to the influence of the dominant over the tonic.[21]

It was precisely this melancholy heritage of functional harmony that was passed on to the Soviet mass-song, depriving its rhythm of individuality and reducing its harmony to reliance on the tonic and dominant.

We have dwelt on this question not only in order to emphasize the technical primitiveness of the mass-song, but also to indicate the basic creative resources employed by Soviet orthodox composers. Functional harmony, with its seventeenth century "homophonic textures," became one of the most active elements in Soviet music as a whole and a dominant characteristic of "socialist realism" in music. Under the conditions of Soviet reality it has enslaved the ear and consciousness of Soviet composers by its mechanically pre-established chords. Fixing the vertical line as the basis of musical texture, it has broken up the theme into single abstract moments of emphasis and at the same time has weakened the interplay between the elements comprising the musical texture (harmony, melody and rhythm). It has thus forced Russian music back to the beginning of the seventeenth century, to a time when harmony was regarded as something independent, self-contained and functionally predetermined, with ensuing "spotted" harmonization, i.e., the placing of harmonic voices (chords) under separate melodic points.

The turning point in the development of Soviet music towards "democratism and realism," which was widely proclaimed in the Soviet press, really meant the movement toward the mass-song and the encouragement of choral and vocal music in general with political propaganda texts.

This turning point can be clearly seen in the cardinal change which has taken place recently in the presentation of Soviet music. It is highly significant that during recent years the leading role in the central Soviet music institutions has definitely and consistently been assumed by choral musicians.

Thus, for example, Sveshnikov, the leader of the State Chorus of Russian Song, was appointed director of the Moscow Conservatory.

In Moscow itself, although there exist only a few symphonic orchestras, there are five large professional choral organizations which constitute the central point of "Soviet democratic musical culture" as a whole. These are the Ensemble of Songs and Dances of the U.S.S.R., the Pyatnitski Chorus, the Chorus of Russian Song, the State Russian Choral Capella, and the Song Ensemble of the All Union Radio-Committee.

B. THE FORMS OF SOVIET MUSIC

1. *ORATORIOS AND CANTATAS*

The extensive cultivation of small musical forms, particularly the mass-song, with the obvious aim of reducing music to a means of political propaganda, has had a noticeable effect on large choral forms such as the oratorio and the cantata. In the actual practice of Soviet composers, however, these "larger forms" are in reality nothing but augmented mass-songs.

The initiative in creating such works belongs again to RAPM, aided by the favourable attitude of the Party. The first model of such musical orthodoxy on a large scale was a cantata entitled *The Way of October* composed by a Prokol collective in commemoration of the tenth anniversary of the October Revolution (1927). This work, which in reality is only a suite of mass-songs, was followed by numerous similar compositions, such as *U.S.S.R., Shock Brigade of the World Proletariat* by A. Krein; the *Requiem in Memory of Kirov,* and the *Song of Spring and Joy* dedicated to the Stalin Constitution by Yudin; the *Jubilee Cantata,* written to commemorate the twentieth anniversary of the October Revolution, by Vasilenko; *A Tale of the Partisans* by Koval'; *The Return of the Sun* by Golub'yov (in which Stalin is represented as a mythical hero fighting with the black raven who blots out the sun); *A Toast* by Prokof'yev in commemoration of Stalin's sixtieth birthday and the same composer's *Cantata* on a text compiled from the works of Marx, Engels, Lenin, and Stalin (a work, incidentally, which was never performed); and a host of other similar compositions, insincere, forced and antimusical.

It is true that Soviet composers have scored some successes in this branch of composition, for example, Koval's *Yemel'yan Pugachov,* Shaporin's *The Field of Kulikovo* and especially Prokof'yev's *Aleksandr Nevski.* These works, which were composed on historical themes, are more sincere and profound in their musical content than those mentioned above. This is particularly true of Prokof'yev's *Aleksandr Nevski.* The magnificent description of the "Battle on the Ice," the final chorus, "Arise Ye Russian People" (is this only an inspired exultation on the occasion of Nevski's victory or is it a general call to arise?), and the deeply mournful episode of the "Field of the Dead," written in the style of ancient lamentation–passages such as these make this work unquestionably the best ever written by a Soviet composer in this form. Naturally, therefore, this work in no way corresponds to the standard propagandistic definition of the cantata.

Themes drawn from the Second World War have been extensively employed by Soviet composers in their large choral and vocal works. Numerous compositions in cantata-oratorio form have been written on such subjects, e.g., *The Great Holy War* by Koval'; *The People's Home Guard* by Enke; *Great Fatherland* by Kabalevski; and *A Tale of the Battle for the Russian Land* by Shaporin. These works are saturated with the defensive slogans of Soviet war-time and postwar propaganda.

During recent years Soviet composers have been urged to create compositions in oratorio form dedicated to the "Stalinist reconstruction of the Soviet land." For example, the Soviet press has loudly acclaimed Shostakovich's *Song of the*

Forests as "one of the most significant and joyful musical creative events of recent times."[22] Judging by the contradictory evaluation which this work has received from the Soviet critics, it is difficult to say to what degree it can be described as a "joyful event" for Soviet music as a whole. It can definitely be said, however, that in the creative development of its composer the work can hardly be considered a cause for great joy.

Prior to this work Shostakovich's musical language was original and profound in content and consequently incomprehensible to many. It is hardly necessary to point out that to be able to speak a language "comprehensible to the masses," it is not necessary that one's language should be especially profound or significant. The music of the *Song of the Forests* reveals the extremely simplified musical idiom now employed by the composer. Unfortunately there is no basis in this for Shostakovich to be jubilant.

Nevertheless, Shostakovich's new style is that of a composer who remembers that he also knows how to use another language; the primitive style of Soviet composers whose ability is far from Shostakovich's, however, is another matter.

A typical example of a work in this style is the patriotic cantata by Ye. Zhukovs'kyi entitled *Glory to Thee My Country,* which was awarded a Stalin Prize in 1949. In an article in *Soviet Music* devoted to this cantata a critic writes that "the theoretical importance of the musical idiom of Zhukovs'kyi's poem lies in its clear-cut national character—the Ukrainian national melody and the typically national forms."[23] The musical excerpts from this work cited by *Soviet Music* however, make it clear that the composer has depended mainly on elementary folk music devices.

Concerning one aria from the work the Soviet critic writes, "[it is] written in the beautiful traditions of the Russian classics (certain themes from Musorgsky's operas come to mind)."[24]

It is bad enough if one is reminded of certain themes from Musorgsky's operas when listening to the music of a Stalin

Prize winner but it is far worse when these themes are brought to mind whenever one hears recent Soviet music as a whole. The truth is that little of the recent music by orthodox Soviet composers is original. Eclecticism, reminiscences of what is most popular in the Russian classics, and most of all reworking and rearrangement of folk song themes—these are in actual fact the most characteristic features of contemporary Soviet music.

2. OPERA

The steady conquest by the mass-song movement of a dominating position in the life of Soviet music and its deep influence on the structure and texture of Soviet choral works inevitably led to an extension of its influence to other fields of music as well. The impact of the mass-song upon Soviet opera has been particularly significant.[25]

Even during the early years of the Soviet regime opera came under strong influence from the mass-song. Many Soviet composers at this period devoted particular attention to plots concerning popular uprisings and rebellions (e.g., *The Eagle Mutiny* by Pashchenko and *The Kamarinski Peasant* by Zhelobinski) or episodes from the Civil War (e.g., *Ice and Steel* by Deshevov and *The Black Cliff* by Pashchenko). The mass-song with its sharply emphasized accentuation, its poster-like tunes, its choppy, staccato texts, and its chanted slogans, began to play a basic role in the formation of operatic texture, giving rise to short episodic dramaturgy in place of broad-scale dramatic construction.[26]

This primitive operatic dramaturgy found its most characteristic expression in Ivan Dzerzhinski's opera *The Quiet Don,* which was accepted by many Soviet composers as a return to lyricism and popular realism.

No one in the Soviet Union would dare to suggest that the "operas" of Dzerzhinski—*The Quiet Don* and *Virgin Soil Upturned*—are not epoch-making works which, comparable to the reforms of such great operatic composers as Gluck, Musorgsky,

Verdi, Wagner, and Debussy, have laid the foundation for a new form, that of "Soviet opera." In reality, however, there is little in common between Dzerzhinski's works and the opera as such. *The Quiet Don*, the first Soviet opera acclaimed by the Party and the government as a work of historical significance, has a skillfully compiled libretto based on the novel by Mikhail Sholokhov. It is doubtful, however, whether the score adds anything to the libretto. Dzerzhinski's music, as a matter of fact, merely completed the process of returning grand opera to the principles of vaudeville or the "drama of manners" in which songs and dances are interspersed in a literary drama. In place of the essential features that constitute the peculiarity of opera as a musical form—arias, ensembles and complex orchestral passages integrally related to the motivation of the plot—in Dzerzhinski's "opera" the dominant characteristics are solo and choral mass-songs with elementary four-square structure, while the orchestra serves merely as an instrumental accompaniment, supporting or doubling the melody of the songs.

The musical dramaturgy of *The Quiet Don*, as well as that of Dzerzhinski's other fairly numerous operas and those of his followers (e.g., Zhukovs'kyi's *With All One's Heart* and Dan'kevych's *Bohdan Khmel'nyts'kyi*), has its origins in the first attempts at opera by Russian composers during the late eighteenth century, i.e., vaudeville and popular plays with music. The fully developed classical model of such dramaturgy is Aleksandr Serov's opera *The Power of Evil* (1871). It is no accident, therefore, that the revival of this opera at the Moscow Bol'shoi Theatre in 1950, after half a century's neglect, was enthusiastically received by the Politburo, or that its producers were awarded a Stalin Prize.[27] Evidently the model is considered worthy of imitation by Soviet composers.

The Power of Evil is a work of genuine talent but from the point of view of operatic dramaturgy it is doubtful that it deserves such serious attention. Its form is that of a song-opera in which the musical development consists of a series of more or less fully elaborated songs. Unlike the songs in *The Quiet Don,* however, those in *The Power of Evil* are not isolated numbers. They are real factors in the musical dramatic development from which more complicated forms are developed. In *The Quiet Don,* however, only the dead scheme of Serov's song-opera has been preserved, without the spirit of artistic life.

Following the performance of *The Quiet Don* on January 17, 1936 at the Leningrad State Academic Small Opera Theater, a special communique was issued under the heading "A Talk Between Comrades Stalin and Molotov and the Authors of the Operatic Spectacle *The Quiet Don.*"[28] What this "talk" between these "comrades" consisted of remains unknown, but the implication was clear: here at last was a genuine Soviet opera, one which would be a model henceforth for Soviet composers. Accordingly, like mushrooms after the rain, there sprang up numerous Soviet operas attempting to rival the orthodoxy of *The Quiet Don.*

Nevertheless, there is still not a single Soviet opera that has held its place in the repertoire as successfully as *The Quiet Don.* Instead there has been a succession of catastrophes, either with the libretto or with the music. The operas produced not only lack the qualities required for the current propaganda line but are gray, lifeless and uninspired, not to mention the fact that they are often mediocre and professionally weak.

Incidentally, a curious incident happened to the composer of *The Quiet Don,* an incident which reflects the sycophancy that fills Soviet musical life. Ivan Dzerzhinski had been a student at the Leningrad Conservatory, but due to his lack of promise as a composer he was obliged to leave the conservatory without graduating. Later, however, when he had composed *The Quiet Don* (incidentally with considerable assistance from Asaf'yev and Shostakovich) and when *Pravda* had published the report on the "historical talk" of the authors with Comrades Stalin and

Molotov, the directors of the Leningrad Conservatory decided to make up for their error and to bask in the reflected glory of Dzerzhinski. In a solemn ceremony they presented the composer with a diploma from the department of composition of the conservatory *O tempora, ô mores!*

EXCURSUS: THE CASE OF THE OPERA WITH ALL ONE'S HEART

A characteristic example of the Soviet operatic style is Herman L. Zhukovs'kyi's opera *With All One's Heart* (based on the novel by Yelizar Mal'tsev). The examples from this opera given in *Soviet Music*[29] indicate that the music is a mixture of borrowings from Musorgsky, Ukrainian folk songs, contemporary mass-songs, the sentimental tunes of nineteenth century Ukrainian folk drama, and traditional Russian operatic melody. Even more significant is the fact that the music is a typical manifestation of popularized simplification and an intuitive "composition by ear" which has nothing in common with operatic structure and which lies altogether outside the field of genuine intellectual creation.

Nevertheless it is worth giving further consideration to this work because of the role it played in the development of Soviet music policy as the result of the attack on it which appeared in *Pravda* on April 19, 1951. It would be tempting but incorrect to place this incident in the same category as the Central Committee resolution concerning Muradeli's opera *The Great Friendship* (1948) or *Pravda's* condemnation of Shostakovich's *Lady Macbeth of Mtsensk* (1936). The attacks on these operas were primarily manifestations of the official opposition to "formalism" in music, or in plain English, to creative freedom. The attack on Zhukovs'kyi's opera, on the other hand, was based on its failure to follow the Party line in its depiction of collective farm existence, rather than on its ideological defects as a work of music.

The history of this work and its composer is curious and instructive. Zhukovs'kyi, to use the customary Soviet expression, is about the same age as the October Revolution, i.e., he was born not long before 1917 (1913); thus he is now about forty. Thus he grew up as a man and as a composer completely under the conditions of the Soviet life. In this sense his music education was typical. As a youth he was busy acquiring the "worker background" necessary at that time for entry into an institution of higher learning. From a job in Kharkov as a railroad worker Zhukovs'kyi entered a "railroad music studio" where he began his study as a pianist. Being undoubtedly gifted musically he was shortly afterwards accepted as a student of the piano department of the Kharkov Conservatory. Although at that time he was far from thinking of dedicating his life to creative work he composed there his first songs, typical examples of the intuitive improvised method of composing. While at the Kharkov Conservatory he also began his activity as an energetic member of the Komsomol although his social status was due to his reputation as an able musician and a worker rather than to his political activity. (Incidentally this is a usual phenomenon in the case of musicians who are Party members. Every conservatory student with any talent is persistently drawn into Party activities. Often such students are entrusted with really fantastic tasks and responsibilities, so acute is the Party's need for members who are also musicians).

The removal of the Ukrainian capital from Kharkov to Kiev in 1934 led to the transfer of a large number of the most active students, including Zhukovs'kyi, to the Kiev Conservatory. There he enrolled in both the piano and the composition departments. His public career developed with dizzying rapidity. At the beginning of the war, while still a student, he was appointed one of the chief musical censors of Glavlit (a Party institution which has charge of issuing permits for all kinds of publications, including books on music and musical scores), notwithstanding the fact that he had absolutely no qualification for this job except his membership in the Komsomol (by that time he may also have acquired his Party membership card.)

At the beginning of the war Zhukovs'kyi had written several songs, some small instrumental pieces and two operas.[30] Were there any indications in these works which would have made it possible to foresee Zhukovs'kyi's future importance? Under normal conditions the path of a conservatory student to the Bol'shoi Theater is not an easy one and is open to only a few composers. There were absolutely no reasons to foresee this accomplishment in Zhukovs'kyi's case on the basis of his prewar musical output. Zhukovs'kyi was one of those rare students to whom learning is not merely secondary but actually unnecessary. He became an infrequent visitor in classes, while it was useless to expect him to meet his assignments. However, this embarrassed him not at all; he continued to write without regard to what was required of him, or even contrary to it. Thus it is not difficult to imagine the artistic value of his compositions of that period. His "creative work" was as far from genuine composition as, let us say, Shostakovich's or Muradeli's work is from dilettantism.

Zhukovs'kyi's compositions were typical uninspired Soviet hack-work and lacked even the basic technical prerequisites. Far from attempting to solve any creative problems he substituted pseudo-music for art and the "popular style" for real mastery. In his work there was absolutely no prevalence of intellectual factors or creative thinking over the instinctive combinations of sounds, no prevalence of moments of creative invention over passive variation and the reproduction of trite phrases. His was a primitive method of composing by memory, the basic feature of which was the attempt to arrange tunes which would please the masses. His compositions contained no trace of any conscious extended musical movement of passages nor even a relatively complex interrelation of sound images. In plain words, he was a typical dilettante of the eighteenth century type who depended upon sentimental melody which he took either directly from folk song or reproduced by combining existing motives and phrases. His harmonic structure did not go beyond simple progressions of the bass and his polyphony was innocent of any but the simplest forms of imitation. His means of developing musical ideas was limited to a single possibility; the reiteration of a four-square stanza. "Resounding orchestration," wrote *Pravda* about his music on one occasion. In the Soviet Union, however, some musicians compose while others orchestrate their works.[31] There are still a number of musicians who know the orchestra, but their services are performed anonymously.

In Zhukovs'kyi's career as a musician there were years which might have been favorable for experiment. For instance, after the first month of the war he was freed from military service by being captured by the Germans, who appointed him conductor of the opera in Kharkov. According to reports he was a fair conductor. His work in this capacity continued until the Germans' retreat from the Ukraine. Zhukovs'kyi then decided (or perhaps it was decided for him) to return to his native land. In Kiev he was given an opportunity, rare for someone who had returned from German captivity, not only of continuing his career but also of pushing ahead rapidly with the production of his opera *With All One's Heart.* The première of this work at the Bol'shoi Theater in Moscow took place on January 16, 1951.[32] Two months later it was officially announced that the composer had been awarded a third prize (25,000 rubles) in the Stalin Prize competition.[33]

Then came the catastrophe of April 19, when by Stalin's personal order the opera was withdrawn from the repertoire on the ground that it did not follow the Party line. On the same day *Pravda* printed an article condemning the opera, following this attack, in the usual Soviet fashion, by a "creative discussion" of the work's defects, which by now were clear to everyone.[34] The inevitable conclusion came on May 11, with the official announcement of the withdrawal of the prize which had been awarded to Zhukovs'kyi.[35]

The case of Zhukovs'kyi's opera is an instructive one for Soviet composers: if they wish to write in the manner of

Shostakovich (of Shostakovich before his "re-education," that is) they are lost; if they wish to write in the manner of Zhukovs'kyi they are likewise lost, notwithstanding the fact that Zhukovs'kyi and his music are typical examples of Soviet musical orthodoxy.

3. *SYMPHONY*

There is no doubt that for Russian music of the past the symphony represented the summit of mental and spiritual development, with the result that the level of Russian symphonic thought was particularly high.

Prior to the publication of the Central Committee's resolution on the opera *The Great Friendship* in 1948, the symphony still enjoyed a vigorous existence in Russia and held a leading position in Soviet music. There can be no doubt that the decline in the level of Soviet musical culture which began long ago, the enslavement of musical creative work by political propaganda and, most important, the sharp turn in Soviet music towards "socialist realism" have had the effect of shifting the emphasis towards "popular musical forms" and away from the symphony, which is officially regarded as a "complicated, textless musical form." These factors have resulted in a lowering of the symphonic style and in the degeneration of the symphony as a specific form. In the words of Asaf'yev,

> To establish with some precision the development of the content and forms of the former Russian symphony of the intelligentsia into the Soviet symphony, that is, into the beginning of an absolutely new quality of music, has thus far proved extremely difficult.[36]

If Asaf'yev had been completely honest he would have had to admit that it is the complete liquidation of symphonic art as a special kind of music which constitutes that "absolutely new quality of music" which he considered it so difficult to define. The degeneration of the "former symphony of the intelligentsia" into the "folk song symphony" or the "potpourri symphony" is in reality that "new quality" of the Soviet symphony to which Asaf'yev refers.

The process by which this decline has come about is one of the most significant in the whole history of Soviet culture, for the symphony held the place of the leading form of Russian music for nearly thirty years of the Soviet regime. To corroborate this statement it is sufficient to refer to the fact that beginning with 1918 (the year Prokof'yev's *Classical Symphony* appeared) and ending with 1945 (the year of Shostakovich's *Ninth Symphony*) more than fifty symphonies were written by Russian composers under the Soviet regime. Symphonic composers included such remarkable artists as Prokof'yev (six symphonies, up to 1945), Shostakovich (nine),[37] Myaskovski (twenty-four), Shcherbachev (four), Shebalin (four) and a number of composers of the younger generation (Khachaturian, Popov, Kabalevski, etc.).

Ever since the late nineteenth century the symphony has been the epitome of creative thought and spiritual depth for Russian music. If under Soviet conditions it continued to live such a relatively long and intensive life, this was due primarily to the tradition of a high creative culture and to the vitality of the people and the country. It was for this reason that the Soviet art policy, which had successfully destroyed the final vestiges of artistic freedom and truth in literature, painting and the theater, remained powerless with regard to the symphony--down to 1948.

The symphony became the sole remaining possibility for the creative soul under the Soviet regime to escape from the hardships imposed on the artist into a world transformed by creativeness. It was inevitable, however, that this submergence in dreams, this escape from the "urgent tasks of socialist construction," should not remain unnoticed by the Soviet cultural politicians. Following a series of indirect attacks on the symphonic form—curtailment of commissions for instrumental works, limitations on publishers' and performers' opportunities--the death-knell of the Soviet symphonic art was sounded by the Central Committee's decree on the opera *The Great Friendship* in 1948. Under the guise of a struggle against formalism and for an ideologically permeated people's art, the decree devoted particularly close attention to the "intolerable attraction of Soviet composers to complex forms of instrumental symphonic and textless music."

The consequences of this decision were soon felt: during the six years which have passed since the decree was issued, there has been a marked decline in the writing of new symphonies by Soviet composers, while those which have been composed--Prokof'yev's *Seventh Symphony* is the best example--are of a significantly lower level than the earlier works of Soviet symphonic composers.

In countries where there is an interest in the production of new symphonies, sonatas and instrumental works, the crisis of contemporary music is self-evident. In the Soviet Union, however, where the state itself declares the uselessness of the symphonic form, one finds not merely a crisis but the death of music, the death of the symphony. And with the death of the symphony in the Soviet Union, there has also died the possibility of the self-determination of the creative will of the peoples under the Soviet regime, which found release from oppressive reality in the pure world of symphonic form.

4. OTHER ORCHESTRAL FORMS

The campaign against instrumental music has had the result that during recent years it has become almost impossible to find any non-program works in Soviet music. The themes of musical works are now almost invariably connected with propaganda campaigns in connection with some political subject such as the expansion of industry or collective farming. Without exception all recently composed suites, overtures or tone poems are primarily weapons of political propaganda and only secondarily musical compositions.

The first explicit use of "Soviet themes" as the basis for such compositions took place during the twenties. Examples are the *Symphonic Monument* by Gnesin in memory of Lenin (1925), the *Funeral Ode* by A. Krein (1926) and *The Poem of Struggle* by Kabalevski. During this period, however, many Soviet composers preferred non-political subjects for their program works, e.g., the *Romantic Suite* by A. Aleksandrov, *The Rose and the Cross* by A. Krein, *Egypt* by Dzegelenok (1920), *The Tales of Buddha* by Knipper (1924), *Chinese Suite* by Vasilenko (1928), and *The Foundry* by Mosolov (1927).

Now that "Soviet themes" and folk music have become the models of the most orthodox purity Soviet composers almost without exception are to be observed having recourse to these fountains of inspiration, chiefly, one suspects, because to do so is to some extent a guarantee of a prosperous life. Characteristic recent works of this type are the *Mariyski Suite* by Rakov, *Dance Suite* by Knipper, *Turkmeniya* by Shekhter, *Mariyski Overture* by Shebalin, *Crimean Suite* by Vitachek, *Dance Suite* by Chemberdzhi, *Song of Triumph* by Veprik, based on Jewish and Ukrainian themes, and *Episodes from the Civil War* by Tomilin, based on Ukrainian folk songs.

A prominent place among compositions of this type is occupied by themes concerning the "leaders" of the Soviet state, for instance, Shebalin's *Lenin*, Khachaturian's *Poem on Stalin*, Myaskovski's *Overture of Welcome*, composed for Stalin's birthday, Muradeli's *Symphony in Commemoration of Kirov*, and Shekhter's *Poem of Gori*.[38]

5. *MUSIC FOR THE BALLET*

The process of decline that is characteristic of the development of the Soviet symphony and opera is less evident in Soviet music for the ballet.[39]

During the first period of Soviet rule ballet continued along the traditional lines of the late nineteenth century (for example, S. Vasilenko's work, *The Handsome Joseph*). Next there appeared ballets which were in reality just as traditional but which were fitted up with new subjects. Typical of these works was Reinhold Glière's ballet *The Red Poppy* (1927), which was built entirely along standard romantic lines but with crudely contrasted "proletarian" and "bourgeois" characters. The former are represented by the lyrical street song "The Little Apple," while fragments of the "International" depict a Soviet captain; the "bourgeois" characters are represented by the "Charleston" and by various waltz themes. The emphasis is not on individual relationships but on mass scenes, as is fitting in a "proletarian" ballet.

In the thirties the picture was sharply changed. Stravinsky's music for the ballet *Pulcinella,* first produced in 1926, led to a development in Soviet ballet which the critics usually brand as "form without content." The most significant examples of this trend were two ballets by Shostakovich, *The Golden Age* (1931) and *The Limpid Stream* (1935). Especially characteristic of these works was the composer's use of musical forms not often found in ballet music, such as the fugue, and the mastery he displayed in the handling of the thematic material, e.g., the brilliant variations on the theme "Tahiti Trot" in the introduction to the third act of *The Golden Age.* As was to be expected, *Pravda* sharply condemned *The Limpid Stream* as a "manifestation of formalism" and, of course, indicated the "correct path" for the development of Soviet ballet: "realistic choreographic spectacle built on the extensive utilization of folk dances."[40]

Although Soviet composers have thus far proved incapable of creating a genuine Soviet ballet on the lines of *Pravda's* recommendations, a tendency towards such "realistic spectacles" has nevertheless been manifest.

A major place in Soviet ballet production was taken by Asaf'yev's ballets with their "realistic aims" and their "scientific-historical methods," to quote the Soviet critics. The first of this composer's fairly numerous ballets was *The Flame of Paris* (1932), a work in the spirit of an epic chronicle. The music incorporates material from the period of the French Revolution (the *Carmagnole,* the *Satyre* and the *Marseillaise,* works by Lully, Gluck and Grétry, and music composed in the same style by Asaf'yev himself). Then there appeared his *Fountain of Bakhchisarai* (1933), a lyrical poem depicting one of the phases of Russian romanticism, with music in the style of the early nineteenth century, followed by *Lost Illusions* (1935) after the novel by Balzac, with musical material based on compositions by Chopin, Liszt and Aubert, interpreted through contemporary means.

Of particular importance not only to Soviet ballet but to Soviet music in general was Prokof'yev's *Romeo and Juliet* (1940). Its consistent symphonic development and its clearly expressed lyricism make this ballet one of Prokof'yev's most profound and inspired works.

6. *CHAMBER MUSIC*

The struggle for freedom of expression became especially acute in the case of chamber music. For a long time there was an official theory of the "decay" of chamber music which, because of its "individualistic nature," had allegedly outlived its usefulness. At one time RAPM even tried to deny the right of chamber music to exist under Soviet conditions, characterizing it as a "socially exclusive genre." This theory is implicit in the Central Committee resolution on the opera *The Great Friendship* which flatly denies the usefulness of everything in music which is "exclusive and which attracts only a small circle of connoisseurs and music lovers."

Nevertheless in opposition to orthodox propaganda concerning the allegedly more democratic character of music with texts, Soviet composers continue to display a clear tendency to commune with themselves and to immerse themselves from time to time in that world of intimate images which is chamber music.

The development of instrumental chamber music is facilitated in the Soviet Union by the existence of such excellent chamber ensembles as the Beethoven Quartet, the GABT and Leningrad Glazunov Quartets, the Armenian Komitas Quartet, and the

Ukrainian Vuillaume Quartet,[41] which were created during the first years of the Revolution. That these chamber ensembles continue to exist is due in large part only to the enthusiasm of the performers.

Soviet propagandists like to boast that in the U.S.S.R. chamber music for the first time in history has become a national possession, and they claim that this is due entirely to the fact that in the U.S.S.R. there are such remarkable ensembles. It goes without saying that the above-mentioned quartets disseminate their art widely also among the working people and even among collective farm audiences. To claim that they have educated new "broad masses of lovers of chamber music," however, would be more than an exaggeration. These ensembles are being heard, but they are appreciated mainly by musical circles and by the few remaining people who have been lovers of quartet music since prerevolutionary times.

Just as in the case of the symphony, so in the case of chamber music compositions, the initiative among Soviet composers belongs to those who in creative work are still in touch with the recent past of Russian music. Prokof'yev (until his death), Myaskovski, Shostakovich, Shebalin, Popov, and a few others constitute the limited number of Soviet composers who, to a certain extent, still continue to maintain the existence of this branch of composition.

Their works in this form consistently reflect the line of development of Russian chamber music which was established long ago. The Moscow group of Soviet composers (including Myaskovski and Shebalin) follows to a considerable degree the traditions of Tchaikovsky and Taneyev, while the Leningrad group, which includes Prokof'yev, Shostakovich and Popov, adheres mainly to the traditions established by Rimsky-Korsakov and Glazunov.

Of course the work of both groups has been greatly influenced by the contemporary Western instrumental chamber music style. It follows that the common characteristics displayed by both groups of Soviet chamber music composers are the extensive employment of polytonal and even atonal writing, a characteristically linear polyphony, a certain repudiation of subjectivism, and a tendency towards sharply delineated episodes and dynamic motion. These features are particularly characteristic of the Leningrad group (for example, in Shostakovich's *Octet*, Popov's *Septet* and Prokof'yev's *Second Quartet*). Shostakovich's chamber style is marked by a tendency towards *cantilena* and ascetic texture, bare of any virtuoso effects, and by a linear polyphonic development of the themes.

During recent years there has been a definite tendency in Soviet music to liquidate the quartet form completely, obviously under the pressure of the official aesthetics of "mass music." Instead the mass-song is to be cultivated for quartet ensembles, using folk songs as thematic material. Typical of this tendency towards the debasement of the quartet style in Soviet music is the *Second Quartet* of A.D. Fylyppenko, for which the composer received a Stalin Prize in 1948. Concerning this work a critic in *Soviet Music* writes,

> Fylyppenko's *Second Quartet*... is an experiment in the composition of a program work in the form of instrumental chamber music. It is dedicated to Hero of the Soviet Union S.A. Kovpak. The quartet was inspired by pictures of the legendary struggle of Ukrainian partisans for their native Soviet Ukraine.[42]

7. *MUSIC FOR SOLO INSTRUMENTS*

The decline of instrumentalism is also displayed in Soviet music for the piano and other solo instruments.[43] During the early years of the Revolution the "constructivist" trends of Western music and its deliberate reaction against emotionalism had a profound influence on Russian piano literature. At the end of the 1920's, however, the musical policy of RAPM, which regarded instrumental music as superseded and which attempted to re-orient Soviet composers towards forms connected with words, led to a sharp decline in both the quantity and the quality of music being composed for the piano. It was only after the dissolution of RAPM in 1932 that the large instrumental forms, as well as music for the piano, began gradually to be revived.

The decisive turn in the development of Soviet piano music took place in the late thirties At that time one could observe a tendency on the part of Soviet piano composers to utilize folklore material, to employ a simplified classical texture, and to lay particular stress on an objective "lyricism" and tone of forced cheerfulness—all, of course, under the pressure of the official political line.

The major exponent of this trend in Soviet piano music was Dmitri Kabalevski, whose elegant, graceful and lyrical music bore no relation to the emotionalism and dramatic fervor which had previously been characteristic of Russian piano music.

More recently an important place in the field of Soviet piano music has been taken by Khachaturian. His piano works manifest a close relation with oriental national music (Armenian, Georgian and Azerbaidzhanian), displayed in their melodic intonations, whimsical themes and pungent harmonies.

Characteristic of the evolution of Soviet composers for the piano is the creative path of the composer S. Feĭnberg. The ecstatic, Scriabinesque mood and the "excessive complexity" which was officially criticized in Feĭnberg's *First Piano Concerto* (1933) were gradually displaced by material more in accord with the bare and elementary texture demanded for Soviet mass music. His *Second Sonata* (1936) shows clearly his "evolution" towards "clarity of thought," while his *Ninth Sonata* (1939), his *Tenth Sonata* (1941) and his *Second Concerto* (1944) are characterized by an attempt to combine moderate classicism with romanticism which is sufficient evidence of the extinction of the real personality of this once brilliant and individualistic composer.

Similarly the late composer A. Aleksandrov's *Eight Pieces on U.S.S.R. Popular Themes* represents a compromise with the official aesthetics. The same thing can be said of Polovinkin's *Postludes* (1938) which are clearly based on folk music themes.

The rehabilitation of RAPM's views on instrumentalism, made official by the resolution on the opera *The Great Friendship,* once more plunged the creative work of Soviet composers for the piano into a crisis. The seriousness of the situation is admitted by the Soviet press itself, for example, in a recent open letter to Soviet composers from the director of the Moscow Conservatory and the members of the conservatory's piano department. The authors of the letter write,

> In accordance with the Central Committee's resolution of February 10, 1948 [concerning the opera *The Great Friendship*] the piano department of the Moscow Conservatory has approached in all seriousness the question of subjecting the student's repertoire to a critical review. During the last three years a special faculty committee has been reviewing the piano compositions of Soviet composers in order to choose the best works.
>
> This survey has revealed the completely unsatisfactory condition of the piano repertoire... As a result, the pianists, who have at their disposal the excellent piano compositions of Tchaikovsky, Rachmaninov, Scriabin, Glazunov, Lyadov, Balakirev, Musorgsky, Chopin, Schumann, Liszt, Mozart, Beethoven, and other composers of the past, do not find that the majority of works by Soviet composers satisfy their creative requirements.[44]

A manifest tendency to subjugate the composer's creative freedom is characteristic also of the Soviet attitude towards compositions for the violin. It goes without saying, of course, that such extreme experiments as the *Violin Concerto* by N. Roslavets (1927), an enthusiastic adherent of atonality, are completely banished from the Soviet composer's general practice. What may appear surprising, however, is the fact that even such compositions as Prokof'yev's *First* and *Second Violin Concertos,* which had acquired a central place in contemporary violin literature, have now been dropped from the approved repertoire. The same fate overtook Myaskovski's *Violin Concerto* (1939), a work of virtuosity, melodic clarity and purity of texture, as well as Shebalin's more intellectual concerto (1940).

It is no wonder, therefore, that Soviet composers are afraid to compose violin concertos since it has proved nearly impossible to combine the "simplicity and accessibility" which are required by the official art policy with the virtuosity and brilliance inherent in the concerto style. One may suspect that it was in an effort to solve this dilemma that Kabalevski composed a *Young People's Violin Concerto,* a work, however, for which "childish" might have been an apter designation.

Almost no one in the Soviet Union now writes solo compositions for the cello or viola. It would appear that Soviet literature for these instruments is confined to the cello concertos by Hamburg, Dzegelenok, Prokof'yev, and Shostakovich and the sonatas for viola of Shirinski and Vasilenko.

8. THE ART SONG

For Soviet composers the writing of *Lieder* or art songs entails considerable difficulties. During the early years of the Soviet regime there was a strong trend towards the popularization of the style of the Russian nineteenth century classics, particularly Tchaikovsky and Musorgsky. This traditionalism was manifested in works by Glière and Vasilenko, who also made extensive use of Chinese, Indian and Turkish folk music themes.

The great majority, however, of those Soviet composers who were influenced by modernism preferred to compose for instruments, and if they turned their attention to vocal music at all it was for the purpose of seeking new means and opportunities for choral idiom.

During the thirties two contrasting trends in the romantic lyric became sharply defined. First, there was an extensive development of song writing by such composers as Myaskovski, Feĭnberg, A. Aleksandrov, Shenshin, and A. Krein, characterized by intimate emotion and symbolism and by refined nuances of feeling expressing a tragic perception of reality. This trend, however, was forced to give way to the mass-song promoted first by Prokol and then by RAPM, written for the use of amateur choruses and soloists and imbued with agitational propaganda.

The result was that the art song, a form which has enjoyed

great popularity in Russia, has now degenerated into or has been replaced by the agitational propaganda mass-song.

C. COMPOSERS: GROUPS AND INDIVIDUALS

1. *THE CREATIVE OPPOSITION*

Let us now consider in greater detail the work of Soviet composers who are the principal objects of criticism by the official guardians of the purity of Soviet music, i.e., the group who may be described most accurately as the creative opposition. These are the composers for whom creative work remains a way of artistic vision and not a mere form of political propaganda. With their whole being these men are freedom-loving and independent. Their attention is concentrated on a world which they wish to create rather than on one which is imposed on them.

It is these composers whom official Soviet critics characterize as "formalists" or as "those who are unable in their creative work to answer the democratic requirements of the masses of the Soviet people." To this group belong, first of all, the "underground artists," a group of first-rank composers whose creative work during the twenties was a major component of Russian music. Tolerating no control from anyone, standing in open opposition to the Soviet aesthetics of "socialist realism," these men by the mid-thirties had either ceased to compose music altogether or carefully concealed what they composed from the Soviet musical public. Only very seldom now do they publish, and then only works which have nothing in common with their creative personality.

For example, anyone at all familiar with Soviet music knows the name of Vladimir Shcherbachov, a composer who is one of the most authoritative professors at the Leningrad Conservatory. His *Second Symphony* (1925) revealed his outstanding talent. Little was to be found in the press, however, concerning the "rout of Shcherbachov's formalist school," an episode of the RAPM campaign following which the composer left Leningrad for Tbilisi. Who knows whether he left of his own accord? Notwithstanding his subsequent formal rehabilitation and his attempt to "reform" by composing a symphony (1936) depicting the rising in the Izhorski industrial plant during the 1905 Revolution, Shcherbachov was again publicly attacked by the critics and soon after ceased entirely to be mentioned in the Soviet press as an important composer.

A similar fate befell Shcherbachov's pupil, Gavriil Popov who proved himself a promising composer, particularly of chamber music, as early as the 1920's.

Especially memorable was the case of Samuel Feĭnberg, the composer of numerous piano sonatas during the twenties, an outstanding pianist and composer with an affinity for Scriabin's style. Have any of his compositions been published or performed since the twenties? (Of course we have in mind original works and not attempts at "reformation.") What about the late Anatoli Aleksandrov, the composer of perhaps ten piano sonatas, many of which were published during those same years? Has anything been heard of him as a composer since the mid-thirties? And Aleksandr Krein (d. 1951), whose opera *Zagmuk* was produced in 1930 at the Bol'shoi Theater—is it really possible that after that date he wrote only a *Suite on Kabardian-Balkar Themes* (1941)? And why on Kabardian-Balkar themes when he was a composer with a clearly defined creative affinity for the European style? Then there is Mosolov, a composer who is well known in European and American modernistic circles who was at one time the secretary of the International Association of Modern Composers. He is a composer who attracted attention during the twenties with his work *The Foundry,* but now he is no longer on the approved list of active composers despite the fact that in 1941 he wrote a composition which was quite unlike his real style. There is something not quite clear about Mosolov's career, particularly his long residence in Central Asia. Was that merely the result of his interest in local folklore? Even more mysterious is the fate of one of the most active Russian disciples of Schoenberg, the author of works of the greatest interest for string ensembles, particularly quartets, a man who at one time (1922) was the director of the Kharkov Conservatory: Nikolai Roslavets, who since the twenties has completely disappeared from musical life and perhaps from life altogether.

Unfortunately it is impossible and perhaps premature to list all the works and all the composers who were silenced by Party criticism. Did these composers stop writing music? Of course not! This could happen to composers who had not yet reached the point where creative work is as necessary as life itself but not to composers of the caliber of those mentioned above. It is certain that these men continue to write but they carefully conceal their work from the Soviet public. This is confirmed by the fact that sometimes it is possible for a few persons to hear behind closed doors a performance of a symphony written "for the desk drawer"—often enough a symphony which will stand comparison with the best works written by Soviet composers.

Among the composers who are most active at present are a number who continue to compose "music intended for a narrow circle of gourmand-aesthetes."[45] In the opinion of the Secretary of the Union of Soviet Composers, Tikhon Khrennikov, and of course in the opinion of those who stand behind him, the members of the Agitation and Propaganda Department of the Party Central Committee, these men also belong to the opposition group. They include the late Sergei Prokof'yev, the late Nikolai Myaskovski, Dmitri Shostakovich, Aram Khachaturian, Vissarion Shebalin, and several others less well known. These men have stubbornly refused to lose their creative individuality for the sake of "socialist realism."

Does this fact not provide convincing testimony that, openly or secretly, in various degrees, the best Soviet composers belong to the creative opposition, the real meaning of which is its political protest against the enslavement of life? One would have to be deliberately nearsighted to fail to see, behind the allegedly "artistic" struggle, behind the "solicitous concern" of the Soviet authorities about music "for the plain people," the truly epic political struggle being waged between the Soviet power and those creative composers whose opposition is a genuine protest against the enslavement of creative thought. This protest acquires added significance from the fact that it is expressed in the form of highly intellectual artistic creations.

It would be a serious mistake, however, to assume that the cracking of the Party's whip for nearly thirty years over the heads of anyone who appeared likely to stray out of line should have affected only the feelings of these composers, leaving their creative work untouched. There can be no question that the degree of creative daring manifested, let us say, by Shostakovich in his *Seventh Symphony* (1942), is far less than in his composition *The Nose* (1926), or that Prokof'yev in his *Scythian Suite* (1914) was more willing to take risks than he was later in his *Seventh Symphony* (1952). Of course, Shostakovich did not begin his composing career as a Zakharov or a Mokrousov, and Prokof'yev never descended to the level of a Dunayevski. The composers of this group still preserve, to a certain degree, even up to the present, the "anti-Zhdanov" trend in their creative work; yet with every new work they become more and more moderate in their creative quest, while their protest grows increasingly muted.

It is an indisputable fact that their creative efforts are the object of artistic and moral sympathy, just as their indomitable opposition is the object of political sympathy, not only among Soviet musicians but also among the general music-loving Soviet public. It should be sufficient to recall the genuine triumph which has been accorded to almost every new symphonic work by Shostakovich. At times these triumphs have assumed the significance of political demonstrations, particularly in the case of the works he composed immediately after the Central Committee's resolution on Muradeli's opera *The Great Friendship*, or the attacks in *Pravda* against his own music. Instances of this kind happened in the case of his *Fifth Symphony* (1937) and his *Piano Quintet* (1940), both of which were acclaimed by the Soviet public as new proofs of vitality in creative freedom. Shostakovich's personal appearance on the platform at conferences has often led to direct intervention by the MVD, who were afraid that the secret feeling of opposition would become obvious, as happened for example during the plenum of the Composers' Union held in Kiev in the spring of 1939, when Shostakovich's appearance called forth an ovation such as had never been accorded even to the "leader" himself, even though demonstrations for the "leader" are inspired by the MVD.

Was not this a spark of the kind which in the past has often enough caused world conflagrations? But unfortunately the MVD agents understand this better than Shostakovich's foreign colleagues, who have never stretched out their hand in sympathy to these heroic rebels. Perhaps only a single voice among the outstanding non-Soviet musicians of our times, that of Sergei Rachmaninov, was raised publicly in solidarity with this opposition. And his voice was heard inside the Soviet Union! It was not for nothing that the members of RAPM bitterly attacked him and for a time organized a consistent boycott of his music in the Soviet Union.

General characteristics of the music of this group of composers. The basic features of the style of this group of composers sharply contradict the model proclaimed by Soviet orthodox critics and display an obvious community of interests with the progressive aspirations of contemporary music.

Perhaps the most characteristic feature of their work, however, is its deep, indissoluble contact with the historical traditions of Russian music, revealed not directly, as is demanded by the Party propagandists, but through the use of the creative experience of Russian composers of the early 1900's, particularly Taneyev, Glazunov, Scriabin, Rachmaninov, and Stravinsky. This contact reflects the opposition of Russian art to everything that stifles man's creative freedom. Like their immediate predecessors and their senior contemporaries, these modern Russian composers make heavy demands on art, seeking through it an answer to the complicated and poignant questions of life.

In this sense, Myaskovski, Prokof'yev and Shostakovich have earned their place in contemporary Russian music primarily as profound philosophers and thinkers. Such qualities in their music as its deep thoughtfulness, its intellectual rigor, its coloristic asceticism, and its fidelity to the principles of symphonic style place them in the foremost ranks of contemporary composers.

The conflict between dream and objective reality, between the joy of the creative personality and external limitations, between the aspiration towards a higher culture and the prevalence of barbarism, between the humanism of the creative spirit and the inhumanity of the environment—this is the basic motif of their existence. The fundamental theme of their work therefore is the formation of personality under the conditions of its enslavement. In this sense these composers are realists, as were their immediate predecessors, Scriabin, with his humanist pathos, Rachmaninov with his moving lyricism and Stravinsky with his "impersonally-personal" music. It is this humanist realism which constitutes the link between their creative work and the deepest roots of classical and contemporary music.

In the creative work of Myaskovski, Prokof'yev and Shostakovich there appears a clearly expressed tendency towards contact with the "neo-classical" trend of contemporary Western music. This tendency represents a synthesis of "constructivism" and emotionalism, classicism and romanticism. In this sense their work tenaciously unites the old with the new. On the level of ideas this synthesis is expressed in the fact that the concept of the "tragic collision" between the artist and society, which dominated the minds of the Russian pre-Soviet artistic intelligentsia, continues to exist in their creative consciousness, only immeasurably deepened and extended by the conditions of Soviet reality. At the same time their work also reflects new ideas and emotions called into vigorous life by contemporary reality. The lyrical humane element as an echo of tradition remains in their creative work, but dynamism, sarcasm, skepticism, and tragedy, deepened by contemporary experience, also influence their style. On the one hand their music contains bright optimism, a certain buoyancy, sociability and tireless activity, on the other a pervasive anxiety and a corrosive melancholy.

Their use of melody. The expression of these qualities is to be found particularly in their melodic idiom. In their music melody is a basic means for the expression of plastic images; it is to them one of the fundamental attributes of creative thought, the soul of music, the basic index of its style. To them, as to The Five and Tchaikovsky and still earlier to Glinka and Dargomyzhsky, the "singing quality" of melody is the essence of musical art, its vital contact with life. It is true that their conception of melody differs significantly from that of their predecessors. Not only do they, in general, avoid direct borrowings from current melodic usage or from folk music, but it can even be said that their conception of melody does not inevitably involve the idea of "singability."

Nevertheless, their notion of melody, like that of their predecessors, is associated with the idea of beauty and sincerity, with that which arises from man's deepest feelings. The accusations by Party critics that these composers have lost touch with true melody and have transformed the mastery of melody into an "empty end in itself" are, of course ridiculous. These composers regard the invention of original, significant melodies as a foremost creative problem. "There is nothing so difficult," wrote Prokof'yev "as to find a melody that can be immediately understood even by an untrained person and at the same time is original. Here a composer is exposed to great danger: he may easily become trivial or vulgar, or he may reproduce that which has already been heard.[46]

The melodies of these composers are firmly based on certain structural types, as is true of classical and romantic music. At the same time there are predominant indications in their music of characteristic elements peculiar to the melody of the Russian composers of the beginning of the twentieth century, such as Scriabin, Taneyev, Glazunov, and Rachmaninov, as well as of Western European composers such as Bruckner, Mahler and Richard Strauss. This can be seen particularly in their use of two types of sharply contrasting structures: themes of broad, extended outline which yield with difficulty to analysis and themes which are short, vigorous and easy to analyze. Examples of both types can readily be found. As examples of the extended themes one may take the secondary theme of Shostakovich's *Fifth Symphony* or that of the second movement of Prokof'yev's *Sixth Symphony*. Characteristic examples of the short themes are those in the finale of Shostakovich's *Fifth Symphony* and the "Battle on the Ice" from Prokof'yev's *Aleksandr Nevski*.

It must be recognized, however, that their melodic structures, in general, are far from any vocal origin with its principle of a succession of sung notes; on the contrary, these structures seem to be rather of instrumental origin, being based on the peculiarities of the instrument for which they were written, its timbre, range and even technique of sound production. Nevertheless, the essential quality of these themes is rooted in Slavic folk music.

In the melodic structure of Prokof'yev, Shostakovich and even of Myaskovski, there is an obvious aspiration for artistic clarity and well-defined outlines (for instance in the scherzo from Shostakovich's *First Symphony* or in the intermezzo of his *Piano Concerto*), and at the same time an inclination for the embellishment of the theme by means of curt, tense, unprepared intervals that tend to efface the clarity of the tonal centre. A strict diatonicism (e.g., in the exposition of the fugue of Shostakovich's *Piano Concerto* or in his *Variations* for string quartet) is also one of the distinguishing attributes of their melodic structure. The latter acquires particular freedom of movement by a partial use of wide intervals and displays an obvious tendency toward modernist linear construction. The almost ascetic bareness or mournful *cantabile* style of many of their themes, especially subordinate ones, is compensated for by the dynamic energy, dramatic impulsiveness and ironic fantasy of the main themes, particularly of the scherzi and finales (e.g., the transformation of the scherzo theme in Shostakovich's *Fifth Symphony*).

Of tremendous importance in the melodic structure of the music of this group of composers are those themes which appear to be based on folk music. For the most part, these are of a broad character resembling the traditional, popular Russian melodies which are still sung. Such melodies are especially characteristic of Myaskovski, as for example, the subordinate theme of the first movement of his *Fifth Symphony* and the theme of the third movement of his *Eighth Symphony* which is based on the song "The Soldier's Wife." To the same category belong their dance themes. The characteristic feature of these is their diatonicism, with a few chromatic passages and sharply differentiated phrases.

Distinct from these is another type of theme characteristic of the music of these composers. These are themes essentially chromatic in nature with broken lines, short pulsations and intermittent breathing, themes which are so purely instrumental in nature that it is doubtful whether they could be sung at all. It is melodies of this type which constitute the pivot upon which is based their entire musical structure.

The principle of melodic construction of these composers is thus closer to the classical tradition of Pergolesi and Bach than to the romantic tradition. Like Stravinsky in his *Dumbarton Oaks Concerto*, they prefer the analytic construction of a theme leading to the deliberate intellectual organization of the melodic matter rather than undisciplined intuition.

These characteristics of their melodic structure determine the methods of thematic development in their music, for example, the combination of the variation form in which the theme is exhibited in various aspects, with the sonata form in which the theme is developed and modified from within.

Their harmony. It follows that the compositions by this group of composers show a tendency towards a combination of homophony with thematic *ostinato* in the secondary parts, as for example, in the exposition of the idyllic second theme of the first movement of Shostakovich's *Seventh Symphony.* More or less repudiating the traditional principles of functional harmony in favor of a harmony based on timbre complexes, these composers are, nevertheless, extremely careful in their harmonic formations, preferring a comparatively clear modal logic to the limited major-minor framework.

Nevertheless their harmonic language was formed under the unmistakable influence of the linear trend of contemporary Western music. Because of their extensive use of a system of independent melodic voices, many of their chord combinations could be analyzed, in terms of traditional harmony, as discords or accidental tone combinations. At the same time, the tonal relationship in their music is based on a solid foundation, the interplay of the tonic and dominant.

These features of harmonic style can be observed even in the music of Taneyev, who also thought in terms of linear polyphony, in contradistinction to Glazunov whose mastery of counterpoint was subordinate to his use of harmony. In the same way the harmony of Myaskovski, Prokof'yev and Shostakovich is based upon the independent movement of the invididual voices, each one of which follows the line of its own development.

The harmony of this group of composers was undoubtedly also influenced by the particular nature of their melodic idiom and by their methods of developing thematic material. As a result, the general impression created by their harmony is one of tenseness rather than repose. The ability of their harmony to give their music a quality of vigorous assertion ("caustic harmony") is exceptionally well manifested, for example, in the brilliantly prepared dynamic climax in the polyphonic episode of Myaskovski's *Seventh Symphony.*

Although the general tendency of their harmony is towards a relatively strict tonal character, the decisive role in it is played by polyphony. Its unmistakably major-minor basis (notwithstanding fairly extensive complications) testifies to the "classical" orientation of their style. In addition, the expressive role played by tonal color is considerable. As an example it is sufficient to refer to the brilliant episode of balanced sonority in the woodwind instruments at the beginning of the development section of the first movement of Shostakovich's *Fifth Symphony*. The purity of tonality, even in polytonal episodes, is completely perceptible (e.g., in the resolution of dissonant harmonies in Shostakovich's *Sixth Symphony*). As a means of achieving tonal purity, the use of tonic-dominant pedal-points assumes great significance (e.g., the work just cited). The attainment of this clarity is promoted also by the reduction of the number of harmonic voices to a minimum (once again Shostakovich's *Sixth Symphony* provides particularly clear examples).

Even in their early works Shostakovich, Prokof'yev and, to some extent, Myaskovski clearly defined the linear structure of development of the voices as the basis for their harmony (e.g., Shostakovich's *First Symphony*). Later this principle of "constructivism" acquires in their works the character of inner creative necessity.

Their use of rhythm. In the music of this group of composers rhythm constitutes an extraordinarily powerful and compelling means of development. The rhythmic elements of their style, in combination with the buoyant, soaring pressure of their melodic themes, creates that dynamic, dashing quality which is characteristic of their music. This can be observed in the main themes of the finales of their symphonies, particularly in Myaskovski's *Second* and *Third Symphonies* and in the symphonies of Prokof'yev and Shostakovich. A typical feature of their compositions is their use of "grouped rhythms" in various forms, without repetition of accented beats. This is a type of rhythm created by means of syncopation, pauses, interruptions, tied notes, strong accents, and more or less insistent tones. Rhythm, it is clear, is to these composers one of the basic components of expressive melody.

Orchestration. Without doubt the main tool in the hands of this group of composers is the orchestra. Superficially, perhaps, their orchestration is similar to that of Glazunov (it is no accident that all of them were students at the St. Petersberg Conservatory), but such a comparison fails to give an accurate idea of the qualities of their orchestration. Glazunov's orchestra, in its fullness and solidity, is extremely colorful, picturesque, descriptive, and shot through with light. Nevertheless, it is the highly colored light of sunset rather than that of early morning. The orchestration of Prokof'yev, Shostakovich and especially Myaskovski does not possess that luminescence which is inherent in Glazunov's "coloristic" scores but recalls rather the scores of Brahms in which, as one conductor remarked, "the sun never shines." Neither Prokof'yev nor Shostakovich is a colorist, nor is Myaskovski. Their orchestral mastery is a mastery of "black and white," of somber, deep and even gloomy colors. In their orchestration there is not the slightest hint of mannerism or extravagance; its nature is rooted in the individuality of thematic lines and closely approaches the principles of chamber music instrumentation. In their orchestral compositions there is an abundance of duets (e.g., the two flutes accompanied by a harp in the third movement of Shostakovich's *Fifth Symphony* or the duet at the beginning of Prokof'yev's *Fifth Symphony*). There is an extensive use of octaves in the high and low registers and of unisons, and a masterful employment of themes for the celeste, xylophone, triangle and timpani as solo instruments. Frequent use is made of the piano, not only for the sake of color but also for its dynamic effect (e.g., in the scherzo of Shostakovich's *Fifth Symphony*). Frequently they restrict the orchestra to pure timbres (recitatives, tremolos, pizzicati, etc.).

As a whole their orchestration is a highly individual re-evaluation of the most significant tendencies of world symphonic literature, especially of their contemporaries such as Mahler, Hindemith and Stravinsky.

The structural principles of their music. Undoubtedly the most important element of their creative work is their faithful adherence to the principle of sonata construction and of the symphonic cycle in general, and at the same time their recreation of the most important principles of contemporary symphonism.

The individual development of their thoughts leads Myaskovski, Prokof'yev and Shostakovich towards the conception of related cycles of compositions and large symphonic forms. Their predominantly intellectual approach to creative work, which exerts its influence on every expressive detail, results in the strict subordination of the parts of the cycle to the whole. Casting aside what is antiquated, artificial and exhausted, they search for what is rational, permanent and vital in the symphonic form which has been developed as the result of the long evolutionary process of European music. Their work is a consequence of the historical logic of music, of its "natural selection"; it is a phenomenon showing the inexhaustible possibilities of the traditional symphonic form and its still developing resources.

The profound content of their creative work and the moving emotionalism of their music are the natural continuation and development of the historically formed symphonic principles of European music on the one hand and the symphonic style of Taneyev and Glazunov on the other.

One more extremely important circumstance: it is perhaps only in the eighteenth century, in the golden age of pure instrumentalism, that one finds composers who wrote so many symphonies as did, for example, Myaskovski. "Inspiration does not come to those who are lazy"—this principle of work, known so well to Rimsky-Korsakov and Tchaikovsky, governs the activity of Myaskovski, Prokof'yev and Shostakovich. Inspiration and hard work are the inseparable companions of their creative intensity.

The character of their themes. It is important to point out that their music preserves a deep, organic contact with contemporary life. It is nourished by contemporary idioms and grows out of the living language which surrounds them. But at the same time, as Prokof'yev once said of Myaskovski, their music "never winks at the public." This quality of creative responsibility to oneself is profoundly characteristic not only of Myaskovski but also of Prokof'yev and Shostakovich, and it is only the pressure of the Soviet art policy which has compelled these composers occasionally to alter their principles and lose sight temporarily of their artistic aspirations.

It will by now be obvious that at the very basis of their work there lies a stylistic compromise, in that their music combines in itself the progressive features of the contemporary style of music with concessions to the late romantic tradition (e.g., "every-day" phrases, the modal and tonal logic of classicism and consistent sonata-form construction). But it would be entirely unjustifiable to think that this "compromise" is merely a consequence of the smothering of creative freedom by the conditions of Soviet reality. The basic reason for their relative traditionalism undoubtedly lies in the very nature of Russian national musical thinking, in which a predilection for folk music and for popular melodies still exists. These melodies, with their narrative development of the musical fabric which is based ultimately on the music of Glinka and which is apparent in the works of the present masters' immediate predecessors (e.g., Scriabin), are still attractive to Russian composers. Therefore, the forms of musical expression characteristic of their music and the very principles of its construction are the consequence of the historical development of Russian music, which has not ceased to inspire their creative work.

In this connection one's attention is attracted by the role played in their music by the extended period, and its reserve, force and intensity, and by the influence of this intensity on the construction of the separate elements of the melody, its abbreviation and extension, its rhythmic rise and fall. Their conception of the theme as a nucleus, as a stimulus for action, together with the lyric character of their themes, creates a sensation of genuine breadth, of a broad-scale development of thought.

It is a well-known fact that the rhetoric of oral speech has always had a profound influence on music. Accordingly the dynamics and construction of contemporary spoken Russian during the Soviet period, with its sharpened rhetoric (e.g., the "meeting diatribe"), has also left its mark on the music of these composers. This explains, perhaps, the choice and relationship of thematic elements typical of their music—fourths and fifths at the outset of their works, sixths and sevenths at the culminations, and octaves and unisons in cadences—elements which give their music a certain oratorical coloring. It may also be the basis for their characteristic exaggeration of dynamic accents, their individual technique of caesuras and pauses, their fondness for music of the people, for naturalistic "mass music" (e.g., the over-emotional lyricism of Shostakovich's *Fifth Symphony*) (insofar, of course, as these elements represent a genuine creative impulse and not a concession to political pressure).

Yet there is often a feeling of doom in their works, for example, in the kettle drum episode of Prokof'yev's *Fifth*

Symphony, in the aria "On the Field of Death" from his *Aleksandr Nevski*, in the andante of Shostakovich's *Eighth Symphony*, and in the many pages of Myaskovski's compositions which are filled with inconsolable anxiety.

With all the apparent balance of their compositions, there is little discipline in the individual themes, which are frequently hurled up like outcries, or in the vaulting connections between the whole structure and its component parts, which often appear as improvisations. Everything is strongly bound together, however, by means of the unity of the directing will. In many respects their music, to counterbalance the concreteness of its sensual coloring, is abstract (it is not for nothing that they prefer the programless symphonic form!) and even surrealistic in the sense of extreme generalization of thought. Not infrequently there appear in it features of purely decorative construction, but it is always genuine music in the sense that it is always a reaction to the soullessness of surrounding life.

Their relation to life. The creative work of this group of composers is inseparable from the life that surrounds them. It expresses what is personal and what has been experienced, and it is consequently autobiographical to the core. In seeking to define the meaning of its expression, one is struck by its clear-cut and definite character: it is at one point characterized by gentle, pensive and deeply subjective lyricism, at another by nervous, malicious fantasy, at a third by elemental outbursts of irrepressible emotion.

It is perhaps the lyrical nature of their music, however, even in its dramatic episodes, which is most characteristic of their work. In this sense they are observers first of all: quiet, thoughtful, always preserving a lyrical, gentle love for life but concealing this love in the inmost recesses of their heart.

Just as was the case with Tchaikovsky, the festive episodes in their music do not signify a positive solution of their problem but only its temporary postponement. The power and completeness of the embodiment of personal feeling, an impassioned love for life, tense emotionalism in defending its rights, are opposed in them to the forces that stifle life.

Hence one of the basic characteristics of their music is that from time to time in the midst of its enchanting carelessness there suddenly arise gusts of bitter, tragic grief, as though the soul, filled with daring and overflowing with noble aspirations, had suddenly felt the harsh blast of reality, causing it to wince and cry out in pain. At times they seem to express an indifference and contempt for everything "romantic" or personal; at other times, remaining alone with themselves, they immerse themselves with all the passion of hopelessness in this "romanticism" which is so hateful to their enslavers.

To these composers creative work is the unfolding of spiritual life: it is a diary not only of the composer but of a human being, of someone whom one recognizes as a brother in adversity, as a thinking and feeling observer of life. Their music, with all its vital completeness and tragedy, becomes something intimate and essential to its listeners. Such it will remain in the history of musical literature, the reflection of a world of tragic images—at once lyrical confessions and monumental fantasies.

Are these composers contemporary in the sense that their music can be considered characteristic of modernism? They are far removed, of course, from those aspects of modernism in which a master absorbs and assimilates all existing influences. In this sense their music, one might say, is immature and even somewhat unnecessarily melodramatic. But it has, along with the clumsiness of youth and with premature old age, its own essential secret of charm and loveliness: an entrancing reluctance, or inability, to find repose, lucidity and equilibrium. This music is close to its hearers not only in the Soviet Union but in the free world as well because what it expresses is familiar and intimate as is everything genuinely human.

Basic philosophy. From this summary of the purely musical aspects of the works of this group of composers let us turn now to a consideration of their underlying assumptions and philosophy of art as manifested in their music.

As has been mentioned already, the decisive period in the formation of the aesthetic views and musical tastes of the great majority of the leading Soviet composers was the twenties and early thirties, i.e., the period during which the influence of modernism upon Soviet artists was most intense.

The Russian philosophy of art and musical criticism at this time was still strongly under the influence of a sort of "neo-Schelling" movement which had been particularly flourishing at the end of the nineteenth century. Subsequent developments had resulted in modifications of detail, but they left unchanged the basic points of view on art and aesthetics characteristic of this movement.

At that time art was still regarded as a kind of bridge between the existing world and a world beyond, and the artist was considered as a kind of "medium" who, during moments of inspiration, is able to see that which is invisible to others. The source of his creative power is not the "unseen world" nor subjective feelings, but a kind of platonic realm of ideas. The intuitive, integral apperception of the world which is inherent in art was considered to be inaccessible to science, which studies the fragmentary manifestations of nature. Consequently, irrationality and freedom from practical concerns and from an interest in everyday reality were then regarded as the prerequisites of genuine art. For art to serve as the vehicle for any kind of tendency was regarded as destructive of its true nature. Later a similarly negative evaluation of the concept of the "social tasks" of art was obviously directed against the Soviet art policy with its political propagandistic conception of art.

In accordance with this conception of the world, art was called upon to play a major role in which the function of the artist and of inspiration assumed a place of paramount importance in creative work. In this view of the problem creation becomes the product of the artist's spiritual understanding. The artist hears the unhearable, sees invisible forms and creates under the influence of fleeting visions. Inspiration is a state of ecstasy, of abstraction during which the artist breaks away from contact with people and from the world of social relationships which surrounds him.

The significant point with regard to this system of ideas in the present context is that it underlies a great deal of the creative work of that group of Soviet composers which we have been discussing. Their obvious "social passivity," existing side by side with an implacable will and colored by psychological mysticism, makes clear their inner affinity with Tchaikovsky and to a lesser degree with Scriabin. Of course, it is a matter here not so much of the contact of ideas as of common philosophical and music sources, springing from the specific qualities and nature of Russian music. Like Tchaikovsky, all these composers–Myaskovski, Prokof'yev, Shostakovich, and, in certain respects, Khachaturian–belong in this sense more to the "Moscow school" than to that of Leningrad, because their moods of dejection which constitute the basis of their lyricism are only rarely resolved into a joyful, optimistic perception of life and nature.

One other essential peculiarity of their lyricism attracts attention. Their creative work seems to be centered around the image of a hero–the "I." The listener receives the impression that he is hearing a kind of lyrical diary, that attention is fixed on certain biographical facts.

Thus the elements of contemporary objectivity are combined in their music with the traditions of romantic subjectivity, just as romantic nostalgia is combined with motives of repulsion from Soviet life. They are not afraid of using plain words and commonplace or even banal musical formulas. The power of their creative work is not based on farfetched images or on unusual "semantic changes," but on spontaneity of lyrical feeling, sincerity and even naïvete.

Thus the human theme occupies a basic place in their music. Moreover, a certain thematic monotony in their works attracts attention: all their works, with few exceptions, seem to be dedicated to the question "I and the environment." Such a consistent appeal to one and the same subject is extremely significant. Their choice of themes is directly connected with the fundamental traits of their philosophy of art.

Fantasy to them is one of the ways of breaking out of the circle of lyrical emotions, but even more significantly it serves as a vehicle to express their disrespectful, emphatically skeptical attitude to the life around them and their parody of false patriotic pathos and the insincerity of Soviet official propaganda.

The elements of their fantasy are anachronism, incongruous combinations of style, conclusions that do not correspond to premises, and utilization of comically exaggerated "Slavonic" phrases and foreign reminiscences.

Their world outlook was formed during the twenties when their horizon of ideas was broadened and their musical experience was enriched. During that period they greedily drank in the impressions of a new creative world that was opening before them. Their character—deeply original, active, forceful, sharply defined in all its features—was already formed by that time. But shortly after, life revealed its negative aspects; their faith in its values was shaken, and there remained to them only creative work, the independence of the artist and the free and proud service of art.

During those years there was defined the sharp contradiction between their social and artistic outlook and that social and political way of life which had begun to manifest itself and in which they were fated henceforward to live and create.

The attraction they felt for world art by no means killed the great feeling of national pride which was inherent in them, but their patriotism had nothing in common with stubborn inertia and chauvinistic intolerance; they did not think of the national culture of the Russian people as something alien to universal culture. The attraction they felt towards the new European spirit was to them only a problem in the working out of a new philosophical, socio-political and artistic world outlook. They regarded the culture of the Russian people as one of the contributing factors of a universal movement, which was nevertheless to remain Russian, sacrificing nothing of its historically formed national originality.

The dramatic collision of contradictions in man, particularly of the "hero" and his environment, defined the problem posed by the times as the creation of "civic" music, impregnated with socially significant ideas and capable of arousing a love for the common good and a hatred for arbitrariness and oppression. Thus there arose the basic conflict between their creative work and the Soviet art policy, the purpose of which was the replacement of the ideals of art by the ideal of service for the political interests of the Party.

In their creative work, consequently, one finds not only satire, fantasy and skepticism but also the theme of heroism; not only debunking but also the apotheosis of elevated civic passions. Occasionally genuinely cheerful, wholesome in feeling, vital and simple, their music is basically concerned with the unfolding of the development of human thought in which its dramatic intensity corresponds to the inner development of their personal character.

To reflect the real historical conflicts of the contemporary epoch with its crises and its great changes—the central theme of contemporary Russian art and of social thought as a whole—became their basic aim. The concept of the "distinctness" of the people and intelligentsia from the government, an eternal theme of Russian art, appears in their creative work also as a leading motif. For culture is immortal, as immortal as the peoples who create it. And as the banner of the struggle for its immortality is raised ever higher, we may speak with a legitimate feeling of pride of this mighty manifestation of the freedom-loving spirit.

Individual composers: Sergei Prokof'yev. At the head of this group of composers until his death stood Sergei Prokof'yev (1891-1953), an artist of impressive power for whom music was always a world in itself which had no place for cheap experiments in "art for everyone" and whose music was sufficiently strong to resist the poverty of "socialist realism." Whoever has listened closely to Prokof'yev's music, from the *Scythian Suite* and the *Classical Symphony* to *Aleksandr Nevski, Romeo and Juliet* and *War and Peace,* knows the breadth and depth of his craftmanship. Soviet musicians were happy in the knowledge that Prokof'yev was living among them, with his unbroken artistic will providing an example of responsible creativity and consistent independence.

Prokof'yev's music includes an enormous variety of forms and is characterized by inexhaustible resourcefulness. The legacy he has left is huge: seven operas, seven ballets, six cantatas and oratorios, seven symphonies and many other symphonic works, nine instrumental concertos, fourteen sonatas, chamber ensembles, music for motion-pictures and the theater, for children and brass bands, many piano pieces, songs and romances. Not all of course is of equal value. Prokof'yev lived a broad, even contradictory, creative life and frequently felt the constraining influence of the life surrounding him. Nevertheless the healthy life-asserting principle of his talent, elemental in its range, was always victorious.

The more than twenty years during which Prokof'yev lived under the conditions of the Soviet regime (he left Russia in 1918 and returned to the U.S.S.R. only in 1933) hardly constituted the decisive influence on his music. He was and remained a consistent and confirmed supporter of "contemporary" music with his unique musical thought and intolerance of any kind of attempt to thwart the creative freedom and independence of the composer's thought. He was unquestionably the mentor whose creative work left its imprint on his gifted younger contemporaries (Shostakovich, Khachaturian, Popov, and others).

It is true that his *Seventh Symphony*, completed a few months before his death, like his repeated attempts to turn to subjects dictated by Soviet propaganda (for example, *A Toast* and his cantata on quotations from Marx, Engels, Lenin, and Stalin) provide evidence of a profound creative crisis and of the decline of his former resourcefulness and inventiveness. However, one must not look for the cause of this crisis merely in the pressure exerted on him by the various decrees of the Central Committee concerning music, since it was under similar conditions of the suppression of creative thought that he also wrote such works as *Aleksandr Nevski, Romeo and Juliet*, the *Fifth* and *Sixth Symphonies, War and Peace* and many other profoundly original instrumental compositions.

The essence of his creative crisis was not fortuitous. It was the result of a certain feeling of life which gradually took possession of his soul under the influence of what he saw or perceived in life about him. It was a feeling of life like that which eventually compelled Tolstoi to reject "the depiction of 'invented' persons" and to change to portraying "people who participate in every-day human life."

Prokof'yev ceased to live in the world of artistic images he had created. It is significant that all his creative work written under Soviet conditions—with the possible exception of *A Toast*, an official composition for a state occasion, and his propaganda mass-songs— is devoted to subjects of the past, even the remote past, which is in decided contrast to the contemporary Soviet world. It is as though Prokof'yev, in the very act of creating, renounced "participation in life" and limited himself to the contemplation of it. This conclusion is strengthened by his extraordinary attention to "children's subjects" (not a single composer of the past or present, including Schumann and Musorgsky, has paid such tribute to the children's world as did Prokof'yev in his later years).

It was life in general rather than the individual life which became the fundamental domain of Prokof'yev's creative thought under the conditions of the Soviet years, years which imbued him with the desire to renounce participation in life. Hence the complete withdrawal of his music into retrospection, into the contemplation of life from afar; hence his gradual transformation from an active and life-affirming artist into a recorder of the idyllic and the picturesque. Hence also the element of all-absorbing lyricism, characteristic of his later works, for example, in the scenes between Andrei and Natasha or between Natasha and Anatol in *War and Peace.*

There is no doubt that this somber conclusion to the composer's creative life, which had begun long before his physical death, was not so much the consequence of persecution by the politicians of Soviet music—which Prokof'yev regarded as nothing more than the yelping of curs—as it was of his profound realization of the death of his fondest hopes, the catastrophic degeneration of a once rich and humane Russian culture as well as the unprecedented subjugation of nations and the establishment of undisguised slavery.

In his autobiographical article "Youthful Years"[4] the composer himself defines the peculiarities of his creative work as follows:

> I should like to dwell on an analysis of the main lines along which my creative work has advanced. The first line is the classical, originating as far back as early childhood when I heard Beethoven's sonatas played by my mother. Sometimes it assumes the neo-classical form (sonatas and concertos); at times it imitates the classicism of the eighteenth century (gavottes, the *Classical Symphony*, in part the *Sinfonietta*). The sec-

ond line is that of the innovator, stemming from a meeting with Taneyev at which he referred to my "rather simple harmonies." At first it was a search for my own harmonic idiom, later it turned into a search for an idiom to express strong emotions (*The Vision, Despair, Temptation, Sarcasms, Scythian Suite,* to some extent the *Romances,* op. 23, *The Gambler, Seven, They Are Seven,* the *Quintet,* and the *Second Symphony*). Although it is chiefly concerned with the harmonic idiom, innovation also affected the intonation of melodies, instrumentation and dramaturgy. The third line is the toccata, or if you prefer, the motor form, stemming probably from Schumann's *Toccata* which at the time [I first heard it] greatly impressed me (*Etudes* op. 2, *Toccata* op. 11, *Scherzo* op. 12, the scherzo of the *Second Concerto,* the toccata of the *Fifth Concerto,* the repeated forceful figures in the *Scythian Suite,* and in the *Age of Steel,* passages in the *Third Concerto*). This line is probably the least valuable. The fourth line is the lyrical. At first it appears as lyrical-contemplative, at times not entirely connected with melodics, at least with extended melody (*Fairy tale* op. 3, *Dreams, Autumn Moods, Romances* op. 9, *Legend* op. 12), sometimes on the other hand connected with a comparatively long melody (the choruses to lyrics by Bal'mont, the opening of the *First Violin Concerto,* songs on texts by Akhmatova, and *Tales of a Grandmother*). This line remained unnoticed or received notice only later. For a long time my lyric vein was generally denied, and lacking encouragement, it developed slowly. Subsequently, however, I paid ever increasing attention to it.

I would like to limit myself to these four lines and to consider a fifth, "the grotesque," which some have tried to ascribe to me, rather as deviations from the preceding lines. In any event I protest the very word *grotesque* which with us has become hackneyed to the point of disgust. The meaning of the French word *grotesque* has been corrupted to a significant degree. With regard to my own music, I would prefer to replace it by the term *skertsoznost'* [a coined term meaning the spirit or form of the scherzo], or if you prefer by three Russian words which give its gradations: jest, laughter, mockery.[*shutka, smekh, nasmeshka*].[48]

No matter how the aesthetic and artistic value of Prokof'yev's music is interpreted, there is no doubt that it was a reaction of the basic forces of freedom against coercion. As a consequence of that system of values which Prokof'yev in his private and public life insisted upon for himself as a conscious participant in life, his music reveals with great force his most characteristic trait—irreconcilability with any limitations whatsoever on the creative freedom of music as original, self-sufficient artistic thought. For him the aim of such a protest was by no means creative independence merely for the sake of novelty. His innovations, as with few of his contemporaries, were the result of an unfailing perception of life, of sincerity and the spontaneity of artistic reaction.

For Russian music under the Soviet regime Prokof'yev was a living indictment of its more than thirty years' distortion to please the political aims of totalitarianism. For Russian Soviet-dominated music he is irreplaceable. With him died its will to resist.

Myaskovski. Like Prokof'yev, Nikolai Yakovlevich Myaskovski (1881-1950) exerted a profound influence upon his junior contemporaries. He is unquestionably one of the most fertile composers of our time, having written twenty-four symphonies, eight string quartets, four piano sonatas, and numerous instrumental and vocal works.

Although he was educated in the St. Petersburg Conservatory, where he was a student of Rimsky-Korsakov, Lyadov and Vitol's, in his creative work he was a consistent follower of the "Moscow school," insofar as his predilection for a psychological approach to music is concerned. As the result of his self-absorption, the texture of his music tends toward somber colors, low registers and cloudy, broken harmonies. His use of melody is characterized by vague, diffuse contours and a preference for polyphonic, linear exposition.

To Myaskovski the symphonic idiom was a form of philosophical thinking complete in itself. He composed nothing for the theater and had an unmistakable dislike for opera. As a genuine symphonist he preferred music that does not illustrate something but which develops exclusively in conformity to its own laws. Hence, form to him is the living embodiment of creative thought and not an external scheme that connects separate musical episodes.

A man of rare spiritual qualities, Myaskovski, with all his remarkable modesty, was straightforward and honest. It is doubtful whether any other Soviet musician was loved so much by his contemporaries or so highly valued by those who knew him personally or through his music.

According to the conductor N. Malko, who was the first to perform many of Myaskovski's earlier symphonies, the composer once casually remarked that his even-numbered symphonies were composed for the public, the odd-numbered ones for himself. Malko adds that in Myaskovski's odd-numbered symphonies there is more depth, personal sadness, contemplation, and complexity. Does this fact not confirm the profoundly subjective character of Myaskovski's creative work and his clearly expressed introspection as well as a certain esoteric tendency?

As in the case of Prokof'yev, there is nothing surprising in the interpretation by Soviet critics of Myaskovski's role in Soviet music. "The symphonic tradition of N. Ya. Myaskovski," we read in a book summarizing the "creative discussions" of 1948,

> with his exaggerated attention to textless instrumental genres, with the predominance of somber subjective moods and abstract rationalist thinking, began to outlive its usefulness as early as the thirties; this was particularly evident in the creative work of Myaskovski's numerous imitators.... A reflection of the formally acquired methods and turns of Myaskovski's symphonic style could be discovered at various times in D. Kabalevski, L. Knipper, N. Peiko, and G. Kirkor and many other Muscovites [composers of the Moscow school].
>
> A gradual clarification of style and the use of broader and more melodic construction could not completely safeguard Myaskovski's music from symptoms of inertia, formlessness and cold artificiality. Thus, side by side with attractive lyrical expressions (the *Twenty-first Symphony* and a number of

> quartets) there were his numerous symphonic-diaries, narrowly abstract, contemplative, subjectivist, although without any decadent intricacies. Recently the composer has turned to the renovation of his typically modernist works, which had long since ceased to elicit any response (new editions of the *Third* and *Fourth Symphonies* and others). In Myaskovski's cantata *The Kremlin at Night* (1947) there was a flagrant contradiction between the poetic text, which describes military headquarters of the socialist state—the Kremlin—and the darkly contemplative music of a nocturnal landscape. The composer's detachment from contemporary life, from the natural element of intonation which is being created by the present-day life of our country, was fully evident in this work.[49]

The author of this critique is basically correct in his characterization of the nature of Myaskovski's creative work, particularly in his concluding statement, which excellently characterizes the composer's creative independence from the persistent attempts on the part of the Soviet art policy to enslave his creative thought. In another passage the Soviet critic writes as follows:

> In [Myaskovski's] creative work, particularly in his symphonies, one cannot but see the profound and intense search and desire to break through the closed circle of intimate subjective experiences, a desire to respond to the great historic changes called forth by the Revolution. These aspirations were evident in the emotional lucidity of the *Fifth Symphony*. ... and in the program subject conceptions of several of his symphonies —the *Sixth* and *Eighth* (devoted to the figure of Stenka Razin) and later the *Twelfth (Kolkhoz)*. The most significant document of his search and of the complex contradictions in N. Myaskovski's outlook in that period is his monumental *Sixth Symphony* (1923), which represents a response to the events of contemporary revolutionary reality. One cannot but agree with the composer himself who later wrote that this reflects "an intellectual, neurasthenic and sacrificial perception of the Revolution and the war." To the confused mind of the artist the Revolution appeared as something alien, as a violent hurricane which was shattering creative life. In his music there predominate gloomy images of death (the medieval religious funeral chant [i.e., the *Dies Irae*] and the ancient Russian funeral motif), while to express the revolutionary forces of the contemporary

> world songs from the epoch of the French Revolution are used.
> In the *Sixth Symphony*, as well as a number of later symphonies (especially the *Seventh, Ninth, Tenth,* and *Eleventh*) Myaskovski's idiom is characterized by complexity of harmony, affectedness of melodic line, expressionist exaggerations, and concentration of emotions.[50]

Thus it may be said that not only did Soviet reality not promote the lucidity of Myaskovski's style, but on the contrary it further deepened his tendency towards seclusiveness.

Shostakovich. Without doubt one of the most typical composers of Soviet reality, one whose work reflects the entire contradiction of the composer's life under Soviet conditions, is Dmitri Dmitriyevich Shostakovich (born 1906).

In recent years the Soviet press has been able joyfully to inform its readers that Shostakovich has composed either a *Song of the Forests* or a "March of the Red Army" in collaboration with Khachaturian, or "Ten Poems," with strictly orthodox political texts. Does it not follow from this that Shostakovich at last has really reformed and that from an "inveterate formalist" he has turned into a dependable executor of musical tasks imposed upon him by the Party? Let us examine his case.

While Prokof'yev, Myaskovski and other Soviet composers of the senior generation belong, in some measure, to the pre-Soviet period of development of Russian music, it has been Shostakovich's lot to play a thankless historical role: not only to continue the development of the best traditions of Russian music but to preserve them unsullied through more than thirty troubled and violent years during which the Communist Party has displayed an undisguised hatred towards everything creatively original and especially towards music itself as a deeply lyrical human activity. The bitterness of Shostakovich's role is greatly intensified by the fact that with all his modesty, his affectionate nature and his hatred of crowds, he has become, through the malicious will of the representatives of the Soviet art policy, a kind of musical-political representative of the Soviet power. To further their exterior political aims, the Soviet strategists have utilized Shostakovich's creative work as a trump card to demonstrate the "advantages" of a system of life which, they claim, promotes the production of artistic values. At various "peace conferences," Shostakovich's name has been used to cover up the inhumanity and aggressiveness of the Soviet "peace-makers." He is cited as an example of the "careful regard" shown by the authorities for the human being, and as proof that they can re-educate an "inveterate formalist" and "cosmopolitan" into a "devoted fighter for the ideals of the world revolution." The tragedy of this situation is underlined by the fact that Shostakovich himself undoubtedly understands perfectly well the role which has been imposed upon him. Yet in many respects he nevertheless contrives to remain himself in his creative work.

In this he is helped first of all by the fact that he, more perhaps than any of his contemporaries, is a composer of symphonies. The history of the development of the symphony shows the existence of a trend towards a psychological unity of creative thought, accomplished by means of the growth and development of broad significant generalizations. The combination of the disciplined mind and the sensitive heart has always been a characteristic feature of genuine symphonic thinking. Shostakovich not only holds firmly to this capability of the symphonic style for generalized thought and emotion but strictly adheres to that traditional symphonic form without which it is difficult even to imagine the complete embodiment of his creative conceptions. The four-movement classical symphonic cycle remains for Shostakovich the best possible means of securing the unity and intensity of development of his creative thought. It is possible that it is due to just this fact that his symphonic style can be grasped with such precision as a phenomenon deeply predetermined by his creative will. Listening to his music one would hardly suspect that this vital will is nourished not by a full sensation of life but rather by a thirst for it; that it is rooted not in psychological confidence in life but only in an aspiration to confide in life. To put it bluntly, the sources of the composer's musical thought are not the abundance of his spiritual forces but rather their impairment. In what other contemporary composer is the completeness and intensity of musical pulsation accompanied by such strong sensations of fading light and gathering dusk? In Shostakovich's music there exists not only a healthy quality and a certain gaiety but also something creeping, hating, suffering. The psychological structure of Shostakovich's music sometimes strikes us with gleams from a world of sensations and images in which it was forced to exist while developing to maturity.

Like his elder contemporaries Stravinsky and Prokof'yev, Shostakovich has thoroughly mastered the traditions of Russian music, its sensitivity to life, its unity with the experience of Russian national melody and its cultivation of professionalism. In his music there exist two evenly balanced aesthetic necessities: an individual expression of ideas in new sonorities, which might be called romanticism, and an aspiration for established standards of musical expression which can be called classicism. These tendencies are combined and reconciled by his profound feeling for the historical development of music. It is in this synthesis that there lies the special attraction exerted by his work; it is this which explains his ability to speak of a new world conception in a language which everyone can understand.

Even in his *First Symphony* (1925) spontaneity and resolute temperament were combined with professional maturity and profound thought. From the great composers of the nineteenth century he had learned precision, intelligibility and monumentality of thought. His senior contemporaries, particularly Stravinsky and Prokof'yev, helped him to develop a fascination with sheer sound and trained him to handle with unusual ease the most complicated techniques and to use them not according to moribund rules and academic canons, but in accordance with his own human needs.

Having broken away from scholastic academicism, Shostakovich moved consistently towards contemporary modernism, with its intellectual constructivist approach to mastery of the thematic material. Linear clarity, the play of melodic lines and harmonic complexes, of timbres and rhythms, an admirable facility in the invention of expressive ideas, all combined with vital, emotionally picturesque content—such were the distinctive characteristics of his style in his early compositions (e.g., his "Aphorisms" for piano and his *Second Symphony*, dedicated to the October Revolution). Later the expressionistic exaggerations that appeared with great force first in *The Nose* (1928-29) and then in *Lady Macbeth of Mtsensk* (1934) provided evidence that Shostakovich had studied the models of the most recent theater music of Western Europe with great attention and responsiveness. The *Piano Concerto* (1933) and the *Fourth Symphony* (1936) which followed demonstrated his increasingly profound adherence to modernism, with its ideals of absolute creative freedom and its dislike of the beaten track.

The brilliance of Shostakovich's individuality had an immediate effect on the development of Soviet music as a whole. Even orthodox Soviet criticism is compelled to recognize the fact that Shostakovich exerted a profound influence on Soviet composers:

> While Myaskovski's influence began to fade markedly by the middle of the forties, the trend headed by D. Shostakovich became ... most influential and fashionable. The majority of young composers who already stood on their own feet (Yu. Sviridov, Yu. Levitin, M. Veinberg, R. Bunin), as well as those still within the walls of the Moscow and Leningrad Conservatories, were under the very strong hypnosis of Shostakovich's symphonic style. In the mid-forties this was as extensive and undoubtedly harmful a "mania" as was in its time the universal imitation of Scriabin. ...51

But to Soviet musical orthodoxy the influence of Shostakovich upon his younger contemporaries, as well as his own creative work, is nothing but the consequences of a failure to overcome "bourgeois relapses" against which, in their opinion, it is necessary to fight as one fights the plague. In reality, of course, this influence is a natural, regular process of the transmission from one generation to another of historically accumulated experience, a process which not only promotes the progress of music but is a necessity for its development. For it is only through the consolidation of past experience in the composer's consciousness that new creative problems arise. There is nothing unnatural and harmful in the fact that the best Soviet composers gravitate towards modernism, because the uniformity of the creative contemporary style leads to a uniformity of the creative search. Nor is it surprising that the most essential element in the uniformity of this search is its independence and freedom, thanks to which art maintains its meaning as "the highest manifestation of the power which exists in man" (Tolstoy). To the Soviet authorities, however, the manifestation of the "power which exists in man" is a highly dangerous phenomenon. Having discovered the organic contact between Shostakovich's works and modernism and his steadily increasing influence upon the creative work of the younger Soviet composers, the Soviet authorities concentrated all the power of their punitive apparatus, accusing him of "formalism," "cosmopolitanism" and other sins of "bourgeois decadence."

The *Pravda* articles "Confusion Instead of Music" and "Falsification of the Ballet" (1936), which were directed against Shostakovich, were in reality the first signals for the total enslavement of Soviet music.[52] For Shostakovich personally they were the condemnation of an artist and humanist who believed in man's intellect and creative powers.

Is it surprising that following this attack Shostakovich seemingly became an entirely different composer? At first he apparently tried to submit and obediently bowed his head (his *Fifth Symphony* and to some extent his *Piano Quartet*), but then, having evidently decided that *Pravda's* articles were only some sort of ambiguous high politics that had no direct relation to him personally, he tried to be himself once again. Something in his soul, however, had been silenced forever. Instead of his former joy and sparkle, there now creeps into his music that "eternal theme" of Russian art which brings him close to Tchaikovsky, Tolstoy and Dostoyevsky: a passionate rebellion against every kind of death and decay, whether physical or spiritual (e.g., the andante of the *Eighth Symphony* and the recitative of the *Ninth Symphony*, in which there is a predilection for dark coloring and "unearthly images."). The reaction to this mood is a desire to be among people, to be in the midst of tumult and commotion, to lose one's own ego and to be merged into the mass. This mood is dominant particularly in the finales of his later works, which produce the impression that the composer is afraid of being isolated and lost.

Complacent lyricism and gentle melodies gradually disappear from his creative work; in their place one finds thematic material colored by grotesque and pessimistic moods. The atmosphere of poignancy, of feverish observation, of sorrowful, agonizing self-confessions becomes more characteristic of his music. This fact is duly noted by the Soviet critics:

> The strongest influences he [Shostakovich] receives are linked with the expressionist hysteria and strident pessimism of Mahler's later symphonies and with the decadent neo-Bach style of Stravinsky's period of the *Symphony of Psalms*. The range of his creative efforts becomes narrowed; he completely repudiates the opera form, hardly composes any theater or choral music, any romances or songs.[53]

Even the "patriotic" *Seventh Symphony*, with its programmatic reference to the siege of Leningrad, is unacceptable to the Soviet critic:

> Shostakovich's *Seventh Symphony*, which played a significant role in the patriotic musical literature of the war years, was less of a unity than the *Fifth Symphony*, to which it is akin. Essentially only the first movement of the *Seventh Symphony*,

> because of its specific programmatic features, was accepted by the broad mass audiences. Shostakovich's musical conception was more effective in its expression of the sinister images of fascism than in the embodiment of the positive heroic images of our contemporary society. The abstractness of intonation, the cosmopolitanism of the musical idiom of Shostakovich, who even during the war did not set himself the task of coming closer to the national and folk musical idiom, was a barrier to the prolonged popularity of the *Seventh Symphony* among the Soviet people.[54]

After his *Eighth Symphony* (1943) with its infinite adagio, the only movement of this kind since Beethoven which can be compared with that composer's works for range and profundity, a movement which "by the power of its human emotion surpasses everything else created in our time" (Koussevitsky), Shostakovich turned his attention to the world of chamber music (the *Trio,* the *Second* and *Third Quartets* and the chamber music *Ninth Symphony*). Concerning his works of this period the Soviet critic writes as follows:

> With accentuated interest [Shostakovich] persistently revives in a decadent and affected manner archaic instrumental forms in particular: fugues, passacaglias, ancient forms of variations, and recitative constructions in the spirit of the seventeenth and eighteenth centuries. ...[55]

One is forced to regard as a protest this retreat on the part of the composer from the primitive Soviet mass-song into the realm of the Renaissance, "that gigantic laboratory where musical forms were just taking shape" (Asaf'yev). Once more Shostakovich avoided taking ready-made schemes, immersing himself rather in the study of the laws of formation. Here one has yet another proof of his deep organic connection with the progress of contemporary modernist music.

Recent developments in the music of Shostakovich are summarized by the Soviet critic as follows:

> In his [recent] large-scale compositions two worlds of images, poles apart, predominate: on the one hand frightening, phantasmagoric visions carried to the pitch of ecstasy. ...; and on the other hand a feeling of the realization of his own doom, of

> weariness and of unbearable anguish. The first world of images finds expression in the piling up of chords and timbres, in mechanical rhythms, strident melodic formulas, and persistently reiterated *ostinato* hammer blows; the second is embodied in artificially impoverished and sparse linear figures, lacking color, animated movement and natural harmonic fullness. These contrasts are presented with special force in such scores as the *Eighth Symphony* or the *Piano Trio.*[56]

From the brilliant embodiment of bright, life-affirming conditions to the depiction of dark harsh elements—such is the logic of the creative path followed by Shostakovich, a path darkened by the sterile life of his environment, with its materialist utilitarian conception of the world, its applied aesthetics of musical propaganda, and its totalitarian violence and tyranny.

Shostakovich's most recent creative activity shows a new—perhaps the last—zigzag of his creative evolution. His obviously enforced repudiation of the symphonic idiom and his turning towards the elements of the mass-song (e.g., *Song of the Forests,* "March of the Red Army," "Ten Poems,")—does this not signify the end of Shostakovich as a composer and his inevitable transformation into a functionary of propaganda? Nevertheless, in 1951 *Izvestiya* wrote that in his new "Twenty-Four Preludes and Fugues for the Piano," Shostakovich again "deviated significantly from his recent realistic stand."[57]

Truly, the nature of this great and genuine artist is strong—perhaps it is unbreakable!

Khachaturian. Undoubtedly one of the most talented and brilliantly individual Soviet composers is Aram Khachaturian (born 1904). His creative work is connected with that line of musical development in the Soviet Union which has less relation to the earlier traditions of Russian music than has the music of the composers we have considered so far. Even in his early works (his *First Symphony* (1934), *Piano Concerto*

(1937), *Symphonic Poem on Stalin* (1938), and *Violin Concerto* (1940)) the national Georgian-Armenian characteristics of his music were announced with such power that it was obvious that in him they had overcome not only the long-standing traditions of Russian music which had dominated nineteenth century Georgia and Armenia but also those direct ties and influences which had been exerted upon his creative work by the Moscow school of composers and their creative environment.

It is sufficient to call attention to the originality of his themes and rhythms to demonstrate the truth of this assertion. Undoubtedly the decisive role here is played by the inherent character of Caucasian popular melodies even more than by his creative individuality. For many years the composer's symphonic work drew its inspiration from Armenian folk music and was marked by captivating temperament, emotionalism and optimism. The persistent taming of Khachaturian's individuality by the Soviet critics, however, has been under way for a long time. Their primary target has been his clearly expressed nationalism. The results of this taming process can be seen, for example, in his ballet *Gayne* (1942), the music of which betrays not only the watering down of national features but also a tendency towards the impersonal trivialities demanded by Soviet aesthetics.

The deterioration of Khachaturian's talent has been traced with considerable accuracy by a Soviet critic in the following words:

> It is known that in the thirties Khachaturian was successful in creating works of a realistic nature (the *Poem About Stalin*, the *Violin Concerto*), while his *Piano Concerto* (1937) gave rise to a whole series of imitations in the creative work of composers of the national republics. However, from the outset of the composer's career his style included, along with healthy folklore elements, traits of French impressionist influences. Later, by the middle of the forties, enticed by the pseudo-innovative "discoveries" of Shostakovich, Prokof'yev and others, in pursuit of "technical craftmanship" incorrectly understood, Khachaturian began to digress from his previous

> achievements. He likewise avoided theatrical musical forms, despite the fact that attention to the ballet (*Gayne*, 1942) brought him deserved success.
>
> Even in his *Second Symphony* (1943), a work whose emotional excitement is characteristic of Khachaturian, it was possible to observe an exaggerated compactness of harmonic means, a hypertrophy of heavy, massive sonorities, and a prolixity of form. Khachaturian's *Cello Concerto*, which appeared in 1946, is based to a considerable extent on a reworking of his previous compositions.
>
> The composer's talent, out of touch with the life-giving popular-national basis, has not found stimuli for further development. ... Khachaturian became less and less productive; he seldom turned to vocal and programmatic symphonic forms, and finally, in his latest work, the *Symphonic Poem*, he engaged in superficial tonal invention lacking musical images having content. The precariousness of his aesthetic positions, his creative self-assurance, the rejection of general cultural and professional perfection—all of this has had a most harmful effect on Khachaturian's creative work and has brought him to a formalistic impasse.[58]

Khachaturian's creative dilemma is the result of his attempt to combine the demand of Soviet aesthetics for "music for the people" and for "socialist realism" with his own talent for devising novel combinations of timbre and rhythm. The impossibility of following his own creative bent has led Khachaturian into frustration and impotence. Such an outcome is inevitable, however, in the case of composers who, like Khachaturian, have not had time to strengthen their individual mastery of their material before being subjected to the Party's exigent demands.

Note.—We have deliberately not included in the group of composers under discussion the name of Dmitri Kabalevski, one of the "leading" Soviet composers and one whose works are comparatively widely known beyond the Soviet borders.

Kabalevski, the author of a significant number of musical works of the most varied forms and especially of piano music, began his creative activity when he joined that progressive group of composers under the Soviet regime whose opposition to official Soviet aesthetics was already sufficiently clear, inasmuch as they consciously followed that trend of Russian modernistic music which treasured above all the creative freedom and independence of the composer's thought. Kabalevski, however, soon not only disclosed a lukewarmness in his creative quest but accepted completely the basic principles of socialist realism.

The real significance of Kabalevski's creative development, however, lies in the fact that he was one of the most talented Russian composers who not only accepted completely the role of "Soviet" composer but, what is especially important, in his musical and public activity and particularly in his journalistic work, devoted himself to unrestricted propaganda of the principles of socialist realism. Kabalevski and his companion in arms Tikhon Khrennikov became for Russian music under the Soviet regime its evil geniuses; in their critical work they made a significant contribution to the enslavement of Soviet music.

For a considerable period editor of *Soviet Music* and author of a vast array of "guiding" reports and articles, Kabalevski, more perhaps than any other sub-Soviet composer, is a typical representative of Soviet sycophancy.

2. *THE TRADITIONALISTS*

Another group of Soviet composers, the traditionalists, consists mainly of representatives of an older generation—such men as Gnesin, Krein, Shteinberg, Glière, Goedicke, Vasilenko, Ippolitov-Ivanov, Glazunov, and Shaporin. These men, mostly former pupils of Rimsky-Korsakov and Lyadov or of Tchaikovsky and Taneyev, show a close relationship to their teachers in their creative aims.

They have always followed a moderate line, combining the stylistic features of The Five with those of the Moscow school.

The group as a whole has been honored by the Party and

government more perhaps than any other. Most of its members are professors at the conservatories and have received various honorary titles and prizes. Their real merit lies in their long and selfless work in educating young composers[59] and in their composing activity which is responsible for the creation of that "basic repertoire" of the Soviet opera and concert hall which is distinguished by its irreproachable subject matter and middle-of-the-road means of expression.

The works of these composers, in form and spirit, are survivals of a "moderate modernism" which is generally anemic and lacking in temperament and breadth of development. Essentially a development of the classical traditions of Russian music, the work of several of them nevertheless shows traces of the influence of pre-Soviet Russian modernism.

The composers of this group have produced a great many "revolutionary compositions," for example, Pashchenko's *The Eagle Mutiny* on a theme from the history of the peasant uprisings of the eighteenth century, *Zagmuk* by Krein, also on a theme from the revolutionary movement, *The Decembrists* by Zolotar'ov, and Glière's ballet *The Red Poppy.* Their symphonic compositions are often associated with "revolutionary" or "Soviet" themes, for instance, the "Symphonic Monument" by Gnesin and the "Funeral Ode in Memory of V.I. Lenin" by Krein, *Turksib* by Shteinberg, a symphony dedicated to the construction of a main railroad line, and Vasilenko's *The Soviet East.* There are also a number of compositions in monumental oratorio form, for example, Shaporin's *On The Field of Kulikovo* and *The Tale of the Battle for the Russian Land.* Finally there are the numerous compositions dedicated to Stalin.

Musically these compositions often have little in common with their titles; in general, they have little to say although most of them are well written within the limits of the classical-romantic style and impress the overseers of the purity of Soviet music by their melodiousness and harmonic clarity.

Such works have not played a significant role in the opera

and concert life of the Soviet Union, with the exception perhaps of Glière's *Red Poppy* and Shaporin's *On The Field of Kulikovo* and *The Tale of the Battle for the Russian Land,* which have not only remained securely in the repertoire but have been widely imitated. But because these compositions were the works of authoritative professors who did not disdain to utilize Soviet themes, they played a tremendous but somewhat equivocal role in Soviet musical life. With these works there began an intensive development of similar music written for particular occasions. Even more important is the fact that these works laid the foundation for that "creative compromise" which dulled the will of Soviet composers and disoriented the Soviet musical world. For Soviet propaganda such "creative work" became an important trump card in the struggle between the Soviet power and the individual artist. These works made it clear that music could be tamed to serve political aims since it was possible to point to the fact that even such composers as Glière, Gnesin, Krein, and others, men of venerable age with extensive creative experience, had come along "hand in hand" with the Party and that consequently their younger pupils, such as Shostakovich, Khachaturian, etc., were "in error" because, being young, they failed to see the "genuinely creative road" pointed out to them by the Party.

In reality, the "unforced" rapprochment between these composers and the demands of the Soviet art policy was merely the result of their eclecticism. Although in general these composers are unquestionably talented and frequently possess even certain traits of originality (for example, Vasilenko and Shaporin) and although they are excellently trained, they never rise above the level of talented imitators and stylists. Reflecting the influence of Rimsky-Korsakov and Tchaikovsky, although at times altogether externally, and immersed in a realm of romantic refinement, their music is invariably well within the limits of moderation and creative mediocrity. To the not overly fastidious Kremlin "aesthetes," however, it is acceptable because of its accessibility and cheap emotionalism.

Among the composers of this group—leaving aside Glazunov and Ippolitov-Ivanov, whose creative work was essentially completed before the full establishment of the conditions of Soviet reality—S.N. Vasilenko (born 1872) stands out particularly. Long a professor at the Moscow Conservatory, Vasilenko is the author of many vocal and instrumental compositions. His music is distinguished by refined taste, delicacy, lyricism, and coloristic inventiveness. His most pronounced characteristic as a composer is his tendency towards the use of an impressionistic style. Paying little attention to what was going on around him and, in particular, oblivious of the decrees of the Party and government concerning music—or perhaps in order to escape from the importunity of those decrees—Vasilenko was immersed in his own world of images and regularly and consistently, though perhaps not very intensively, continued to compose up to the end of his life, now and then paying tribute to "Soviet subject matter."

Like Vasilenko, his younger contemporary Yuri Shaporin (born 1889) is one of the more original composers among this group. A typical traditionalist and an admirer of The Five on point of principle, particularly of Musorgsky, Shaporin nevertheless is also inclined to a certain radicalism chiefly for coloristic descriptive purposes, at times allowing himself a harmony and a certain amount of discordant polyphony as a means of intensifying tension. On the whole, however, his work remains within the bounds of the long-established canons of musical thinking.

Perhaps the most typical representative of this group of composers is Reinhold Glière (born 1875) who was for many years a professor at the Moscow Conservatory and who is the author of a great number of compositions in the most various forms. Possessing considerable mastery within the limits of the classical-romantic tradition but lacking the necessary originality for creative individuality, Glière found it easier to follow the Party line in aesthetics than did some other composers of the senior generation. More than that of other composers, his music appeals, if not to "socialist realism," at least to "traditional realism," for all of his compositions remain within the circle of the well-tested in form and theme.

Although the work of this group of composers is of no importance for the future of music, it has certainly left its mark upon Soviet music because it officially represents the limits of the creative horizon beyond which it is dangerous to roam. The fact that it has been elevated by Party orthodoxy to the level of a model for art (more by means of encouraging the composers with Stalin Prizes and decorations than by Party decrees) has accelerated the process of levelling down Soviet music. To Soviet musical orthodoxy the work of this group of composers represents the limit of the creative quest and a model of tradition. To the oppositional group of composers, however, it has always been and still remains the purest eclecticism, lying outside the sphere of their concern.

3. *ORTHODOX COMPOSERS (VOLUNTARY AND INVOLUNTARY)*

To the last and most numerous group of Soviet composers belong the great majority of those who grew up and were trained under the conditions of Soviet reality.

It would seem that a period of more than a quarter of a century should be entirely adequate for raising a generation of creatively active composers. Yet the Soviet power—and this fact must be emphasized very emphatically—although it has greatly encreased the *number* of composers, has, at the same time, and evidently quite deliberately, catastrophically lowered their *professional level.* There is not a single composer among the younger group who stands out as a representative of the new generation. Yet music attracts ever new generations of composers, men who are frequently not less talented than those of the preceding generations.

The most significant aspect of this situation, and perhaps the most alarming, is that the level of the spiritual culture of the Soviet peoples has continually declined. The new generation of the Soviet intelligentsia is made up, in the main, of peasants by birth or persons originating from the working masses, persons who are without any kind of inherited cultural influences and who lack even a feeling of the necessity for art. Nor is the deficiency supplied by Soviet music education, in which the basic conception of music as an art is lacking, as is any breadth of creative outlook and even an elementary creative curiosity. Everything which served to transmit the rich musical tradition of the past is gradually disappearing—the people who were once devoted to it, the concert life that grew up around it and the musical way of life engendered by it. That which still survives of this tradition is consistently degraded and the new generation is being brought up in a spirit of hatred and contempt for creative thought.

The great majority of representatives of the new generation of Soviet composers already sincerely detest everything connected with the musical culture of the past, and they are particularly outspoken in their disdain for the contemporary art of the West. It is not merely that they tend to belittle modernism because of the official attitude of condemnation towards it; they actually do not understand contemporary Western music. Even late romanticism appears to them as something arbitrary, artificial and useless.

Having been brought up to view music as a means to an end, compelled to be entirely at the service of the Soviet political system, they restrict their horizon to musical propaganda and regard the mass-song as the only legitimate form of music. In this way there has been produced the real Soviet type of composer, the typical composer of "smaller forms"—songs and choral works. Such, essentially, are the majority of the younger orthodox composers. They are frequently referred to as "platform composers" (*estradniki*), a designation indicating not their concert activity but the political function of their work. Until recently this nickname was pronounced with a nuance of scorn, for the "platform" in the Soviet Union during the thirties was associated rather with the circus than with concert activities. But it was precisely in the theater that there began the process of replacing the former concert repertoire by the new Soviet propaganda repertoire—the propaganda mass-songs, the instrumental music designed for diversion, the popular songs with their sentimental overtones, the instrumental pieces with their superficial brilliance and virtuosity, and the program symphonies which are actually nothing but mass-songs arranged for orchestra. It was as the result of this development that the nickname "platform composer" or the designation "worker among the masses" became honorable titles more and more sought after by members of the Composers' Union.

Many Soviet orthodox composers, however, have no rooted aversion to the opera and the symphony. In fact it is even considered a duty by such composers to "transplant" the principles of the mass-song to symphonic and operatic forms. It is hardly necessary, however, to add that such operas and symphonies, which are merely inflated mass-songs, are as unlike genuine works in these forms as vaudeville, for example, is unlike opera. Nevertheless, the initiative of these "composers for the masses" has become the leading factor in Soviet opera and symphony, as we have already pointed out.

Surveying the numerous unmusical, often professionally incompetent programmatic symphonic poems and overtures written for some particular occasion by the great number of young Soviet composers, it is difficult to select the most representative of them, since they are all colorless and monotonous. Yet they have positively and irrevocably transformed Soviet instrumental music into a means of propaganda and have compelled even genuine composers to follow in their footsteps. Myaskovski's *Twelfth (Kolkhoz) Symphony* is an illustration of this fact.

Of course there is no reason whatever to regard the orthodox group of Soviet composers as something integral and monolithic, composed of standardized "Soviet production units." Among these composers are some who are compelled, for the sake of their continued existence, to be tactful and amenable to the demands of Soviet art policy. But there are also those who are genuinely Soviet, to whom the composition of music has ceased to be a creative activity and has become a mere tool for propaganda. It is with these latter composers that we are concerned at present. They represent that "new type" of composer of the Communist future which in the opinion of the Party is to replace the "old-fashioned composer," the "formalist." They are the forerunners of the type of composer which the Soviet power is nursing with such care. Like the "new Soviet man," the "new Soviet composer" has his own moral and ethical level and his own perception of aesthetic problems. Frequently he is not lacking in external culture (or rather an alluvial deposit of civilization), but his most characteristic features are his unscrupulousness in the employment of the means of success, flattery and grovelling before those in power, rudeness to the weak, and most of all, an impudent attitude toward everything connected with the concept of humanity. The new Soviet musician is a member of the Party and an important person in the field of music policy. Human qualities are not obligatory; what is important is loyalty to the myth about the "golden age" of Communism.

The professional requirements demanded from the "new Soviet composer" are extremely limited. To compose a mass-song is an act requiring little professional culture. It is sufficient to limit oneself to the trade of functional harmony which one learned in school and to know how to gather together the necessary thematic material from that old reliable source, folk music. The great majority of contemporary Soviet composers live and work within the limits of such requirements. After all, it is not important what creative resources they possess so long as their "creative" work serves to support the regime in power.

FOOTNOTES TO PART V

1. *Assotsiatsiya Sovremennoi Muzyki.*

2. *Rossiiskaya Assotsiatsiya Proletarskikh Muzykantov.*

3. *Ob''yedineniya Revolyutsionnikh Kompositorov i Muzykal'nykh Deyatelei.*

4. For the full titles of these publications see the bibliography.

5. A group of French composers formed during the 1920's. The members were Georges Auric, Louis Durey, Arthur Honegger, Darius Milhaud, François Poulenc, and Germaine Tailleferre.

6. For a discussion of this resolution and its consequences see Part I, Section D, above.

7. "Doklad T.N. Khrennikova" [Report by T.N. Khrennikov], *Sovetskoye iskusstvo* [Soviet Art], No. 17 (1105), April 24, 1948.

8. *Puti,* pp. 18-19.

9. "Doklad B.V. Asaf'yeva" [Report by B.V. Asaf'yev], *Sovetskoye iskusstvo,* No. 17 (1105), April 24, 1948.

10. *Ibid.*

11. See for example Zhdanov's warning against "one-sided enthusiasm for instrumental symphonic music without text," (quoted in *Puti,* p. 82). "The neglect of program music," Zhdanov wrote, "is also a departure from progressive traditions." And the editor of *The Ways of Development of Soviet Music,* following in Zhdanov's footsteps, writes quite unambiguously about the necessity of "combining instrumental music with choral solo singing," and states that "the most important problem for Soviet composers is the creation of contemporary opera rich in content, full of artistic value and reflecting perfectly the life, aspirations and ideals of the Soviet people." (*Ibid.,* pp. 83-84).

12. *Ocherki sovetskovo muzykal'novo tvorchestva,* Moscow-Leningrad, 1947. (Hereafter cited as *Ocherki*).

13. Asaf'yev, B.V., "Puti razvitiya sovetskoi muzyki," *ibid.*, Vol. I. pp. 5-19.

14. *Ibid.*, p. 5.

15. *Ibid.*

16. *Ibid.*, pp. 6-7.

17. See Nest'yev, I., "Massovaya pesnya" [The Mass Song], *ibid.*, pp. 246-253, and *Puti*, pp. 44-45.

18. *Proizvodstvennyi kollektiv studentov nauchno-kompozitorskovo fakul'teta Moskovskoi Konservatorii* [Production Collective of Students of the Scientific Compositional Faculty of the Moscow Conservatory].

19. *Ocherki*, p. 253.

20. "Doklad T.N. Khrennikova" [Report by T.N. Khrennikov], *Sovetskoye iskusstvo*, No. 17 (1105), April 24, 1938.

21. Asaf'yev, *Intonatsiya*, pp. 41-42.

22. Bernandt, G., "'Pesn' o lesakh' D. Shostakovicha" [Shostakovich's *Song of the Forests*], *Sovetskaya muzyka*, December 1949, No. 12, p. 60.

23. Protopopov, V., "Patrioticheskaya kantata ('Slav'sya, otchizna moya! ') Ye. Zhukovskovo," *ibid.*, April 1950, No. 4, p. 19.

24. *Ibid.*, p. 20.

25. For a valuable analysis of the historical origins of the contemporary crisis in Soviet opera see the article by Asaf'yev, B.V., "Opera," in *Ocherki*, pp. 20-38.

26. In his article on Soviet opera, *op. cit.*, Asaf'yev gives an excellent characterization of the stylistic degeneration caused by the influence of the mass-song on operatic dramaturgy. The role of the recitative in Soviet opera, he writes, was reduced to a dry and primitive naturalistic narration of prosaic speech, employing

musical intervals. Rhythm became impoverished. The use of mass-song marching rhythms became the inevitable formula for all climactic scenes. "Stage-business" for dramatic action designed to depict the course of events degenerated into the cliche, "Let's have a talk, then go and sing." The art of ensembles, previously the high point in opera, disappeared entirely. Melody degenerated into fragmentary songs in couplet form with trite or sentimental progressions. Mass choral effects, which are essential to give a note of realism, led to the decline of the aria as a means for expressing passion and profound feeling.

27. For an illustration of the set for this performance of Serov's opera (by the stage designer V.V. Dmitriev) see *Bol'shaya Sovetskaya Entsiklopediya* [Large Soviet Encyclopedia], 2nd ed., Vol. XIV, plate facing p. 564.

28. "Beseda tovarishchei Stalina i Molotova s avtorami opernovo spektaklya 'Tikhii Don,'" *Pravda,* No. 20 (6626), January 20, 1936.

29. Kukharski, V., "Opera 'Ot vsevo serdtsa'" [The Opera *With All One's Heart*], *Sovetskaya muzyka,* March 1951, No. 3, pp. 25-34.

30. One of these works was based on Wanda Wassilevska's novel *The Rainbow,* the theme of which was the "reunion" of the "liberated" western regions of the Ukraine with the Soviet motherland.

31. For a recent critical reference in the Soviet press to this practice see Grachev, Mikhail, "Muzykal'nye polyfabrikaty" [Musical Semi-finished Products], *Krokodil,* Vol. XXXI, 1953, No. 11 (1337), p. 5. Grachev's immediate target is the operetta composer Yu. Milyutin.

32. See "Novaya sovetskaya opera v Bol'shom Teatre 'Ot vsevo serdtsa'" [A New Soviet Opera at the Bol'shoi Theatre, *With All One's Heart*], *Pravda* and *Izvestiya,* January 17, 1951.

33. "V Sovete Ministrov Soyuza SSSR. O prisuzhdenii Stalinskikh Premii za vydayushchiyesya raboty v oblasti nauki, izobretatel'stva, literatury i iskusstva za 1950 god" [In the U.S.S.R. Council of Ministers: The Awarding of Stalin Prizes for Outstanding Work in the Fields of Science, Invention, Literature, and Art for 1950], *Pravda* and *Izvestiya,* March 17, 1951.

34. "Neudachnaya opera: O postanovke opery 'Ot vsevo serdtsa' v Bol'shom Teatre" [An Unsuccessful Opera: Concerning the Production of the Opera *With All One's Heart* at the Bol'shoi Theater], *Pravda,* April 19, 1951. Reprinted in *Sovetskaya muzyka,* May 1951, No. 5, pp. 8-12.

35. "V komitete po Stalinskim Premiyam v oblasti literatury i iskusstva" [In the Committee on Stalin Prizes in Literature and Art], *Pravda* and *Izvestiya,* May 11, 1951, and "V Sovete Ministrov SSSR" [In the Council of Ministers of the U.S.S.R.], *Pravda* and *Izvestiya,* May 13, 1951.

36. Asaf'yev, B.V., "Simfoniya" [The Symphony], *Ocherki,* p. 68.

37. In December 1953 the Soviet press announced the first performance of Shostakovich's *Tenth Symphony.* For criticism of this work, see Annex D, pp. 305-310.

38. On the consequences of the development of musical compositions of this type, see further Section V.c.2., below.

39. See Kisélev, "Balet" [Ballet], *Ocherki,* pp. 39-59.

40. *Pravda,* February 6, 1936. See note 52, on next page.

41. The Vuillaume Quartet is named for the violin maker Jean-Baptiste Vuillaume (1798-1875), "a most prolific maker of eminently clever copies of Cremonese masters" (*Grove's Dictionary of Musicians,* 3rd ed., Vol. V, p. 518a). GABT is an abbreviation for *Gosudarstvennyi Akademicheskii Bol'shoi Teatr* [State Academic Great Theater]. The Komitas Quartet is believed to be named for S.G. Komitas, an Armenian composer (1869-1935).

42. "Novye uspekhi sovetskoi muzyki" [New Successes of Soviet Music], *Sovetskaya muzyka,* April 1949, No. 4, p. 4.

43. See Solovtsov, A.A., "Fortepiannaya muzyka" [Piano Music], *Ocherki,* pp. 160-197.

44. "Bol'she vnimaniya fortepiannoi muzyke. Otkrytoye pis'mo kompozitoram" [More Attention to Piano Music. An Open Letter to Composers], *Sovetskoye iskusstvo,* No. 50 (1334), June 23, 1951.

45. "Doklad B.V. Asaf'yeva," *op. cit.*

46. Prokof'yev, S., "Vystupleniye na sobranii kompozitorov i muzykovedov g. Moskvy" [Speech at the Meeting of Composers and Musicologists of Moscow], *Sovetskaya muzyka,* January-February 1948, No. 1, p. 66.

47. "Yunye gody," *Sovetskaya muzyka,* April 1941, No. 4.

48. *Ibid.*, p. 85.

49. *Puti,* pp. 67-68.

50. *Ibid.*, pp. 37-38.

51. *Puti,* p. 68.

52. "Sumbur vmesto muzyki—ob opere 'Ledi Makbet Mtsenskovo uyezda' " [Confusion Instead of Music: on the Opera *Lady Macbeth of Mtsensk District*], *Pravda,* No. 27 (6633), January 28, 1936. English translation in Seroff, Victor I., *Dmitri Shostakovich: The Life and Background of a Soviet Composer,* New York, Knopf, 1943, pp. 204-207.

"Baletnaya fal'sh' (Balet 'Svetlyi ruchei,' libretto F. Lopukhova i Piotvorskovo, muzyka D. Shostakovicha. Postanovka Bol'shovo Teatra)" [Falsification of the Ballet (The Ballet *Limpid Stream* with libretto by F. Lopukhov and Piotvorski and Music by D. Shostakovich. Performance by the Bol'shoi Theater)], *Pravda,* No. 36 (6642), February 6, 1936. English translation in Seroff, *op. cit.*, p. 207.

53. *Puti,* p. 68.

54. *Ibid.*, p. 63.

55. *Ibid.*, p. 69.

56. *Ibid.*

57. Koval', Marian, "O tvorchestve Dmitriya Shostakovicha"[On the Creative Work of Dmitri Shostakovich], *Izvestiya,* November 8, 1951.

58. *Puti,* pp. 71-72.

59. During the first years of the Soviet rule Glazunov, Ippolitov-Ivanov and Glière were at the head of the largest conservatories, those of Leningrad, Moscow and Kiev respectively. *Puti*, p. 36.

PART VI

National Schools

A. GENERAL PREMISES

Officially Soviet culture is a "multi-national" phenomenon to which the creative efforts of the different peoples inhabiting the Soviet Union have made significant contribution. The Soviet ideologists always ignore the obvious fact that the centrifugal forces at work in the Soviet Union are becoming so much stronger with every decade that one can speak of the unmistakable growth of a tendency towards the formation of nationally distinctive cultures among the various national groups within the Soviet Union.[1]

There is absolutely no reason, however, to think the Soviets have solved the question of national cultural self-determination. On the contrary, the Marxist-Leninist theory itself in relation to this question confirms unequivocally its imperialist essence in Stalin's well known "Report on the National Question" at the Third All-Russian Congress of Soviets in March, 1918, in which he said,

> All this [discussion] points to the necessity of interpreting the principle of self-determination as the right to self-determination not of the bourgeoisie but of the working masses in a given nation. The principle of self-determination must be an instrument in the struggle for socialism and must be subordinated to the principles of socialism.[2]

This attitude towards the question of cultural self-determination has defined actual Soviet practice which, particularly in the field of art, boils down to the "inalienable right" of the authors, artists, poets, and musicians of all the peoples inhabiting the Soviet Union to glorify the Soviet power in their native languages. As Stalin wrote on one occasion, "Is it possible that our comrades are not familiar with the well-known formula by Marxists concerning the fact that present-day Russian, Ukrainian, Byelorussian, and other [Soviet] cultures are socialist in content and national in form, i.e., in language?"[3]

Yet even if the existence of the Soviet national republics is problematical and illusory, still their external national characteristics have taught their inhabitants to realize that they represent a certain "national whole" not identical with other parts of the Soviet empire. Particularly the national languages employed in the institutions of the various republics—the language of the press, the school, literature, and the theater—could not but leave deep traces in the consciousness of the masses of the population of the Ukraine, Byelorussia, Georgia, Armenia, and the other national republics, teaching them to regard themselves as members of a definite cultural unit.

On the other hand the developing process of cultural interaction among independent ethnic groups in the Soviet Union has had the effect of strengthening the ties of cultural unity. The historical tradition of Russian literature, theater and music (based on their ability to comprehend and appreciate the rich originality of the inner world and culture of the non-Russian peoples) fostered mutual understanding and respect among the peoples of Russia and still continues to make itself felt. Even if one ignores the noisy clamor of Soviet propaganda, it is impossible not to recognize the unquestionable growth in the minds of the Soviet people of the conception of equality among the peoples regardless of their racial and national origin. Notwithstanding the use of national languages in the schools and the formation of national institutions of higher education, scientific institutions and musical and theatrical establishments in the national republics, the authority and significance within the Soviet empire of what was formerly Russian culture and the power of attraction of its cultural centers is not only unabated but on the contrary is becoming steadily more powerful. Among men of culture and art in Moscow and Leningrad one frequently encounters the names of people from the Ukraine, the Caucasus or Central Asia; similarly, the reverse process of an influx of Russian cultural forces into the national republics is being felt ever more strongly.

If the national genius of the peoples of the Soviet Union could only free itself from the Soviet policy of depriving the peoples of their individuality and if the peoples could obtain the right to free creative work within their native culture, there would become manifest the beneficial effect of a general interchange of spiritual values for mutual cross-fertilization between the different national cultures and for the development of historically conditioned principles for a culture and civilization common to all mankind.

In our time the question of national cultures, particularly in music, has been greatly exaggerated, especially in the Soviet Union. Musical culture has always been characterized by what unites rather than by what separates. "German," "French," "Italian," or "Russian" music is "national" not so much because the majority of composers of these schools were consistent interpreters of the "national soul" of their people as because they were followers of the school of the greatest representatives of their music.

Thus "national traits" in music manifest themselves less in the specifically "national" idiom of the composer than in the vividness of the creative system of thinking represented by a great individuality. Music is characterized by cultural integration rather than by differentiation.

In our time composers are most easily distinguished by the signs of the system which they profess (e.g., the followers of Schoenberg, Stravinsky or Hindemith) rather than by national traits—providing, of course, that they are not deliberate "folklorists." Even in the latter case, however, it is often possible to recognize the "national" character of their music only through a "folklore microscope" (e.g., the music of Béla Bartók).

To put it more simply: for the creation of a national musical culture the local folklore treasures of a people are less important than the presence of a genuinely great master able to create a school.

Thus arises the central problem of national musical cultures, the problem of "cadres" as it is called in the Soviet Union. It is, of course, a matter not simply of "cadres" who possess an academic technique and musical education and who are able to attain the level of contemporary creative mastery; it is a question of composers of outstanding importance, able to grow beyond the general level and to enrich the musical culture of the world with the new qualities of their own "national" originality.

Looked at in this way, it is clear that one could hardly expect the creation of national musical cultures where musical creative work has only recently entered the stage of the writing of music, as is the case in several of the Soviet republics.

This judgment is eloquently confirmed by the picture of musical life in the Central Asiatic republics presented in an article in *Soviet Music* entitled "A Decisive Turning Point is Necessary" concerning conditions of musical life in the Soviet republics of Central Asia—an article signed by A. Maldÿbayev, a People's Artist of the U.S.S.R., S. Shakhidi, Honored Artist of the Tadzhik S.S.R., M. Tulebayev, Honored Art Worker of the Kazakh S.S.R., and the composers Ashir Kuliyev of the Turkmen S.S.R., and M. Burkhanov of the Uzbek S.S.R..[4]

The authors of the article present a number of flagrant examples of bad composing practice, including the following: "The joint creative work of a composer-melodist[5] and a trained composer was frequently reduced to a point where one author would do work enough for two while another would only compose a melody, then sign his name on the manuscript of the finished composition as its rightful author";[6] "a number of composers who graduated from Tashkent Conservatory in 1945 are still not able to compose independently";[7] "the pedagogical staff also does not meet the requirements of a higher school; the training of musical cadres in Tadzhikistan and in the Kirghiz Republic is in a still more deplorable state";[8]

"some music schools accept absolutely untrained people of the local nationality just in order to be able to increase artificially their 'percentage'."[9]

The authors arrive at the conclusion that "in several Republics *there are at the present time no trained composers.*"[10]

> Without waiting until the schools produce national cadres, it is necessary now to send out fresh, trained creative forces. A great creative work must be developed in folklore studies. The field of musicology and music criticism must be stimulated. For this purpose it is necessary to send young musicologists graduated from the metropolitan conservatories to the republics of Central Asia.
>
> The creative forces brought from outside the republic, in addition to work on opera and ballet, should be able to help in creating a concert repertoire for philharmonic societies and radio committees. Choral work must attract composers and concert organizations.[11]

Of course no "fresh, trained creative forces" can be of any help where there are "at the present time no 'trained composers'." They could not help even if such "trained composers" existed in these republics. A national culture is established not by trained touring artists but by a full-blooded culture taking shape through centuries and, most of all, by a mature mastery of art by its representatives.

Under existing conditions it is natural that the "national" music that is created in these republics with the help of "trained composers," the emissaries of the Union of Soviet Composers, bears the unmistakable stamp of hybridization of that mass-song style that dominates all Soviet music, mechanically combined with local folk music.

B. THE UKRAINIAN NATIONAL MUSIC MOVEMENT[12]

1. DEVELOPMENT

The maturing of Ukrainian music is perhaps more significant, broad and many-sided than that of the music of any other Soviet national republic except Georgia and Armenia.

Prior to the present century, the Ukraine had a very weakly developed national school of music. There was only a limited number of professional composers there who had acquired a good technique and who were capable of expressing their own national originality within the scope of larger musical forms. At present, however, the number of Ukrainian composers has been considerably increased and there are some among them who reach the level of contemporary requirements.

The aspiration of Ukrainian composers towards the mature manifestation of a national style has encountered extremely complicated and unfavorable conditions. On the one hand, even as early as the 1920's voices were heard calling "away from Russian music" (this slogan, proclaimed by Professor M. Hrinchenko in his *History of Ukrainian Music* published in 1922, subsequently made a great deal of trouble for him); on the other hand there has been a powerful movement among Ukrainian composers for direct contact with Russian music. Finally the actual conditions of the development of Ukrainian music during the Soviet period have been conditioned by the imperatives of the Soviet art policy, with all its ensuing consequences.

Nevertheless it can be said that the basic characteristic of the "new" contemporary stage in the history of Ukrainian music is its aspiration towards universalism and completeness of creative mastery. If heretofore Ukrainian composers turned mainly to their national past, to history and to the national folklore, at present the fundamental characteristic of their creative work is its search for an integral ideal combining originality and the absolute, perfect and unchangeable features common to all music, to all mankind. Behind the distinct, the particular, the national, there appear human community and unity—the signs of a mature equilibrium of style.

This process is manifested especially in the fact that Ukrainian music is overcoming the intuitive creation and constructional improvisation characteristic of it in the past, with the predominance of small forms and vocal music and dependence on local folklore. In the place of a generalized conception of composition there is a striving for mastery of larger creative scope and a tendency towards pure instrumental media and towards attainment of the contemporary level of expressive means. Mature professionalism with its many-sided manifestation of creative thought, its universality of forms and means of expression and its pathos of affirmation has now become characteristic of the Ukrainian national school of music.

Even in the early twenties there was concentrated in Kiev, the center of Ukrainian culture, an important group of musicians who assisted in the new rise of Ukrainian national music by their creative, performing and organizational activities. Particularly noteworthy members of this group were the semi-professional composers Kyrylo Stetsenko (1882-1922), Yakiv Stepovyi (Yakymenko) (1883-1921), Mykola Leontovych (1877-1921), and Oleksander Koshyts' (1875-1945).

In the work of these men one still feels the strong attraction of the national musical tradition of the second half of the nineteenth century. This tendency is characteristic also of the works of Mykola Lysenko (1842-1912), one of the most important propagandists of Ukrainian national music during the late nineteenth century. This tradition is characterized by the predominance of material drawn from folk song, by the primacy of vocal genres and "arrangements" of folk songs, and by populist concepts and "melancholy" emotions. But these composers, particularly Leontovych, in their extensive use of folk music were trying to comprehend and embody creatively the many-sided manifestation of popular songs as an original form of national musical thought. Particularly in Leontovych's work, the basic principle is the personification of the separate voices of Ukrainian folk song in which each participant is a real force, an actual personage, a characteristic phenomenon. It is thanks to this dynamic understanding of the expressive qualities of folk song that the polyphony in the music of these composers loses its abstract associations, while the musical fabric becomes organically interwoven, unified by a texture in which each voice lives its own complete life in accordance with its expressive function. The homophonic principle of construction with a predetermined base of functional harmony that constituted one aspect of Ukrainian music of the past (particularly in the music of Lysenko) gradually disappears; harmonic polyphony or polyphonic harmony gives place to a dynamic polyphony which is rooted in the very nature of Ukrainian native song. Thus the active principle in Ukrainian folk music becomes the motive force directing the further development of the style of Ukrainian music.

It is mainly as the result of this feature that in the work of this group of composers the importance of an active treatment of the musical material is stressed, the limits of form are broadened and the role of individualized solo singing to some extent free from ethnographism is particularly developed (examples may be found in the songs for solo voice by Stetsenko and Stepovyi to texts by Shevchenko and Franko). In contradistinction to the choral arrangement of folk songs, a movement develops towards the creation of original choral works with a considerably augmented scope (e.g., *In Springtime* and *A Dream* by Stetsenko and *Shchedryk* [A Christmas Song], *The Fife-Player* and *The Thaw* by Leontovych). At the same time there is a growth in the level of individual professional mastery in the enrichment of harmony, in the utilization of more intricate tonal-modal relationships and the modal peculiarities of song and in the diversification of texture in general (instead of simply combining folk songs as had been done in the past, there is now a thematic development).

The increasingly individualized approach to creative problems is particularly evident in the experiments made by these composers with larger musical forms. Particularly noteworthy is their effort to get away from the "patchy" dramaturgy of the dramas of everyday life with inserted musical numbers of which there used to be a great number, and their attempt to master the principle of operatic composition (e.g., *The Haidamaks* and *Iphigenia in Tauris* by Stetsenko, *The Fires of St.*

John's Eve by Pidhorets'kyi and *A Mermaid's Holiday* by Leontovych). Many of the composers of this group had taken an active part in political life of the revolutionary epoch, a period when Ukrainian cultural organizations were especially active. It was at this time that there were organized the Ukrainian state choruses—the "Republican Capella" under the direction of Koshyts' which later became widely known through its appearances in Europe and America and the choral group "Dumka", directed at first by Stetsenko and later by Nestor Horodovenko, which for nearly a quarter of a century was the main representative of Ukrainian choral music.

During those years there was also organized the Lysenko Musical Institute on the basis of Lysenko's music school in Kiev. This school became the chief institution of higher musical education in the Ukraine and, prior to its "reorganization" as a conservatory in 1933, the major center for the education of national musical cadres. Also at that time there were organized, on the basis of former Russian opera houses, the first Ukrainian national opera houses in Kiev, Odessa and Kharkov, as well as philharmonic societies, music publishing houses, etc.

Thus was strengthened the broad movement of Ukrainian musical culture towards new horizons, a movement that was rooted in the cultural rebirth experienced by all the Soviet-dominated peoples at that time but which has been the object of harsh and unremitting repression by the Soviet power ever since the mid-twenties.

The establishment of Soviet power in Ukraine led to the complete rout there of national creative forces and sharply changed not only the form of the Ukrainian musical movement but the nature of its manifestation as well.

The outright physical destruction of several of the most important composers (e.g., Leontovych, who was killed in 1921 by agents of the secret police), the untimely death of many composers resulting from unbearable repressions and exile (e.g., Stetsenko and Stepovyi) or emigration (e.g., Akimenko, Koshyts' and Horodovenko); the liquidation of many institutions which had been created (e.g., the Lysenko Musical Institute)—such is the record of the Soviet national policy in the field of Ukrainian musical culture. From the time of the Soviet triumph everything was subordinated to carrying out Stalin's slogan "a culture national in form but socialist in content" and to the implementation of the policy of suppressing any free expression of creative development.

The full weight of this policy was felt by the new generation of Ukrainian composers who entered the field of musical activity in the mid-twenties. The organization around which was centered the activity of this new generation of Ukrainian composers was the "Leontovych Association" which had been organized as a committee to preserve the heritage of the composer and in which was preserved the atmosphere of creative activity that had been characteristic of the first years of the Revolution.

The most important representatives of this group were the composers Levko Revuts'kyi (born 1889), Borys Lyatoshyns'kyi (born 1895), Viktor Kosenko (1896-1938), Valentyn Kostenko (1895-1944?), Mykhaylo Verykivs'kyi (born 1896), and Pylyp Kozyts'kyi (born 1898); the historian of Ukrainian music Mykola Hrinchenko (1888-1945); the ethnographer and music critic Dmytro Revuts'kyi (1891-1942); and the music critic Masutin (exiled in 1935).

During the twenties and thirties another important Ukrainian national musical movement grew up in Lvov (western Ukraine), under substantially different conditions, prior to the establishment of Soviet power there in 1939. This movement was represented by such composers as Stanyslav Lyudkevych (1879-1950), Vasyl' Barvins'kyi (born 1888), Nestor Nyzhankivs'kyi (1894-1940), and Mykola Kolessa (born 1904). This group, working parallel to the composers of the Kiev group, played an important role in raising the level of maturity and originality of Ukrainian music.

Even in the mid-twenties, however, the Soviet art policy in the Ukraine clearly manifested its intention of transforming music into an applied means for political propaganda. In accordance with this policy the forms of organization of Ukrainian musical life were radically changed. A complete and systematic control by the Party was established in all sectors of musical activity. Everything that directly or indirectly served the aims of Bolshevism was encouraged while whatever was opposed to those aims was ruthlessly suppressed.

Even during the first years of the Soviet regime there began in the Ukraine, just as in the other parts of Soviet Russia, an intensified differentiation of creative forces, inspired by the Soviet authorities with the aim of facilitating their struggle against the nonconformists. Just as in Moscow and Leningrad there were established in the Ukraine several competing creative organizations with conflicting aims and ideals.

Side by side with the Leontovych Association—which after five years of existence was reorganized under political pressure as the "All-Ukrainian Association of Revolutionary Musicians" (abbreviated VUTORM)[13]—there were organized several unnecessary, ineffective bodies such as the "Association of Proletarian Musicians of the Ukraine" (abbreviated APMU),[14] which was in reality a branch of RAPM, and the "Association of Revolutionary Composers of the Ukraine" (abbreviated ARKU).[15] Attempts were even made to revive the activity of the Association of Contemporary Music (ASM). But whereas ASM, APMU and ARKU, with small memberships and weakened by internecine strife, left no trace on the musical life of the Ukraine, the All-Ukrainian Association of Revolutionary Musicians, tenaciously preserving the enlightened traditions of the Leontovych Association, was able to unite around its activities almost all the more important composers of the middle generation. The activity of this organization continued until nearly 1932, i.e., until the date of the Central Committee resolution "On the Reorganization of Art and Literary Organizations" which applied to art throughout the Soviet Union.

Following this resolution and particularly after the organization of the Union of Soviet Composers of the Ukraine in 1934 (actually a branch of the Union of Soviet Composers), there began a new stage of the complete enslavement of Ukrainian music, which in turn called forth a subversive opposition by Ukrainian music against the Soviet art policy. The struggle for the subordination of music to political aims became particularly acute in the Ukraine, being directed not only against any contact between Ukrainian music and contemporary Western music (labelled as "formalism" and "cosmopolitanism") but—and this is particularly important—against any and all manifestations of the desire of Ukrainian music to achieve its own originality.

Even in its external signs the development of Ukrainian Soviet music prior to 1934 strikes one by its intensive creative life, its variety of musical forms, its mastery and development of the techniques of contemporary writing, and its assimilation of larger forms, not merely in traditional vocal forms but also in instrumental music which had previously been little developed. Sonatas, suites, chamber works, concertos, and even symphonies and operas were being composed.

It was chiefly during the period before 1934 that Ukrainian composers wrote a number of major compositions of a quality never previously attained in Ukrainian music, e.g., Kozyts'kyi's choral works *The Wonderful Fleet* and *The New Atlantis;* the oratorio *Marusya Bohuslavka* and the *Requiem in Memory of Lysenko* by Verykivs'kyi; the suite *Kateryna* for chorus, orchestra and soloists by Zolotar'ov; choral works by Revuts'kyi on texts by Shevchenko and Tychyna; *The All-Seeing Eye* by Radziyevs'kyi; the operas by Yanovs'kyi *Explosion* and *Thoughts of the Black Sea;* Kostenko's operas *Karmelyuk* and *The Carpathians;* Zolotar'ov's *Khves'ko Andyber;* Lyatoshynski's opera *The Golden Hoop;* the *Romantic Symphony* of Kostenko; *Springtime* by Verykivs'kyi; the symphony and orchestral suite of Lyatoshyns'kyi; the *Heroic Overture* of Kosenko; a great number of instrumental sonatas, concertos and works for instrumental ensembles; and finally, the most important composition of those years, the *Second Symphony* of L. Revuts'kyi. Revuts'kyi's symphony is one of the most typical works in the Ukrainian repertoire. Its thematic material is deeply rooted in Ukrainian folk song, but nevertheless the composer has not used this material in a "documentary" way but has interpreted it creatively as the manifestation of an original system of musical thought.

Almost simultaneously there appeared several professionally mature compositions among the Lvov group of Ukrainian composers, for example, S. Lyudkevych's oratorio for chorus and orchestra *The Caucasus* to a text by Shevchenko and the same composer's symphonic poem *Stonemasons* after a poem by Franko; the orchestral rhapsody *Springtime*, the *Piano Concerto*, the *Sextet*, and other compositions by V. Barvins'kyi; and *The Lemko Wedding*, the *Ukrainian Suite* and the *Variations for Symphonic Orchestra* by Mykola Kolessa.

While their immediate predecessors depended mainly on the academic resources of the classical tradition, the Ukrainian composers mentioned above clearly display a tendency to absorb the influences of contemporary Western music, a tendency which is particularly manifest in such compositions as Lyatoshyns'kyi's *Second Symphony*, Revuts'kyi's *Second Piano Concerto* and Kolessa's *Variations for Symphonic Orchestra*.

What attracts attention in their means of expression is their broad and free treatment of folk music material which they employ as a thematic basis, their extensive application of the variation principle of development and elaboration, the complexities of their harmony, their frequent use of semitone intervals, and in general their tendency towards complex harmonic timbres and freedom of linear exposition and textural development. Like their predecessors this group of Ukrainian composers depends on national folk music as the principal source for the development of a national style. In their works, however, folk music is still to a considerable degree a material for stylization and arrangement rather than an organic language.

Such an upswing in creative work could not but contribute to a general rise of Ukrainian musical life as a whole. There was an extensive development in theatrical and concert life, musical education and amateur musical activity. The nationalization of the opera houses led inevitably to the creation of a Ukrainian operatic repertoire, based on such earlier works as Lysenko's *Taras Bul'ba* as revised and orchestrated by Revuts'kyi and Lyatoshyns'kyi, and the revisions of Hulak-Artemovs'kyi's *The Dnieper Cossack on the Danube* and Lysenko's *Natalka Poltavka*. The philharmonic societies and symphony orchestras which were organized in many cities, the music schools and conservatories in Kiev, Odessa and Kharkov, and the numerous choral groups and orchestras, particularly those composed of national instruments (bandores),[16] promoted the development of Ukrainian musical culture as a whole.

Naturally these developments called forth increased repression on the part of the Soviet Authorities, who were not at all interested in centrifugal aspirations in their "provinces." The All-Union Committee for Art Affairs with its "national branches" and its subsidiary organs (particularly the Union of Soviet Composers) began to exercise a watchful control over all aspects of Ukrainian musical life, imposing a firm limit to the further development of Ukrainian music.

By the mid-thirties numerous new groups of composers and musical workers who had been brought up in the Sovietized music schools began to make their appearance. The most striking peculiarity of this new generation of Ukrainian composers was the deep dichotomy manifest in their activities: on the one hand, a steadily increasing passivity and an external appearance of obedience to the will of the Party and the government, on the other an increasingly sharp but secret protest against the suppression of national and creative freedom.

Since that time the general development of Ukrainian music has followed the same path as that of Soviet music as a whole—the curbing of individuality and the lowering of musical culture. The subject matter of creative work has been decisively changed. Composers more and more, willingly or otherwise, turn their attention to themes of present-day Soviet life with its propagandistic political demands, employing that standardized "socialist realism" which is the expression of this creative levelling. Themes of the glorification of great and small leaders, of industrialization and collectivism of Soviet patriotism, of the mobilization of Party vigilance, of the current zigzags of the Party's internal policy—all this has gradually come to form the entire scope of the uninspired trade of Ukrainian, as of Soviet music.

It is particularly difficult for Ukrainian composers, however, to handle the theme of glorification of the leaders. First of all it is necessary for them to propitiate the local viceroys, who are often removed with a speed like that at which Soviet-made shoes wear out. A song composed in honor of some Lyubchenko, Postyshev, Kossior, or Dubovyi may become an immediate casualty and the composer may disappear from the horizon for many years unless he knows how to repent convincingly. Intimidated by such "creative" failures, therefore, Ukrainian composers often played safe by writing odes in praise of Stalin himself. It would seem that the composers of no other Soviet republic have written so many songs glorifying Stalin as have Ukrainian composers, and no wonder! There are so many dangers around that it is much better to insure one's safety ahead of time.

Another peculiarity in the creative work of the newer Ukrainian composers is their sharply changed attitude to the national Ukrainian song, which until recently was the basis for the formation of a national style. Now the Ukrainian folk song does not attract the composers' attention. On the contrary, even composers of the older generation, to safeguard themselves from accusations of "nationalist bias," make more extensive use of Russian folk song material. Russian song, they seem to think, is the original source of all musical cultures, as the composer Kozyts'kyi, who had formerly been one of the theoretical adherents of Ukrainian folk song, declared over the radio on one occasion. Naturally such an attitude makes everything much simpler. No one would dare to accuse the Russians of chauvinism!

A process of deliberate levelling of the national originality of Ukrainian music has set in, with everything being reduced to the academic standards of the school classics legalized by Soviet aesthetics. Every trace of individualization is being suppressed in order to avoid violating the thesis of the "mass" and "popular" character of Soviet music. The very structure of musical life has been simplified. The system of state planning has been applied to art as well, reducing the complicated process of interaction among composer, performer, listener, and state to a direct relationship in which everything is subject to state and Party control, from the composer's personal life to the satisfaction of the listener's needs. Under this system the Composers' Union distributes the orders handed out by the Committee for Art Affairs, supervises their execution, determines their "artistic"—or rather propaganda—value, and then arranges for their performance.

Thus Ukrainian composers and performers have been gradually transformed into functionaries of the propaganda apparatus. From time to time the decrees of the Party and government "take stock" of the progress of Soviet art and "direct" its further development. These decrees provide the occasion for yet another purge which helps to achieve a change of features not of Ukrainian but of Soviet music. As a result of such operations everything that in one form or another betrays a tendency to rise above the level of the official standard simply disappears from musical life, while everything that is in accord with the new course is elevated, with the aid of Stalin Prizes and various decorations, to a superlative degree as a model, an example to be imitated. As a result of such purges one hardly hears anything in recent years about the composers of the senior generation.[17] Instead the horizon of creative and organizational life of Ukrainian music is filled with new names, e.g., the Stalin Prize winners Zhukovs'kyi and Fylyppenko, whose only merit is that they are politically reliable. The stormy development of Ukrainian music during the twenties has given way to a feeble trade serving a bureaucratic system of propaganda and having nothing in common with live creation.

2. *THE CHARACTERISTICS OF UKRAINIAN MUSIC*

Nevertheless, in the Ukraine as in other parts of the Soviet Union, the vital sources of art are not exhausted and the necessity for freedom to breathe the atmosphere of creative work—the freedom which Ukrainian music enjoyed in the recent past—is still strongly felt. Ukrainian composers are still not reconciled to the harsh oppression of free creative thought, as one can readily see from the recurring necessity the Soviet authorities feel to shout at them—as though they were not already frightened and confused!

One of these peremptory shouts was the resolution of the Central Committee of the Communist Party of the Ukraine which was published following the All-Union Central Committee's resolution concerning Muradeli's opera *The Great Friendship.* In this resolution, on orders from the Kremlin, the "anti-popular formalist trend in Ukrainian music, as expressed in the works of composers B. Lyatoshyns'kyi (particularly in his second symphony), G. Taranov, I. Bėlza, M. Tits, M. Gozenpud, and others," was subjected to "sharp criticism."[18]

According to the resolution,

> ...the danger and great harm of the formalist trend in Ukrainian music is aggravated by the fact that individual Ukrainian composers have not yet rid themselves completely of a bourgeois nationalist ideology which is one of the most tenacious remnants of capitalism in the minds of people for whom servility and obsequiousness towards the bourgeois West have always been characteristic. ...Whereas one group of contemporary Ukrainian composers (Lyatoshyns'kyi and others)

> cover themselves with folk song motifs and create what are essentially "general European" compositions that are without any vital thoughts and which do not reflect the life of our people, another group (Verykivs'kyi and others) evaded Soviet reality by a retreat into the past and, under pretense of the preservation of national art, cultivated the outmoded, reactionary aspects of the past.

Finally the resolution reproaches Ukrainian composers for their attitude towards popular art:

> Among Ukrainian composers there is a considerable group of musicians whose attitude towards the people's musical and vocal creative work is superficial and passively dependent. In their works they do not display the ideational-artistic content and musical originality of the folk song; they do not understand it creatively and do not enrich it by the heroism of contemporary life. The music of these composers is dull, passively contemplative, emotionally colorless and vulgarly sentimental.

This resolution served as a basis for the report made on April 19, 1948 to the First All-Union Congress of Soviet Composers by the Secretary General of the Union of Soviet Composers of the Ukraine, Shtogarenko, who described the condition of musical creative work in the Ukraine. (Shtogarenko, by the way, had secured the confidence of the Party dignitaries by his cantata *My Ukraine* which is actually a dithyramb in honor of Stalin.)

According to Shtogarenko "the most flagrant example of the formalist trend" was B. Lyatoshyns'kyi. "Most of Lyatoshyns'kyi's vocal works composed during the twenties," Shtogarenko reported,

> were written to decadent and mystical texts and his instrumental music disclosed a tendency towards expressionism. In those works in which Lyatoshyns'kyi made use of Ukrainian folk song he emptied it of its content of ideas and destroyed its naturalness and simplicity. [His] opera *The Golden Hoop* is without tunefulness and expressiveness—its vocal parts are almost unsingable. In his second symphony, published in 1945, he continues to remain in the same formalist positions.[19]

Thus Shtogarenko once more (how often it has happened!)

attacked a man who is undoubtedly one of the most gifted, interesting and experienced Ukrainian composers, a man who even received an official decoration in 1939 in connection with the twenty-fifth anniversary of the Kiev Conservatory where he had taught composition for many years, a man who is a former chairman of the Composers' Union of the Ukraine, the author of three symphonies, two operas and a great number of instrumental and vocal works.[20]

Besides attacking Lyatoshyns'kyi who has long had the reputation in the Soviet Union of being an "incorrigible formalist," Shtogarenko asserted that in the symphony of G. Taranov dedicated to the thirtieth anniversary of the October Revolution and in his sextet dedicated to the memory of Zoya Kosmodemyanskaya,[21] there was a "clearly expressed orientation towards Western bourgeois culture."[22] Just think of it: in a sextet dedicated to a partisan heroine one can find not only "formalism" but a "clearly expressed orientation towards Western bourgeois culture"! Indeed, this is a "crime" which no amount of repentance could expunge!

But even this was not enough for the speaker. Shtogarenko was zealous in revealing "class enemies" and went on to attack the creative work of Klebanov, "in whose symphony the feeling of hopelessness and doom predominates." Indeed! How dare a Soviet composer not merely display hopelessness and doom in his work but even entertain such feelings while living in the Soviet conditions of—let us not say life but veritable holiday?

But the real point does not concern Klebanov who, incidentally, is an exceptionally gifted, comparatively young composer—the real point concerns the speaker himself. Shtogarenko, who is a graduate of the Kharkov Conservatory (1935 or 1936) is a talented but not very well educated composer who, having attracted attention by his unusual modesty, suddenly received a Stalin Prize for his cantata *My Ukraine* and was "promoted" to the chairmanship of the Composers' Union of the Ukraine. Evidently from fear of losing his position he became insolent and, confusing matters, attacked not only such officially recognized, so to say, "formalists" as Lyatoshyns'kyi and such "pessimists" as Klebanov but also completely moderate composers who sincerely love folk music and who have dedicated to it their entire not particularly easy creative life.

Shtogarenko himself, having been brought up in the atmosphere of Ukrainian interests, was always a "confirmed Ukrainian." In the Soviet Union to be a "confirmed Ukrainian," however, and to love and encourage one's own national aspirations is a very dangerous business. Shtogarenko, therefore, in order to take out insurance against his own Ukrainianism, decided to accuse others not of nationalist tendencies but—and this is simply staggering—of "national narrow-mindedness"! "National narrow-mindedness," he said at the Congress, "is characteristic of the creative work of M. Verykivs'kyi. He mechanically transfers popular song into his music without unfolding its deep content."[23] Truly a dramatic casuistry!

Is it any wonder that the Ukrainian composers have grown to fear Ukrainian folk music like fire? Who except the Party Central Committee and Shtogarenko can define the limit of "unfolding its deep content?" Wouldn't it perhaps be better not to try to "unfold" it at all? But then, ceasing to be a "nationalist," one would become a "formalist." It's a two-edged weapon! Ukrainian composers came to realize that the only way to preserve their very lives was to follow in the footsteps of Shtogarenko and glorify Stalin.

As was to be expected the greater number of "formalists" was found among the composers of the Lvov group, for they have experienced the "beneficial influence" of Soviet music policy only briefly. But Shtogarenko referred to them in rather muted tones—after all, it might be embarrassing, as those composers were newcomers, almost like the "foreign guests" in the Soviet Union.

He therefore merely remarked that "there are also certain

composers in Lvov who are lagging behind the spiritual interests of the Soviet people. Utilizing national melodies they frequently dress them up in an impressionistic manner."[24] To "lag behind the spiritual interests of the people" in the Soviet Union is a serious transgression, equivalent to feeling oneself free of Party obligations, i.e., feeling oneself to be not the slave of the "socialist state." Moreover, to "dress up national melody in an impressionistic manner" means not only "lagging behind the spiritual interests of the people" (i.e., of the Party), but attempting to oppose these interests with something of bourgeois origin, especially with something as exotic as impressionism. This is altogether bad!

A noteworthy characteristic of the creative work of the Lvov composers is their extensive use of local folk music. One of the distinctive features of folk music which has not yet been sufficiently investigated and explained is the role of musical dialects. The use of such local musical dialects had played an important role in the works of such prominent reformers of contemporary music as Béla Bartók. In the present context it is a matter of the "Hutzul" idiom which has acquired a definite individuality and significance. Its employment and development by composers would contribute significantly to the development of the national originality of Ukrainian music.

The internal and external dependence of contemporary music on local life and its organic contact with local folk music determined the characteristics of the music of the Lvov group of Ukrainian composers, particularly M. Kolessa. The deliberate disregard of this circumstance by the Soviet music policy certainly cannot promote the development of national musical cultures. Moreover the very methodology of Soviet music, "national in form and socialist in content," which is the basis of Soviet musical orthodoxy as applied to national musical culture, has nothing in common with the genuine essence of development of creative practice in the music of the peoples of the Soviet Union. Mechanically dividing the concepts of "form" and "content," this methodology inevitably pursues aims that are diametrically opposed to those of musical creation which, however it may be retarded, continues to develop in accordance with its inner laws.

The general enslavement of Ukrainian music has attained an even greater intensity during recent years. In the rise and fall of the waves of its development there is undoubtedly hidden a certain regularity corresponding to the rise and fall of political activity of the Kremlin politicians.

In 1951 *Pravda* again attacked the Ukrainian intellectuals, including the composers, accusing them of the gravest "ideological mistakes," which actually means covert opposition to the Party and the government.[25]

Even an orthodox composer like K. Dan'kevych was compelled to write a penitential letter to *Pravda* (July 25, 1951) in which he acknowledged the "errors" Pravda had pointed out in his opera *Bohdan Khmel'nyts'kyi.*[26] A tested member of the Komsomol, later in all likelihood a member of the Party, Dan'kevych had always been outstanding in his adherence to the Party and the government. His strong temperament had been lavishly devoted to the service of the "great Soviet people and the great Party of Lenin and Stalin," to quote the letter to *Pravda* in which he promises to "dedicate his life" to this service.

Dan'kevych had been extremely active not only as a composer but also as a "social worker" (it was no accident that he was "elected" chairman of the Ukrainian Union of Soviet Composers before World War II). In his work he was never interested in seeking creative originality, nor was he greatly troubled by creative problems in general; he was definitely hostile to those composers for whom such problems were more important than propaganda. From his very first compositions to his most recent ones (particularly his ballet *Stolen Happiness,* which for a long time was kept in the repertoire and in which he cleverly used political agitators as dancers), Dan'kevych has been a typical propagandist. Every bar of his primitively melodic and harmonically functional music, composed in the rigid style of seventeenth century symphonic music, is packed with Soviet propaganda. Yet even he had to repent for his "mistakes."

C. OTHER NATIONAL SCHOOLS

The development of the musical cultures of other peoples of the Soviet Union has followed a course analogous to that of Ukrainian music. Here, too, the national music movements which had made their appearance in pre-Soviet Russia in the form of "musical populism," with a preference for nationalist subjects and national folk music, reached their highest point during the 1920's and by the late thirties had been fully converted into outlying possessions of the Union of Soviet Composers.

The so-called "travelling sessions" which are organized periodically by the administration of the Union of Soviet Composers resemble in spirit the visitations of Ivan the Terrible's dreaded *oprichniki,*[27] although outwardly they look like vacation trips by the inhabitants of Moscow and Leningrad to Kiev, Tbilisi, Yerevan, Baku, Minsk, etc. Such occasions end, as a rule, with the complete rout of the "nationalist opposition," under cover of a struggle against "formalism" and "cosmopolitanism."

Even worse was the First All-Union Congress of Composers held in Moscow in 1948. There it was absolutely essential for the representatives from the national republics to discover not only in themselves but also in their national colleagues the most heinous sins. Thus the Georgian speaker at this convention, like his Ukrainian colleague, spared no words in attacking the "criminal activity" of Georgian "formalists" and "cosmopolitans."[28]

In his opinion the Union of Georgian Composers, containing nearly seventy composers and musicologists, had recently achieved great success in creating a number of compositions in the most diverse forms. But Georgian composers, "[who] for the most part are well acquainted with popular art," were accused of limiting themselves "to a merely superficial utilization of folklore." Furthermore, "in the work of some Georgian composers" was displayed "a disregard for the principles of Soviet aesthetics." For example, the composer Kiladze, who "made a successful debut in the symphonic form, and who created such remarkable pieces as his first orchestral suite and his symphonic poem *Gandegili,*" in his recent compositions did not give the melodic side of music "proper development." Also, in the opinion of the speaker, Mshvelidze, his own opera *The Tale of Tariele* "suffers from an overloading of the orchestra and from melodies which cannot be retained in the memory."

Altogether bad is the case of Balanchivadze who "in his ballet *The Heart of the Mountains,* his symphonic intermezzo *Lake Rits* and a number of his piano compositions has recently departed from the realistic basis of music." Moreover all is not well in the works of many other composers. In Tuskiya's *Violin Concerto* "the composer's melodic gift does not find free development"; Gokieli "in reworking the opera *Patara Kakhi* has transformed the national hero of the Georgian people into a hero of melodrama"; in the *First Symphony* of Machavariani and the compositions of Gabichvadze, "deliberate factors predominate," and so forth and so on. The speaker particularly deplored the fact that Georgian composers are "unhealthily attracted" to large forms and neglect the composition of songs.[29]

In his final statement, which has just been paraphrased, the speaker is entirely correct. Georgian composers obviously prefer large instrumental works to the mass-songs of political propaganda. Having had a good schooling (for many years Spendiarov, an excellent teacher and a pupil of Rimsky-Korsakov, taught in Georgia) Georgian composers not only can handle the larger forms with ease but employ in them the extremely interesting and original rhythms and intonations of Georgian national music.

There is also no doubt that such a "bias" towards larger forms and pure instrumentalism and towards the working out of the elements of a national style are deeply progressive phenomena, testifying to the high level of mastery of the Georgian composers, to their independence and their devotion to the ideals of creative freedom. By the same token these characteristics testify to the desire of Soviet Georgian composers not to have anything to with the primitive musical means and the thematics of Soviet propaganda imposed upon them by the Soviet art policy.

At the Congress of Soviet Composers in 1948 even more severe criticism was addressed to the Armenian and Azerbaidzhanian composers.

Of the Armenian composers it was said that "they are carried away by historical subjects and pay little attention to Soviet life," that "the great majority of [their] compositions do not find recognition among the people"; that they are "out of touch with the popular and national basis and disregard the national principle in music"; that they "complicate musical language," etc.[30] But the most horrible confession made by the Party speaker was that "one can observe a movement towards the principles of the formalist trend in the works of young Armenian composers," a fact fraught with serious consequences!

Armenian music, like that of Georgia, has long since outgrown populist ethnographism. With such composers as Aro Stepanyan, Ter Mairosyan, Araratyan, Kirakosyan, and Khachaturian—who is kept in Moscow by the Committee for Art Affairs as an exhibit for export—Armenian music is an independent, originally national and highly professional culture. The fact, for example, that Khachaturian's music is taking a secure place in world culture testifies to the high level of Armenian music. It would be a great loss for contemporary music if the creative work of Armenian composers were to lose its national individuality under pressure of the Soviet art policy. Yet symptoms have already appeared of a levelling of Armenian national characteristics in Khachaturian's music. Such symptoms can be detected in his ballet suites *Gayne* and *Masquerade* in which the compromise with mastery and taste is obvious.

The music of Azerbaidzhanian composers is less strongly original and less professional than that of Armenian and Georgian composers. They too, however, according to the Central Committee of the Azerbaidzhanian Communist Party, "have broken away from popular taste, pay no attention to the classical tradition and ignore and distort popular art."[31]

Thus Kara Karayev's *First Symphony*

> displays a complete absence of contact with popular song, abstractness of melodic material and a predilection for dissonant chords. Also formalist is the *Third Symphony* of A. Gadzhiyev in which a monotonous mechanical motion predominates. Formalism is likewise evident in F. Amirov's *Sonata* for piano and in his *Piano Concerto,* with an orchestra of national instruments written in association with Babayev. Inferior musical dramaturgy, superficiality of musical characterization and monotony of expressive means are the main shortcomings of Niyazi's opera *Khosrov and Shirin.*[32]

Even on the basis of this distorted criticism one is bound to recognize the fact that the composers of a number of Soviet national republics have not only mastered the larger forms but are also trying to keep pace with contemporary Western music, disregarding the demands of Soviet art policy, consistently developing the music of their own people and raising it to the level of a high and original culture.

Byelorussian music lives a comparatively undeveloped creative life. A rather weak professionalism testifies to the prevalence of ethnographism. Yet Byelorussian music has matured considerably in comparison with its past.

The long pedagogical activity in Minsk of Zolotar'ov, an

important pupil of Rimsky-Korsakov, helped promote the education of several Byelorussian composers who are perhaps caught in the snare of Party musical aesthetics only because of their professional weakness. Yet even so, the speaker at the 1948 Congress, a certain Bogatyryov (a rather elementary composer, not to be confused with S. Bogatyrev, an outstanding professor formerly at the Kharkov, now at the Moscow Conservatory) found it necessary to report that the opera *Kastus' Kalinovski* by D. Lukas was "professionally helpless"; that the songs by N. Sokolovski were "without ideas, vulgar and reminiscent of the gypsy style." and that in Aladov's music "modernist influence are in evidence."[33]

Incidentally Bogatyryov, in his capacity as guardian of the Party purity of Byelorussian music, also called attention to the treatment of Byelorussian folk songs by the composers of the Republic. In his opinion such songs were "always in a minor key, reflecting the hard life of the Byelorussian people in the past." Perhaps one might deduce from this circumstance that the present Soviet life also seems somewhat unattractive to Byelorussian composers.

The musical creative life of the other Soviet republics is extremely weakly developed. These republics have neither national composers of their own nor a sufficient basis for their development, since their artistic consciousness has not yet been developed. At best ethnographism flourishes and even that only within the limit of harmonization of folk songs.

As a rule experienced composers are periodically sent out to these areas on missions from Moscow; they collect ethnographic material and then, back in Moscow, write a "national opera" for yet another musical festival in Moscow. There is a well-established tradition by now of how to "compose" such works: the subject must describe the "hard life of the people in the past and their happiness in the communist present"; with regard to the music, local folk music is harmonized in accordance with the rules of functional harmony as presented during the first year of musical education.

Such "parades"–the festivals of national art of the Soviet Republics–always appear flying the banner of "gratitude" by the particular national group in question to the Party, the government and its leaders for their "happy life."

However, the guarantee for the duration of this happy life is extremely undependable. As a rule festivities end with the award of prizes and the simultaneous condemnation of everything displayed at the "parade" and even the exile of those who put on the display.

FOOTNOTES TO PART VI

1. The Soviet ideologist are of course well aware of this situation and in actual practice the Soviet power carries on an implacable struggle against "nationalist" tendencies.

2. Stalin, Joseph, "Doklad po natsional'nomu voprosu," *Sochineniya* [Works], Moscow, 1947, Vol. IV, pp. 31-32.

3. Stalin, Joseph, "Otnositel'no marksizma v yazykoznanii" [On Marxism in Linguistics], *Pravda,* June 20, 1950.

4. "Neobkhodim reshitel'nyi perelom! (O sostoyanii muzykal'novo iskusstva v respublikakh Srednei Azii)" [A Decisive Turning Point is Necessary (On the State of Music in the Republics of Central Asia)], *Sovetskaya muzyka,* January 1949, No. 1, pp. 98-103.

5. A "composer-melodist" is a native who can sing folk melodies; a "trained composer" is someone who has been sent out from Moscow by the Composers' Union to "assist" the composer-melodist in "creating" national operas, symphonies, ballets, etc.

6. *Ibid.*, p. 100.

7. *Ibid.*, p. 101.

8. *Ibid.*

9. *Ibid.*, p. 102.

10. *Ibid.* My italics.—A.O.

11. *Ibid.*

12. Part of the material in this section has appeared in Ukrainian in the author's article "XX st." [The Twentieth Century], in the section "Istoriya muzyky" [The History of Music] in *Entsyklopediya ukrainoznavstva* [Encyclopedia of Ukrainian Knowledge], Munich-New York, Naukove tovarystvo im. Shevchenka, 1949, Vol. 1, Part III, pp. 873-876. The article was written under the pseudonym Ye. Olens'kyi.

13. An abbreviation for *Vseukrainskoye Tovarishchestvo Revolyutsionnykh Muzykantov.*

14. *Assotsiatsiya Proletarskikh Muzykantov Ukrainy.*

15. *Assotsiatsiya Revolyutsionnykh Kompozitorov Ukrainy.*

16. A stringed musical instrument widely used in the Ukraine.

17. It is noteworthy, for example, that *Soviet Music* in 1949 "regretted" the "weak creative activity" displayed by L. Revuts'kyi in recent years: Kiselev, G., "L. N. Revutski (K 60-letiyu so dnya rozhdeniya)" [L.N. Revutski (For His Sixtieth Birthday)], *Sovetskaya muzyka,* April 1949, No. 4, p. 38.

18. "Pervyi vsesoyuznyi s"yezd sovetskikh kompozitorov. Sodoklady predstavitelei soyuznikh respublik" [First All-Union Congress of Soviet Composers. Reports by Representatives of the Union Republics], *Sovetskoye iskusstvo,* No. 17 (1105), April 24, 1948. Referred to hereafter as *Sodoklady.*

19. *Ibid.*

20. It is a curious fact that when it is necessary to display the creative mastery of Soviet composers, the Soviet organizers turn to the "formalists" and particularly to the music of Lyatoshyns'kyi. Thus in a series of concerts given after the war in Eastern Berlin as a demonstration of the achievement of Soviet music, Lyatoshyns'kyi's quartets were frequently performed and received most flattering critiques in the Berlin press. But that was Berlin! It is quite a different thing in Moscow where criticism is guided by considerations, not of music but of politics.

21. A heroine of the partisan warfare against the Germans during World War II.

22. *Sodoklady, op. cit.*

23. *Ibid.*

24. *Ibid.*

25. "Ob opere 'Bogdan Khmel'nitski'" [Concerning the Opera *Bohdan Khmel'nyts'kyi*], *Pravda,* July 20, 1951. For English translation

of text see *Current Digest of the Soviet Press*, Vol. III, No. 25, 1951, pp. 12-13.

26. Konstantyn Dan'kevych, "V redaktsiyu gazety 'Pravda'" [To the Editors of *Pravda*], *Pravda*, July 24, 1951. For English text see *Current Digest of the Soviet Press*, *op. cit.*, p. 23.

27. A special group of semi-military officials organized by Ivan IV.

28. *Sodoklady*, *op. cit.* See also "Vsesoyuznyi s"yezd sovetskikh kompozitorov" [All-Union Congress of Soviet Composers], *Pravda*, April 22, 1948.

29. *Sodoklady*, *op. cit.*

30. *Ibid.*

31. *Ibid.*

32. *Ibid.*

33. *Ibid.*

PART VII

Conclusion

In a recent issue of *Soviet Music* a reviewer of Thomas Mann's novel *Doctor Faustus* quotes the author's words to the students of Zurich: "Today a work has value only if it assists in some way in creating the atmosphere for a new humanism."[1]

The Soviet critic twists this thought to mean that a work of art has value only when it has been transformed into a tool in the political struggle for the aims of Bolshevism, since it is allegedly only in this way that it can serve to create the "atmosphere of a new humanism."

In the general problem of contemporary art such a presentation of the question is, of course, merely an ominous detail in the eternal argument about freedom of art, an argument that simultaneously raises another question: freedom from what?

Which aspects of human life ought to be banished from art by force? Is it those aspects to which art on this side of the Iron Curtain devotes its strength and skill, or those with which the Central Committee of the Communist Party is so concerned?

Of course it would be strange and unnatural if contemporary art were not to reflect the entire reality of life and were to withdraw into the realm of poetic fantasy of the romantic past—or into the world bounded by Communist Party resolutions. Is the proper sphere of art contemplation or personal feeling or political considerations? Has art not the right to explore *every* aspect of the world and to live a vital and many-sided life? Defending the thesis

---

1. "Kniga o gibeli burzhuaznovo iskusstva" [A Book About the Downfall of Bourgeois Art], *Sovetskaya muzyka,* 1951, No. 5, p. 119.

that art has the right to take its material from everywhere, even from the decrees of the Communist Party Central Committee, is therefore not in itself equivalent to demanding the deformation of art. In this sense the Soviet cultural politicians' belief in "socialist realism," "art for the masses" etc., might not lead to the decline of art.

The chief cause of the tragic deformity of Soviet art is not so much the fact that it serves the aims of communism as that it must serve those aims by *compulsion*, by *force*, by *order*. The demand that art should serve the cause of communism results not from any creative impulse on the part of the artists themselves but from the decrees of the Central Committee. Soviet art's attempts at orthodoxy in line with the Party aesthetics are non-artistic not so much because the artist has tried to create his work within the framework of communist policy as because the sources of his inspiration have been forcibly transplanted to the offices of the Party.

Here, precisely, lies the tragic meaning of the question of artistic expediency in Soviet art. The fact that the struggle to compel art in the Soviet Union to become the mouthpiece of communist ideology is so stubborn, protracted and strained is evidence that this struggle not only has no organic foundation but is hostile to the very nature of art. The world outlook that is being imposed upon the Soviet artist is strange and incomprehensible to him and powerless to kindle in him the desire to serve it. Art's service to the aims of communism is a matter of the artist's taste, honesty and conscience and in no way an organic problem of contemporary art.

Soviet propaganda's hypnotic phrases about "serving the people," which actually mean serving the Party policy, do not seem to have had such an effect upon the representatives of Soviet art that it is necessary to despair of the fate of art. But the question of compulsion of the artist, of the enforced reduction of art to a tool of propaganda, of the usurpation of art by the government Party and by dictatorship is another matter entirely. This is a question not merely of what art should express but of the very destiny of art, its future, its life or death—not only the life or death of Russian art or of the art of the peoples of the Soviet Union but of art as a whole.

The musical culture of the world is a treasure house of many centuries and of many peoples. It is multiform and common to all mankind. One of its component parts, and by no means the least important, is Russian music. In all its manifestations Russian music breathed the same creative air as world music; it had the same aspirations, the same creative conceptions. The Communist dictatorship, however, fences off Russian culture from the rest of the world by an Iron Curtain, forcibly disrupting its contact with world culture; it prevents the free development of creative forces among the peoples it dominates, and it reduces their creative originality to nonexistence.

Russian culture, particularly music, is undergoing the agony of a dark night in its history. True, Russian culture has not yet died and will not die as long as the people who have created it still exist. Sooner or later it will regain its freedom and will enter upon the road of cooperation with other peoples, with all mankind; but this fact does not minimize the acuteness of the present situation of Soviet music.

The pronouncements of the Soviet government in the field of music, like the propaganda carried on by the Soviet press to support them, are clumsy and ignorant, but to those who do not know the actual state of affairs, who still are ready to believe the Soviet myth about a "golden age," these declarations, with their hypocritical concern for "music for the masses," are unfortunately still attractive. How many people are there outside the Soviet Union who realize that the personal and creative lives of Soviet composers, even the greatest of them, depend completely and unreservedly on the overt and covert intrigues of the Politburo and its apparatus of coercion? How many are aware of the fact that a thorough, detailed and brutal check-up on the loyalty of Soviet musicians is one of the ordinary, day-to-day, "lawful" methods of "re-educating" Soviet musicians in conformity with the decrees of the Party and government?

The artist lives only when he is able not merely to preserve his inner life but to carry it to completion. It is to the exalted and intense inner lives of Russian composers that Russian music is indebted for its genuine and invaluable creative treasures, in contrast to the incompetent works of political propaganda which the Soviet authorities offer as models of "Soviet art." But none of the successes of Soviet composers achieved under pressure of the Soviet art policy can replace that inner world in which the artist is called upon to live, a world which is perhaps hidden deeply in the inmost recesses of his heart but which from time to time breaks through in brief gleams, leaving its traces in the pages of his scores.

Mankind in general and the artist in particular live by something more than the mere will to survive and the necessity for material success. One may call this urge "the lure of distance," the lure of the future, or the call of immortality, for the dream of the future is the basis of immortality. And the brighter this dream, the more effectively it has been embodied in art, the more joyful it is, the more profound is the feeling it imparts of the immortality of the creative spirit. Is it strange that Soviet artists in their work also strive towards this joy? And if in the creative work of even the best of them this faith in the future has expired, the fault is in no way theirs; the guilty ones are those who have deprived them of this faith, those who have disseminated the lie about the "golden age" in order to conceal their own lack of faith—their lack of that faith which is absent from materialist Soviet communism itself.

All the innumerable material, moral and artistic sacrifices

which Soviet life has brought with it have been made for the sake of those who are to come, for the future. What would be their value if these sacrifices had been made merely in order to achieve material well-being? The aesthetics of the Soviet music policy which requires that music limit itself to the political tasks of the moment—this is in all literalness the aesthetics of spiritual poverty.

Under the conditions of Soviet life spiritual values have catastrophically declined; crude "realism" increasingly saps the spiritual power of the artist, forcing him to strive for success in terms of political propaganda. Soviet musicians are deprived of their right to make use of the achievements of the world's musical culture; their responsibility for the future of music, for the continuation of its age-long development, is reduced to the service of a cheap and vulgar naturalism. Worst of all, it seems that a time has arrived when the younger generation of composers, whose tastes have been poisoned, feels no need for either the genuine creative spirit or for music itself as the "lure of distances." The humiliation of the creative spirit by political reality more and more compels not only artists of modest talents but even those whose gifts are outstanding to submit to the domination of ignorance and tastelessness.

Contemporary art, with its love of life and of the world, its deliberate rejection, under the pressure of materialism, of metaphysics and mysticism, its aspiration to create a "poetry of objective life" in opposition to the symbolism of the recent past, its concentration on the exterior world and the "objective" experiences of the "wholesome" personality—contemporary art generally is inclined to stress those aspects of creative work which stands in opposition to the art of the past which aspired to interpret man's inner states of mind and to penetrate into the inmost secrets of the world.

Soviet art policy, however, with its aesthetics of "socialist realism," destroys outright the art which opens up unsuspected depths within the heart, which helps man feel his hidden reserves of tenderness, sadness and delight, of thirst for happiness; and in its place it offers only the primitive aesthetics of the "classics" of the 1860's which have long since outlived their usefulness.

Every work of art, of course, is based on a modification and development of what the artist has learned; but whoever repeats himself in art will die, for the artist's dream is to express himself differently from others and even differently from what he himself was once. In the Soviet Union the highest premium is placed on the ability "to express everyone's thoughts through one's own expression," to give voice to the general feeling; otherwise, it is claimed, art will not be understood by the masses. It goes without saying that genuine simplicity is excellent, but it is accessible only to exceptional people. In Soviet art "simplicity" becomes prosaic and bare, whereas in genuine art everything simple, everything natural, is genuinely beautiful.

The tragedy of Soviet composers lies in the fact that they are forcibly restrained from following the dream of beauty which beckons to them. Not only as musicians but also as men they are unusually complex and contradictory. The exalted spirituality of the most outstanding among them and their genuinely religious nature, brought up in the spiritual culture of the past, are combined with the dark, elementally sensuous bases of Soviet life. Extremely sensitive in their creative work, they give expression to the most complicated trends of their epoch, embodying in their music all its contradictions: the sense of approaching doom, the struggle of faith against unbelief, the poignant moral resistance against darkness, pity for humanity, conscience, shame, and the fateful desire for an immediate catastrophe. It is as though the most delicate vibrations of the best which mankind has created resound in their music, coming into collision with the dark, elemental forces encroaching upon their souls from the destructive elements of Soviet reality.

Whatever takes place behind the Iron Curtain relates in equal measure both to Soviet artists and to all those outside the Soviet empire who value art. For the agony of the art of the peoples of the Soviet Union is the consequence not of its creative exhaustion but of its unprecedented enslavement by political authorities bent on subordinating art to their aggressive aims.

The symptoms of the agony of Soviet music have a deeper and broader significance than their relation to the present day and to music alone. They are component parts of that gigantic struggle in which the contemporary world is engaged concerning the question: which is more important, man or the system which enslaves him, the personal or the impersonal, the spiritual or the material? The struggle of the Soviet power against the freedom of music is only a sinister detail in this controversy. For the composer, for the musician in general—as for all mankind today—this is not merely a controversy over the "atmosphere of a new humanism"; it is a choice between man and the system, man and an abstract principle, man and a political idea. It is a struggle for life, a defense of humanity against barbarism.

The agony of the music of the peoples of the Soviet Union is more profound than it might seem at first glance. It is rooted in the materialistic nihilism of Soviet art policy, in its deliberate negation of the spiritual creative meaning of life, in its suppression of man's right to freedom of thought and feeling.

But in the world of enslavement where the very idea of art is being killed, no social reforms can save mankind from hopeless degradation. The safeguarding of creative freedom, particularly the *freedom of contemporary art,* is therefore the most urgent task of our times.

During its historical development art has gone through many styles, schools and trends. It has experienced many disappointments and setbacks, but always its unconquerable essence has remained firm, even during the days when the earth trembled: the breath of creative freedom without which thought becomes deadened, expressive power grows numb, talents wither, and the divine spark of artistic insight is extinguished. Like goodness and truth, creative freedom is an eternal and primary urge which human nature, unencumbered by the burden of lies, always strives to achieve. Every depreciation and perversion of creative freedom inevitably becomes a repudiation and profanation of the divine principle in man. And in the end art will also survive the abyss of the troubled Soviet times. But to attain this goal it is essential that the enslaved peoples should again take heart and revive their former will to fight, their ability to withstand violence. The pledge of their revival lies in the creative work of the best Soviet composers—those in whose hearts the music of freedom still sounds—and in the fact that among the broad masses of Soviet-dominated peoples the need for genuine art has not yet been suppressed.

The heart of art is still alive in the Soviet Union. The experiments carried out on it by the Communist Party and the secret police have not yet destroyed it. Its power lies in the fact that not only the best Soviet composers but the Soviet people as a whole know and believe that

> Although clouds obscure the sun,
> It still remains radiant.

ANNEX A

Text of the decree "On the Reorganization of Art and Literary Organizations," issued by the Central Committee of the Communist Party of the Soviet Union (Bolsheviks) on April 23, 1932:[1]

The Central Committee ascertains that, as a result of the considerable successes of socialist construction, literature and art have, in the past few years, exhibited a considerable growth, both in quality and quantity.

Some years ago, when literature was still under the strong influence of certain alien elements, which flourished particularly in the first years of the NEP, and when the ranks of proletarian literature were still comparatively feeble, the Party helped, by every means in its power, in the creation of special proletarian organizations in the spheres of literature and art, with a view to strengthening the position of proletarian writers and art workers.

Now that the cadres of proletarian literature have had time to grow, and new writers have come forward from factories, mills, and collective farms, the framework of the existing literary organizations (VOAPP, RAPP, RAPM, etc.)[2] has become too narrow and holds back the serious growth of literary creation. This situation creates the danger that these organizations may be transformed from a means for the greater mobilization of Soviet writers and artists around the tasks of socialist construction into a means for the cultivation of group insulation, for isolation from the political tasks of the day, and from those significant groups of writers and artists who now sympathize with the aims of socialist construction.

Hence the necessity for an appropriate reorganization of the literary-artistic associations and for the extension of the basis of their work.

Therefore the Central Committee resolves:

---

1. "O perestroike literaturno-khudozhestvennykh organizatsii," *Pravda,* April 24, 1932. Translation, used with permission of the publishers, from Brown, Edward J., *The Proletarian Episode in Russian Literature,* New York, Columbia University Press, 1953, pp. 200-201.

2. VOAPP: All-Union Organization of Associations of Proletarian Writers. RAPP: Russian Association of Proletarian Writers.

1) To liquidate the Association of Proletarian Writers (VOAPP, RAPP):

2) To unite all writers upholding the platform of the Soviet power and striving to participate in Socialist construction into a single Union of Soviet Writers with a Communist fraction therein;

3) To promote a similar change in the sphere of other forms of art;

4) To entrust the Organization Bureau with the working out of practical measures for the application of this resolution.

ANNEX B

Text of the decree "On the Opera *The Great Friendship* by V. Muradeli," issued by the Central Committee of the Communist Party of the Soviet Union (Bolsheviks) on February 10, 1948:[1]

The Central Committee of the All-Union Communist Party considers the opera *The Great Friendship* (music by Vano Muradeli, libretto by G. Mdivani) produced at the Bol'shoi Theater of the U.S.S.R. on the Thirtieth Anniversary of the October Revolution to be vicious and inartistic in both its music and its subject matter.

The basic defects of the opera lie first of all in the music. The music is feeble and inexpressive. It contains not a single melody or aria to be remembered. It is confused and disharmonious, built on complicated dissonances, on combinations of sound that grate upon the ear. Some lines and scenes with pretensions to melodiousness are suddenly broken by discordant noises wholly strange to the normal human ear and oppressive to the listener. Between the musical accompaniment and the development of the action on the stage there is no organic connection. The vocal part of the opera—the choral, solo, and ensemble singing—produces a miserable impression. As a result of all this, the potentialities of the orchestra and the singers are not exploited.

The composer has not made use of the wealth of folk melodies, songs, tunes, and dance motifs in which the creative life of the people of the U.S.S.R. is so rich, and especially the artistic creation [tvorchestvo] of the peoples of the North Caucasus where the action of the opera is laid.

In the pursuit of a false "originality" in music, the composer, Muradeli, has neglected the best tradition and the experience of the classic opera in general and Russian classic opera in particular, which is distinguished by inner substance, by richness of melody and breadth of diapason, by popularity [narodnost'] of appeal, by grace, beauty, and clarity of musical form. These characteristics have made Russian opera the best in the world, a species of music loved by and comprehensible to the wide masses of the people.

---

1. "O opere 'Velikaya Druzhba' V. Muradeli, Postanovleniye TsK VKP (b) ot 10 fevralya 1948 g.," *Sovetskaya muzyka,* 1948, No. 1, pp. 3-8. Translation used by permission of the authors and publishers from Counts, George S. and Nucia Lodge, *The Country of the Blind: The Soviet System of Mind Control,* Houghton Mifflin, Boston, 1949.

The plot of the opera, which pretends to portray the struggle for the establishment of Soviet power and friendship of peoples in the North Caucasus in 1918-21, is historically false and fictitious [iskusstvennyi]. The opera creates the erroneous impression that the peoples of the Caucasus, such as the Georgians and the Ossetians, were at that time hostile to the Russian people. This is historically false. It was the Ingushi and Chechen who opposed the establishment of friendship among peoples of the North Caucasus at that time.

The Central Committee of the Party holds that the failure of Muradeli's opera is the result of the formalistic path which he has followed—a path which is false and injurious to the creative work of the Soviet composer.

The conference of Soviet musicians, conducted by the Central Committee of the Party, showed that the failure of Muradeli's opera is not an isolated case. It is closely linked with the unsatisfactory state of contemporary Soviet music, with the spread of a formalistic tendency among Soviet composers.

As far back as 1936, in connection with the appearance of Dmitri Shostakovich's opera *Lady Macbeth of Mtsensk, Pravda,* the organ of the Central Committee of the Party, subjected to sharp criticism the anti-popular formalistic perversions in his music and exposed the harm and danger of this tendency to the future development of Soviet music. Writing then on instructions from the Central Committee of the Party, *Pravda* formulated clearly the Soviet people's requirements of their composers.

Notwithstanding these warnings, and also in spite of instructions given by the Central Committee of the Party in its decisions on the journals *Zvezda* and *Leningrad,* on the moving picture *Great Life* [*Bol'shaya Zhizn'*], and the repertoire of the dramatic theatres and measures for its improvements, no reorganization took place in Soviet music. The individual successes of some Soviet composers in the creation of widely popular songs, in the composition of music for the cinema, and so on, do not alter the general situation. The state of affairs is particularly bad in the field of symphonic and operatic music. The question at issue concerns composers who adhere to the formalistic anti-popular tendency. The very fullest expression of this tendency is found in the works of such composers as Dmitri Shostakovich, Sergei Prokof'yev, Aram Khatchaturian, Vissarion Shebalin, G. Popov, N. Myaskovski, and others whose compositions represent most strikingly the formalistic perversions and anti-democratic tendencies in music which are alien to the Soviet people and their artistic tastes. The characteristic marks of this music are the negation of the basic principles of classical music: the cult of atonality, the dissonance and discord supposedly expressive of "progress" and "novelty" in the development of musical form, the rejection of such a vital principle of musical composition as melody, and enthusiasm for confused, neuropathological combinations which transform music into cacophony, into a chaotic medley of sounds. This music reeks strongly of the odor of the contemporary, modernistic, bourgeois music of Europe and America which reflects the decay of bourgeois culture, the total negation, the impasse of musical art.

An essential mark of the formalistic tendency is also the rejection of polyphonic music and singing based on the simultaneous arrangement and development of a series of independent melodic lines and an enthusiasm for monotonous unisonic music and singing, often without words. This constitutes a violation of the many-voiced system of music and singing native to our people, and leads to the impoverishment and decadence of music.

Many Soviet composers despise the best traditions of Russian and Western classical music, reject these traditions as supposedly "obsolete," "old-fashioned," and "conservative," and contemptuously regard composers who strive conscientiously to master and develop the methods of classical music as advocates of "primitive traditionalism" and of "epigonism." In the pursuit of mistakenly understood innovation, they have lost contact in their music with the needs and artistic taste of the Soviet people, formed a narrow circle of specialists and musical gourmands, lowered the high social role and narrowed the significance of music, confining it to the satisfaction of the perverted tastes of esthetic individualists.

The formalistic tendency in Soviet music has bred in a section of Soviet composers a one-sided enthusiasm for complex forms of instrumental symphonic textless music and a disdainful attitude toward such musical forms as opera, choral music, popular music for small orchestras, for popular instruments, vocal ensembles, and so on.

The inevitable result of all of this is that the foundation of vocal culture and dramaturgic mastery will be lost and that composers will forget how to write for the people. Evidence of this is the fact that not a single Soviet opera on the level of the Russian classical operas has been written in recent times.

The loss of contact with the people by some Soviet composers has resulted in the propagation of the putrid "theory" that the failure of the people to understand the music of many Soviet composers is due to the fact that the people allegedly are not yet sufficiently "mature" to understand their complex music, that they will understand it in centuries to come, and that the lack of popular appeal of certain musical works is nothing to worry about. This thoroughly individualistic and fundamentally anti-popular theory has still further encouraged some composers and musicologists to draw off from the people, from the criticism of the Soviet public, and to retire into little individual worlds of their own.

The cultivation of these and similar views brings the greatest harm to Soviet musical art. A tolerant attitude toward such views signifies the spread among representatives of Soviet musical culture of alien tendencies which lead to a blind alley in the development of music, to the liquidation of musical art.

The vicious anti-popular formalistic tendency in Soviet music also has a baleful influence on the preparation and education of young composers in our conservatories and, first of all, in the Moscow Conservatory (the Director of which is Comrade Shebalin) where the formalistic tendency is dominant. Respect for the best traditions of Russian and Western classical music is not inculcated in the students, and love for popular creative art and democratic musical forms is not nurtured in them. The work of many students in the conservatories is a blind imitation of the music of Shostakovich, Prokof'yev, and others.

The Central Committee of the Party finds the state of Soviet musical criticism utterly intolerable. The opponents of Russian realistic music, the partisans of decadent and formalistic music, hold a leading position among the critics. They interpret every new composition by Prokof'yev, Shostakovich, Myaskovski, or Shebalin as a "new conquest of Soviet music." They glorify the subjectivism, the constructivism, the extreme individualism, and the technical complexity of the language of this music, that is, precisely everything that should be subjected to criticism. Instead of smashing views and theories harmful and alien to the principles of socialist realism, musical criticism assists in the spread of these views by praising and proclaiming as "advanced" those composers who in their work share erroneous creative purposes.

Musical criticism has ceased to express the opinion of Soviet society, the opinion of the people, and has been converted into a speaking trumpet for individual composers. Some music critics, instead of giving objective criticism based on principle, have taken to humoring and fawning on certain leaders of music and praising their work to the skies, for reasons of personal friendship.

All of this means that some Soviet composers, nourished on the influence of contemporary decadent West European and American music, have not yet shaken off the vestiges of bourgeois ideology.

The Central Committee of the Party considers this unfavorable situation on the front of Soviet music to be the result of the incorrect line in the field of Soviet music which has been pursued by the Committee on Art Affairs under the Council of Ministers of the U.S.S.R. and the Organizational Committee of the Union of Soviet Composers.

The Committee on Art Affairs under the Council of Ministers of the U.S.S.R. (of which Khrapchenko is chairman) and the Organizational Committee of the Union of Soviet Composers (headed by Khachaturian), instead of developing the realistic tendency in Soviet music which is founded on a recognition of the tremendous progressive role of the classical heritage, and particularly the traditions of the Russian musical school, actually encouraged the formalistic tendency which is alien to the Soviet people. They failed to utilize and develop this heritage with its emphasis on union of high content with artistic perfection of musical forms, on honesty and realism, on deep organic connection with the people and their musical and vocal art, on high level of professional artistry combined with simplicity and comprehensibility of musical works.

The Organizational Committee of the Union of Soviet Composers has become the tool of a group of composers of the formalistic school and the main nursery of formalistic perversions. In the Organizational Committee a stale atmosphere has been created; creative discussions are lacking. The heads of the Organizational Committee and the musicologists grouped around them sing the praises of anti-realistic, modernistic compositions undeserving of support, while works which are distinguished by their realistic character and by an effort to continue and to develop the classical heritage are declared to be second-rate, remain unnoticed, and are treated in a supercilious manner. Composers who pride themselves on being "innovators" and "arch revolutionaries" in music conduct their activities in the Organizational Committee like champions of the most backward and mouldy conservatism, showing a contemptuous intolerance toward the slightest suggestion of criticism.

The Central Committee of the Party considers that the situation and the attitude toward the tasks of Soviet music which are found in the Committee on Art Affairs under the Council of Ministers of the U.S.S.R. and in the Organizational Committee of the Union of Soviet Composers can no longer be tolerated because they do immeasurable harm to the development of Soviet music. During recent years the cultural needs and the level of artistic taste of the Soviet people have advanced greatly. The Soviet people expect from composers works of high quality and ideological content in all categories—in operas, in symphonic music, in song writing, in choral and dance music. In our country composers enjoy unlimited opportunities for creative work and all the conditions essential for the genuine flowering of musical culture. Soviet composers have an audience such as no composer of the past has ever known. For them to fail to make use of all these rich possibilities and to direct their creative efforts along the correct realistic path would be inexcusable.

The Central Committee of the All-Union Communist Party resolves:

1. To condemn the formalistic tendency in Soviet music as against the people and as leading actually to the liquidation of music.

2. To propose to the Department of Propaganda and Agitation of the Central Committee and the Committee on Art Affairs that they endeavor to correct the situation in Soviet music, liquidate the shortcomings set forth in the present resolution of the Central Committee, and ensure the development of Soviet music in the direction of realism.

3. To call upon Soviet composers to become aware of the lofty demands made on musical art by the Soviet people, to clear away everything that weakens our music and hampers its development, to ensure that upsurge of creative work which will advance Soviet musical culture rapidly and lead to the creation of finished works of high quality, worthy of the Soviet people, in every branch of music.

4. To approve organizational measures of the appropriate Party and Soviet organs directed toward the improvement of musical affairs.

ANNEX C

Excerpts from and comment on an article by G. Dombayev, "O nekotorykh voprosakh kontsertnoi raboty" [Concerning Certain Questions of Concert Work], *Sovetskaya muzyka* [Soviet Music], April, 1950, No. 4, pp. 39-47.

In reviewing Dombayev's article, the editor of *Soviet Music* writes:

> Dombayev's article touches upon extremely important questions concerning the organization of concert activity in our country. The author quite correctly points to serious shortcomings in the work of Soviet musical institutions and offers a number of useful suggestions to raise the ideological and artistic level of concert work.

Dombayev begins:

> There is no need to demonstrate the importance of the problems facing our philharmonic societies which have been called upon systematically, according to plan and in a well-thought-out manner to propagate among the broadest strata of the Soviet people the best compositions of the musical art of the past and present and the achievements of our talented musical performers in all forms.

As one of the basic reasons for the unsatisfactory work being done by individual philharmonic societies, Dombayev cites poor planning:

> The plan of the philharmonic society should reflect the ideological and artistic spiritual interest of the broad strata of Soviet society. The plan must be realistic. Nevertheless it usually is drawn up in the art director's office and is then passed on from office to office for approval. Often the performers themselves only learn of its existence after it has been approved.

Naturally, with such "planning" of the work of the philharmonic societies, it is impossible to "spare the public from joyless, boring and uninteresting concert seasons, lacking in serious ideological and artistic content, and discouraging the public's desire to attend concerts." Insufficient consideration is given "to the level of musical development of the audience of each philharmonic society," and the "actual performing ability of conductors and orchestras."

> Superficial and immature performance of an ideologically significant and technically complex composition creates a wrong impression among the public; as a result a deserving work may be dropped from the society's repertoire for a long time. To restore later on the authority of a composition which has been undeservedly discredited requires much time and considerable effort. ... We think that it is not always expedient to arrange programs consisting entirely of new works by Soviet composers. Such concerts usually bear the stamp of haste and slovenliness, and create a negative impression upon the audience.

There is no doubt that behind this superficially safe formulation on the subject of programs dedicated entirely to Soviet composers, there is hidden a more profound evaluation of the creative work itself which does indeed create "a negative impression upon the audience."

In the seemingly small details to which Dombayev draws our attention there is evidence of that slovenliness which Soviet audiences invariably encounter in the organization of concerts.

> It is high time we learned to issue good posters (incidentally, literate ones without fail!), to post them in advance, rather than a day or two before the concert, in different sections of the city, especially in workers' districts, student settlements, theaters, cinemas, and other public places.
>
> It is high time to revive in the outlying districts the tradition of issuing a printed program at the beginning of each concert. ... And would it not be desirable, at least at the beginning and end of the season, to print in the program the names of artists of the symphony orchestra and the other collectives of the philharmonic society? ... The Committee on Art Affairs under the U.S.S.R. Council of Ministers, through Muzgiz, can commission highly qualified musicologists to write a series of "Guide Books for Concerts"—short annotations to all the standard and new symphonic works. ... The time is long overdue for the publication of a small dictionary of musical terms containing a description of musical instruments and an explanation of the forms of musical compositions. ...

> In recent years a new form of musical propaganda—the musical lecture bureau [lektorii]—has been used on a wide scale. These lecture bureaus have accumulated significant experience. ... But many philharmonic societies have lost interest in the lecture bureaus and at present in many instances they exist [only] formally, as if for reports.

Dombayev devotes considerable attention to the "touring concerts by leading masters of Soviet musical performance." "The management of all touring concert work in the country," he writes,

> is entrusted to the Touring Bureau of the Committee on Art Affairs under the U.S.S.R. Council of Ministers. However, this organization has more obligations than rights and is frequently not in a position, therefore, to be responsible for the execution of the touring plans. ... Some of the leading performers, particularly the vocalists, not only do not manifest an interest in touring trips to the outlying districts, but even avoid them by every means. ... We could name tens of excellent performers in Leningrad who remain in the city without leaving it for years.

It seems to us that this is the veiled expression of a perceptible lack of interest on the part of some outstanding Soviet performers in giving concerts in outlying districts. Is this because the public in such districts has ceased to attend concerts saturated with political propaganda, or because it has forgotten how to distinguish between a performance of genuine mastery and mere hack-work?

A similar situation exists in the concert field in regard to talented youths, "The training of our talented artistic youth is carried out with extreme sluggishness and without initiative," writes Dombayev.

> Artistic young people enter the joyful path of concert service to the people with an unpleasant feeling of being a "burden" to both the Concert Touring Bureau and the philharmonic societies.

Dombayev mentions the lack of publicity, owing to which the "public does not fill our concert halls to hear our young artists." However, here also it is not difficult to see that the catastrophic decline of musical culture as a whole is basically responsible for the moribund condition of concert life in the Soviet Union.

"There is almost no concern over the development of artists for symphony orchestras," Dombayev continues.

> As a result of all this the artistic and ideological "temperature" of the orchestra is gradually declining. ... Even with regard to our conductors all is not well. Many orchestras lack conductors who are adequately trained, mature and able to train orchestral ensembles. Alongside the true masters of their trade, it seems that journeymen [remeslenniki] are at work in the field. Such "conductors" come to rehearsals without any prepared plan of interpretation of the musical composition and they have nothing to say to the orchestra. Senselessly and briskly they wave their hands, and that is the limit of their "direction" of the orchestra. Is it necessary to say that such "conductors" lead to the disqualification of their orchestras?

In conclusion Dombayev draws attention to deficiencies in the training of young musicians, pointing out that

> the education of valuable cadres of Soviet musicians is impossible without a vital and substantial concert atmosphere in a city. ...
>
> In turn, the directors of the philharmonic societies must understand that music students are not only a qualified audience sensitively reacting to and thirsting for everything that is new, but also that they are the reservoir from which the philharmonic societies are drawing and will draw new cadres of soloists, orchestral and chamber performers and musicologists.

The administration of the whole system of musical life in the Soviet Union is least of all able to cope with its task. "Practice has shown," writes Dombayev,

> that the Main Board of Music Institutions in the Committee on Art Affairs is unable to direct effectively all the philharmonic societies in the Soviet Union and respond to all their numerous requests, while the affiliates of the Committee on Art Affairs in the Union Republics, as a rule, have only one official in each musical section, who is in addition not always sufficiently qualified.
>
> On the staff of any philharmonic society one will find a director, administrators and clerical workers of all grades, but not art officials, with the exception of the art director. (Inci-

dentally, in a number of the philharmonic societies the directors are not musicians, while the art directors, as a rule, hold more than one office—conductors of the symphony orchestra overburdened with creative work in the orchestra, frequently with no interest in the other aspects of the society's activity.)

Even more eloquent is the information presented by representatives of various localities in response to Dombayev's article. Thus, for example, one musician, in an article entitled "Create Normal Conditions for Work of the Philharmonic Societies,"[1] writes:

> How can one speak of any serious creative work when, for more than two decades, our philharmonic society has been cooped up in various kinds of basements. During all these years the workers have haunted the doorsteps of the city officials and have used up piles of paper in addressing the Moscow directors for help in creating tolerable conditions at least for the creative work of the musical organizations. But all in vain.
>
> The symphony orchestra, quartets, choral capellas, soloists—all roam from one institution to another in search of a tenderhearted building official willing to permit them to rehearse for an hour or two. The question of course is not the lack of premises—there are plenty in Saratov—but the fact that here it has become a peculiar "tradition" to consider the philharmonic as an institution not so important or deserving of attention as, for example, the dramatic theater, the opera house, the technical academy, and others.

Another member of a philharmonic society describes not only the conditions of work, but also—and this is especially characteristic—the quality of the touring performers who do have a place to rehearse.[2] "It is necessary to devote particular attention," he writes,

---

1. D. Andreyev (lecturer at the Saratov Philharmonic Society), "Sozdat' normal'nye usloviya dlya raboty filarmonii," *Sovetskaya muzyka,* August, 1950, No. 8, pp. 57-58.

2. S. Veikhman (lecturer at the Molotov Philharmonic Society) and M. Blyumin (Art Director of the Kuibyshev Philharmonic Society), "Bol'she vnimaniya gastrol'nym kontsertam" [Greater Attention to the Concert Tour Concerts], *Sovetskaya muzyka,* August, 1950, No. 8, p. 58.

to the activity of that large group of concert performers who form the entourage of well-known "stars." In all probability these pianists and singers consider their participation in a concert as marking time. How otherwise can one explain the absence of creative enthusiasm in many of these artists, their careless execution, sour notes and extremely limited repertoire? It is sad that those responsible for planning concert tours are reconciled to this situation, not seeing a live performer behind the word "entourage."

ANNEX D

Some Additional References from the Soviet Press, 1953-1954

Note: The original Russian text of Mr. Olkhovsky's work was completed in late 1951. During the time required for translation, editing and publishing, a number of articles have appeared in the Soviet press which exemplify, corroborate or modify statements in the text. For technical reasons it was not possible to include references to such articles in the text. Extracts from a number of the most significant ones are therefore presented here in translation, with references to the subjects and sections in the text to which they refer.

The translations used are those published originally in the *Current Digest of the Soviet Press*, used by permission of Mr. Leo Gruliow, Editor of the *Current Digest*.

Music journalism and criticism.—p. 87.

"Razvivat' i sovershenstvovat' sovetskuyu muzyku" [(editorial) Develop and Perfect Soviet Music], *Pravda*, Feb. 10, 1953, p. 1. (Translation of complete text given in *Current Digest of the Soviet Press*, March 21, 1953, Vol. V, No. 6, p. 14.)

. . . .

One cause of the many defects in Soviet music's development is the unsatisfactory state of musical criticism. The newspaper *Sovetskoye iskusstvo* [Soviet Art] avoids serious, fundamental criticism of musical work; it avoids raising and discussing the most important problems of music esthetics. Criticism is poorly developed in the magazine *Sovetskaya muzyka* [Soviet Music].

. . . .

Records and record players.—p. 104.

Orlov, Vladimir, "Neobyknovennaya plastinka" [An Unusual Record], *Izvestiya*, Dec. 27, 1953, p. 3. (Translation of condensed text given in *Current Digest of the Soviet Press*, Feb. 10, 1954, Vol. V, No. 52, pp. 34-35.)

. . . .

The grateful Soviet listener will find in the broad stream of long-playing records issued this year many of his favorite works from the high points of our own and foreign musical classics.

It is disturbing, though, that with all the richness of the repertoire, several elementary desires remain unsatisfied. It is good that many of Glazunov's symphonic works are in the repertoire, but it is bad that Borodin and Musorgsky are represented by only one-fifth and one-seventh as many recordings respectively. Most listeners would undoubtedly first of all like to acquire Tchaikovsky's celebrated *First Concerto* and then Saint-Saëns' *Concerto No. 5*, Musorgsky's opera *Khovanshchina*, Gluck's *Orpheus*, Rossini's *The Barber of Seville*, and then his *Cinderella*. However, this is not possible. To the present time, such great works have not been recorded as Mozart's *Requiem*, Beethoven's *Symphony No. 9* and Berlioz' *Fantastic Symphony*. There are very few recordings of works by the late S. Prokof'yev, which evoke lively interest. T. Khrennikov's work is represented by two short songs only. N. Obukhova's artistry is one-sidely represented, mainly in love songs of dilettante composers; the excellent V. Barsova has not even been recorded. Many similar comments could be made. ...

. . . .

Unfortunately, the limited output of record players hinders distribution of long-playing records. It is very difficult to find an electric record player in department stores. An even greater rarity is the special radio-phonograph put out by the Elfa Factory. ...

. . . .

Opera—pp. 104, 169.

Koval', Marian, "Glubzhe izuchat' zhizn', sovershenstvovat' masterstvo!" [Study Life More Deeply, Perfect Mastery!], *Izvestiya*, March 4, 1953, p. 2 (Translation of condensed text given in *Current Digest of the Soviet Press*, April 18, 1953, Vol. V, No. 10, pp. 23-24.)

. . . .

The acute lag of creative music behind the growing artistic demands of the people appears most sharply in that most important sphere of music; opera.

Without a complete display in operatic works of all of the means of musical and dramatic expressiveness—arias, ensembles, choruses, recitatives and the symphonic techniques—there can be no full-valued operatic art. It is inconceivable without profound assimilation and further development of the best traditions of classical opera, without penetration into the life and historical creative work of our own people, without persistent mastery of the entire complicated technique of musical dramaturgy.

The creation of contemporary operas has still not become a central task in all composers' organizations. The Committee on Art Affairs has not displayed the proper skill and flexibility in guiding the creation of operatic work. Writers of operas receive such an abundance of contradictory instructions and opinions that it only confuses them and reduces their sense of responsibility toward their work. But the greatest blame for the prolonged lag in the opera genre falls on the composers themselves for not showing enough creative energy in working on operas.

. . . .

Theaters and concert halls—p. 129.

Orlov, Vladimir, "Razmyshleniya nad skripkoi" [Thoughts on the Violin], *Izvestiya,* Feb. 27, 1953, pp. 2-3. (Translation of condensed text given in *Current Digest of the Soviet Press,* April 11, 1953, Vol. V, No. 9, pp. 38-40.)

. . . .

Here is what [Russian Republic People's Artist Ivan Petrovich Lobanov] writes [to *Izvestiya*]:

"Last November working people in the city of Kalinin and the company of the province drama theater received a wonderful gift: a new and magnificently finished theater building. Everything would have been wonderful if it had not been for the sound...A word uttered from the stage sounds good only in the first and last rows; in the center of the hall and in the grand tier it loses its clarity and all that can be heard is a jumbled, unintelligible mumbling...This has greatly complicated our creative work. In our concern for members of the audience in the 'dead space' we actors are compelled to strain our voices considerably, to pronounce each word separately, waiting until the rumble it sets off dies down... This destroys the realism of the performance..."

The people of Kalinin are, alas, not the only sufferers. The Victory Theater in Stalingrad cost several million rubles to build and has a marble staircase and a beautiful auditorium for 900 persons. Careful measurements by physicists show, however, that the rumble from bass notes lasts three whole seconds! In order to obtain tolerable sound definition it was necessary to interfere radically with the theater's first-class equipment: to exclude the sections which produce bass notes. In other words, the contrabasses and cellos had to be removed from the orchestra.

Audiences in the Tchaikovsky Hall and the Central Theater of the Soviet Army in Moscow and in the magnificent Novosibirsk

Theater risk sitting in "dead zones." Mention can also be made of the Ordzhonikidze Motion Picture Theater in Kharkov, the Young Pioneer Motion Picture Theater in Saratov, the Palace of Culture in Kirovsk—of a long list of beautiful buildings plagued by one and the same evil.

The architects are to blame for this fault; they forgot about that invisible but principal figure in every theater; sound. ...

The rich synthesis of arts which is architecture should also embody the art of the musician. Now, however, the architect has stronger support than the instinctive feeling of the old masters. There is such a thing as architectural acoustics. ...

Builders often underestimate this science, however. Acoustics specialists are hardly ever consulted in drawing up plans for theaters. Acoustics specialists had little to do even with the planning of the Radio Broadcasting Committee's large Moscow radio center with its dozens of auditoriums and studios.

The acoustics specialist comes into the picture only at the end of the project, when disaster threatens. The builder is often unable to carry out the recommendations of the acoustics specialist, however, because there is a shortage of sound-absorbing materials.

And so sound is often neglected in our buildings. Acoustics are missing in some theater buildings. People sit in an auditorium but do not hear the concert; on the other hand, when they sit at home they are forced to hear a continual "concert": sound travels freely throughout the building and penetrates the walls between apartments.

A Neglected Realm of Science.—Wishing to become familiar with contemporary problems of architectural acoustics we thumbed carefully through Soviet journals and compendiums on physics, construction and architecture for the past ten to twelve years, and nowhere did we find any major writings on this important problem. We decided to look in on the research institutes which are supposed to take up problems of architectural acoustics.

In the U.S.S.R. Academy of Sciences' Lebedev Physics Institute we found neglected equipment and instruments without people, while in the U.S.S.R. Academy of Architecture's structural acoustics laboratory we found neglected people without equipment or instruments. Old-fashioned equipment is used there only to make crude measurements of sound penetration of walls and ceilings. Sound absorption cannot be measured because equipment is lacking. How can one expect serious scientific work here?

And yet, it developed from a talk with Comrade Timofeyev, the director of the laboratory, that he has no complaints to make to the Presidium of the Academy. In choosing which to safeguard—architectural acoustics or the peace and quiet of his superiors—Comrade

Timofeyev evidently decided long ago that the peace and quiet of his superiors were most in need of protection.

In the acoustics laboratory of the Radio Broadcasting Committee's Sound Transcription Research Institute we found personnel busy making a wired sound model of a concert hall on the corner of a table.

Work in the acoustics laboratory of the U.S.S.R. Ministry of Cinematography's Acoustics Research Laboratory is more fruitful, but even this laboratory is becoming a first-aid center to cover up the mistakes of careless motion picture theater builders.

The lack of published scientific works on architectural acoustics is due to the fact that the work of the laboratories is so poor theoretically that it cannot be published.

Who is responsible for the serious lag in architectural acoustics in the country?

The Presidium of the U.S.S.R. Academy of Architecture, the Committee on Construction Affairs and the U.S.S.R. Academy of Sciences' Commission on Acoustics (Chairman: Corresponding Member of the U.S.S.R. Academy of Sciences N.N. Andreyev; Vice-Chairman: Doctor of Technical Sciences L.D. Rozenberg). There is a large gap in the architectural acoustics front but the commission has failed to call attention to it for years on end.

The commission also says nothing about work having stopped on the science of hearing in recent years, about the fact that almost no young people are being trained in acoustics and that the few acoustics specialists graduated from the higher educational institutions are assigned to work other than what they have been trained to do, or about the fact that acoustics are not included in the programs of general physics courses of higher technical educational institutions or even in the courses of the physics faculties.

A person can be graduated from a higher educational institution and still be a stranger in the world of sound.

. . . .

Operetta—p. 134.

Grosheva, Ye., "Vazhnyi zhanr muzykal'novo iskusstva. O gastrolyakh Sverdlovskovo Teatra Muzykal'noi Komedii" [Important Genre of Musical Art. Concerning Tours of Sverdlovsk Musical Comedy Theater], *Pravda,* August 28, 1953, p. 4. (Translation of condensed text given in *Current Digest of the Soviet Press,* Oct. 10, 1953, Vol. V, No. 35, p. 40.)

. . . .

Thus, in trying to furnish Moscow audiences productions new to them the Sverdlovsk Theater has inadvertently raised questions of musical comedy long overdue.

In their careful search for material the theaters either lose the discrimination necessary in regard to selecting operettas or turn to the repertoires of related genres—vaudeville, comedy and even commonplace melodrama. It is no accident that some of the theaters' operetta productions have begun to be called "musical extravaganzas." This means that the operetta has begun to lose its chief weapon—laughter—and its distinctive quality—music.

Everybody knows that the skill of the actor is closely dependent upon the repertoire. The crude musical material in many operetta theater performances requires no vocal skill on the part of the performers. One seldom hears good singing on the operetta stage, and although the musical discipline of the Sverdlovsk Theater is somewhat higher than that of many others, vocal work is not its actors' strong point. ...

Problems of developing the genre are closely related to the state of creative writing. There are very few authors working in the operetta field and almost none of them possess the skill required for it. Absolutely no young dramatists or composers are taking up operetta. This genre is foreign to many masters of Soviet music and the art of comedy.

The U.S.S.R. Ministry of Culture's Chief Administration on Affairs of the Arts has badly managed its work in preparing repertoires for the musical comedy theaters.

The creative problems relating to the work of the operetta theaters have long been critical, yet no real help has been given this necessary genre. The time has come to back up words with action. The Unions of Soviet Writers and Composers as well as the corresponding agencies of the Ministry of Culture must take decisive steps to provide the musical comedy theaters with worthwhile repertoires. ...

. . . .

Radio broadcasting—pp. 140-142.

Kazakov, G., "Ustranit' ser'yoznye nedostatki v radioveshchanii" [Eliminate Grave Shortcomings in Radio Broadcasting], *Pravda*, Jan. 30, 1953, p. 2. (Translation of condensed text given in *Current Digest of the Soviet Press*, March 28, 1953, Vol. V, No. 7, pp. 40-41.)

. . . .

No less than half the radio broadcasting time is taken up by music programs. The role of radio in propagandizing music is generally known. Thanks to sound recording, radio broadcasting has tens of thousands of musical works in reserve, yet this wealth is poorly used in broadcasts. The impression is created that only a few works are being presented, with variations.

The repertoire of radio concerts, particularly in basic programs, is poor and monotonous. It is difficult to hear an opera, operetta, or major symphonic work. If one works or studies on Thursday evenings, one usually will not hear a single opera over the radio, because they are played only during the daytime.

Frequently the very same artists, predominantly Radio Committee performers, perform several times a day and, moreover, from one and the same repertoire. A great deal of just censure is provoked by the unsatisfactory quality of Sunday programs.

The Radio Broadcasting Committee is not manifesting the necessary concern for educating the listeners' musical tastes, and underestimates the Soviet peoples' interest in outstanding musical compositions. That is why for months one cannot hear on the basic program concertos and symphonies by Tchaikovsky, Balakirev, Borodin, and Musorgsky, which are loved by the people. Few vocal works of the peoples of the Soviet Union are translated into Russian and performed on the radio, and even fewer operatic arias, songs and romances by Russian composers are broadcast in the languages of other peoples.

. . . .

Amateur musical activity—p. 142.

Massalitinov, K., "Samodeyatel'nym kollektivam—polnotsennyi repertuar" [Supply Amateur Groups with Rich Repertoire], *Izvestiya,* March 19, 1954, p. 3. (Translation of condensed text given in *Current Digest of the Soviet Press,* April 28, 1954, Vol. VI, No. 11, pp. 32-33.)

. . . .

Matters are no better in regard to the repertoire for rural chorus groups. The Union of Soviet Composers takes little interest in writing new songs for the village. Composers devote almost no time to arranging folk songs. It is many years now since we have seen in magazines for amateur groups choral works by distinguished composers like Shostakovich, Glière, Knipper, Khachaturyan, Khrennikov, Dzerzhinski and others. Their work is virtually never heard in rural amateur productions.

Even song writers whose works are printed in collections for amateur performances do not study the unique features of folk choruses, with the result that their songs for the most part lack vitality and do nothing for the art of singing. It is no accident that the villagers perform only a small portion of what was written and published last year in collections of the State Cultural-Enlightenment Publishing House and in the magazine *Molodyozhnaya estrada.* [Young People's Stage]. ...

Rural chorus groups listen enthusiastically to broadcasts by professional choruses such as the Pyatnitski, Northern, Urals and Voronezh groups. But neither the State Music, State Cultural-Enlightenment nor the Young Guard Publishing Houses have published collections from the repertoire of these choruses in many a long year. Village chorus groups have to adapt the songs as well as possible, listening to them on the radio or on phonograph records and singing them by ear. Under such circumstances distortion of the songs is inevitable.

If a composer is to write good songs for the people, he must know life and have close bonds with the creative singing of the people. And what is actually happening? Composers seldom spend any time in collective farm villages but avoid such visits. During the last decade not a single Moscow composer has been to song-loving Voronezh Province, the home of two professional folk choruses, the Pyatnitski and the Voronezh. Is it any wonder, then, that folk songs are often written or adapted by composers without taking national chorus singing into account, without preserving and developing its special features?

The problem of creating a valuable repertoire for rural performers came to a head long ago and will admit no delay. The U.S.S.R. Ministry of Culture must coordinate the work of all organizations and institutions called on to guide amateur activities; they are, in effect, left to themselves. Why, for example are so many publishing houses busy with putting out repertoire materials for amateur performances, thereby duplicating one another? Would it not be better to concentrate on the creation of a good repertoire for amateur performances in one place?

Literature on methods, which is prepared by people's art centers, should greatly assist amateur work. But there is clearly a shortage of such literature, and what there is is not competently compiled. Magazines and collections for amateur performances reach the district in two or three copies.

. . . .

The mass-song—Part V, Section 3, pp. 157-166.

Khubov, Georgi, "O pesne" [Concerning Songs], *Pravda*, Feb. 8, 1954, p. 3. (Translation of condensed text given in *Current Digest of the Soviet Press*, March 24, 1954, Vol. VI, No. 6, pp. 33-35.)

. . . .

... In recent years our talented composers and poets have written many beautiful songs which have won the love and recognition of the broadest masses. These songs, gracing the work and life of Soviet man and educating young people in a spirit of patriotism and the fight for peace and friendship among peoples, live and will always live, for beautiful songs never die.

This has also been clearly confirmed by a plenary session held recently in Moscow of the U.S.S.R. Union of Composers' board, which was devoted to problems in developing Soviet song writing. Many excellent songs from past years resounded again and again in the concert programs of the plenary session, and one could see how warmly and joyfully the large audiences which filled the concert halls and clubs of the capital welcomed them.

But life progresses by leaps and bounds. Socialist culture, enriched by the experience of building communism in our country, is developing with tempestuous speed. The spiritual and esthetic requirements of the people are growing constantly. The present day poses important and challenging tasks before both composers and song writers, the more so since the song is the most popular and most militant and effective genre of lyric music.

During the all-Soviet "plenary song session" listeners naturally awaited with particular impatience *new* and talented songs of our time from composers and poets, songs varied in content, each striking in form. But, alas, there were too few such songs.

It cannot be said that composers and poets have "soured" on the song genre and seldom turn to it. No, a multitude of songs are being composed. After all, more than 400 songs, a large number of which originated in recent years, were chosen for the plenary session concerts. Some among them are undoubtedly good: V. Muradeli's "The Party Is Our Pilot" (lyrics by S. Mikhalkov), V. Solovyov-Sedoi's "Vyorsts" (lyrics by L. Oshanin), M. Blanter's "Distant Path, an Eagle's Flight" (lyrics by A. Surkov), S. Tulikov's "We Are for Peace" (lyrics by A. Zharov), V. Zakharov's "Russian Beauty" (lyrics by P. Kazmin), and others.

A number of interesting and uniquely national works testify that song writing in the fraternal republics has revived noticeably. ...

Nevertheless, the song writing of Soviet composers markedly

lags behind life. Its present condition and rate of development in no measure satisfy the people's present-day demands.

* * *

The successes of past years have obviously turned the heads of many composers and songwriters. A complacent self-confidence has begun to stifle the restless urge for the new, the joy of bold creative searchings, the keen desire to study life in its development and to perfect artistic craftsmanship. They have forgotten the glorious tradition of the folk quality of the Soviet song and, instead of keeping ever in step with life, going ever forward, they turn to the easier "repetition of the past," tolerating stereotype and routine in songs, reciting dull sermons in a clumsy style.

This explains the many weak and mediocre songs, monotonous in theme and usually without subject. Living, graphic expression is replaced in them by rhymed rhetoric of general phrases and standard turns of speech, which wander from one song to another.

During the plenary session many "examples" were cited of such writing, where a more or less successful line from a song is endlessly repeated in others—with a few "freshening" word changes. For example: "Your Hand, Distant Comrade" (A. Sofronov), "Your Hand, Comrade, and We Shall Win" (G. Rublev), "Give Me Your Hand, Unknown Comrade" (Dm. Sedykh), and so forth.

The listener often senses similarities even in the music of songs, which rehash one and the same long familiar melodic, harmonic and technical treatment. It is clear that no one will accept songs lacking in creative inspiration, originality and craftsmanship, even if they are played every day in concerts and over the radio. The minute they begin they are misted with the grey cobweb of boredom.

Composers and poets are not making a sufficient study of life, of the tempestuously developing art of the folk song; their creative imagination does not always penetrate the heart of life's phenomena. Yet without a comprehensive knowledge of life, which molds the people's characters, one cannot write true-ringing songs.

In light songs even stirring themes and figures of our times are reflected in a banal, superficial and impoverished manner. An example is D. Lvov-Kompaneyets' recently released song "From Distant Tambov'," with words by L. Oshanin. It depicts a standard "dark-browed youth," who "is going to his home collective farm," where he will marry his Natasha (of the "dark braids," of course), and who at the same time will "raise—unprecedented crops," since:

"He goes with an education
And an eager heart (!)—"

In a crudely stylized folk form [chastushka], the writers of "What Will Come" (words by O. Fadeyeva, music by M. Tabachnikov) chose, among other things, to sing of a collective farm cowshed. Whether they ever visited a collective farm is not known, but their capricious imagination poured into the mold of the most unabashed hackwork: "We built palaces for cows and for calves. And only showers and hardwood floors and radio phonographs do we lack! Wait, wait, it all will come!"

Another song—"They Go to the Village" (music by L. Lyadova and words by G. Khodosov)—is not much better. Its authors are obviously totally unfamiliar with the life of the Soviet countryside and imagine collective farmers as some sort of wild peasants who make a noisy, bluntly "operatic" fuss over the arrival of engineers and agronomists in the village "for good."

We could cite other songs as examples of dull mediocrity (for example, M. Fradkin's "Wind, Bend Not the Birch," with words by A. Kovalenkov.)

Songs like these are written easily, by a hackneyed formula: the person who writes the lyrics rhymes general phrases "on the theme of the day," gives them a striking title (which changes the subject), and the composer adapts them to a "primitive motif" set to an artless accompaniment with garish accordion interludes.

Unfortunately, many such pseudo-folk works are being written. The Union of Composers is fairly indifferent toward them (and toward song genres in general, incidentally), music critics are "used" to them and remain silent, while undiscriminating officials of the State Music Publishing House willingly print them, even with pretentious headings: "Collective Farm Amateur Library."

Participants in the thousands of collective farmers' and workers' amateur groups speak the truth in chiding musical institutions, composers and poets for their inertia and indifference to the growing spiritual requirements of the people. ...

Folk quality is the basis of the realistic method in art in general and in songs in particular. ...

To this day the esthetic concept of folk quality still frequently undergoes philistine reduction to a concept of popular appeal. Everything which is truly folk in art is unconditionally popular, but far from everything which is popular has a truly folk character, since for various reasons works which are haphazard, even weak, mediocre and later inevitably discarded and completely forgotten can also enjoy temporary (sometimes even noisy) success. Folk quality is the first sign of ideological purity of style, unfading beauty and high artistic taste.

The music of a song can express more than the words, but to do so it also needs a poetic and meaningful text, a graphic embodiment of a subject, thought and mood which are true to life. Is it necessary to stress that pictorial specificity of thematic development in a song enables it to portray the typical features of the new more profoundly, more clearly and sharply?

Very few good thematic songs have appeared of late. A sort of arithmetical standard for song texts has been worked out which is so general and tenuous that separate couplets or even lines can be thrown out or rearranged without detriment.

This situation, which has arisen not without the influence of the harmful "no-conflict theory," cannot be tolerated. It is necessary to promote in every way the creation of living thematic songs of various types and on present-day themes—heroic, work, lyric, comic, music hall, etc. ...

One senses of late a particularly acute lag in lyric, everyday, satiric and comic genres of song writing. The composers and poets are not the only ones to blame for this, but critics and some high-ranking figures of music institutions and professional organizations as well. One still finds "theoreticians" who in almost every lyric or music hall song are ready to see the banal and commonplace. Matters have been reduced to the point where even in B. Mokrousov's beautiful lyric song "Lone Concertina" (set to the profound and poetic lyrics of M. Isakovski) some music excerpts have begun to perceive—the commonplace.[1] Judgments like this stem from esthetic ignorance and a bigoted attitude toward the lyric genre of Soviet song. To consider a lyric or music hall song commonplace simply because it is a lyric or music hall song is to prate banalities and to injure art. ...

Many of those who spoke during the plenary sessions sharply criticized bureaucratic methods of guidance of song writing in music broadcasts and in the U.S.S.R. Ministry of Culture's Music Institutions Administration. Severe criticism was directed at major shortcomings in the work of the Union of Composers, its secretariat and song-and-chorus committee, the State Music Publishing House and local professional organizations.

---

1. For a report that Mokrousov has been ousted from the Union of Soviet Composers on a charge of plagiarism, see the *New York Times*, June 30, 1954. The author's comments on this event, analyzing its significance, are contained in his article, "Tol'ko li plagiat?" [Merely Plagiarism?], *Novoye Russkoye Slovo*, New York, Vol. XLI, No. 15, 417, July 13, 1954.

The most serious conclusions must be drawn from this legitimate criticism. It is necessary to draw our outstanding composers and poets into active creative work in various song genres on a broader scale, to advance talented young people more energetically and boldly and to develop profound criticism and self-criticism in professional organizations. ...

. . . .

The music of Shostakovich—p. 215.

Koval', Marian, "Novye muzykal'nye proizvedeniya" [New Musical Compositions], *Pravda,* Feb. 5, 1953, p. 3. (Translation of complete text given in *Current Digest of the Soviet Press,* March 14, 1953, Vol. V, No. 5, pp. 42-43.

. . . .

At the concert on the opening day of the [sixth] plenary session, [of the board of the U.S.S.R. Union of Soviet Composers], Dm. Shostakovich's new cantata *Over Our Motherland Shines the Sun,* devoted to the 19th Party Congress, was performed. There is much beautiful, bright and joyful music in the cantata. The composer continues to develop his creative talent in a realistic direction, turning to the great themes of present-day life.

The work begins with the lyrical strains of a boys' chorus. There is a particularly moving quality in the children's clear voices telling in a touching way about the beloved and happy motherland. The cantata then tells about the hard battles for freedom during the revolutionary struggle and the great patriotic war. Here the composer builds in the energetic rhythms of revolutionary songs. The colorful, emotional music, majestically orchestrated, convincingly expresses the essence of the struggle. The brilliant musical theme "Communists, forward!" presented by the chorus, then taken up by the orchestra, captivates the listener with its challenging ring.

The work ends glorifying the motherland, glorifying the Party. It testifies to the fact that the composer has deeply penetrated the graphic structure of Russian revolutionary songs and has successfully worked this rich source of musical inspiration into his creative work. He bases the lyrical melody in his music on the slow, flowing meditative Russian folk song [protyazhnaya], but he does not always use it boldly enough.

It should be noted that the cantata's text, written by the poet Yevgeni Dolmatovski, is not very expressive and lowers the artistic level of the work.

. . . .

The music of Shostakovich.

Khachaturyan, Karen, "Kantata D. Shostakovicha" [(a review of) A cantata by D. Shostakovich], *Vechernyaya Moskva*, Nov. 24, 1952, p. 3. (Translation of condensed text given in *Current Digest of the Soviet Press*, Jan. 17, 1953, Vol. IV, No. 49, p. 52.)

These days, while the entire Soviet people are celebrating the 35th anniversary of Great October, in the large hall of the Moscow Conservatory there resounded for the first time a new cantata by Dmitri Shostakovich entitled *Over Our Motherland Shines the Sun* (words by Ye. Dolmatovski). The cantata was written for a children's chorus, a mixed chorus and a symphony orchestra augmented by a section of brass winds. ...

Shostakovich's cantata begins with light, lyrical music, conveying the majesty and loveliness of our motherland, and is filled with the powerful and inexhaustible creative spirit of the forces which are joyfully and confidently building their new, peaceful life. ...

The cantata next tells of the revolutionary past of our people, who have won their "good fortune in severe fights and battles," and of the leading roles which our wise party and its great leaders Lenin and Stalin have played in this struggle. ...

Later, the cantata returns to its initial theme, the theme of the homeland portrayed in all the scope of its plans and designs, in all the grandeur of its huge construction projects. The Soviet people, rallied around the Communist Party and around dear, beloved Stalin, firmly and tirelessly march toward communism. The words resound with confidence and enthusiasm: "Our generation will see communism! Our people will build communism!"

The concluding part of the cantata, the culmination of the work, sounds forth triumphantly, with the power and strength of a hymn. It ends with an oath of loyalty to the Communist Party and with the militant summons: "Comrades, forward to the glory of the party of Lenin and Stalin."

This new cantata by Shostakovich makes a valuable contribution to Soviet music. It is marked by profound ideological content and is clothed in a plain, clear form. Its images are vivid and true. It is melodious and has been written in simple, comprehensive language. ...

. . . .

The music of Shostakovich.

"Zrelost' i masterstvo. Zametki o desyatoi simfonii D. Shostakovicha." [Maturity and Skill. Notes on D. Shostakovich's Tenth

Symphony.], *Sovetskaya kultura* [Soviet Culture], Feb. 27, 1954, pp. 2-3. (Translation of condensed text given in *Current Digest of the Soviet Press*, April 14, 1954, Vol. VI, No. 9, pp. 17-18.)

Dmitri Shostakovich's *Tenth Symphony* is one of the most important and outstanding works of recent times. It would be idle to try to deal in one single article with all the questions arising from it. Consequently we confine ourselves for the time being to first impressions and first remarks concerning this work.

Shostakovich has recently experienced a great creative upswing. He literally does not lay down his composer's pen; new works of various genres follow upon one another without pause. One sees in this the ardent endeavor of the patriotic Soviet musician to participate by his work in the general creative enthusiasm of the Soviet people.

In addition to the well-known oratorio *Song of the Forests*, a long cycle of poems for unaccompanied chorus and the cantata *Over Our Motherland Shines the Sun*, Shostakovich has written two volumes of preludes and fugues for the piano, and the last three months of 1953 saw the performance of his two new string quartets (No. 4 and No. 5) and his *Tenth Symphony*.

Whereas much has been written about *Song of the Forests* and the choral works, the critics have not ventured a single word concerning the others, such as the *Fourth Quartet*, with its superb second movement (andantino). The cycle of preludes and fugues also has not been thoroughly evaluated. Yet these works, which lead up to the *Tenth Symphony*, especially the cycle of preludes and fugues, are significant and thought-provoking, though individual sections may be criticized.

In his best preludes and fugues Shostakovich has demonstrated a new piano style. Without indulging in comparisons, one cannot but be struck by Shostakovich's bold determination to repeat the immortal achievement of the great J.S. Bach, whose two-volume "Well-Tempered Clavichord" includes 48 preludes and fugues.

In many of the preludes and fugues themes from Russian songs can be detected. ...

The cycle of preludes and fugues demonstrates clearly the composer's recent interests and musical development.

We immediately think of Bach and Musorgsky when we hear the solemn and somber quietude of the *Tenth Symphony's* introductory bars. The music of the first movement is tragic. It sings of woe and suffering which cannot be forgotten or ignored. Its sorrow is concentrated and unforgettable, a sorrow too deep for tears, at the same time tender and severe, neither expecting nor demanding consolation. ...

The tragic element in Shostakovich's music always springs from the counterposing of two irreconcilable, conflicting principles; the struggle of man in the new world, with new consciousness, against the dark forces of reaction, obscurantism and death. In the *Seventh Symphony* and many succeeding works the composer presents the forces of evil, hurtling against the bright new socialist world, as the terrible images of fascism and war. In the first movement of the *Tenth Symphony* the composer, having, as it were, taken the listener by the hand,once more leads him in the wake of the recently raging war to graves of the cherished. Pictures from the past rise up before the eyes, and at times there is in the music a reminder of the pains, pangs and violent passions of battle. There are moments when it seems that the powers of darkness and misanthropy are once more about to rejoice in blood, while leaden clouds rise over the horizon and threaten to blot out the sun.

The second movement of the symphony deviates from the usual scherzo, for, by the nature of its music and its significance in the dramatic conception of the whole work, it reaches to our minds, far beyond the confines of the traditional scherzo of the four-movement symphonic pattern. ...

This movement gives the impression of a whirlwind, powerful, threatening, absorbing everything in its path. In this music one senses an aspiring surge of huge masses of people, full of incomprehensible life forces, of invincible and inexhaustible energy. ...

The third movement, andante, could be called "Disturbed Rest." ... A flourishing march from out of nowhere disrupts and confuses the little world of homely human joys and comfortable well-being. It is interesting to find in this march a theme which will play a significant role in the fourth movement too. ...

In the andante there are also at times motifs—sounds and colors—from nature. They are not the vivid colorings of midday, but the lulling, subdued tints of twilight. When the storm and fury of the march gradually die away, a French horn rings out through the clear, transparent air like some far-off hunting horn, and the pizzicato of the strings surges up like a flock of blackbirds frightened from sleep. The long evening shadows stretch out. Dusk deepens. The intent ear catches the frightening, dull rumble of distant thunder. Sleep slowly creeps over all. Only a single violin plays the same short theme repeatedly. But even this sounds ever more faintly, until it dies away altogether. The orchestra freezes into immobility in the middle of a statement and then the last four notes, falling like four heavy drops, restate the motif of the march theme.

The second and third are undoubtedly the best movements of the *Tenth Symphony*. Now we come to the fourth and last. Here, too, there are significant and resplendent passages. In the introductory andante, the recitative—in which the cellos and double basses "converse," now with the oboe, now with the flutes, now with the bassoon—is profoundly touching and literally attains the expressiveness of human speech. ... The other episodic themes of the allegro are completely transitory, in that they do not attract sufficient attention to themselves. The main point about this finale is that it displays no "finality," no summing-up, no final rounding-off.

True, the finale is distinguished by fiery movement and stormy temperament. There is action here, but the results of the action are not shown. Consequently the finale does not give a general summary of all that has gone before, nor bring about the denouement of the tragic concept running through the whole symphony. ... As it stands, the finale weakens the artistic and therefore to some extent also the philosophical conception of the *Tenth Symphony*. Such are its substantial shortcomings.

Can these shortcomings be explained as organic defects in the tragic genre itself, when applied to present-day conditions, as Shostakovich has many times been assured? By no means. This must be stated frankly and unambiguously. The struggle of the new world with the old, which is going on before our very eyes, in which we ourselves are participants, by its very essence includes elements of the tragic. The old will not give way voluntarily, will not yield without a struggle. And the struggle to affirm the new cannot proceed without bloodshed, it is often tense with sufferings and sacrifices, with the destruction of superb, altruistic people. And so the present splendid struggle which advanced mankind is waging against the dark forces of reaction actually provides ample material for tragic art. Therefore Shostakovich's favoring of tragic subjects and feelings is perfectly justified and most certainly requires no special explanation or apology. The point is not whether tragic themes should resound throughout the *Tenth Symphony* or not, but rather that the symphony should give fuller and more vivid voice to the triumph of the powers of light, which in actual life are far stronger than those of darkness and death. Then the democratic, humanistic ideals of our culture and society would find more profound and adequate expression.

In the *Tenth Symphony*, for the first time—and this is what is fundamental and new in it—we find images of the great mass movement, invincible in its might, ready to overcome any obstacle, freedom-loving; images of tremendous, powerful energy. What draws the listener's attention in the *Tenth Symphony* is the invincibility of movement, the confidence in victory, the dramatic struggle and the mass, collective nature of its endeavors.

But is must be added that the *Tenth Symphony,* to our mind, depicts not accomplishment but accomplishing. Falling back on visual associations, one might say that one sees powerful, courageous people with clenched fists, contracted brows, eyes of pain and wrath; but even at the very end of the symphony, in the last stage of unfolding its content, one does not see the happy smile of conquerors. That is the problem; in the music of the *Tenth Symphony* there is little smiling, little light, little sunshine—yet these are absolutely indispensable! They are demanded by the very musical conception of the work, as well as by our Soviet conception of the tragic as bearing within itself its own negation. The facts of our contemporary life demand this.

The path along which Shostakovich's art is progressing is no straight, smooth, well-beaten one. At times in his music the new and the old come together in a most curious manner, interweaving and conflicting. ... The *Tenth Symphony* has shortcomings and contradictions but at the same time much that is new, powerful and splendid. It is probably a transitional work for Shostakovich. We can be proud to add such a score to Soviet music. It is one of the most vivid evidences of the remarkable flourishing of symphonic music in our country, and also proclaims the flowering of the tremendous, mature talent of Shostakovich, his growth and steady progress. At the same time the *Tenth Symphony* points up certain stumbling blocks in this growth and progress.

One thing more, in conclusion. Shostakovich's progress is invariably bound up with work on contemporary themes. At the same time, he is progressing toward deeper creative mastery of the classical traditions. Therefore it seems fit and important to us to recall a certain classical tradition which Soviet composers should not overlook, one which is simultaneously of ethical and of purely artistic nature. The composers of the past always strove in their works to inspire the listeners, to instill in them love of life and faith in life. This tradition has been firmly established over the centuries, and it would be foolish to say that there is nothing essential in it. The victorious finales of classical symphonies are the climaxes of their entire conception of the world and their mode of creative thought; such finales are demanded by the very conception of their symphonic canvasses. In a word, the great tragic musicians were invariably optimists in their works. One of the best-known of them finished his *Ninth Symphony* with the "Ode to Joy," while another ended his tragic opera with the chorus "Rejoice," which was indeed a Russian "Ode to Joy'."

The Soviet people await a new, contemporary hymn to joy in the music of their composers. Dmitri Shostakovich should compose a Soviet "Ode to Joy." The composer, rising to the height of classical art, will hear this song in his heart and will reiterate it in new and splendid works. We are convinced of this. Yes, it will be so.

Note: For an extensive discussion of Shostakovich's *Tenth Symphony*, see *Sovetskaya Muzyka*, June 1954, No. 6, pp. 119-134; translation of condensed text in *Current Digest of the Soviet Press*, August 4, 1954, Vol. VI, No. 25, pp. 8-12. For the author's comment on this discussion, see "Ocherednoi proval sovetskoi 'khudozhestvennoi politiki'" [A Regular Failure of the Soviet "Artistic Policy"], *Novoye Russkoye Slovo*, New York, No. 15,450, August 15, 1954.

The music of Glière—p. 228.

"Nad chem rabotayut kompozitory" [What Composers Are Working On], *Vechernyaya Moskva*, [Evening Moscow], Jan. 30, 1953, p. 3. (Translation from *Current Digest of the Soviet Press*, March 14, 1953, Vol. V, No. 5, p. 43.)

An eminent Soviet composer—U.S.S.R. People's Artist R. Glière—has frequently turned to themes glorifying the Armed Forces of the Soviet Union. He has composed many works for military brass bands.

In connection with a coming holiday—the 35th anniversary of the Soviet Army—R. Glière has begun on a new composition which praises the exploits of Soviet soldier-patriots. A cantata devoted to the Soviet Army celebration will be written to the words of the poet Ya. Belinski.

Ukrainian music—Part VI, Section c, pp. 255-261

Gordeichuk, N., "Vyshe uroven' tvorchestva kompozitorov Ukrainy" [Raise Level of Ukrainian Composers' Work], *Pravda Ukrainy*, May 17, 1953, pp. 2-3. (Translation of condensed text given in *Current Digest of the Soviet Press*, June 27, 1953, Vol. V, No. 20, p. 17-18).

. . . .

Ukrainian composers are much more active in symphonic work. At the eighth plenary session of the board of the Composers' Union, strong symphonic compositions, including seven symphonies, were performed. ... But the growth in quality of Ukrainian symphonic work lags considerably behind growth in quantity.

Unfortunately, not one new symphonic work fully meets the great ideological and artistic standards set for Soviet music.

A favorable aspect of symphonic work of recent years is the composers' striving for program music, their striving to communicate with the people through comprehensible and concrete thoughts and images invested with corresponding artistic form.

However, in this field of program music theoretic muddle and confusion have reigned up to now. One group of composers thinks program music is only that which involves explicit literary formulation and includes development of a plot. Others think program music is only that which has idea-content and images defined and made concrete by a title which generalizes the music. A third group considers that a program work must have merely its own implicit program, known only by the composer.

Both the first and second kinds of program music are perfectly possible; they occur frequently in classical, especially Russian music. Therefore there is no basis for quarrelling over which is better; the essence of the matter lies not in the form of the program music but in the quality of the embodiment in musical terms of the great symphonic whole.

As to so-called "implicit program music" it also exists in classical music, but can it have a place in our life? In our opinion it cannot. Progressive composers of the past did not disclose the program thought of some compositions because of adverse social conditions, because of severe censorship, which defended the ruling classes' interests and dealt harshly with the slightest sign of humaneness, progressiveness and love of freedom in art. The artist in socialist society, devoted to the people's service, need not hide the genuine meaning of his work.

The programs of most symphonies of Ukrainian composers are superficially external, poster-declarative and sometimes even particularly abstract. Most often they are as follows: first part—picture of the Soviet people's struggle (it is often unclear what the struggle is for); second—nature scene; third—genre scene (the life of Soviet people)—incidentally, the second and third can be reversed; and, finally, fourth—a popular celebration, scenes of victory, triumph, etc. Amid the welter of these very common situations in music one often cannot see the living Soviet man, with his emotions and experiences; there is no reflection of the difficulties against which our people fight in their steady advance toward communism. The program of such a symphony is reduced to a wordless label, because it is not revealed dialectically. Composers must reach the point of triumphant conclusion only after showing a stubborn and prolonged struggle, clashes of qualitatively different images, and on this foundation present the essential point and convincingly convey this essential point to the listener. The notorious no-conflict theory persists in the work of several Ukrainian Soviet composers. ...

Shostakovich on creative originality in music.

Shostakovich, D., "Radost' tvorcheskikh iskanii" [The Joy of Creative Searchings], *Sovetskaya Muzyka,* 1954, No. 1, pp. 40-42. (Translation of condensed text given in *Current Digest of the Soviet Press,* Feb. 10, 1954, Vol. V, No. 52, pp. 3-4)

The year 1954! A new historical frontier on the Soviet people's path to communism. ...

For us musicians 1954 has its own special significance. This year the peoples of the Soviet Union will commemorate the 150th anniversary of the birth of the great genius of Russian music Mikhail Ivanovich Glinka. This is a memorable date.

"Glinka year" should be a new stage in popularizing the heritage of the composer, in careful study of his inspiring work. It is an honorable task of Soviet musicians to learn from Glinka, to follow his wise counsels and creatively to develop the great Glinka traditions. ...

Soviet composers meet the new year, 1954, with well known achievements. In the past year the repertoire of our music theaters has been enriched with operas on historical themes—Yu. Shaporin's *The Decembrists,* K. Dankevich's *Bogdan Khmel'nitski* (revised version), N. Peiko's Bashkirian opera *Aikhylu,* and the ballet *On the Shores of the Sea* by the young Lithuanian composer J. Juzeliunas. The Bol'shoi Theater is ready to produce S. Prokof'yev's ballet *The Stone Flower.* Several valuable works have appeared also in the genres of symphony and oratorio music (I wish to note V. Salmanov's symphony, cantatas by A. Chimakadze and V. Chistyakov, the symphonic poem *Pavlik Morozov* by Yu. Balkashin, and A. Balanchivadze's concerto), chamber, instrumental and vocal music (A. Babadzhanyan's trio, Yu. Levitin's *Quartet No. 7,* Yu. Sviridov's splendid vocal poem "My Motherland" with verses by A. Isaakyan, which was first heard last November). The recently held seventh plenary session of the board of the Union of Soviet Composers acquainted us also with new popular songs.

For all that, what we accomplished last year still cannot meet the growing esthetic demand of the Soviet people. Our young composers did not work hard enough. They have open to them all paths, all opportunities for indefatigable creative search, for improving their mastery. Yet after their first success some young composers surrender to self-satisfied complacency. It must be said that this reproach applies also to some masters of the older generation who work uninspiredly, without genuine creative absorption, without the necessary intensity. One cannot consider it reasonable that a composer who turns out two or three songs a year considers his mission fulfilled. Creative passivity inevitably leads to decline of talent and dilettantism.

The great Soviet composers S. Prokof'yev and N. Myaskovski, who always worked at the full of their creative powers, set examples of high professionalism in art. Although they had created numerous works in all genres, they continued to work with tremendous intensity to the last days of their lives. An untiring professional is R. Glière, a great master of the oldest generation of Soviet composers. When he finishes one work he has already begun another, unswervingly fulfilling his extensive "production plan."

That is how we all should work—both the composers of the older generation and our talented youth. ...

In 1954 there must resound new and good operas, ballets, symphonies, oratorios, instrumental works, choral works and art songs. We want to hear new, enjoyable popular songs, and witty and vivid stage music.

It must be hoped that in 1954 the work of the Union of Soviet Composers will improve. This organization still suffers from bureaucratic evils. The unnecessary bureaucratic fuss which flourishes in the Union often takes the place of living creative discussions of interesting works (even if [they are] of the kind which is subject to discussion!) It is necessary that creative discussions be boldly presented in the pages of our magazine also; the magazine [Soviet Music] should be the initiator and inspirer of arguments, an arena for living clash of opinions.

The recent declaration by *Pravda* concerning the production of *The Storm* at the Moscow Drama Theater seems to me extremely noteworthy and important. This article warmly supports the artist's right to daring search for originality.

"One of the worst calamities which can befall art is indulgence in levelling, forcing art into a single fixed pattern, even though it be the best," says *Pravda*. "Such treatment of a work of art obliterates individuality, gives rise to stereotype and imitation, hinders the development of creative thought and eliminates from art the joy of the quest."

> Socialist realism opens up vast scope for the artist's thought and provides the greatest freedom to creative individuality and development of the most varied genres, trends, and styles. That is why it becomes so important to support an artist's daring efforts at times, to study his creative style and, in judging the merits and shortcomings of his handling of an artistic problem,

to bear in mind the artist's right to independence, boldness and originality.

These wise words cannot, of course, go unnoticed in the Union of Soviet Composers, as in other organizations. In solving any creative problem the chief thing determining success is true idea direction, talent and mastery. One cannot forget this in analyzing and judging this or that artistic phenomenon. In our disputes the most important argument should be whether the work has lofty ideas and artistic qualities, not whether its author or composer belongs to this or that tendency.

It seems to me that the Union should not "guard" our composers from search for the new, from following independent, untrod paths of art. We should fear not daring creative originality but "safe" superficiality, dullness and stereotyped work.

The effort to smooth over sharp edges in creative work seems to me one of the manifestations of the erroneous "no-conflict" theory. The sooner we reject these levelling tendencies, the better it will be for the development of Soviet art.

I believe ardently in the bright future of our Soviet music. It is strong in vivid talents, great realistic traditions, indivisible ties with the people and with the people's strivings and interests.

We Soviet composers have before us a boundless field of activity.

May 1954 be marked by great new achievements of Soviet music, may there grow and develop truthful, advanced, daring Soviet music, rich in thought and dear and close to the people!

BIBLIOGRAPHY

The bibliography includes the following types of material:

1. Books and articles published in the Soviet Union by and about Soviet composers and musicologists.

2. Books and articles about pre-Soviet composers of the Russian Empire published under the Soviet regime.

3. Books and articles about Soviet music by non-Soviet authors.

4. Source and autobiographical material on Russian contemporary composers who have left the Soviet Union.

Except for periodicals, the bibliography has been compiled primarily from the card catalogues of the New York Public Library and Columbia University Library; *A Catalog of Books Represented by Library of Congress Printed Cards Issued to July 31, 1942,* 167 vols., Washington, D.C.; the two supplements to this work for the years 1942-1947 and 1948-1952, 42 and 23 vols.; and the *Monthly List of Russian Accessions,* published by the Library of Congress. The *Monthly List of Russian Accessions* provides an index of articles published in the Soviet journal *Sovetskaya muzyka* [Soviet Music].

An asterisk preceding a name indicates that a biography of that person can be found in the second edition of *Bol'shaya sovetskaya entsiklopediya* [Large Soviet Encyclopedia], Moscow, 1949–.

A dagger preceding a name indicates that the person in question is a Stalin Prize winner and that a biography of him can be found in Bernandt, *Sovetskiye kompozitory (q.v.).*

Abbreviations Used:

L. Leningrad
M. Moscow
P. Petrograd
SI *Sovetskoye iskusstvo* [Soviet Art], Moscow (newspaper).
SM *Sovetskaya muzyka* [Soviet Music], Moscow.

Abbreviations of Libraries:

CLU University of California at Los Angeles, Calif.
CSt-H Hoover Library of War, Revolution and Peace, Stanford

University, Stanford, Calif.

CU	University of California, Berkeley, Calif.
CaTU	University of Toronto, Toronto, Canada.
CtY	Yale University, New Haven, Conn.
DLC	Library of Congress, Washington, D.C.
DS	U.S. Department of State, Washington, D.C.
DSI-M	U.S. National Museum, Smithsonian Institute, Washington, D.C.
ICU	University of Chicago, Chicago, Ill.
InU	Indiana University, Bloomington, Ind.
MH	Harvard University, Cambridge, Mass.
MiDW	Wayne University, Detroit, Mich.
NIC	Cornell University, Ithaca, N.Y.
NN	New York Public Library, New York, N.Y.
NNC	Columbia University, New York, N.Y.
NNM	American Museum of Natural History, New York, N.Y.
NhD	Dartmouth College, Hanover, N.H.
OCl	Cleveland Public Library, Cleveland, Ohio.
WaU	University of Washington, Seattle, Wash.

I. BOOKS AND ARTICLES

Abraham, Gerald Ernest Heal (1904-), *Eight Soviet Composers*, London, Oxford University Press, 1943, 102 p. [DLC; NN; NNC]

——, *On Russian Music: Critical and Historical Studies. . .*, London, Reeves, New York, Scribner, 1939, 279 p. [DLC; NN; NNC]

Abramova, A., *Musorgski: kinostsenarii* [Musorgsky: Film Scenario], M., 1951, 101 p. [DLC]

Adorno, Theodor W., "Die gegängelte Musik," *Der Monat*, Berlin-Dahlem, Vol. V, No. 56, May 1953, pp. 177-183. [DLC; NN; NNC]

Analysis of communiqué of the Communist-controlled Second International Congress of Composers and Music Critics held in Prague. General and fairly technical considerations on music under Soviet dictatorship.

Akademiya nauk SSSR. Institut istorii iskusstv [U.S.S.R. Academy of Sciences. Institute of the History of the Arts], *Pamyati akademika Borisa Vladimirovicha Asaf'yeva: sbornik statei o nauchno-kriticheskom nasledii* [In Memory of Academician Boris Vladimirovich Asaf'yev: Collected Articles on (His) Critico-Scientific Heritage], M., 1951, 93 p. [DLC]

Akymenko *(pseud.)*, *see* Yakymenko, Fedir.

Alabev, *see* Alyab'yev.

* †Aleksandrov, Aleksandr Vasil'yevich (1883-1946). *See* Polyanovski.

* †Aleksandrov, Anatoli Nikolayevich (1888-). *See* Belyayev, V.M.

* †Aleksandrov, Boris Aleksandrovich (1905-).

Alekseyev, A.D., *Russkiye pianisty: ocherki i materialy po istorii pianizma* [Russian Pianists: Essays and Materials on the History of the Piano], M., 1948, 313 p. [DLC]

Al'shvang, Arnol'd Aleksandrovich, *Aleksandr Nikolayevich Skryabin: k 25-letiyu so dnya smerti* [Aleksandr Nikolayevich Scriabin: For the Twenty-fifth Anniversary of His Death], M., 1940, 62 p. [NN]

——, *M.P. Musorgski: populyarnyi ocherk* [M.P. Musorgsky: A Popular Essay], M., 1946, 19 p. [DLC]

——, *"N.A. Rimsky-Korsakov," VOKS Bulletin*, M., 1942, No. 3-4, pp. 78-82. [DLC]

——, *Opyt analiza tvorchestva P.I. Chaikovskovo: 1864-1878* [An Attempt at an Analysis of the Work of P.I. Tchaikovsky: 1864-1878], M.-L., 1951, 255 p. [DLC; NN]

——, *Sovetskii simfonizm: populyarnyi ocherk* [The Soviet Symphony: A Popular Essay], M., 1946, 19 p. [DLC]

Altayev, Al. *(pseud.)*, *see* Yamshchikova.

*Alyab'yev, Aleksandr Aleksandrovich (1787-1851). *See* Dobrokhotov.

American Russian Institute of Southern California, Hollywood, *On Soviet Music: Documents and Discussion*, Hollywood, 1948, 22 p. [DLC; NNC]

Includes text of the Party resolution on Muradeli's opera *The Great Friendship*, pp. 1-6, as printed in the *U.S.S.R. Information Bulletin*, Wash., D.C., February 28, 1948; also statements by Aram I. Khachaturian, pp. 12-13, Vano I. Muradeli, pp. 13-15, Sergei S. Prokof'yev, pp. 9-11, and Dmitri D. Shostakovich, pp. 7-9.

*†Amirov, Fikret Meshadi Dzhamil ogly (1922-).

*Andriashvili, Akaki Kirillovich (1904-).

Angert, G.A., *100 oper: libretto oper, kharakteristiki i biografii kompozitorov* [One Hundred Operas: Opera Librettos, Profiles and Biographies of Composers], ed. by Leonid L. Sabaneyev, M., 1927, 277 p. [NN]

Apraksina, O.A., *Muzykal'noye vospitaniye v russkoi obshcheobrazovatel'noi shkole* [Musical Training in the Russian School of General Education], M., 1948, 146 p. [DLC; NN]

*†Arakishvili (Arakchiyev), Dmitri Ignat'yevich (1873-), *Kratkii istoricheskii obzor gruzinskoi muzyki* [Short Historical Review of Georgian Music], Tbilisi, 1940, 69 p. [DLC]

____. *See* Begidzhanov.

*Arkhangel'ski, Aleksandr Andreyevich (1846-1924).

Artemovski, *see* Hulak-Artemovs'kyi.

*†Arutyunyan, Aleksandr Grigor'yevich (1920-).

*†Asaf'yev, Boris Vladimirovich (Igor' Glebov, *pseud.*) (1884-1949), *Anton Grigor'yevich Rubinshtein v yevo muzykal'noi deyatel'nosti i otzyvakh sovremennikov (1829-1929)* [Anton Grigor'yevich Rubinstein in His Musical Activity and in the Opinions of Contemporaries (1829-1929)], M., 1929, 181 p. [NN]

____, *Chaikovski* [Tchaikovsky], P., 1921, 25 p. [NN]

____, *Chaikovski: opyt kharakteristiki* [Tchaikovsky: An Attempt at a Characterization], P.-Berlin, 1923, 48 p. [NN]

——, *"Charodeika": opera P.I. Chaikovskovo: opyt raskrytiya intonatsionnovo soderzhaniya* [*The Enchantress*, an Opera by P.I. Tchaikovsky: An Attempt to Shed Light on Its Intonational Content], M., 1947, 38 p. [DLC; NN]

——, ed., *De Musica: sbornik statei* [De Musica: A Collection of Articles], P., 1923, 122 p. [DLC]
Articles by Boris V. Asaf'yev, Aleksei V. Finagin, Semyon L. Ginzburg, Roman I. Gruber, and Boris Zotov.

——, "Doklad B.V. Asaf'yeva" [Report by B.V. Asaf'yev], *SI*, No. 17(1105), April 24, 1948. [NN]

——, *Glazunov: opyt kharakteristiki* [Glazunov: An Attempt at a Characterization], L., 1925, 128 p.

——, *Glinka*, M., 1947, 306 p.; 2nd ed., 1950, 308 p. [DLC; NN; NNC]

——, *Instrumental'noye tvorchestvo Chaikovskovo* [The Instrumental Work of Tchaikovsky], P., 1922, 69 p. [DLC; NN]

——, *Izbrannye raboty o M.I. Glinke* [Selected Works on M.I. Glinka], M., 1952, 398 p. (*Izbrannye trudy* [Selected Works], Vol. I.) [NN]

——, *Izbrannye stat'i o russkoi muzyke* [Selected Articles on Russian Music], 2 vols., M., 1952. [DLC]

——, "J.A. Šaporin" [i.e., Yu. A. Shaporin], *Tempo*, Prague, Vol. XIX, No. 6-7, 1947, pp. 192-195. [NN]

——, *K vosstanovleniyu "Borisa Godunova" Musorgskovo: sbornik statei* [Towards a Restoration of *Boris Godunov* by Musorgsky: A Collection of Articles], M., 1928, 72 p. [NN]

——, *Kniga o Stravinskom* [Book About Stravinsky], L., 1929, 398 p. [NN; NNC]

——, "Kratkii otchot o deyatel'nosti Rossiiskovo instituta istorii iskusstv" [Brief Report on the Activity of the All-Russian Institute for the History of the Arts], in the collection *Zadachi i metody izucheniya iskusstv* [Tasks and Methods in Studying the Arts], P., 1924, pp. 169-229. [NN]

——, "Mjaskovjskji" [i.e., N. Ya. Myaskovski], *Tempo,* Prague, Vol. XIX, No. 2-3, 1946, pp. 56-59. [NN]

——, *Musorgski: opyt kharakteristiki* [Musorgsky: An Attempt at a Characterization], M., 1923, 69 p. [DLC; NN]

——, *Muzykal'naya forma kak protsess* [Musical Form As Process], Vol. I, M., 1930.

——, *ibid.,* Vol. II, *Intonatsiya* [Intonation], M., 1947, 163 p. [DLC; NN]

——, *Nikolai Andreyevich Rimski-Korsakov (1844-1944),* M., 1944, 90 p. [DLC; NN; NNC]

——, *P.I. Chaikovski: 1840-1893* [P.I. Tchaikovsky: 1840-1893], P., 1921, 19 p. [NN]

——, "Portréty sovětských skladatelů: Šostakovič" [Portraits of Soviet Composers: Shostakovich], *Tempo,* Prague, Vol. XIX, No. 6-7, 1947, pp. 188-192. [NN]

——, *Rimski-Korsakov: opyt kharakteristiki* [Rimsky-Korsakov: An Attempt at a Characterization], P.-Berlin, 1923, 56 p. [DLC; NN]

——, *Russkaya muzyka ot nachala XIX stoletiya* [Russian Music from the Beginning of the Nineteenth Century], M.-L., 1930, xiii+319 p. [NN]

——, ed., *Russkii romans: opyt intonatsionnovo analiza: sbornik statei* [The Russian Romance: An Attempt at Intonational Analysis: A Collection of Articles], M., 1930, 167 p. [NN]
Articles by Boris V. Asaf'yev, Yelizaveta L. Dattel', Zinaida V. Ewald, S.D. Maggid, Aleksandr S. Rabinovich, Yelena Tynyanova, and R.I. Zaritskaya.

——, "Šebalin" [i.e., Vissarion Yakovlevich Shebalin], *Tempo,* Prague, Vol. XIX, No. 8, 1947, pp. 248-251. [NN]

——, *Sergei Prokof'yev: ocherk* [Sergei Prokof'yev: An Essay], L., 1927, 37 p. [NN]

——, "Sergěj Prokofěv," *Tempo*, Prague, Vol. XIX, No. 4, 1947, pp. 111-115. [NN]

——, *Simfonicheskiye etyudy* [Symphonic Etudes], P., 1922, 328 p. [DLC; NNC]

——, *Skryabin: opyt kharakteristiki* [Scriabin: An Attempt at a Characterization], P.-Berlin, 1923, 50 p. [DLC; NNC]

——, *Skryabin, 1871-1915*, P., 192-?, 26 p. [NN]

——, *Slovar' naiboleye neobkhodimykh muzykal'notekhnicheskikh oboznachenii* [Dictionary of the Most Essential Musical-Technical Terms], P., 1919, 102 p. [NN]

——, *Tschaikowskys "Eugen Onegin": Versuch einer Analyse des Stils und der musikalischen Dramaturgie*, Potsdam, Athenaion, 1949, 150 p. [DLC]

——, "Volnuyushchiye voprosy: vmesto vystupleniya na tvorcheskoi diskussii" [Stirring Problems: In Lieu of a Speech at the Creative Discussion], *SM*, May 1936, No. 5, pp. 24-27. [NN]
Concerning the *Pravda* articles on Shostakovich's ballet *Limpid Stream* and his opera *Lady Macbeth of Mtsensk*. For material on the "Creative Discussion," see the article "Protiv formalizma i fal'shi. . . ."

——, ed., *Voprosy muzyki v shkole: sbornik statei* [Problems of Music in School: A Collection of Articles], L., 1926, 284 p. [NN]

——. See *Akademiya nauk SSSR. Institut istorii iskusstv;* Bogdanov-Berezovski; Hoffmann-Erbrecht; [*Leningradskaya filarmoniya*]; Zhitomirski.

——, and Vasili V. Yakovlev, eds., *P.I. Chaikovski* [P.I. Tchaikovsky], P., 1920, 184 p. (*Proshloye russkoi muzyki: materialy i issledovaniya* [The Past of Russian Music: Materials and Research], Vol. I.) [CU; DLC; NN; NNC]

* †Ashrafi, Mukhtar Ashrafovich (1912-).

* †Azmaiparashvili, Shalva I'lich (1902-).

B., "God raboty universiteta muzykal'noi kul'tury TsDKA im. M.V. Frunze" [A Year of Work by the University of Musical Culture of the M.V. Frunze Central House of the Soviet Army], *SM*, July 1949, No. 7, p. 89.

*Baiganin, Nurpeis (1860-1945).

*Baizakov, Isa (1900-1946).

Bal y Gay, Jesús, "Musica intramuros: la situación de la música en la U.R.S.S.," *Nuestra musica*, Mexico, July 1948, pp. 163-187. [NN]

*Balakirev, Mily Alekseyevich (1836-1910), and Vladimir Vasil'yevich Stasov (1824-1906), *Perepiska M.A. Balakireva s V.V. Stasovym (1858-1869)* [The Correspondence of M.A. Balakirev with V.V. Stasov (1858-1869)], ed. with foreword and commentary by Vlad. Karenin, introduction by Grigori L. Kiselyov, M., 1935, 276 p. [NN]

Balakirev, Mily Alekseyevich (1836-1910), and Nikolai Andreyevich Rimsky-Korsakov (1844-1908), "Perepiska M.A. Balakireva i N.A. Rimskovo-Korsakova" [Correspondence of M.A. Balakirev and N.A. Rimsky-Korsakov], *Muzykal'nyi sovremennik* [Musical Contemporary], P., 1917, No. 7-8, pp. 56-76. [NN]

Balakirev. *See* Bunimovich; Fyodorova.

* †Balanchivadze, Andrei Melitonovich (1906-).

Balanchivadze, Meliton. *See* Khuchua.

* †Balasanyan, Sergei Artyom'yevich (1902-).

"Baletnaya fal'sh': balet 'Svetlyi ruchei,' libretto F. Lopukhova i Piotvorskovo, muzyka D. Shostakovicha. Postanovka Bol'shovo Teatra" [Falsification of the Ballet: The Ballet *Limpid Stream* with Libretto by F. Lopukhov and Piotvorski and Music by D. Shostakovich. Performance by the Bol'shoi Theater], *Pravda*, No. 36(6642), February 6, 1936.

Barenboim, L.A., and Vladimir Il'ich Muzalevski, comps., *Khrestomatiya po istorii fortepiannoi muzyki v Rossii: konets XVIII i pervaya polovina XIX vekov* [A Reader for the History of Piano Music in Russia: The End of the Eighteenth and the First Half of the Nineteenth Centuries], M., 1949, 323 p. [DLC]

*Barkhudaryan, Sergei (Sarkis) Vasil'yevich (1887-).

Barski, Sergei, "Kniga o gibeli burzhuaznovo iskusstva: 'Doktor Faustus' Tomasa Manna" [A Book About the Downfall of Bourgeois Art: Thomas Mann's *Doctor Faustus*], *SM*, May 1951, No. 5, pp. 117-119.

Begidzhanov, A., *Dmitri Arakishvili*, M., 1953, 176 p.

*Belyayev, Mitrofan Petrovich (1836-1904). *See* Scriabin.

Belyayev, Viktor Mikhailovich (1888-), *Aleksandr Alekseyevich Shenshin*, M., 1929, 32 p. Text in Russian and German. [DLC; NN; NNC]

——, *Aleksandr Konstantinovich Glazunov: materialy k yevo biografii* [Aleksandr Konstantinovich Glazunov: Materials for His Biography], Part I, *Zhizn'* [Life], P., 1922, 150 p. [DLC; NN; NNC]

——, *Anatoli Nikolayevich Aleksandrov*, M., 1927, 38 p. Text in Russian and German. [DLC; NN; NNC]

——, *Belorusskaya narodnaya muzyka* [Byelorussian Folk Music], L., 1941.

——, *Georgi L'vovich Katuar: George Catoire*, M., 1926, 40 p. Text in Russian and German. [DLC; NN]

——, *Igor Stravinsky's Les noces: An Outline*, tr. from Russian by S.W. Pring, London, Oxford, 1928, 37 p. [DLC; NN; NNC]

——, *Muzykal'nye instrumenty Uzbekistana* [Musical Instruments of Uzbekistan], with musical score examples, sketches by A. Mazayev, M., 1933, 133 p. [DLC; NN: lacks chart]

——, *Nikolai Yakovlevich Myaskovski*, M., 1927, 30 p. Text in Russian and German. [DLC; NN; NNC]

___, *Samuil Yevgen'yevich Feinberg,* M., 1927, 24 p. Text in Russian and German. [DLC; NN; NNC]

___, *Sergei Nikiforovich Vasilenko,* M., 1927, 42 p. Text in Russian and German. [DLC; NN]

* †Belyi, Viktor Aronovich (1904-).

Bėlza (Boelza), Igor' Fyodorovich (1904-), *A.P. Borodin,* M., 1944, 53 p. [DLC; NN]; 1947, 69 p. [DLC]

___, *A.P. Borodin: populyarnyi ocherk* [A.P. Borodin: A Popular Essay], M., 1946, 16 p. [DLC]

___, *B.M. Lyatoshyns'kyi,* Kiev, 1947, 61 p. [DLC; NN; NNC]; Russian ed., M., 1947, 53 p. [DLC]

___, *Dvadtsat' pervaya i dvadtsat' sed'maya simfonii N. Ya. Myaskovskovo* [The Twenty-first and Twenty-seventh Symphonies of N. Ya. Myaskovski], M., 1951, 34 p. [DLC; NN]

___, *Handbook of Soviet Musicians,* ed. by Alan Bush, 2nd ed., London, Pilot Press, 1944, xiv+101 p. [NN; NNC]
First ed., September 1943.

___, *Russkiye klassiki i muzykal'naya kul'tura zapadnovo slavyanstva* [Russian Classicists and the Musical Culture of Western Slavdom], M., 1950, 66 p. [DLC]

___, *S.I. Taneyev i russkaya opera: sbornik statei* [S.I. Taneyev and Russian Opera: A Collection of Articles], M., 1946, 167 p. [DLC; NN; NNC]

___, *S.V. Rakhmaninov i russkaya opera: sbornik statei* [S.V. Rachmaninov and Russian Opera: A Collection of Articles], M., 1947, 197 p. [CLU; DLC; NN]

___, *V. Ya. Shebalin,* M., 1945, 58 p. [DLC]

___, *Vtoraya (Bogatyrskaya) simfoniya Borodina: Poyasneniye* [The Second *(Bogatyr)* Symphony of Borodin: Comments], M., 1951, 20 p. [DLC]

Beregovski, M., comp., *Yevreiskii muzykal'nyi fol'klor* [Jewish Musical Folklore], ed. by M. Viner, Vol. I, M., 1934. [NNC]

Berkman, T., *A.N. Yesipova: zhizn', deyatel'nost' i pedagogicheskiye printsipy* [A.N. Yesipova: Her Life, Work and Pedagogical Principles], ed. and introduction by G.M. Kogan, M.–L., 1948, 141 p. [DLC]

Berkov, Pavel Naumovich (1896-), ed., *Russkaya komediya i komicheskaya opera XVIII veka* [Russian Comedy and Comic Opera of the Eighteenth Century], M., 1950, 731 p. [DLC; MH; NN]

Berkov, Viktor Osipovich, *Garmoniya Glinki* [The Harmony of Glinka], M., 1948, 252 p. [DLC; NN]

____, *Gogol' o muzyke* [Gogol on Music], M., 1952, 31 p. [NN]

____, *Uchebnik garmonii Rimskovo-Korsakovo: znacheniye, teoreticheskiye osnovy, metodika: ocherk* [The Manual of Harmony by Rimsky-Korsakov: Its Significance, Theoretical Bases and Methodology: An Essay], M., 1953, 70 p. [DLC]

Berlyand-Chernaya, Ye., *Pushkin i Chaikovski* [Pushkin and Tchaikovsky], M., 1950, 141 p. [NNC]

Bernandt, G.B., "'Pesn' o lesakh' D. Shostakovicha" [D. Shostakovich's *Song of the Forests*], *SM*, December 1949, No. 12, pp. 60-65.

____, *S.I. Taneyev*, M., 1950, 377 p. [DLC; NN]

____, *S.I. Taneyev*, M., 1951, 28 p. [DLC]

____, comp., *Sovetskiye kompozitory–laureaty stalinskoi premii: spravochnik*, [Handbook of Soviet Composers, Stalin Prize Winners], M., 1952, 137 p. [DLC; NN]

Composers whose names appear in the bibliography preceded by a dagger (†) are listed in Bernandt. In addition, short biographies of the following composers are also included:

Afanas'yev, Leonid Viktorovich (1921-); Babadzhanyan, Arno Arutyunovich (1921-); Bunin, Vladimir Vasil'yevich

(1908-); Chernetski, Semyon Aleksandrovich (1881-1950); Dekhterev, Vasili Aleksandrovich (1910-); Dzhangirov, Dzhangir Shirgesht ogly (1921-); Ernesaks, Gustav Gustavovich (1908-); Fylyppenko, Arkadiy Dmytrovych (1912-); Gadzhibekov, Sultan Ismail ogly (1919-); Galynin, German Germanovich (1922-); Gomolyaka, Vadim Borisovich (1914-); Ivanov-Radkevich, Nikolai Pavlovich (1904-); Karayev, Kara Abul'faz ogly (1918-); Kats, Sigizmund Abramovich (1908-); Kochurov, Yuri Vladimirovich (1907-); Korchmarev, Klementi Arkad'yevich (1899-); Kos-Anatols'ki, Anatoli Iosifovich (1909-); Krasev, Mikhail Ivanovich (1898-); Kryukov, Nikolai Nikolayevich (1908-); Kuzham'yarov, Kuddus Khodzham'yarovich (1918-); Kyrver, Boris Vol'demarovich (1917-); Leman, Al'bert Semyonovich (1915-); Levitin, Yuri Abramovich (1912-); Lukin, Filipp Mironovich (1913-); Lyuban, Isaak Isaakovich (1906-); Machavariani, Aleksei Davidovich (1913-); Maiboroda, Platon Illarionovich (1918-); Makarov, Valentin Alekseyevich (1908-); Manevich, Aleksandr Mendeleyevich (1908-); Massalitinov, Konstantin Irakliyevich (1905-); Mazayev, Arkadi Nikolayevich (1909-); Meitus, Yuli Sergeyevich (1903-); Milyutin, Yuri Sergeyevich (1903-); Mokrousov, Boris Andreyevich (1909-); Morozov, Igor' Vladimirovich (1913-); Mshvelidze, Shalva Mikhailovich (1904-); Mukhatov, Velimukhamed (1916-); Muravlyov, Aleksei Alekseyevich (1924-); Nikolayeva, Tat'yana Petrovna (1924-); Nyaga, Stepan Timofeyevich (1900-1951); Peiko, Nikolai Ivanovich (1916-); Pokrass, Dmitri Yakovlevich (1899-); Reiman, Villem Madisovich (1906-); Rustamov, Seid Ali ogly (1907-); Sadykov, Talib (1907-); Satyan, Ashot Movsesovich (1906-); Shvedas, Ionas Izidoryaus (1908-); Skul'te, Adol'f Petrovich (1909-); Starokadomski, Mikhail Leonidovich (1901-); Stepanov, Lev Borisovich (1908-); Stepanyan, Aro Leonovich (1897-); Svechnikov, Anatoli Grigor'yevich (1908-); Tallat-Kelpsha, Iosif Antonovich (1888-1949); Toradze, David Aleksandrovich (1922-); Tsintsadze, Sulkhan Fyodorovich (1925-); Tulikov, Serafim Sergeyevich (1914-); Vainyunas, Stasis Andreyevich (1909-); Yudakov, Solomon (Suleiman) Aleksandrovich (1916-); Zarin', Marger Ottovich (1910-).

"Beseda tovarishchei Stalina i Molotova s avtorami opernovo spektaklya 'Tikhii Don' " [A Talk Between Comrades Stalin and Molotov and the Authors of the Operatic Spectacle *The Quiet Don*], *Pravdá,* No. 20(6626), January 20, 1936.

* †Blanter, Matvei Isaakovich (1903-).

*Blazhevich, Vladislav Mikhailovich (1881-1942).

Blok, M., "Vazhnyi etap v razvitii sovetskovo muzykoznaniya: Vsesoyuznaya nauchnaya sessiya po muzykoznaniyu" [An Important Stage in the Development of Soviet Musicology: The All-Union Scientific Session on Musicology], *SM*, April 1950, No. 4, pp. 48-54.

*Blumenfel'd, Feliks Mikhailovich (1863-1931).

Boelza, *see* Belza.

Bogatyrev, S. S., *Dvoinoi kanon* [The Two-Part Canon], M.–L., 1947, 128 p. [DLC; NN]

* †Bogatyryov, Anatoli Vasil'yevich (1913-).

Bogdanov-Berezovski, Valer'yan Mikhailovich (1868-), *B.V. Asaf'yev*, L., 1937, 28 p. [NN]

____, "B.V. Asaf'yev: opyt kharakteristiki" [B.V. Asaf'yev: An Attempt at a Characterization], *Novyi mir* [New World], M., 1935, No. 5, pp. 275-288. [NN]

____, *Opernoye i baletnoye tvorchestvo Chaikovskovo: ocherki* [The Operatic and Ballet Work of Tchaikovsky: Essays], L., 1940, 117 p. [DLC; NN]

____, *Sovetskaya opera* [Soviet Opera], ed. by M.A. Glukh, L–M., 1940, 261 p. [DLC; NNC]

____, *Yu. A. Shaporin i yevo simfoniya* [Yu. A. Shaporin and His Symphony], L., 1934, 29 p. [NN]

Bol'shaya sovetskaya entsiklopediya [Large Soviet Encyclopedia], 2nd ed., 22 vols. to date, M., 1949- .
Composers whose names appear in the bibliography preceded by an asterisk (*) are listed in *Bol'shaya.*

"Bol'she vnimaniya fortepiannoi muzyke: otkrytoye pis'mo kompozitoram" [More Attention to Piano Music: An Open Letter to Composers], *SI*, No. 50(1334), June 23, 1951.

Bol'shemennikov, A., "O rabote muzykal'novo izdatel'stva" [On the Work of the Music Publishing House], *SM*, January 1951, No. 1, pp. 58-63.

*Borodin, Aleksandr Porfir'yevich (1833-1887), *Muzykal'no-kriticheskiye stat'i* [Articles of Musical Criticism], M., 1951, 64 p. [NN]

____, *Pis'ma A.P. Borodina* [The Letters of A.P. Borodin], introduction and notes by Sergei A. Dianin, 4 vols., M., 1927-1950. [DLC; NN]

1857-1877, Vols. I-II, 1927-1928; *1878-1887*, Vols. III-IV, 1949-1950.

____. *See* Bélza; Braudo; Figurovski; Khubov; Kremelev; Marshak; Popova, T.V.; Remezov.

*Bortnyansky, Dmitri Stepanovich (1751-1825). *See* Dobrokhotov.

*Brandukov, Anatoli Andreyevich (1859-1930). *See* Ginzburg, L.

Braudo, Yevgeni Maksimovich (1882-), "A.P. Borodin," *Apollon* [Apollo], P., 1917, No. 2-3, pp. 50-59. [NN]

____, *Aleksandr Porfir'yevich Borodin: yevo zhizn' i tvorchestvo* [Aleksandr Porfir'yevich Borodin: His Life and Work], P., 1922, 151 p. [DLC; NN]

____, *"Boris Godunov" Musorgskovo* [Musorgsky's *Boris Godunov*], M., 1927, 45 p. [NN]

____, *Borodin*, P., 1922, 15 p. [NN]

____, *Istoriya muzyki: szhatyi ocherk* [A History of Music: A Condensed Essay], 2nd ed. corrected and supplemented, M., 1935, 463 p. [DLC]

____, *Osnovnye voprosy opernoi politiki* [Fundamental Problems of Opera Policy], ed. by L. Obolenski, L., 1929, 20 p. [DLC]

____, *Osnovy material'noi kul'tury v muzyke* [Elements of Material Culture in Music], M., 1924.

____, "Tsezar' Antonovich Kyui: 1835-1918" [Cesar Antonovich Cui: 1835-1918], *Apollon* [Apollo], P., 1917, No. 8-10, pp. 8-12. [NN]

____, *Vseobshchaya istoriya muzyki* [General History of Music], 2 vols., P.–M., 1922-1925. [DLC; NN]; Vol. III, M.–L., 1926. *Do kontsa 16 stoletiya* [To the End of the Sixteenth Century], P., 1922, Vol. I, 205 p.; *Ot nachala 17 do serediny 19 stoletiya* [From the Beginning of the Seventeenth to the Middle of the Nineteenth Century], M., 1925, Vol. II, 566 p.

____, and Nikolai Ernestovich Radlov (1889-), eds., *"Ekspressionizm": sbornik statei* ["Expressionism": A Collection of Articles], P., 1923, 232 p. [NNC]

Brazhnikov, M.V., *Puti razvitiya i zadachi rasshifrovki znamennovo rospeva XII-XVIII vekov: primeneniye nekotorykh statisticheskikh metod k issledovaniyu muzykal'nykh yavlenii* [The Development and Problems in Ciphering the Neumatic Chant of the Twelfth-Eighteenth Centuries: The Application of Statistical Methods in the Investigation of Musical Phenomena], L., 1949, 101 p. [CtY; NN]

Bruk, M., *Marian Koval'*, M.–L., 1950.

*†Brusilovski, Yevgeni Grigor'yevich (1905-). *See* [*Leningradskaya filarmoniya*].

*Bryusova, Nadezhda Yakovlevna (1881-), *Russkaya narodnaya pesnya v russkoi klassike i sovetskoi muzyke* [The Russian Folk Song in Russian Classics and in Soviet Music], M., 1948, 135 p. [DLC; InU; NN]

____, *Vladimir Zakharov*, M., 1949, 45 p. [DLC]

____. *See* "Protiv formalizma...."

*†Budashkin, Nikolai Pavlovich (1910-).

Budyakovski, Andrei Yevgen'yevich (1905-), *Chaikovski: kratkii ocherk zhizni i tvorchestva* [Tchaikovsky: A Brief Sketch of His Life and Work], 2nd ed. corrected and supplemented, L., 1936, 38 p. [NNC]

____, *P.I. Chaikovski: simfonicheskaya muzyka* [P.I. Tchaikovsky: Symphonic Music], L., 1935, 273 p. [DLC; NN]

Bugoslavski, Sergei Alekseyevich (1888-), *Mikhail Ivanovich Glinka,* M., 1943, 25 p. [NN]

____, *M.M. Ippolitov-Ivanov: zhizn' i tvorchestvo* [M.M. Ippolitov-Ivanov: Life and Work], M., 1936, 54 p. [DLC]

____, *Reingol'd Moritsevich Glier: R.M. Glière,* M., 1927, 59 p. Text in Russian and German. [DLC; NN]

____, and Ivan Petrovich Shishov (1888-), comps., *Russkaya narodnaya pesnya* [The Russian Folk Song], ed. by M. Grinberg, M., 1936, 190 p. [NNC]

Bunimovich, Vladimir Il'ich (Muzalevski, *pseud.*), *M.A. Balakirev: kritiko-biograficheskii ocherk* [M. A. Balakirev: A Critico-Biographical Essay], L., 1938, 135 p. [DLC]

____, *Russkaya fortepiannaya muzyka: ocherki i materialy po istorii russkoi fortepiannoi kul'tury (XVIII - pervoi poloviny XIX st.)* [Russian Piano Music: Essays and Materials on the History of Russian Piano Music (The Eighteenth and the First Half of the Nineteenth Centuries)], L., 1949, 358 p. [DLC; NN; NNC]

____. *Starsheishii russkii khor: k 225-letiyu leningradskoi gosudarstvennoi akademicheskoi kapelly* [The Oldest Russian Chorus: The Two Hundred Twenty-fifth Anniversary of the Leningrad State Academic Choir], L., 1938, 72 p.[NN]

____. *See* Barenboim.

Burkhanov, Mutal Muzainovich (1916-). *See* "Neobkhodim...."

*Catoire (Katuar), Georgi L'vovich (1861-1926), *Muzykal'naya forma* [Musical Form], 2 parts, M., 1934-1936.

____, *Teoreticheskii kurs garmonii* [Theoretical Course of Harmony], 2 parts, M., 1924-1925. [DLC?]

____. *See* Belyayev, V.M.

Cazden, Norman, "What's Happening in Soviet Music?," *Masses and Mainstream*, New York, Vol. I, No. 2, April 1948, pp. 11-24. [DLC; NN; NNC]

Chaikovski, *see* Tchaikovsky.

Chelyapov, Nikolai Ivanovich (1889-), ed., *Muzykal'nyi al'manakh: sbornik statei* [Musical Almanac: A Collection of Articles], M., 1932, 119 p. [NN]

——. *See* "Protiv formalizma...."

†Chemberdzhi, Nikolai Karpovich (1903-1948). *See* "Protiv formalizma...."

Chemodanov, Sergei Mikhailovich (1888-), *Istoriya muzyki v svyazi s istoriei obshchestvennovo razvitiya: opyt marksistskovo postroyeniya istorii muzyki* [A History of Music in Connection with the History of Social Development: An Attempt at a Marxist Construction of the History of Music], Kiev, 1927, 203 p. [NN]

——, *Mikhail Mikhailovich Ippolitov-Ivanov*, M., 1927, 56 p. Text in Russian and German. [DLC; NN]

——, *Mikhail Mikhailovich Ippolitov-Ivanov: k 50-letiyu muzykal'noi deyatel'nosti* [Mikhail Mikhailovich Ippolitov-Ivanov: For the Fiftieth Year of His Musical Activity], M., 1933.

——, *Sotsial'no-ekonomicheskiye osnovy muzyki* [The Socio-Economic Bases of Music], ed. by Nikolai A. Roslavets and Yevgeni M. Braudo, M., 1925, 34 p.

Chernyi, Osip, "Dmitri Shostakovich," *Novyi mir* [New World], M., 1945, No. 10, pp. 140-147. [NN]

Chernyshevsky, Nikolai G. (1828-1889), "Esteticheskiya otnosheniya iskusstva k deyatel'nosti" [The Aesthetical Relationship of Art to Reality], *Estetika i poeziya* [Aesthetics and Poetry], St. P., 1893, pp. 1-108. [NNC]

Chkhikvadze, G., *Kompozitory Gruzinskoi SSR: kratkiye biografii* [Composers of the Georgian S.S.R.: Short Biographies], Tbilisi, 1949.

†Chulaki, Mikhail Ivanovich (1908-), *Instrumenty simfonicheskovo orkestra* [Instruments of the Symphonic Orchestra], L., 1950, 211 p. [DLC]

Chyshko, Oleksander Semenovych (Oles' Chishko) (1895-). *See* [*Leningradskaya filarmoniya*].

Cui (Kyui), Cesar Antonovich (1835-1918), *Izbrannye stat'i* [Selected Articles], comp., introduction and notes by I.I. Gusin, L., 1952, lxvii+690 p. [DLC; NN; NNC]

____. *See* Braudo.

Danilevich, L., *A.N. Skryabin*, M., 1953, 110 p. [DLC]

____, *I.O. Dunayevski*, M., 1947, 37 p. [DLC]

____, "'Master iz klamsi': opera D. Kabalevskovo" [*The Craftsman of Clamecy:* An Opera by D. Kabalevski], *SM*, December 1937, No. 12, pp. 35-47. [NN]

____, *Muzyka na frontakh Velikoi Otechestvennoi voiny* [Music on the Front Lines of the Great Patriotic War], M., 1948, 86 p. [DLC]

____, *P.I. Chaikovski* [P.I. Tchaikovsky], M., 1950, 59 p. [DLC]

____, "Vtoroi fortepiannyi kontsert D. Kabalevskovo" [The Second Piano Concerto of D. Kabalevski], *SM*, October 1936, No. 10, pp. 54-56. [NN]

Dan'kevych, Konstantyn, "V redaktsiyu gazety 'Pravda'" [To the Editors of *Pravda*], *Pravda*, July 24, 1951.

____. *See* "Ob opere 'Bohdan....'"

Dargomyzhsky, Aleksandr Sergeyevich (1813-1869), *Avtobiografiya: pis'ma: vospominaniya sovremennikov* [Autobiography: Letters: Recollections of Contemporaries], ed. by Nikolai F. Findeizen, P., 1921.

____, *Izbrannye pis'ma* [Selected Letters], ed. and introduction by Mikhail S. Pekelis, Vol. I, M., 1952, 75 p. [DLC]

——. *See* Martynov; Pekelis; Shlifshtein.

*Davidenko, Aleksandr Aleksandrovich (1899-1934).

*Davydov, Karl Yul'yevich (1838-1889). *See* Ginzburg, L.; Ginzburg, S.L.; Gutor.

Derzhanovski, Vladimir Vladimirovich, *A.K. Glazunov: 1882-1922*, M., 1922, 19 p. [DLC]

Derzhavna konservatoriya [State Conservatory], Kiev, *P.I. Chaykovs'kyi na Ukraini: materialy i dokumenty* [P.I. Tchaikovsky in the Ukraine: Materials and Documents], arranged by L.D. Faynshteyn, O.Ya. Shreyer and T.M. Tikhonova, ed. and foreword by Andriy V. Ol'khovs'kyi, Kharkov, 1940, 141 p. [DLC]

Derzhavna ordena Lenina konservatoriya im. P.I. Chaikovs'koho [The Tchaikovsky State Conservatory (Order of Lenin)], Kiev. *Kafedra istorii muzyky* [Department of the History of Music]: *kerivnyk* - prof. A.V. Ol'khovs'kyi [Director, Professor Andriy V. Ol'khovs'kyi], *Ukraïns'ka muzykal'na spadshchyna: zbirnyk stattey* [Musical Heritage of the Ukraine: Collected Articles], Kh., 1940, 157 p. [NN]
Articles by V. Dyachenko, M. Heylih, Andriy V. Ol'khovs'kyi, Dmytro M. Revuts'kyi, T. Sheffer, and T. Tikhonova.

Dobrokhotov, V., *A.A. Alyab'yev: kamerno-instrumental'noye tvorchestvo* [A.A. Alyab'yev: Instrumental Chamber Music], M., 1948, 29 p. [DLC]

——, *A.N. Verstovski: zhizn', teatral'naya deyatel'nost', opernoye tvorchestvo* [A.N. Verstovski: Life, Theatrical Activity and Operatic Works], M., 1949, 125 p. [DLC; NN]

——, *D.M. Bortnyanski*, M., 1950, 55 p. [DLC; InU]

——, *Ye. I. Fomin*, M., 1949, 72 p. [NN]

Dobrynina, Ye., *Pyataya simfoniya Glazunova* [The Fifth Symphony of Glazunov], M., 1953, 20 p.

*Dolidze, Semyon Vissarionovich (1903-).

*Dolidze, Viktor Isidorovich (1890-1933). *See* Korev, S.

Dolzhanski, A.N., *Kratkii muzykal'nyi slovar'* [Short Musical Dictionary], L., 1952, 479 p. [DLC; NN]

Dovzhenko, Valer'yan D., ed., *M.D. Leontovych: zbirka stattey ta materialiv* [M.D. Leontovych: A Collection of Articles and Materials], Kiev, 1947, 101 p. [DLC; NN; NNC]

——, *V.S. Kozenko: kompozitor 1896-1938* [The Composer V.S. Kozenko: 1896-1938], Kiev, 1951, 126 p. [DLC]

Downes, Olin, "The Discussion on Soviet Music," *Soviet Russia Today*, New York, April 1948, p. 15.

*Dranishnikov, Vladimir Aleksandrovich (1893-1939).

*Drigo, Richard Yevgen'yevich (1846-1930).

Drozdov, Anatoli Nikolayevich (1889-), *Mikhail Fabianovich Gnesin: Michail Fabianowitsch Gnessin*, M., 1927, 48 p. Text in Russian and German. [NN]

Druskin, Mikhail Semyonovich (1905-), *Ocherki po istorii tantsoval'noi muzyki* [Essays on the History of Dance Music], L., 1936, 204 p. [DLC; NN]

——, *Voprosy muzykal'noi dramaturgii opery: na materiale klassicheskovo naslediya* [Problems of the Musical Dramaturgy of Opera: Based on Material from the Classical Heritage], L., 1952, 343 p. [DLC]

Dubovski, I., *et al.*, *Uchebnik garmonii* [Manual of Harmony], M.–L., 1939, 3rd revised ed., 1947, 339 p. [DLC]

*†Dunayevski, Isaak Osipovich (1900-). *See* Danilevich; [*Leningradskaya filarmoniya*]; Yankovski.

*†Dvarionas, Balis Dominikovich (1904-).

*†Dzerzhinski, Ivan Ivanovich (1909-). *See* [*Leningradskaya filarmoniya*].

*Dzhambul Dzhabayev (1846-1945). *See* Vishnevskaya.

Emsheimer, Ernst, "Musikethnographische Bibliographie der nichtslavischen Völker in Russland," *Acta musicologica*, Copehagen, Vol. XXV, 1943, pp. 43-63. [DLC]

Engels, Friedrich (1820-1895). *See* Marx.

Erlich, Victor, "The Russian Formalist Movement," *Partisan Review*, New York, Vol. XX, No. 3, May-June 1953, pp. 282-296. [DLC; NN; NNC]

Eshpai, Yakov Andreyevich (1890-), *Natsional'nye muzykal'nye instrumenty mariitsev* [National Musical Instruments of the Mari], Ioshkar-Ola, 1940, 39 p. [DLC]

†Feinberg, Samuil Yevgen'yevich (1890-). *See* Belyayev, V.M.

Ferman, V., *Istoriya novoi zapadnoyevropeiskoi muzyki* [A History of Modern West European Music], Vol. I, M.–L., 1940.

——. *See* "Protiv formalizma...."

Ferman, Val., "Nemetskaya romanticheskaya opera" [German Romantic Opera], *SM*, June 1936, No. 6, pp. 12-33. [NN]
One of his *Ocherki po istorii zapadnoyevropeiskoi opery XIX v.* [Essays on the History of West European Opera of the Nineteenth Century], n.p., before June 1936.

Figurovski, N.A., and Yu.I. Solov'yov, *Aleksandr Porfir'yevich Borodin*, M., 1950, 210 p. [DLC; NN; NNC]

Filippov, Vladimir Aleksandrovich (1889-). *See* Kolosova.

Finagin, Aleksei Vasil'yevich (1890-), *Russkaya narodnaya pesnya* [The Russian Folk Song], P., 1932, 92 p. [DLC; NN]

Findeizen, Nikolai Fyodorovich (1868-1928), *Glinka*, P., 1922, 20 p. [NN]

——, *Kamernaya muzyka Chaikovskovo* [The Chamber Music of Tchaikovsky], M., 1930, 38 p. [NN]

———, ed., *Muzykal'naya etnografiya: sbornik statei* [Musical Ethnography: A Collection of Articles], L., 1926, 51 p. Text in Russian and French. [DLC; NN]

———, *Ocherki po istorii muzyki v Rossii s drevneishikh vremyon do kontsa XVIII veka* [Essays on the History of Music in Russia from the Most Ancient Times to the End of the Eighteenth Century], 2 vols., 7 parts, M.–L., 1928-1929. [DLC]

Finkelstein, Sidney, "The Discussion on Soviet Music," *Soviet Russia Today,* New York, April 1948, p. 15.

Fomin, Yevstignei Ipat'yevich (1761-1800). *See* Dobrokhotov.

Fried, E.L., *Modest Petrovich Musorgski: k 100-letiyu so dnya rozhdeniya* [Modeste Petrovich Musorgsky: For the One-hundredth Anniversary of His Birth], L., 1939, 39 p. [NN]

Fyodorova, Galina, *A.K. Glazunov,* M.–L., 1947, 51 p. [DLC]

———, *M.A. Balakirev,* M., 1951, 78 p. [DLC; NN]

*Gabichvadze, Revaz Kondrat'yevich (1913-).

*†Gadzhibekov, Uzeir Abdul Husein ogly (1885-1948), *Osnovy azerbaidzhanskoi narodnoi muzyki* [Fundamentals of Azerbaidzhan Folk Music], Baku, 1945, 112 p. [MH]

———. *See* Kasimov; Vinogradov.

*†Gadzhiyev, Akhmed Dzhevdet Ismail ogly (1917-).

Galatskaya, V.S., *Muzykal'naya literatura zapadnoyevropeiskikh stran: uchebnoye posobiye dlya muzykal'nykh uchilishch* [Musical Literature of West European Countries: Textbook for Music Schools], ed. by A. Khokhlovkina, Vol. I, M., 1952, 401 p. [DLC]

*Galkauskas, Konstantin Mikhailovich (1875-).

*Garbuzov, Nikolai Aleksandrovich (1880-), *Drevnerusskoye narodnoye mnogogolosiye* [Ancient Russian Folk Polyphony], M.–L., 1948.

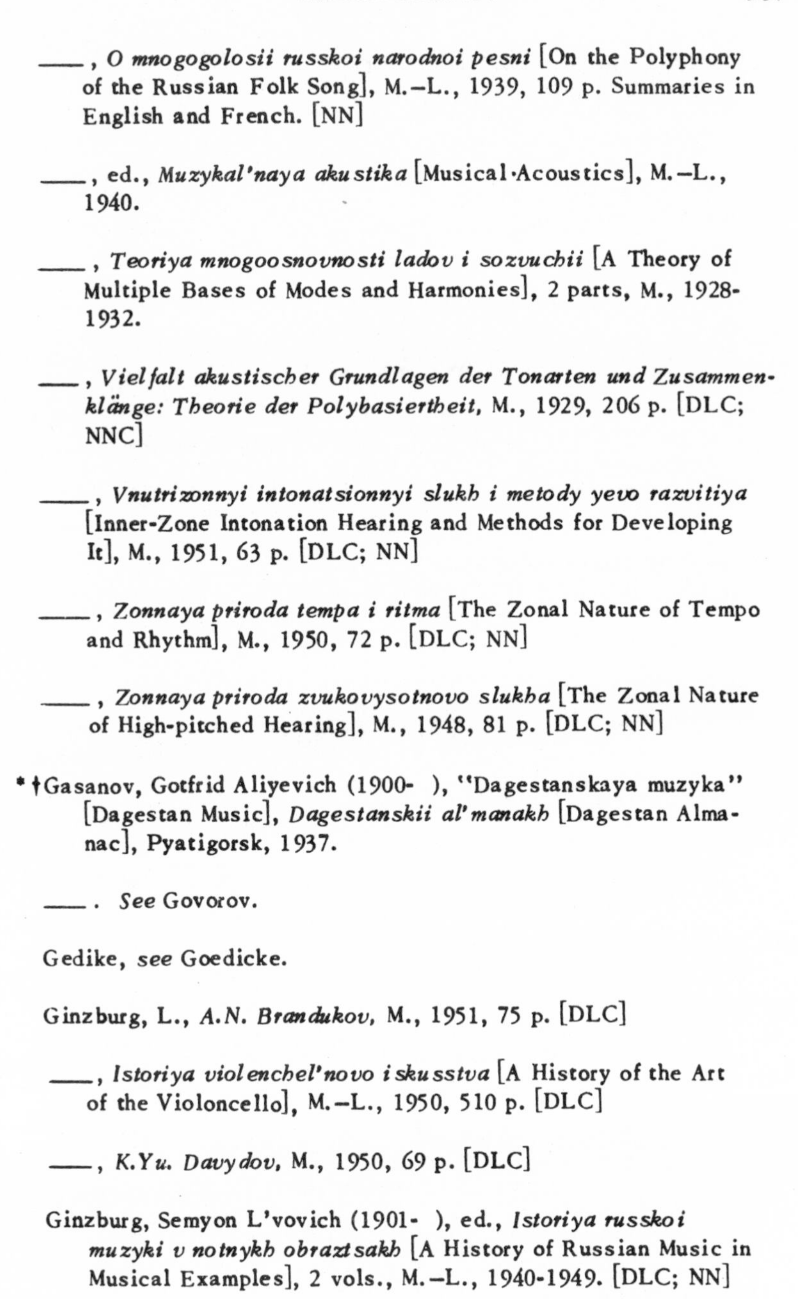

———, *O mnogogolosii russkoi narodnoi pesni* [On the Polyphony of the Russian Folk Song], M.–L., 1939, 109 p. Summaries in English and French. [NN]

———, ed., *Muzykal'naya akustika* [Musical·Acoustics], M.–L., 1940.

———, *Teoriya mnogoosnovnosti ladov i sozvuchii* [A Theory of Multiple Bases of Modes and Harmonies], 2 parts, M., 1928-1932.

———, *Vielfalt akustischer Grundlagen der Tonarten und Zusammenklänge: Theorie der Polybasiertheit*, M., 1929, 206 p. [DLC; NNC]

———, *Vnutrizonnyi intonatsionnyi slukh i metody yevo razvitiya* [Inner-Zone Intonation Hearing and Methods for Developing It], M., 1951, 63 p. [DLC; NN]

———, *Zonnaya priroda tempa i ritma* [The Zonal Nature of Tempo and Rhythm], M., 1950, 72 p. [DLC; NN]

———, *Zonnaya priroda zvukovysotnovo slukha* [The Zonal Nature of High-pitched Hearing], M., 1948, 81 p. [DLC; NN]

*†Gasanov, Gotfrid Aliyevich (1900-), "Dagestanskaya muzyka" [Dagestan Music], *Dagestanskii al'manakh* [Dagestan Almanac], Pyatigorsk, 1937.

———. *See* Govorov.

Gedike, *see* Goedicke.

Ginzburg, L., *A.N. Brandukov*, M., 1951, 75 p. [DLC]

———, *Istoriya violenchel'novo iskusstva* [A History of the Art of the Violoncello], M.–L., 1950, 510 p. [DLC]

———, *K.Yu. Davydov*, M., 1950, 69 p. [DLC]

Ginzburg, Semyon L'vovich (1901-), ed., *Istoriya russkoi muzyki v notnykh obraztsakh* [A History of Russian Music in Musical Examples], 2 vols., M.–L., 1940-1949. [DLC; NN]

____, *K.Yu. Davydov: glava iz istorii russkoi muzykal'noi kul'tury i metodicheskoi mysli* [K.Yu. Davydov: A Chapter from the History of Russian Musical Culture and Systematic Thought], L., 1936, 211 p. [DLC; MH; NN]

____, ed., *Puti razvitiya uzbekskoi muzyki: sbornik statei* [Paths of Development of Uzbek Music: A Collection of Articles], L.–M., 1946, 207 p. [DLC]

____, comp., *Russkii muzykal'nyi teatr 1700-1835 gg.: khrestomatiya* [The Russian Musical Theater 1700-1835: A Reader], L.–M., 1941, 306 p. [DLC; NN; NNC]

Gippius, Yevgeni Vladimirovich (1903-), "Intonatsionnye elementy russkoi chastushki" [Intonational Elements of the Russian *Chastushka*], *Sovetskii fol'klor* [Soviet Folklore], M., April-May 1936, No. 4-5, pp. 97-142. [NN]

*Glazunov, Aleksandr Konstantinovich (1865-1936). *See* Asaf'yev; Belyayev, V.M.; Derzhanovski; Dobrynina; Fyodorova; Malkov; Ossovski; Vanslov.

Glebov, Igor' *(pseud.), see* Asaf'yev.

*†Glière (Glier), Reinhold Moritsevich (1875-). *See* Bugoslavski; Korev, Yu.; Sezhenski; Slonimsky.

*Glinka, Mikhail Ivanovich (1804-1857), *Avtobiografiya: zametki ob instrumentovke* [Autobiography: Notes on Instrumentation], ed. by Semyon L. Ginzburg, L., 1937, 34 p. [NN; NNC]

____, *Literaturnoye naslediye* [Literary Heritage], Vol. I, *Avtobiograficheskiye i tvorcheskiye materialy* [Autobiographical and Creative Materials], L.–M., 1952. [DLC]; Vol. II, *Pis'ma i dokumenty* [Letters and Documents], M.–L., 1953 or 1954, 890 p.

____. *See* Asaf'yev; Berkov, V.O.; Bugoslavski; Findeizen; Inch; Karintsev; Kuznetsov; Laroche; Livanova; Lyapunova; Martynov; Orlova, A.; Ossovski; Popova, T.V.; Protopopov; Remezov; Serov; Shlifshtein; Stasov; Strel'nikov; Uspenski, Vsevolod; Yamshchikova; Zagurski.

Glukh, M.A., ed., *Leningradskiye kompozitory: kratkiye biografii* [Leningrad Composers: Short Biographies], M., 1950, 133 p. [DLC]

*†Gnesin, Mikhail Fabianovich (1883-), *Nachal'nyi kurs prakticheskoi kompozitsii* [Elementary Course in Practical Composition], M., 1941, 142 p. [NN]

——. See Drozdov; [*Leningradskaya filarmoniya*].

*†Goedicke (Gedike), Aleksandr Fyodorovich (1877-). *See* Levik; Yakovlev.

*†Gol'denveizer, Aleksandr Borisovich (1875-).

*Golovanov, Nikolai Semyonovich (1891-).

Gordeyeva, Ye., *Iz istorii russkoi muzykal'noi kritiki XIX veka* [From the History of Russian Musical Criticism of the Nineteenth Century], M., 1950, 73 p. [DLC]

Gorodetskaya, Zinaida Izrailevna, *"Pskovityanka": opera N.A. Rimskovo-Korsakovo* [*The Maid of Pskov:* An Opera by N.A. Rimsky-Korsakov], M., 1936, 92 p. [DLC]

Gorodinski, V.M., *Molodye muzykanty* [Young Musicians], M., 1949, 133 p. [DLC]

——, *Muzyka dukhovnoi nishchety* [The Music of Spiritual Poverty], M.–L., 1950, 135 p. [DLC; NN; NNC]

Gosudarstvennaya akademicheskaya filarmoniya [State Academic Philharmonic Society], Leningrad, *Desyat' let simfonicheskoi muzyki, 1917-1927* [Ten Years of Symphonic Music, 1917-1927], ed. by Nikolai A. Mal'ko, Yakov M. Gessen and Pavel P. Kristi, L., 1928, 177 p. [DLC]

——, *Knigi o simfonicheskoi muzyke* [Books on Symphonic Music], L., 192-?. [DLC?]

Gosudarstvennyi akademicheskii malyi opernyi teatr [State Academic Small Opera Theater], Leningrad, *Imeniny: opera v 4 aktakh (6 kvartinakh): muzyka V.V. Zhelobinskovo:*

sbornik statei i materialov k postanovke opery v Gosudarstvennom akademicheskom malom opernom teatre [*Name-Day:* An Opera in Four Acts (Six Scenes): Music by V.V. Zhelobinski: A Collection of Articles and Materials in Connection with the Staging of the Opera in the State Academic Small Opera Theater], L., 1935, 49 p. [NN]

Gosudarstvennyi akademicheskii teatr opery i baleta [State Academic Theater of Opera and Ballet], Leningrad, *"Zhar-Ptitsa": balet: programma* [*The Firebird* Ballet: A Program], P., 1921, 31 p. [NN]

Gosudarstvennyi ordena Lenina akademicheskii teatr opery i baleta imeni S.M. Kirova [S.M. Kirov State Academic Theater of Opera and Ballet (Order of Lenin)], Leningrad, *Leningradskii gosudarstvennyi ordena Lenina akademicheskii teatr opery i baleta imeni S.M. Kirova,* ed. by Aleksandr M. Brodski, L., 1940, 228 p. [DLC; NN]

Articles by Valer'yan M. Bogdanov-Berezovski, Aleksandr M. Brodski, Mikhail S. Druskin, Yuri O. Slonimski, S.A. Tsvetayev, and Nikolai D. Volkov.

Gosudarstvennyi institut istorii iskusstv [State Institute of the History of the Arts], Leningrad, *Muzyka i muzykal'nyi byt staroi Rossii: materialy i issledovaniya* [Music and Musical Life in Old Russia: Materials and Researches], Vol. I, *Na grani XVIII i XIX stoletii: sbornik rabot istoricheskoi sektsii O[tdela] T[eorii] i I[storii] M[uzyki]* [Between the Eighteenth and Nineteenth Centuries: Collected Works of the Historical Section of the Department of the Theory and History of Music], L., 1927, 212 p. [NN]

Articles by Boris V. Asaf'yev, A.V. Druzhinin, Aleksei V. Finagin, V.A. Prokof'yev, and Andrei N. Rimsky-Korsakov.

Govorov, S., *Laureat Stalinskoi premii kompozitor G.A. Gasanov* [Stalin-Prize Winner Composer G.A. Gasanov], Makhachkala, 1949.

Gozenpud, *see* Hozenpud.

Grachev, Mikhail, "Muzykal'nye polyfabrikaty" [Musical Semi-finished Products], *Krokodil* [Crocodile], M., Vol. XXXI, No. 11(1337), 1953, p. 5.

*Grechaninov, Aleksandr Tikhonovich (1864-), *Catalogue des compositions de Alexandre Gretchaninoff*, Paris, Imp. de Navarre, 1931, 26 p. [NNC]

——, *Moya muzykal'naya zhizn'* [My Musical Life], Paris, 1934, 151 p. [NN]

——, *Moya zhizn'* [My Life], New York, Novyi zhurnal, 1951, 153 p. [DLC; NNC]

——, *My Life*, tr. by Nicolas Slonimsky, New York, Coleman-Ross, 1952, 204 p. [DLC; NN]

——, *Spisok sochinenii A.T. Grechaninova* [List of the Works of A.T. Grechaninov], M., 1924, 15 p. Text in Russian and German. [NN]

Grigorovich, Dmitri Vasil'yevich (1822-1900), *Literaturnye vospominaniya* [Literary Reminiscences], with an appended complete text of P.M. Kovalevski's Recollections, introduction, ed. and notes by V.L. Komarovich, L., 1928, xxxii+ 515 p. [DLC; NN]

Material on Mikhail I. Glinka.

Grinberg, M., and N. Polyakova, eds. and comps., *Sovetskaya opera: sbornik kriticheskikh statei* [Soviet Opera: A Collection of Critical Articles], M., 1953, 478 p. [DLC; NN]

Grinberg. *See* "Protiv formalizma...."

Grinchenko, *see* Hrinchenko.

Grosheva, Ye.A., *et. al.*, eds., *Sovetskaya muzyka na pod''yome: sbornik statei* [Soviet Music on the Ascent: A Collection of Articles], M., 1950, 276 p. [DLC; NN]

Gruber, Roman Il'ich, *Istoriya muzykal'noi kul'tury* [History of Musical Culture], Vol. II, M., 1953, 414 p. [DLC; MH]

——, *Istoriya muzykal'noi kul'tury: s drevneishikh vremyon do kontsa XVI veka* [History of Musical Culture: From The Most Ancient Times to the End of the Sixteenth Century], Vol. I, 2 parts, M.–L., 1941. [DLC; NN]

Do vtoroi poloviny XI v. [To the Second Half of the Eleventh Century], Part I. *Vtoraya polovina XI - nachalo XV v.* [From the Second Half of the Eleventh to the Beginning of the Fifteenth Century], Part II.

____, *Muzykal'naya kul'tura drevnevo mira* [Musical Culture of the Ancient World], L., 1937, 258 p. [DLC]

____, "O vozmozhnosti i predelakh ispol'zovaniya v muzykovedenii ekonomicheskikh kategorii" [Concerning the Possibilities and Limits of Using Economic Categories in Musicology], *Muzykoznaniye* [Musicology], L., Vol. IV, 1928, pp. 40-62. [NN]

*Gruodis, Yuozas Matveyevich (1884-1948).

Gumretsi, *Nikolai Faddeyevich Tigranov i muzyka Vostoka* [Nikolai Faddeyevich Tigranov and Music of the Orient], foreword by Nikolai Ya. Marr and Aleksandr A. Spendiarov, L., 1927, 46 p. [NN]

Gutor, V., *K.Yu. Davydov, kak osnovatel' shkoly* [K.Yu. Davydov As the Founder of a School], ed. with foreword and notes by L.S. Ginzburg, M.–L., 1950.

Hoffmann-Erbrecht, Lothar, "B.W. Assafjew-Glebow," *Musik und Gesellschaft,* Berlin, Vol. II, No. 7, July 1952, pp. 5-7. [NN]

Honegger, Arthur, "Old Ears for New Music: Our Listening Habits Are Outdated," *Musical Digest,* March 1947, pp. 6-7, 16. [DLC; NN]

Hozenpud, A., *Operna dramaturhiya Chaikovs'koho: narysy* [The Operatic Dramaturgy of Tchaikovsky: Essays], Kharkov, 1940, 145 p. [DLC]

Hrinchenko, Mykola (1888-1945), *Istoriya ukraïns'koï muzyky* [History of Ukrainian Music], Kiev, 1922.

____, "Ukraïns'ka muzykal'na tvorchist' za radyans'kykh chasiv" [Ukrainian Music in the Soviet Period], *Zhyttya y revolyutsiya* [Life and Revolution], Kiev, 1927, No. 10-11.

*Hulak-Artemovs'kyi (Artemovski), Semen Stepanovych (1813-1873). *See* Kiselyov, G.L.

*Ibragimov, Khaibibulla Kalimullovich (1894-).

Ikonnikov, Aleksei A., *Myaskovsky: His Life and Work*, tr. from Russian, New York, Philosophical Library, 1946, 162 p. [DLC; NN; NNC]

Ilyukhin, A., *Russkii orkestr* [The Russian Orchestra], M., 1948, 124 p. [DLC]

Inch, Herbert Reynolds (1904-), "A Bibliography of Glinka," New York, 1935, 28 p., typescript. [NN]

Ioffe (Joffe), Iyeremiya Isayevich, *Krizis sovremennovo iskusstva* [The Crisis of Contemporary Art], L., 1925, 64 p. [NNC]

——, *Kul'tura i stil': sistema i printsipy sotsiologii iskusstv: literatura, zhivopis', muzyka natural'novo tovarno-denezhnovo industrial'novo khozaistva* [Culture and Style: The System and Principles for a Sociology of the Arts: The Literature, Painting and Music of a Natural Industrial Monetary Goods Economy], L., 1927, 366 p. [NN]

——, *Muzyka sovetskovo kino: osnovy muzykal'noi dramaturgii* [Music of the Soviet Film: The Fundamentals of Musical Dramaturgy], L., 1938, 165 p. [NN]

——, *Sinteticheskaya istoriya iskusstv: vvedeniye v istoriyu khudozhestvennovo myshleniya* [A Synthetic History of the Arts: Introduction to a History of Artistic Thought], L., 1933, 568 p. [NN]

*Ippolitov-Ivanov, Mikhail Mikhailovich (1859-1935), *50 let russkoi muzyki v moikh vospominaniyakh* [Fifty Years of Russian Music in My Recollections], M., 1934, 159 p. [DLC]

——. *See* Bugoslavski; Chemodanov.

Iskusstvo Buryat-Mongol'skoi ASSR [The Art of Buryat-Mongol A.S.S.R.], M.–L., 1940, 101 p. [DLC]

Articles by G. Arkhincheyev, A. Georgiyev, Georgi A. Polyanovski, and Isidor Ryk.

Iskusstvo Gruzii [The Art of Georgia], M.–L., 1937, 194 p. [DLC] Material by Dmitri I. Arakishvili and Sh. Aslanishvili.

Iskusstvo Sovetskoi Belorussii: sbornik [The Art of Soviet Byelorussia: A Collection], M., 1940, 145 p. [NNC]

Iskusstvo Sovetskoi Kirgizii: sbornik statei [The Art of Soviet Kirghizia: A Collection of Articles], M., 1939, 173 p. [DLC; NNC]

*†Ivanov, Yanis (Ivan) Andreyevich (1906-).

*Ivanov-Boretski, Mikhail Vladimirovich (1874-1936), ed., *Materialy i dokumenty po istorii muzyki* [Materials and Documents for a History of Music], 2 vols., M., 1934. [DLC]

____, *Muzykal'no-istoricheskaya khrestomatiya* [Musical-Historical Reader], 3 parts, M., 1929; 2 parts, 2nd ed., M., 1933-1936.

____, ed., *Muzykal'noye nasledstvo: sbornik materialov po istorii muzykal'noi kul'tury v Rossii* [Musical Legacy: A Collection of Materials for a History of Musical Culture in Russia], M., 1935. [DLC]

____, *Pyat' let nauchnoi raboty Gosudarstvennovo instituta muzykal'noi nauki (Gimna), 1921-1926* [Five Years of Scientific Work of the State Institute of Musical Science (*Gimn*), 1921-1926], M., 1926, 59 p. [NN]

Jelagin (Yelagin), Juri, "Muzykal'naya politika Kremlya" [The Kremlin's Music Policy], *Narodnaya pravda* [Peoples' Truth], New York-Paris, November 1951, No. 17-18, pp. 17-18. [DLC; NN]

____, *Taming of the Arts,* tr. from Russian by Nicholas Wreden, New York, Dutton, 1951, 333 p. [DLC; NN; NNC]

____, *Ukroshcheniye iskusstv* [Taming of the Arts], New York, Izdatel'stvo imeni Chekhova, 1952, 434 p. [DLC; NN; NNC]

Joffe, *see* Ioffe.

"K novomu pod"yomu muzykal'novo obrazovaniya" [Towards a

New Improvement in Music Education], *SM*, August 1950, No. 8, pp. 3-8. (editorial)

*†Kabalevski, Dmitri Borisovich (1904-). *See* Danilevich; "Protiv formalizma...."

*Kalinnikov, Vasili Sergeyevich (1901-). *See* Paskhalov.

*Kalninš (Kalnin'sh; Kalnyn'), Alfreds Yanovich (1879-1952).

Kaltat, L., *T.N. Khrennikov*, M., 1946, 46 p. [DLC; NN]

Kann-Novikova, Ye., *M.I. Glinka: novye materialy i dokumenty* [M.I. Glinka: New Materials and Documents], 2 vols., M., 1950-1951. [NN; DLC: Vol. I]

——, *Sobiratel'nitsa russkikh narodnykh pesen Yevgeniya Linyova* [Yevgeniya Linyova: Collector of Russian Folk Songs], ed. and introduction by Yevgeni V. Gippius, M., 1952, 182 p. [DLC]

*†Kapp, Artur Iosifovich (1878-1952).

*†Kapp, Eugen Arturovich (1908-). *See* Polyanovski.

*Karashvili, Andrei Nikolayevich (1857-1925).

Karatygin, Vyacheslav Gavrilovich (1875-1925), *I. Musorgski; II. Shalyapin* [Part I: Musorgsky; Part II: Chaliapin], P., 1922, 82 p. [DLC; NN]

——, *V.G. Karatygin: zhizn', deyatel'nost', stat'i i materialy* [V.G. Karatygin: Life, Work, Articles, and Materials], L., 1927, 267 p. [NN; NNC]

Karenin, Vlad. *(pseud.), see* Komarova-Stasova.

*Kargareteli, Il'ya Georgiyevich (1867-1939).

Karintsev, Nikolai Aleksandrovich (1866-), *Glinka: kartiny iz zhizni* [Glinka: Pictures from His Life], M., 1936, 102 p. [NN]

Karp, S., "K voprosu o podgotovke muzykal'nykh kadrov" [On the Problem of Training Music Cadres], *SM*, April 1949, No. 4, pp. 51-53.

*†Kashkin, Nikolai Dmitriyevich (1839-1921), *Stat'i o russkoi muzyke i muzykantakh* [Articles About Russian Music and Musicians], ed., introduction and notes by S.I. Shlifshtein, M., 1953, 82 p. [DLC]

____, *Uchebnik elementarnoi teorii muzyki* [Manual of Elementary Theory of Music], M., 1929, 74 p. [NN]

____. *See* Yakovlev.

Kasimov, K., *Uzeir Gadzhibekov*, Baku, 1949.

*Kastal'ski, Aleksandr Dmitriyevich (1856-1926), *Osnovy narodnovo mnogogolosiya* [Elements of Folk Polyphony], ed. by Viktor M. Belyayev, M., 1948, 360 p. [DLC]
First ed. appeared as *Osobennosti narodno-russkoi muzykal'noi sistemy* [Peculiarities of the Russian Folk Music System], M.–P., 1923, 58 p. [DLC; NN]

Katuar, *see* Catoire.

*Keldysh, Yuri (Georgi) Vsevolodovich (1907-), *Istoriya russkoi muzyki* [History of Russian Music], 2 vols., M., 1947-1948. [DLC; NN: missing?]
Vol. I, 472 p.; *Vtoraya polovina XIX veka* [The Second Half of the Nineteenth Century], Vol. II, 388 p.

____, *M.P. Musorgski: k pyatidesyatiletiyu so dnya smerti, 1881-1931* [M.P. Musorgsky: For the Fiftieth Anniversary of His Death, 1881-1931], M., 1931, 16 p. [DLC]

____. *See* "Protiv formalizma...."

†Khachaturian, Aram Il'ich (1904-), "O gruzinskoi muzyke" [On Georgian Music], *SM*, October 1936, No. 10, pp. 43-46. [NN]

____, "O tvorcheskoi smelosti i vdokhnovenii" [Concerning Creative Boldness and Inspiration], *SM*, November 1953,

No. 11, pp. 7-13. (Complete tr. in *Current Digest of the Soviet Press,* New York, Vol. V, No. 46, December 30, 1953, pp. 3-5.)

___. *See* [*Leningradskaya filarmoniya*]; Martynov; Slonimsky.

Khanukayev, Kh., and M.I. Plotkin, *Dagestanskaya muzyka* [Dagestan Music], Makhachkala, 1948.

Khinchyn, L., *P.I. Chaikovs'kyi, 1840-1940* [P.I. Tchaikovsky, 1840-1940], Kharkov, 1940, 157 p. [NN]

Khokhlov, Pavel Akinfiyevich (1854-1919). *See* Yakovlev.

†Khrennikov, Tikhon Nikolayevich (1913-), "Doklad T.N. Khrennikova" [Report by T.N. Khrennikov], *SI,* No. 17(1105), April 24, 1948.

___, "O neterpimom otstavanii muzykal'noi kritiki i muzykovedeniya" [Concerning the Intolerable Lag in Music Criticism and Musicology], *SM,* February 1949, No. 2, pp. 7-15; also in *SI,* No. 8(1148), February 19, 1949.

___, "Tvorchestvo kompozitorov i muzykovedov posle postanovleniya TsK VKP(b) ob opere 'Velikaya Druzhba'" [The Work of Composers and Musicologists Following the Decree of the Central Committee of the All-Union Communist Party (Bolsheviks) Concerning the Opera *The Great Friendship*], *SM,* January 1949, No. 1, pp. 23-56.

___, "Vystupleniya na plenume: T. Khrennikov (zaklyuchitel'noye slovo)" [Speeches at the Plenum: T. Khrennikov (Concluding Speech)], *ibid.*, pp. 55-56.

___. *See* Kaltat; [*Leningradskaya filarmoniya*]; "Protiv formalizma...."

Khrestomatiya po muzykal'noi literature dlya detskikh muzykal'nykh shkol [A Reader of Musical Literature for Children's Music Schools], Vol. I, No. 1, M., 1952 [CU]

Khubov, Georgi Nikitich, *A.P. Borodin, 1833-1887*, M., 1933, 125 p. [DLC; NN]

___, *O zadachakh razvitiya sovetskoi muzyki* [Tasks in the Development of Soviet Music], M., 1953, 37 p. [DLC]

___, *Zhizn' A. Serova* [The Life of A. Serov], M., 1950, 138 p. [DLC]

___. *See* "Protiv formalizma...."

Khuchua, P., *Meliton Balanchivadze,* Tbilisi, 1952.

Khvostenko, Vladimir, "Muzyka narodov SSSR: materialy k bibliograficheskomu ukazatelyu, 1917-1936" [Music of the Peoples of the U.S.S.R.: Materials for a Bibliographical Index, 1917-1936], *SM,* April 1937, No. 4, pp. 104-108. [DLC; NN]

*† Kiladze, Grigori Varfolomeyevich (1903-). *See* [*Leningradskaya filarmoniya*].

Kirgizskii muzykal'nyi fol'klor [Kirghiz Musical Folklore], M.–L., 1939.

Kiselyov, Grigori Leonidovich, "L.N. Revutski: k 60-letiyu so dnya rozhdeniya" [L.N. (M.) Revuts'kyi: For the Sixtieth Anniversary of His Birth], *SM,* April 1949, No. 4, pp. 34-38.

___, *L.N. Revutski, narodnyi artist SSSR* [L.N.(M.) Revuts'kyi, People's Artist of the U.S.S.R.], Kiev, 1951, 50 p. [DLC]

___, *S.S. Gulak-Artemovski* [S.S. Hulak-Artemovs'kyi], Kiev, 1951, 27 p. [DLC]

Kiselyov, V.A., ed., *N.A. Rimski-Korsakov: sbornik dokumentov* [N.A. Rimsky-Korsakov: A Collection of Documents], M., 1951, 289 p. [CU; DLC; NN]

___, *P.I. Chaikovski: zhizn' i tvorchestvo* [P.I. Tchaikovsky: Life and Work], M., 1947, 47 p. [DLC]

*†Knipper, Lev Konstantinovich (1898-). *See* "Protiv formalizma...."

Kocharyan, Aram, *Armenskaya narodnaya muzyka: obshchii obzor* [Armenian Folk Music: A General Review], M.–L., 1939, 46 p. [NN; NNC]

•Kolessa, Filyaret Mykhaylovych (1871-1947).

Kolosova, Yevgeniya Mikhailovna, and Vladimir Aleksandrovich Filippov (1889-), eds., *A.N. Ostrovski i russkiye kompozitory: pis'ma* [A.N. Ostrovski and Russian Composers: Letters], M.–L., 1937, 249 p. [NN; NNC]

Komarova-Stasova, Varvara Dmitriyevna (Vlad. Karenin. *pseud.*) (1862-), "Iz detskikh vospominanii o velikikh lyudyakh: Musorgski" [From Childhood Recollections of Great People: Musorgsky], *Muzykal'nyi sovremennik* [Musical Contemporary], P., 1917, No. 5-6, pp. 15-20. [NN]

——, *Vladimir Stasov: ocherk yevo zhizni i deyatel'nosti* [Vladimir Stasov: A Sketch of His Life and Work], 2 vols., L., 1927. [NN; NNC]

•Komitas, Solomon Gevorkovich (Kevorkian) (*pseud.* of Sogomon G. Sogomonyan) (1869-1935).

Kompozitory Sovetskoi Ukrainy: spravochnik [Composers of the Soviet Ukraine: A Handbook], Kiev, Mistetstvo, 1951, 99 p.

"Kompozitory v kolkhozakh" [Composers in the Kolkhozes], *SM*, March-June 1936, Nos. 3-6. [NN]

•Kondrat'yev, Nikolai Vasil'yevich (1846-1921).

Korev, S., *"Keto i Kote" V. Dolidze* [*Keto and Kote* by V. Dolidze], M.–L., 1951.

Korev, Semyon Isaakovich, ed., *Nash muzykal'nyi front: materialy vserossiiskoi muzykal'noi konferentsii (iyun' 1929 g.)* [Our Music Front: Materials of the All-Russian Music Conference, June 1929 (Leningrad)], M., 1929, 259 p. [NN]

Korev, Yu., *"Mednyi vsadnik" R. Gliera* [*The Bronze Horseman* by Glière], M., 1951, 50 p. [DLC]

•Korganov, Vasili Davidovich (1865-1934), *Chaikovski na Kavkaze* [Tchaikovsky in the Caucasus], Yerevan, 1940.

•†Koval' (*pseud.* of Kovalyov), Marian Viktorovich (1907-),

"O tvorchestve Dmitriya Shostakovicha" [On the Creative Work of Dmitri Shostakovich], *Izvestiya,* November 8, 1951.

____. *See* Bruk.

Kovalyov, *see* Koval' *(pseud).*

Kozenko, Viktor S. *See* Dovzhenko.

*Krein, Aleksandr Abramovich (1883-1951). *See* Sabaneyev.

Kremelev, Yu., *A.P. Borodin: k stoletiyu so dnya rozhdeniya* [A.P. Borodin: For the One-hundredth Anniversary of His Birth], L., 1934, 87 p. [DLC]

____, *Leningradskaya gosudarstvennaya konservatoriya, 1862-1937* [The Leningrad State Conservatory, 1862-1937], M., 1938, 177 p. [DLC]

____, *Voprosy muzykal'noi estetiki* [Problems of Musical Aesthetics], M., 1953, 75 p. [DLC]

Kretzschmar (Krechmar), Hermann (1848-1924), *Istoriya opery* [A History of Opera], tr. and choice of illustrations by P.V. Grachov, ed. and foreword by Igor' Glebov, L., 1925, 406 p. [NN; NNC]

Kruzhkov, V.S., *Gimn Sovetskovo Soyuza* [Hymn of the Soviet Union], M., 1944, 30 p. [DLC]

Kryzhanovski, Ivan Ivanovich (1867-1924), *The Biological Bases of the Evolution of Music,* tr. from an unpublished manuscript by S.W. Pring, London, Oxford University Press, 1928, 57 p. [DLC; NN; NNC]

Kukharski, V. "Opera 'Ot vsevo serdtsa'" [The Opera *With All One's Heart*], *SM,* March 1951, No. 3, pp. 25-34.

Kulakovski, Lev Vladimirovich (1897-), *"Snegurochka": opera N.A. Rimskovo-Korsakovo* [*The Snow Maiden:* Opera by N.A. Rimsky-Korsakov], 3rd ed., M., 1935, 83 p. [DLC]

____. *See* "Protiv formalizma...."

Kulikovich, Mikola, *Belaruskaya muzyka: karotki narys historii belaruskaha muzychnaha mastatstva* [Byelorussian Music: A Brief Outline of the History of Byelorussian Musical Art], Part I, New York, 1953. [DLC; NN; NNC]

Kuliyev, Ashir. *See* "Neobkhodim...."

Kurt, Ernst (1886-1946), *Grundlagen des linearen Kontrapunkts: Einführung in Stil und Technik von Bach's melodischer Polyphone*, Berne, Drechsel, 1917.

——, *Romantische Harmonik und ihre Krise in Wagner's "Tristan"*, Berne-Leipzig, Haupt, 1920.

*Kuznetsov, Konstantin Alekseyevich (1883-1953), *Etyudy o muzyke* [Studies on Music], Odessa, 1919, 61 p. [NN]
Material on Dargomyzhsky, Glinka, Rimsky-Korsakov, Scriabin, and Tchaikovsky.

——, *Glinka i yevo sovremenniki* [Glinka and His Contemporaries], M., 1926, 70 p. [NN]

——, *Muzykal'no-istoricheskiye portrety: biografii kompozitorov, izbrannye stranitsy ikh tvorchestva* [Musico-Historical Portraits: Biographies of Composers, Selected Pages of Their Work], M., 1937, 198 p. [NN]

——, "Serge Rachmaninoff's Musical Life," *VOKS Bulletin*, M., 1945, No. 6, pp. 40-51. [NN]

Kvitka, Klyment Vasyl'ovych (1880-), *Profesional'ni narodni spivtsi y muzykanty na Ukraïni: prohrama dlya doslidu ïkh diyal'nosty y pobutu* [Professional Folk Singers Among Musicians in the Ukraine: A Program for the Study of Their Effect upon the Mores], Kiev, 1924, 114 p. [NN]

——, *Ukraïns'ki pisni pro ditozhubnytsyu* [Ukrainian Songs About a (Mother) Child-Murderer], Kiev, 1927, 60 p. [NN; NNC]

——, *Ukraïns'ki pisni pro divchynu, shcho pomandruvala z zvodytelem: systematyzatsiya, uvagy, ta novi materiyaly* [Ukrainian Songs About the Lass Who Went Off with Her

Seducer: Systematization, Considerations and New Materials], Kiev, 1926, 40 p. [NN]

Kyui, *see* Cui.

Lahuti, Abul'kasin (Abul'gasem Lakhuti) (1887-). *See* Vishnevskaya.

Lapshin, Ivan Ivanovich (1870-), *Khudozhestvennoye tvorchestvo* [Art Work], P., 1922, 331 p. [NN; NNC]
Material on Musorgsky, Rimsky-Korsakov and Scriabin.

___, *N.A. Rimski-Korsakov i yevo znacheniye v istorii russkoi muzyki* [N.A. Rimsky-Korsakov and His Significance in the History of Russian Music], Prague, Russkaya uchonaya akademiya, 1945, 109 p. [CU]

___, *Rimski-Korsakov: dva ocherka* [Rimsky-Korsakov: Two Essays], P., 1922, 74 p. [DLC; NNC]

___, *Ruská hudba: profily skladatelů* [Russian Music: Profiles of Composers], tr. from Russian by Zofie Pohorecka, Prague, Za svobodu, 1947, 522 p. [DLC]

*Laroche (Larosh), German Avgustovich (1845-1904), *Izbrannye stat'i o Glinke* [Selected Articles on Glinka], ed., foreword and notes by S.I. Levit, M., 1953, 195 p. [DLC]

___, *Sobraniye muzykal'no-kriticheskikh statei* [Collected Articles of Musical Criticism], Vol. II, 2 parts, *O P.I. Chaikovskom* [On P.I. Tchaikovsky], ed. by Vasili V. Yakovlev, M.–P., 1922-1924. [NN]

Lebedinski, L., *Novyi etap bor'by na muzykal'nom fronte* [A New Stage in the Struggle on the Musical Front], M., 1931, 80 p. [NNC]

___. *See* "Protiv formalizma...."

Lenin, Vladimir Ilyich (1870-1924), "Otstalaya Yevropa i peredovaya Aziya" [Backward Europe and Progressive Asia], *Sochineniya* [Works], 4th ed., M., 1948, Vol. XIX, pp. 77-78. (Reprinted from *Pravda,* No. 113, May 18, 1913.)

——, "Partiinaya organizatsiya i partiinaya literatura" [Party Organization and Party Literature], *Sochineniya* [Works], 4th ed., M., 1947, Vol. X, pp. 26-31.

[*Leningradskaya filarmoniya* (Leningrad Philharmonic Society)], *Sovetskiye kompozitory* [Soviet Composers], ed. by M.I. Chulyaki, L., 1938, 95 p. [DLC; NN]

Short biographies of Boris V. Asaf'yev, Yevgeni G. Brusilovski, Oles' S. Chishko (Oleksander Chyshko), Isaak O. Dunayevski, Ivan I. Dzerzhinski, Georgi K. Fardi, Mikhail F. Gnesin, Boris G. Gol'ts, Aram I. Khachaturian, Leon A. Khodzha-Einatov, Tikhon N. Khrennikov, Grigori V. Kiladze, Nikolai Ya. Myaskovski, Georgi N. Nosov, Zakhari P. Paliashvili, Andrei F. Pashchenko, Ruvim S. Pergament, Gavriil N. Popov, David A. Pritsker, Sergei S. Prokof'yev, Feodosi A. Rubtsov, Yuri A. Shaporin, Vladimir V. Shcherbachov, Dmitri D. Shostakovich, Maksimilian O. Shteinberg, Lyubov' L. Shtreikher, Vasili P. Solov'yov-Sedoi, Nikolai M. Strel'nikov, Georgi V. Sviridov, Viktor K. Tomilin, Yuri N. Tyulin, Sergei N. Vasilenko, Yuliya L. Veisberg, Viktor V. Voloshinov, Mikhail A. Yudin, Valeri V. Zhelobinski, Aleksei S. Zhivotov.

Leningradskaya filarmoniya, 1934-1935 [The Leningrad Philharmonic Society, 1934-1935], L., 1935, 79 p. [NNC]

*Leontovych, Mykola Dmytrovych (1877-1921). *See* Dovzhenko.

Levik, B., *Aleksandr Gedike* [Aleksandr Goedicke], M., 1947.

*Linyova, Yevgeniya E. (1854-1919). *See* Kann-Novikova.

Livanova, Tamara Nikolayevna, *Istoriya zapadnoyevropeiskoi muzyki do 1789 goda* [The History of West European Music to 1789], M.–L., 1940, 816 p. [NN]

——, *Kriticheskaya deyatel'nost' russkikh kompozitorov-klassikov* [Work in the Field of Criticism by Russian Classical Composers], M., 1950, 100 p. [DLC; NNC]

——, ed., *M.I. Glinka: sbornik materialov i statei* [M.I. Glinka: A Collection of Materials and Articles], M.–L., 1950, 388 p. [DLC; NN]

___, *Ocherki i materialy po istorii russkoi muzykal'noi kul'tury* [Essays and Materials on the History of Russian Musical Culture], Part I, M., 1938, 352 p. [DLC; NN; NNC]

___, *Pedagogicheskaya deyatel'nost' russkikh kompozitorov-klassikov* [Pedagogical Activity of Russian Classical Composers], M., 1951, 99 p. [DLC; NN; NNC]

___, *Russkaya muzykal'naya kul'tura XVIII veka v yeyo svyazyakh s literaturoi, teatrom i bytom* [Russian Musical Culture of the Eighteenth Century in Its Contact with Literature, the Theater and Everyday Life], 2 vols., M., 1952-1953. [DLC; NN]

Lokshin, D.L., *Vydayushchiyesya russkiye khory i ikh dirizhery: kratkiye ocherki* [Outstanding Russian Choruses and Their Conductors: Short Essays], M., 1953, 131 p. [DLC]

London, Kurt L. (1899-), *The Seven Soviet Arts*, London, Faber, 1937, 381 p. [DLC; NN; NNC]; New Haven, Yale University Press, 1938. [DLC; NN]
Part III, Chapter I concerns music.

Lourié (Lur'ye), Arthur (1892-), "L'évolution de la musique Russe," *Les Oeuvres nouvelles*, New York–Paris, 1945, Vol. V, pp. 121-163. [DLC; NN; NNC]

___, "O Shostakoviche: vokrug 7-oi simfonii" [On Shostakovich: About His Seventh Symphony], *Novyi zhurnal* [New Review], New York, Vol. IV, 1943, pp. 367-372. [DLC; NN]

___, *Sergei Koussevitzky and His Epoch: A Biographical Chronicle*, tr. from Russian by S.W. Pring, New York, Knopf, 1931, xiv+253 p. [DLC; NN; NNC]
Contains material on the early Soviet period.

Lovtski, G., "Muzyka i dialektika: o tvorchestve A.N. Skryabina" [Music and Dialectic: On the Work of A.N. Scriabin], *Sovremennyya zapiski* [Contemporary Annals], Paris, 1920, Vol. II, pp. 124-140. [DLC; NN]

*Lunacharski, Anatoli Vasil'yevich (1876-1933), *Lenin o kul'ture i iskusstve* [Lenin on Culture and Art], M., 1938.

———, "Taneyev i Skryabin" [Taneyev and Scriabin], *Novyi mir* [New World], M., 1925, No. 6, pp. 113-126. [NN]

———, *V mire muzyki: sbornik statei* [In the World of Music: A Collection of Articles], ed. by V.D. Zel'dovich, M.–P., 1923, 91 p. [DLC]

———, *Voprosy sotsiologii muzyki* [Problems of the Sociology of Music], M., 1927, 135 p. [NN: missing since May 5, 1935]

Lur'ye, *see* Lourié.

Lyapunova, S., comp., *Rukopisi M.I. Glinki: katalog* [Manuscripts of M.I. Glinka: A Catalogue], L., 1950.

*†Lyatoshyns'kyi, Borys Mykolovych (1894-). *See* Bėlza.

*Lysenko, Mykola Vytal'ovych (1842-1912). *See Muzey diyachiv nauky ta mystetstva Ukraïny.*

Malkov, N.P., *Shestaya simfoniya Glazunova* [The Sixth Symphony of Glazunov], L., 1941, 51 p. [NN]

Marshak, Il'ya Yakovlevich, *Aleksandr Porfir'yevich Borodin*, M., 1953, 517 p. [DLC]

Martynov, Ivan I., *A.S. Dargomyzhski*, M., 1944, 31 p. [DLC]

———, *A.S. Dargomyzhski*, M., 1947, 46 p. [DLC]

———, *A.S. Dargomyzhski: populyarnyi ocherk* [A.S. Dargomyzhsky: A Popular Essay], M., 1946, 13 p. [DLC]

———, *Aram Khachaturian*, M., 1947, 38 p. [NN]

———, *Dmitri Shostakovich*, M.–L., 1946, 111 p. [NNC]

———, *Dmitri Shostakovich: The Man and His Work*, tr. from Russian by T. Guarlsky, New York, Philosophical Library, 1947, 197 p. [DLC; NN; NNC]

———, *Gosudarstvennyi russkii narodnyi khor imeni Pyatnitskovo* [The Pyatnitski State Russian People's Chorus], M., 1950, 133 p. [DLC?]

____, *M.I. Glinka*, M., 1947, 52 p. [DLC]

____, *M.I. Glinka: kratkii ocherk zhizni i tvorchestva* [M.I. Glinka: A Short Sketch of His Life and Work], M., 1941, 128 p. [DLC; NN]

____, *Mirovoye znacheniye russkoi klassicheskoi opery: stenogramma publichnoi lektsii, prochitannoi v Moskve* [The World Significance of Russian Classical Opera: Verbatim Notes of a Public Lecture Delivered in Moscow], M., 1952, 31 p. [DLC; NNC]

____, *M.P. Musorgski: lektsiya* [M.P. Musorgsky: A Lecture], M., 1951, 25 p. [DLC]

Marx, Karl (1818-1883), and Friedrich Engels (1820-1895), *Literature and Art by Karl Marx and Frederick Engels: Selections from Their Writings*, New York, International Publishers, 1947. [DLC; NN; NNC]

____, *Marks i Engel's ob iskusstve* [Marx and Engels on Art], comp. by Frants P. Shiller and Mikhail A. Lifshits, ed. by Anatoli V. Lunacharski, M., 1933, 279 p. [DLC; NN; NNC]

Matsa, Ivan Lyudvigovich (1893-), "K voprosu marksistskoi postanovki problemy stilya" [Toward a Marxist Formulation of the Problem of Style], *Vestnik Kommunisticheskoi Akademii* [Journal of the Communist Academy] M., 1928, Book XXV, pp. 96-115. [NN; NNC]

____, *Sovetskoye iskusstvo za 15 let: materialy i dokumentatsiya* [Fifteen Years of Soviet Art: Materials and Documentation], comp. by Matsa, L. Reingardt and L. Rempel', M., 1933, 663 p. [DLC; NN]

____, *Tvorcheskiye voprosy sovetskovo iskusstva* [Problems of Creative Work in Soviet Art], M., 1933, 45 p. [NN]

Mazel', Lev Abramovich, *Fantaziya f-moll Shopena: opyt analiza* [Chopin's Fantasy in F-minor: An Essay in Analysis], M., 1937, 183 p. [NN]

____, *O melodii* [On Melody], M., 1952, 299 p. [DLC]

——, "Spetsial'nyi kurs analiza muzykal'nykh proizvedenii" [Special Course in the Analysis of Musical Compositions], unpublished.

——. *See* Ryzhkin.

Medtner (Metner), Nikolai Karlovich (1880-1951), *The Muse and the Fashion: Being a Defence of the Foundations of the Art of Music,* tr. and annotated by Alfred J. Swan, Haverford, Pa., Haverford College Bookstore, 1951, 146 p. [DLC]

——, *Muza i moda: zashchita osnov muzykal'novo iskusstva* [The Muse and the Mode: A Defense of the Foundations of the Art of Music], Paris, Tair, 1935, 154 p. [NN]

——. *See* Yakovlev.

Miliukov, Paul Nikolayevich (1859-1943), *Ocherki po istorii russkoi kul'tury* [Essays on the History of Russian Culture], jubilee ed., 3 vols., Paris, Sovremennyya zapiski, 1930-1937. [DLC?; NN; NNC]

——, *Outlines of Russian Culture,* Part III, *Architecture, Painting and Music,* ed. by Michael Karpovich, tr. by Valentine Ughet and Eleanor Davis, Philadelphia, University of Pennsylvania Press, 1943, 159 p. [DLC; NN; NNC]

Moisenco, Rena, *Realist Music: 25 Soviet Composers,* London, Meridian, 1949, 277 p. [NN; NNC]
  Supplement, London, 1950, 32 p. [NN]

——, *Twenty Soviet Composers,* London, Workers' Music Association, 1943, 64 p. [DLC; NN]

†Muradeli, Vano Il'ich (1908-), "'Preodolet' nedostatki v tvorchestve ukrainskikh kompozitorov" [Overcome Shortcomings in the Work of Ukrainian Composers], *Izvestiya,* May 20, 1953.
  Review of the eighth plenum of the administration of the Union of Soviet Composers of the Ukraine.

——. *See* "Protiv formalizma...."

Musorgsky, Modeste Petrovich (1839-1881), *M. P. Musorgski:*

pis'ma i dokumenty [M.P. Musorgsky: Letters and Documents], prepared for publication by Andrei N. Rimsky-Korsakov and Varvara D. Komarova-Stasova, M.–L., 1932, 576 p. [DLC; NN; NNC]

____, *Pis'ma k A.A. Golenishchevu-Kutusovu* [Letters to A.A. Golenishchev-Kutuzov], commentary by P. Aravin, ed. and introduction by Yuri V. Keldysh, M.–L., 1939, 116 p. [DLC; NN; NNC]

____, "Pis'ma k V.V. Stasovu" [Letters to Vladimir Vasil'yevich Stasov], *Raduga: al'manakh Pushkinskovo doma* [Rainbow: Pushkin House Alamanac], P., 1922, pp. 232-241. [NN]

____. *See* Al'shvang; Asaf'yev; Braudo; Fried; Karatygin; Keldysh; Komarova-Stasova; Martynov; Orlov; Rimsky-Korsakov, A.N.; Sliotov; Stasov; Tumanina.

Muzalevski *(pseud.), see* Bunimovich.

Muzey diyachiv nauky ta mystetstva Ukrdïny [Museum of Science and Art Workers in the Ukraine], Kiev, *Zbirnyk... prysvyachenniy Mykoli Lysenkovi* [Collection... Dedicated to Mykola Lysenko], Kiev, 1930, 178 p. [NN; NNC]

Muzykal'noye iskusstvo Kazakhstana [Music of Kazakhstan], Alma-Ata, 1944.

†Myaskovski, Nikolai Yakovlevich (1881-1950), "Avtobiograficheskiye zametki o tvorcheskom puti" [Autobiographical Notes Concerning My Creative Path], *SM*, June 1936, No. 6, pp. 3-12. [NN]

____. *See* Asaf'yev; Belyayev, V.M.; Belza; Ikonnikov; [*Leningradskaya filarmoniya*].

Nabokov, Nicolas (1903-), "The Music Purge," *Politics*, New York, Vol. V, No. 2, 1948, pp. 102-106. [DLC; NN; NNC]

Includes full text of the Central Committee resolution on *The Great Friendship* as translated in the *Daily Worker*, New York, March 12, 1948.

——, *Old Friends and New Music*, Boston, Little, Brown, 1951, 294 p. [DLC; NNC]

——, "Prokof'yev," *Chisla* [Numbers], Paris, 1930, No. 2-3, pp. 217-228. [NN]

National Council of American-Soviet Friendship, Music Committee, *List of Soviet Music Publications Available in the United States of America*, New York, 1945, 71 p., mimeographed. [DLC; NN; NNC]

"Neobkhodim reshitel'nyi perelom!: o sostoyanii muzykal'novo iskusstva v respublikakh Srednei Azii" [A Decisive Turning Point Is Necessary!: On the State of Music in the Republics of Central Asia], *SM*, January 1949, No. 1, pp. 98-103.

Signed by A. Maldybayev, People's Artist of the U.S.S.R., S. Shakhidi, Honored Artist of the Tadzhik S.S.R., M. Tulebayev, Honored Art Worker of the Kazakh S.S.R., the composers Ashir Kuliyev of the Turkmen S.S.R., and M. Burkhanov of the Uzbek S.S.R.

Nest'yev, Izrail' Vladimirovich (1911-), "Dollarovaya kakofoniya" [Dollar Cacophony], *Izvestiya*, January 7, 1951. (English text in *Current Digest of the Soviet Press*, New York, Vol. III, No. 1, 1951, p. 16.)

——, *Russkaya sovetskaya pesnya: lektsiya* [The Russian Soviet Song: A Lecture], M., 1951, 33 p. [DLC]

——, *Sergei Prokofiev: His Musical Life*, tr. from the Russian by Rosa Prokofieva, introduction by Sergei Eisenstein, New York, Knopf, 1946, xxvii+193+xiv pp. [DLC; NN; NNC]

"Neudachnaya opera: o postanovki opery 'Ot vsevo serdtsa' v Bol'shom Teatre" [An Unsuccessful Opera: Concerning the Production of the Opera *With All One's Heart* at the Bol'shoi Theater], *Pravda* and *Izvestiya*, April 19, 1951. Reprinted in *SM*, May 1951, No. 5, pp. 8-12.

Nikolayev, A.A., *Fortepiannoye nasledstvo Chaikovskovo* [The Piano Heritage of Tchaikovsky], M., 1949, 206 p. [DLC; NN; NNC]

Nikolayev, Leonid Vladimirovich (1878-1942). *See* Savshinski.

Nikolayeva, Nina, *Simfoniya Chaikovskovo "Manfred": poyasneniye* [The *Manfred* Symphony by Tchaikovsky: Comments], M., 1952, 25 p. [DLC]

Nisnevich, I., "Kompozitory BSSR za 30 let" [Composers of the Byelorussian S.S.R. For Thirty Years], *SM*, 1949, No. 3, pp. 29-34.

"Novaya sovetskaya opera v Bol'shom Teatre 'Ot vsevo serdtsa'" [A New Opera at the Bol'shoi Theatre, *With All One's Heart*], *Pravda* and *Izvestiya*, January 17, 1951.

†Novikov, Anatoli Grigor'yevich (1896-), "O sovremennoi muzyke" [Contemporary Music], *Ogonyok* [Flame], M., Vol. XXXI, No. 6, February 1953, pp. 10-11. [NN]

——. *See* Polyanovski.

"Novye uspekhi sovetskoi muzyki" [New Successes of Soviet Music], *SM*, April 1949, No. 4, pp. 3-8.

Nyurnberg, M.V., *Simfonicheskii orkestr i yevo instrumenty: kratkii ocherk* [The Symphonic Orchestra and Its Instruments: A Brief Essay], L., 1950, 150 p. [DLC; NN]

Novosel'ski, A., *Ocherki po istorii russkikh narodnykh muzykal'nykh instrumentov* [Essays on the History of Russian Folk Musical Instruments], M., 1931.

"Ob opere 'Bogdan Khmel'nitski' " [Concerning the Opera *Bohdan Khmel'nyts'kyi*], *Pravda*, July 20, 1951.

Ocherki sovetskovo muzykal'novo tvorchestva [Essays on Soviet Musical Creation], ed. by Boris V. Asaf'yev, Arnol'd A. Al'shvang, *et al.*, Vol. I, M.–L., 1947, 321 p. [DLC?; NN]

Articles by Boris V. Asaf'yev, Yuri V. Keldysh, M.S. Kiselev, Ivan I. Martynov, Izrail' V. Nest'yev, A.A. Solovtsov, V. Tsukkerman, E.E. Tsytovich, V.A. Vasina, and I.M. Yampol'ski.

Short title: *Ocherki*.

Odoyevski, Vladimir Fyodorovich (1803-1869), *Izbrannye muzykal'no-kriticheskiye stat'i* [Selected Articles on Musical Criticism], introduction and commentary by Vl. Protopopov, M., 1951, 117 p. [DLC; NN; NNC]

Ogolevets, Aleksei Stepanovich, *Osnovy garmonicheskovo yazyka* [Fundamentals of the Language of Harmony], M., 1941, 971 p. Summary in French. [NN; NNC]

___, "P.I. Chaikovski" [P.I. Tchaikovsky], *Novyi mir* [New World], M., 1940, No. 7, pp. 192-209. [NN]

___, *Vvedeniye v sovremennoye muzykal'noye myshleniye* [Introduction to Contemporary Musical Thought], M., 1946, 469 p. [CU; NN; NNC]

Ol'khovs'kyi, Andriy V. (i.e., Olkhovsky, Andrey), *Narys istorii̇ ukraïns'koï muzyky* [Outline of the History of Ukrainian Music], Kiev, 1941.

___, "XX st." [The Twentieth Century], in the section "Istoriya muzyky" [History of Music], in *Entsyklopediya ukraïnoznavstva* [Encyclopedia of Ukrainian Knowledge], Munich-New York, 1949, Vol. I, Part III, pp. 873-876.
Written under the pseudonym Ye. Olens'kyi.

Orlov, Georgi Pavlovich (1900-), *Letopis' zhizni i tvorchestva M.P. Musorgskovo* [Chronicle of the Life and Work of M.P. Musorgsky], ed. by Vasili V. Yakovlev, M., 1940, 188 p. [DLC; NN; NNC]

___, *Muzykal'naya literatura: bibliograficheskii ukazatel' knizhnoi i zhurnal'noi literatury o muzyke na russkom yazyke* [Musical Literature: A Bibliographical Index of Books and Articles on Music in the Russian Language], L., 1936, 222 p. [DLC]

Orlova, A., comp., *M.I. Glinka: letopis' zhizni i tvorchestva* [M.I. Glinka: A Chronicle of His Life and Work], ed. by Boris V. Asaf'yev, M., 1952, 540 p. [DLC; NNC]

Orlova, Ye., *Romansy Chaikovskovo* [The Songs of Tchaikovsky], M., 1948, 163 p. [DLC; NNC]

Ossovski, Aleksandr Vyacheslavovich, *Aleksandr Konstantinovich Glazunov: yevo zhizn' i tvorchestvo* [Aleksandr Konstantinovich Glazunov: His Life and Work], St.P., 1908?, 52 p. [NNC]

___, *M.I. Glinka: issledovaniya i materialy* [M.I. Glinka: Research and Materials], L.–M., 1950, 272 p. [DLC; NN]

___, *Mirovoye znacheniye russkoi klassicheskoi muzyki: stenogramma publichnoi lektsii, prochitannoi v 1948 godu v Leningrade* [The World Significance of Russian Classical Music: A Verbatim Record of a Public Lecture Read in 1948 in Leningrad], L., 1948, 27 p. [DLC]

___, "Osnovnye voprosy russkoi muzykal'noi kul'tury XVII i XVIII vekov" [Fundamental Problems of Russian Musical Culture of the Seventeenth and Eighteenth Centuries], *SM*, May 1950, No. 5, pp. 53-57.

Ostrovski, A.L., *Kratkii muzykal'nyi slovar'* [Short Musical Dictionary], L., 1949, 212 p. [NNC]

Paliashvili, Zakhari Petrovich (1872-1933). See [*Leningradskaya filarmoniya*].

Pashchenko, Andrei Filippovich (1883-). See [*Leningradskaya filarmoniya*].

Paskhalov, Vyacheslav Viktorovich (1873-), *V.S. Kalinnikov*, M., 1947, 27 p. [DLC; NN]

___, *Vasili Sergeyevich Kalinnikov: zhizn' i tvorchestvo* [Vasili Sergeyevich Kalinnikov: Life and Work], L.–M., 1951, 226 p. [DLC; NN]

Pavlov, Konstantin, "P.I. Tchaikovsky," *VOKS Bulletin*, M., 1942, No. 3-4, pp. 71-75. [NN]

Pavlyuchenko, S.A., *Elementarnaya teoriya muzyki dlya muzykal'nykh uchilishch i shkol* [Elementary Theory of Music for Music Schools and Schooling], 2nd ed., L.–M., 1940, 158 p. [DLC; NN]

___, *Kratkii muzykal'nyi slovar': spravochnik* [Short Musical Dictionary: A Handbook], ed. by K.K. Rozenshil'd, linguistic ed. A.M. Yevlakhov, M., 1950, 192 p. [DLC]

Pekelis, Mikhail Samoilovich (1899-), *Dargomyzhski i narodnaya pesnya: k probleme narodnosti v russkoi klassicheskoi muzyke* [Dargomyzhsky and the Folk Song: On the Problem of Nationality in Russian Classical Music], M., 1951, 209 p. [DLC; NN; NNC]

___, ed., *Istoriya russkoi muzyki* [A History of Russian Music], 2 vols., M., 1940. [DLC; NN]

Pekker, Yan, *V.A. Uspenski: muzykal'no-etnograficheskaya i kompozitorskaya deyatel'nost' v Uzbekistane i Turkmenii* [V.A. Uspenski: Musico-Ethnographical and Composers' Activity in Uzbekistan and Turkmenia], M., 1953, 154 p. [DLC]

Plotkin, M.I. *See* Khanukayev.

Pokhitonov, Daniil Il'ich (1878-), *Iz proshlovo russkoi opery* [From the Past of Russia Opera], ed. and introduction by Sergei S. Danilov, L., 1949, 262 p. [DLC; NN]

Polyak, N.S., *Pervaya simfoniya S.I. Taneyeva* [The First Symphony of S.I. Taneyev], L., 1937, 24 p. [NN]

Polyakova, N. *See* Grinberg.

Polyanovski, Georgi Aleksandrovich, *A.V. Aleksandrov*, M., 1948, 99 p. [DLC; NN]

___, *A. Novikov*, M., 1948, 39 p. [DLC; NN]

___, *Eugen Kapp*, M.–L., 1951, 47 p. [DLC]

___, *N.A. Rimskij-Korssakow*, Potsdam, Stichnote, 1948, 31 p. [DLC; NN]

___, *S.N. Vasilenko*, M., 1947, 163 p. [MH; NN]

___. *See* "Protiv formalizma...."

†Popov, Gavriil Nikolayevich (1904-). *See* [*Leningradskaya filarmoniya*].

Popova, Tat'yana Vasil'yevna, *A.P. Borodin (dlya shkol'nikov starshevo vozrasta)* [A.P. Borodin (For Older School Children)], M., 1937, 135 p. [DLC; NN]

——, *Borodin*, M., 1953, 222 p. [DLC]

——, comp., *Mikhail Ivanovich Glinka: kratkii rekomendatel'nyi ukazatel'* [Mikhail Ivanovich Glinka: A Brief Recommended Bibliography], ed. by Ye. Levina, M., 1953, 45 p. [DLC]

——, *Muzykal'nyi zhanry i formy* [Musical Genres and Forms], M., 1951, 298 p. [DLC]

——, *Simfonicheskaya fantaziya "Kamarinskaya" M. Glinki* [The Symphonic Fantasy *Kamarinskaya* by M. Glinka], M.–L., 1950.

Postavnichev, K., *Massovoye peniye: s prilozheniyem pesen, not, chastushek i novykh tekstov...* [Mass Singing: With Appended Songs, Sheet Music, *Chastushkas*, and New Texts...], M., 1925, 144 p.

"Prekrasnye traditsii" [Excellent Traditions], *SI*, No. 17(1105), April 24, 1948. [NN]

Preobrazhenski, Antonin Viktorovich (1870-1929), *Kul'tovaya muzyka v Rossii* [Liturgical Music in Russia], L., 1924, 123 p. [DLC; NN]

Prokhorova, I., *"Snegurochka" N.A. Rimskovo-Korsakova* [*The Snow Maiden* by N.A. Rimsky-Korsakov], M., 1952, 47 p. [NN]

†Prokof'yev, Sergei Sergeyevich (1891-1953), *Sergei Prokof'yev: tvorcheskii i zhiznennyi put'* [Sergei Prokof'yev: Life and Work], M., 1932, 23 p. [DLC; NN; NNC]

——, "Vystupleniye na sobranii kompozitorov i muzykovedov g. Moskvy" [Speech at the Meeting of Composers and Musicologists of Moscow], *SM*, January-February 1948, No. 1, p. 66. [DLC]

——, "Yunye gody: iz avtobiografii" [Youthful Years: From My Autobiography], *SM*, April 1941, No. 4, pp. 71-85. [NN]

——, [Prokof'yev Number], *Tempo*, London, Spring 1949, No. 11, 36 p. [DLC?; NNC]

——. *See* Asaf'yev; [*Leningradskaya filarmoniya*]; Nabokov; Nest'yev; Slonimsky.

"Protiv formalizma i fal'shi: tvorcheskaya diskussiya v moskovskom soyuze sovetskikh kompozitorov" [Against Formalism and Falsification: Creative Discussion in the Moscow Union of Soviet Composers (February 10, 13, 15, 1936)], *SM*, March 1936, No. 3, pp. 14-60. [NN]

Speeches delivered in the following order: Chelyapov, Polyanovski, Lebedinski, Sezhenski, Knipper, Kabalevski, Neigauz, Khavenson, G. Bruk, Belyi, Shteinpress, Chemberdzhi, Krasin, Shvarts, Zhitomirski, Sabo, Grinberg, Dovgyallo-Garbuz, Bogosovski, Okayemov, Ryzhkin, Khrennikov, Bryusova, Ferman, Fere, Vinogradov, Valentina Ramm, Gusman, Vasilenko, Kulakovski, Veprik, Muradeli, Girinis, Neimark, Khubov, Keldysh, and Chelyapov.

Protopopov, Vl.L., *M.I. Glinka*, M., 1949, 70 p. [NN]

——, ed., *Pamyati Sergeya Ivanovicha Taneyeva, 1856-1946: sbornik statei i materialov k 90-letiyu so dnya rozhdeniya* [In Memory of Sergei Ivanovich Taneyev, 1856-1946: Collected Articles and Materials for the Ninetieth Anniversary of His Birth], M., 1947, 272 p. [DLC; NN; NNC]

——, "Patrioticheskaya kantata: 'Slav'sya, otchizna moya!' Ye. Zhukovskovo" [The Patriotic Cantata *Glory to Thee, My Country* by Ye. (H.) Zhukovs'kyi], *SM*, April 1950, No. 4, pp. 18-23.

Puti. *See* Shaverdyan.

"Puti sovetskoi operetty" [The Paths of Soviet Operetta], *SI*, No. 11(1399), February 6, 1952.

Rabinovich, Aleksandr Semyonovich (1900-1943), *Russkaya*

opera do Glinki [Russian Opera Before Glinka], M., 1948, 268 p. [DLC; NN]

Rachmaninov, Sergei Vasil'yevich (1873-1943), *Molodye gody Sergeya Vasil'yevicha Rachmaninova: pis'ma; vospominaniya* [Youthful Years of Sergei Vasil'yevich Rachmaninov: Letters and Reminiscences], L., 1949, 188 p. [DLC; NN; NNC]

____, "Pis'ma S.V. Rakhmaninova k Re" [S.V. Rachmaninov's Letters to Re], *Novyi mir* [New World], M., 1943, No. 4, pp. 105-113. [NN]

____, *Rachmaninoff's Recollections Told to Oscar von Riesemann*, New York, Macmillan, 1934, 272 p. [DLC; NN; NNC]

____. *See* Bélza; Kuznetsov; Solovtsov.

Radlov, Nikolai Ernestovich (1889-). *See* Braudo.

†Rakov, Nikolai Petrovich (1908-). *See* Solovtsov.

Ratskaya, Ts., *N.A. Rimski-Korsakov*, M., 1953, 137 p. [DLC]

Rechmenski, N., *Massovye muzykal'nye narodnye instrumenty* [Folk Music Instruments for the Masses], M., 1953, 68 p. [DLC]

Remezov, Ivan Ivanovich, *A.P. Borodin: lektsiya* [A.P. Borodin: A Lecture], M., 1952, 35 p. [DLC]

____, *M.I. Glinka: lektsiya* [M.I. Glinka: A Lecture], M., 1951, 43 p. [DLC]

Revuts'kyi, Dmytro Mykolovych (1891-1942), *Ukraïns'ki dumy ta pisni istorychni* [Ukrainian Ballads and Historical Songs], Kiev, 1919, 300 p. [NN]; 2nd ed., 1930, 273 p. [NNC]

†Revuts'kyi, Levko Mykolovych (1889-). *See* Kiselyov, G.L.

Rimsky-Korsakov, Andrei Nikolayevich (1878-1940), *Maksimilian Shteinberg: Maximilian Steinberg*, M., 1928, 40 p. Text in Russian and German. [NN]

——, *N.A. Rimski-Korsakov: zhizn' i tvorchestvo* [N.A. Rimsky-Korsakov: Life and Work], 5 vols., M., 1933-1946. [NN; NNC: Vols. I, III-V]

——, "'Boris Godunov' M.P. Musorgskovo" [*Boris Godunov* by M.P. Musorgsky], *Muzykal'nyi sovremennik* [Musical Contemporary], P., 1917, No. 5-6, pp. 108-167. [NN]

Rimsky-Korsakov, Nikolai Andreyevich (1844-1908), *Osnovy orkestrovki: s partiturnymi obraztsami iz sobstvennykh sochinenii* [Principles of Orchestration with Musical Examples Drawn from His Own Works], ed. by Maksimilian O. Shteinberg, 2 vols., M., 1946. [DLC; NN]; Eng. tr. by Edward Agate, 2 vols. in one, Berlin, Edition russe de musique, 1927. [NNC]

——, *Prakticheskii uchebnik garmonii* [Practical Manual of Harmony], 17th ed. corrected and supplemented by Maksimilian O. Shteinberg, M.–L., 1949, 170 p. [NN]; Eng. translation from the 12th ed. by Joseph Achron, New York, Fischer, 1930, 142 p. [DLC; NN; NNC]

——. *See* Al'shvang; Asaf'yev; Balakirev; Berkov, V.O.; Gorodetskaya; Kiselyov, V.A.; Kulakovski; Lapshin; Polyanovski; Prokhorova; Ratskaya; Rimsky-Korsakov, A.N.; Solovtsov; Yankovski.

Rogal'-Levitski, Dmitri R., *Sovremennyi orkestr* [The Contemporary Orchestra], Vol. I, M., 1953, 480 p. [DLC]

Rostislavov, A[leksandr Aleksandrovich?], "Oktyabr'skiye sobytiye" [Events of October], *Apollon* [Apollo], P., 1917, No. 6-7, pp. 79-84. [NN]

——, "Revolyutsiya i iskusstvo" [The Revolution and Art], *ibid.*, No. 8-10, pp. 80-87. [NN]

Rubinstein, Anton Grigor'yevich (1828-1894). *See* Asaf'yev.

Russian Symphony: Thoughts About Tchaikovsky, New York, Philosophical Library, 1947, 271 p. [DLC; NN; NNC]
Articles by Arnol'd A. Alshvang, Ksenya Davydova,

Yuri V. Keldysh, Dmitri D. Shostakovich, Vasili V. Yakovlev, B.M. Yarustovski, and Daniil V. Zhitomirski.

"Russkaya muzykal'naya bibliografiya za 1925 g." [Russian Music Bibliography for 1925], *De musica*, L., Vol. II, 1926, pp. 130-138. [NN]

"Russkaya muzykal'naya bibliografiya za 1925 goda (s predisloviyem A.N. Rimski-Korsakova)" [Russian Music Bibliography for 1925 (Foreword by A.N. Rimsky-Korsakov)], *De musica*, L., Vol. I, 1925, pp. 117-124. [NN]

Ryzhkin, I.Ya., "Novoye izdaniye uchebnika garmonii" [A New Edition of a Textbook of Harmony], *SM*, February 1950, No. 2, pp. 108-110.

———, *Russkoye klassicheskoye muzykoznaniye v bor'be protiv formalizma* [Russian Classical Musicology in the Struggle Against Formalism], M., 1951, 151 p. [DLC; NN; NNC]

———. *See* "Protiv formalizma...."

———, and Lev Abramovich Mazel', *Ocherki po istorii teoreticheskovo muzykoznaniya* [Essays on the History of Theoretical Musicology], 2 vols., M.–L., 1934-1939.

Sabaneyev, Leonid Leonidovich (1881-), *Aleksandr Abramovich Krein: Alexander Krein*, M., 1928, 39 p. Text in Russian and German. [DLC; NN]

———, *A.N. Skryabin* [A.N. Scriabin], M., 1922, 31 p. [NN]

———, *Chto takoye muzyka* [What Music Is], M., 1925, 43 p.

———, *Istoriya russkoi muzyki* [A History of Russian Music], M., 1924, 87 p. [NN; NNC]

———, *Modern Russian Composers*, tr. from the Russian by Judah A. Joffe, New York, International Publishers, 1927, 253 p. [DLC; NN; NNC]

———, *Music for the Films: A Handbook for Composers and*

Conductors, tr. by S.W. Pring, London, Pitman, 1935, 128 p. [DLC; NNC]

———, *Muzyka posle Oktyabrya* [Music After October], M., 1926, 165 p. [NN]

———, *S.I. Taneyev: mysli o tvorchestve i vospominaniya o zhizne* [S.I. Taneyev: Thoughts on Work and Recollections of His Life] Paris, Tair, 1930, 217 p. [NN; NNC]

———, *Skryabin*, 2nd revised ed., M.–P., 1923, 201 p. [DLC]

———, *Vospominaniya o Skryabine* [Recollections of Scriabin], M., 1925, 318 p. [NN]

Reviewed by Andrei N. Rimsky-Korsakov in *De musica*, L., Vol. II, 1926, pp. 133-134. [NN]

———, *Vseobshchaya istoriya muzyki* [A General History of Music], M., 1925, 265 p. [NN; NNC]

Saminsky, Lazare (1882-), *Music of Our Day: Essentials and Prophecies*, New York, Thomas Y. Crowell, 1932, 313 p. [DLC; NN]; new enl. ed. 1939, xxvi+390 p. [DLC; NNC]

One section is entitled "New Russians and Their Alma Mater."

Satylganov, Toktogul (1864-1933). *See* Vinogradov.

Savshinski, S., *Leonid Nikolayev: pianist, kompozitor, pedagog* [Leonid Nikolayev: Pianist, Composer, Teacher], L., 1950, 188 p. [DLC]

Schaeffner, André (1895-), and Boris Fyodorovich Schloezer (1884-), "Les courants de la musique russe contemporaine," *Encyclopédie de la musique et dictionnaire du Conservatoire*, Paris, [1913-] 1931, 2e. partie [Vol. I] (1925), pp. 159-175. [DLC; NN]

Schloezer (Shletser), Boris Fyodorovich (1884-), *A. Skryabin* [A. Scriabin], Vol. I, *Lichnost'. Misteriya* [The Personality and the Mystery], Berlin, Grani, 1923. [NN; NNC]

———. *See* Schaeffner.

Schneerson, Grigori, *see* Shneyerson.

Scriabin, (Skryabin) Aleksandr Nikolayevich (1872-1915), *Aleksandr Nikolayevich Skryabin, 1915-1940: sbornik k 25-letiyu so dnya smerti* [Aleksandr Nikolayevich Scriabin, 1915-1940: A Compendium for the Twenty-fifth Anniversary of His Death], ed. by St. Markus, M., 1940, 243 p. [NN; NNC]

___, *Pis'ma A.N. Skryabina* [Letters of A.N. Scriabin], ed. by Leonid L. Sabaneyev, M., 1923, 56 p. [NNC]

___, and Mitrofan Petrovich Belyayev (1836-1904), *Perepiska A.N. Skryabina i M.P. Belyayeva, 1894-1903* [The Correspondence of A.N. Scriabin and M.P. Belyayev, 1894-1903], introduction and notes by Viktor M. Belyayev, P., 1922, 194 p. [NN]

___, "Zapiski A.N. Skryabina" [The Memoirs of A.N. Scriabin], in *Russkiye propilei: materialy po istorii russkoi mysli i literatury* [Russian *Propylaia*: Materials on the History of Russian Thought and Literature], ed. by Mikhail O. Gershenzon, M., 1919, Vol. VI, pp. 95-247. [NN; NNC]

___. *See* Al'shvang; Asaf'yev; Danilevich; Lovtski; Lunacharski; Sabaneyev; Schloezer; Vodarsky-Shiraeff; Yakovlev.

Seroff, Victor Ilyich (1902-), and Nadejda Galli-Shohat, *Dmitri Shostakovich: The Life and Background of a Soviet Composer*, New York, Knopf, 1943, 260 p. [DLC; NN; NNC]

Serov, Aleksandr Nikolayevich (1820-1871), *Izbrannye stat'i* [Selected Articles], ed. with introduction and notes by Georgi N. Khubov, M., 1950, 625 p. [DLC; NN; NNC]

___, *Muzyka yuzhno-russkikh pesen* [Music of the Songs from South Russia], M., 1953, 34 p. [DLC]

___, "Russkaya narodnaya pesnya kak predmet nauki" [The Russian Folk Song As a Subject for Science], *SM*, October 1936, No. 10, pp. 16-42. [NN]

___, *Russkaya narodnaya pesnya kak predmet nauki*, ed. and notes by Aleksei S. Ogolevets, M., 1952, 62 p. [DLC; NN]

___, *Vospominaniya o Mikhaile Ivanoviche Glinke* [Recollections of Mikhail Ivanovich Glinka], M., 1951, 82 p. [DLC; MH; NN]

___. *See* Khubov; Strel'nikov.

Sezhenski, K., *Kratkii slovar' muzykal'nykh terminov* [Short Dictionary of Musical Terms], 2nd corrected and enlarged ed., M.–L., 1950, 118 p. [DLC]

___, *R.M. Glier* [R.M. Glière], 2nd ed., M.–L., 1940.

___. *See* "Protiv formalizma...."

†Shaporin, Yuri Aleksandrovich (1889-), *See* Asaf'yev; Bogdanov-Berezovski; [*Leningradskaya filarmoniya*].
According to Bernandt *(q.v.)* Shaporin was born in 1887.

Shatskaya, V.N., *Muzyka v shkole: khudozhestvennoye vospitaniye sredstvami muzykal'novo iskusstva* [Music in School: Artistic Training Through Music], M., 1950, 173 p. [DLC]

Shaverdyan, Aleksandr Isaakovich, *A.A. Spendiarov: zhizn' i tvorchestvo: kratkii ocherk* [A.A. Spendiarov: Life and Work: A Short Essay], M.–L., 1939.

___, *Puti razvitya sovetskoi muzyki: kratkii obzor* [The Ways of Development of Soviet Music: A Brief Survey], M., 1948, 137 p. [DLC; NN]
Short title: *Puti.*

Shcherbachov, Vladimir Vladimirovich (1889-). *See* [*Leningradskaya filarmoniya*].

†Shebalin, Vissarion Yakovlevich (1902-). *See* Asaf'yev; Bèlza.

Sheibler (Scheibler), T.K., "Iz istorii razvitiya kabardinskoi muzyki za gody sovetskoi vlasti" [From the History of the Development of Kabardinian Music During the Soviet Regime], *Uchonye zapiski Kabardinskovo nauchno-issledovatel'skovo instituta* [Scientific Annals of the Kabardinian Research Institute], Nal'chik, 1948, Vol. IV.

Shenshin, Aleksandr Alekseyevich (1890-). *See* Belyayev, V.M.

Shishov, Ivan Petrovich (1888-). *See* Bugoslavski.

Shletser, *see* Schloezer.

Shlifshtein, S., *A.S. Dargomyzhski: lektsiya* [A.S. Dargomyzhsky: A Lecture], M., 1951, 23 p. [DLC]

——, *Glinka i Pushkin* [Glinka and Pushkin], M., 1950, 95 p. [DLC]

Shneyerson (Schneerson), Grigori Mikhailovich, "The Changing Course of Russian Music," *Modern Music,* New York, Vol. XIII, No. 2, January-February 1936, pp. 19-24. [DLC; NN; NNC]

——, *Muzyka na sluzhbe reaktsii* [Music in the Service of Reaction], M., 1950, 98 p. [DLC; NN]

——, *Sovremennaya amerikanskaya muzyka* [Contemporary American Music], M., 1945, 31 p. [CU]

†Shostakovich, Dmitri Dmitriyevich (1906-), *Message to America from Dmitri Shostakovich, January 4, 1942,* San Francisco, The American Russian Institute, 1942? [NN]

——, "My Seventh Symphony," *VOKS Bulletin,* M., 1942, No. 1-2, pp. 55-56. [NN]

——, "Po puti narodnosti i realizma" [Along the Path of Nationality and Realism], *SM,* November 1952, No. 11, pp. 6-11.

——, "Soviet Music Today," *Saturday Review of Literature,* New York, Vol. XXX, No. 4, January 25, 1947, p. 25. [DLC; NN; NNC]

——, "Symphony of Struggle and Victory," *VOKS Bulletin,* M., 1942, No. 1-2, pp. 57-60. [NN]

——. *See* Asaf'yev; "Baletnaya fal'sh..."; Bernandt; Chernyi; Koval'; [*Leningradskaya filarmoniya*]; Lourié; Martynov; Seroff; "Sumbur...."

Shteinberg, Maksimilian Oseyevich (1883-). *See* [*Leningradskaya filarmoniya*]; Rimsky-Korsakov, A.N.

Shtelin, Yakov, *see* Staehlin.

†Shtoharenko, Andriy Yakovych (1902-). *See* Znosko-Borovs'kyi.

Sidel'nikov, Viktor M., *Russkoye narodnoye tvorchestvo i estrada: populyarnyi ocherk* [Russian Folk Art and the Music Hall: A Popular Essay], M., 1950, 63 p. [DLC; NN]

——, *Suleiman Stal'ski: k 15-letiyu so dnya smerti* [Suleiman Stal'ski: For the Fifteenth Anniversary of His Death], M., 1953, 23 p. [DLC; NN]

Skrebkov, S.S., *Uchebnik polifonii* [Textbook of Counterpoint], M., 1951, 269 p. [DLC; NN]

Skryabin, *see* Scriabin.

Sliotov, Pyotr Vladimirovich, and V.A. Sliotova, *Musorgski,* M., 1934, 239 p. [NN]

Slonimski, Yuri Osipovich, *"Petrushka": muzyka Igorya Stravinskovo* [*Petrushka:* Music by Igor Stravinsky], L., 1935, 26 p. [NN]

——, *Sovetskii balet: materialy k istorii sovetskovo teatra* [The Soviet Ballet: Materials for a History of the Soviet Theater], M., 1950, 365 p. [DLC]

Slonimsky, Nicolas (1894-), "Aram Khachaturian," *American Review on the Soviet Union,* New York, Vol. III, No. 4, 1941, pp. 23-25. [NN]

——, "Development of Soviet Music," *Research Bulletin on the Soviet Union,* Vol. II, No. 4, April 30, 1937, pp. 31-36. [NNC]

Issued by the American Russian Institute for Cultural Relations with the Soviet Union, Inc.

——, "A New Tune in Soviet Music," *Saturday Review of*

Literature, New York, Vol. XXXVII, No. 5, January 30, 1954, pp. 37, 39, 62-64. [DLC; NN; NNC]

____, "Reinhold Glière," *American Quarterly on the Soviet Union*, New York, July 1938, pp. 52-56. [NN]

____, "Serge Prokofiev: His Status in Soviet Music," *ibid.*, Vol. II, 1939, pp. 37-44. [NN]

____, "Soviet Music and Musicians," an offprint from *Slavonic and East European Review*, Vol. XXII, No. 61, December 1944, 18 p. [DLC; NN]

Sodoklady. See [Soyuz Sovetskikh Kompozitorov].

Sogomonyan, *see* Komitas *(pseud.)*

Sokhor, A., *V.P. Solov'yov-Sedoi: pesennoye tvorchestvo* [V.P. Solov'yov-Sedoi: Song Writing], L., 1952, 174 p. [DLC; NN]

Sokolov, Yuri Matveyevich (1889-1941), ed., *Onezhskiye byliny* [Onega Ballads], M., 1948, 937 p. [DLC; NN; NNC]

Solovtsov, A.A., *N.A. Rimski-Korsakov*, M., 1948, 217 p. [DLC; NN]

____, *N.A. Rimski-Korsakov: lektsiya* [N.A. Rimsky-Korsakov: A Lecture], M., 1951, 35 p. [DLC; NN]

____, *S.V. Rakhmaninov*, M., 1947, 111 p. [NN]

____, *Simfoniya N. Rakova: poyasneniya* [The Symphony by N. Rakov: Comments], M., 1951, 23 p. [DLC; NN]

Solov'yov, Yu.I. *See* Figurovski.

†Solov'yov-Sedoi, Vasili Pavlovich (1907-). *See [Leningradskaya filarmoniya]*; Sokhor.

SONGS, Collections of

Belov, L.O., A.I. Voinov, and L.A. Yudkevich, comps., *Pesni o Staline* [Songs About Stalin], M., 1950, 202 p. [DLC; NN]

Bugoslavski, Sergei A., and Ivan Petrovich Shishov (1888-), comps., *Pesni donskikh i kubanskikh kazakov* [Songs of the Don and Kuban Cossacks], M., 1937, 109 p. [NN; NNC]

Dobrushin, Iezekiil Moiseyevich (1883-), and A.D. Yuditski, *Yevreiskiye narodnye pesni* [Jewish Folk Songs], ed. by Yuri M. Sokolov, M., 1947, 279 p. [DLC; NN; NNC]

Druskin, Mikhail S., *Revolyutsionnye pesni 1905 goda* [Revolutionary Songs of 1905], L., 1936, 70 p. [DLC]

Ewald (Eval'd), Zinaida Viktorovna (1895-), ed., *Belorusskiye narodniye pesni* [Byelorussian Folk Songs], M.–P., 1921, 142 p. Text in Byelorussian. [DLC]

Frolov, Markian Petrovich (1892-), and St. Morozov-Ural'ski, eds., *Pesni krasnoi armii* [Songs of the Red Army], Sverdlovsk, 1934, 15 p. [NN]

Gippius, Yevgeni Vladimirovich (1903-), and Zinaida Viktorovna Ewald, eds. and comps., *Pesni Pinezh'ya: materialy fonogramm-arkhiva* [Songs of the Pinega River Region: Materials from the Phonograph Archive], Vol. II, M., 1937, 591 p. (*Akademiya nauk SSSR. Trudy instituta antropologii, etnografii i arkheologii* [U.S.S.R. Academy of Sciences. Works of the Institute of Anthropology, Ethnography and Archaeology], Vol. VII, *Fol'klornaya seriya* [Folklore Series], No. 2.) [DLC; NN; NNC]

Globa, Andrei Pavlovich (1888-), comp. and tr., *Buryatskiye i mongol'skiye pesni* [Buryat and Mongol Songs], M., 1940, 68 p. [DLC; NNC]

——, ed. and tr., *Pesni narodov SSSR* [Songs of the Peoples of the U.S.S.R.], 2nd supplemented ed., M., 1935, 365 p. [DLC]; 1941, 814 p. [NNC]; 1947, 814 p. [NN]

Grebnev, A.F., comp. and ed., *Adygeiskiye (cherkesskiye) narodnye pesni: melodii: sbornik pervykh zapisei* [Adyge (Cherkess) Folk Songs: Melodies: First Collected Records], with introduction, "kriticheskii obzor muzykal'novo tvorchestva naroda adyge (cherkesov)" [Critical Review of the Musical Art of the People of Adyge (Cherkess)], M.–L., 1941.

*Gudkov, Viktor Panteleimonovich (1899-1942), and N.N. Levi, comps., *Pesni narodov Karelo-Finskoi SSR: sbornik karel'skikh, vepsskikh i russkikh pesen* [Songs of the Peoples of the Karelo-Finnish S.S.R.: A Collection of Karelian, Vepse and Russian Songs], Petrozavodsk, 1941.

Kapiyev, effendi (1909-1944), ed., *Pesni gortsev* [Songs of Mountaineers], commentary by Kapiyev, M., 1939, 253 p. [DLC; NNC]

Material on peoples of the Caucasus.

Kedrina, Z., ed., *Pesni kazakhskikh stepei: sbornik proizvedenii kazakhskoi literatury* [Songs of the Kazakh Steppes: A Collection of Works of Kazakh Literature], M., Detgiz, 1951, 382 p. [DLC; NN; NNC]

Khait, Yuli, *Pesni revolyutsii* [Songs of the Revolution], words by Pavel German, music by Yuli Khait, 3 vols., Kiev, 192-? [NN]

Konchevski, Arkadi Karlovich (1884-), comp., *Pesni Kryma* [Songs of the Crimea], ed. by Vyacheslav V. Paskhalov, introduction by Anatoli V. Lunacharski, M., 1929, 49 p. [NN]

Tatar and Bashkir folk songs.

——, comp., *Pesni Vostoka* [Songs of the East], ed. by Vyacheslav V. Paskhalov, M., 1927, 41 p. [NN]

Folk songs of peoples of the Crimea.

Kozyts'kyi, Pylyp Yemel'yanovych (1898-), *Pisnya 30-ho polku* [Song of the Thirtieth Regiment], M. 1943, 5 p. [NN]

Lavrov, F.Ya., *Stalin v ukraïns'komu fol'klori Velykoï Vitchyznyanoï viyny* [Stalin in Ukrainian Folklore of the Great Patriotic War], Kiev, 1947, 30 p. [DLC; NNC]

Litvak, G., tr., *Pesni i dumy Sovetskoi Ukrainy* [Songs and Ballads of Soviet Ukraine], M., 1940, 27 p. [NN]; introduction by M. Ryl'ski, M., 1951, 334 p. [NN; NNC]

Lozanova, Aleksandra Nikolayevna (1896-), *Narodnye pesni o*

Stepane Razine [Folk Songs About Stepan Razin], Saratov, 1928, 277 p. [NN]

——, ed., *Pesni i skazaniya o Razine i Pugachove* [Songs and Tales About Razin and Pugachov], introduction and notes, M.–L., 1935, lxiv+418 p. [DLC; NN]

Milovidov, L., comp., *Pesni sovetskoi molodyozhi* [Songs of Soviet Youth], Book I, M., 1951. [DLC; NN]

Pesni bor'by i pobed: sbornik [Songs of Struggle and Victory: A Compendium], Saratov, 1934, 79 p. [NN]

Pesni krasnoi armii [Songs of the Red Army], M., 1936, 219 p. [NN]

Pesni krasnoi armii, Molotov, 1943, 31 p. [DLC]

Pesni novovo byta [Songs of a New Life], Yerevan, 1930, 28 p. [NN]

Works by Aleksandr G. Arutyunyan, Sp. Melikyan and Mikh. Mirzoyan.

Pesni revolyutsii: sbornik revolyutsionnykh pesen i stikhotvorenii [Songs of the Revolution: A Collection of Revolutionary Songs and Verse], P., 1917, 32 p. [NN]

Pesni sovetskikh lyotchikov (dlya massovovo ispolneniya) [Songs of Soviet Airmen (For Mass Performance)], M., 1932, 18 p. [NN]

Pesni Sovetskoi Moldavii: sbornik proizvedenii moldavskikh kompozitorov [Songs of Soviet Moldavia: A Collection of Works by Moldavian Composers], M., 1951, 75 p. [NN]

Poluyanov, P.N., comp., *Pesni o Moskve* [Songs About Moscow], M., 1947, 85 p. [NN]

In connection with the eight-hundredth anniversary of the founding of Moscow. Songs by Boris A. Aleksandrov, Matvei I. Blanter, Nikolai K. Chembordzhi, Isaak O. Dunayevski, Sigizmund A. Kats, Tikhon N. Khrennikov, Lev K. Knipper, Zinovi L. Kompaneyets, V. Kruchinin, A. Lepin, F. Maslov, Yuri S. Milyutin, Boris A. Mokrousov,

Anatoli G. Novikov, D. Pokrass, Sergei S. Prokof'yev, Dmitri D. Shostakovich, V. Yurovski.

Romansy i pesni sovetskikh kompozitorov [Ballads and Songs by Soviet Composers], M., 1952, 40 p. [DLC]

Rubin, Vl., comp., *Pesni bor'by i gneva: stikhi i pesni o zarubezhnoi molodyozhi* [Songs of Struggle and Wrath: Verse and Songs of Foreign Youth], M., 1936, 61 p. [NN]

Shafir, A., comp., *Pesni: sbornik* [A Collection of Songs], ed. by Nikolai N. Aseyev and Yuri M. Sokolov, M., 1935, 222 p. [NN]

Shiroka strana moya rodnaya: sbornik pesen [Broad Is My Native Land: Collection of Songs], M., 1947, 78 p.; 1952, 95 p. [DLC]

Sokolov, Yuri M., comp., *Russkaya narodnaya pesnya: sbornik dlya uchashchikhsya srednei shkoly* [The Russian Folk Song: A Collection for Pupils of the Secondary School], ed. by B.M. Volin, M., 1938, 150 p. [NNC]

Turganov, Boris Aleksandrovich, comp., *Pesni strany sovetov* [Songs of the Land of the Soviets], 3rd ed. rev. and enl., M., 1937, 198 p. [DLC; NNC]

Vinogradov, Vasili I., *et al.*, comps., *Tatarskiye narodnye pesni* [Tatar Folk Songs], ed. by A.S. Klyucharyov, Vol. I, n.p., 1941.

Yarustovski, B.M., *Pesni Velikoi Otechestvennoi Voiny* [Songs of the Great Patriotic War], M., 1945, 55 p. [DLC]; ed. by L.T. Atovm'yan and M.V. Iordanski, M., 1946, 214 p. [DLC]

Yerikeyev, Akhmed, comp., *Tatarskiye narodnye pesni* [Tatar Folk Songs], M., 1936, 173 p. [NNC]

Zatayevich, Aleksandr Viktorovich (1869-1936), *250 kirgizskikh instrumental'nykh p'yes i napevov* [Two Hundred Fifty Kirzhiz Instrumental Songs and Airs], M., 1934.

____, *500 kazakhskikh pesen i kyui''yev* [Five Hundred Kazakh

Songs and Instrumental Pieces], Alma-Ata, 1931, xxxiv+312 p. [NN]
From Adayevsk, Bukeyevsk, Semipalatinsk, and Uralsk Regions.

——, *1000 pesen kirgizskovo naroda: napevy i melodii* [One Thousand Songs of the Kirghiz People: Airs and Melodies], introduction by Aleksandr D. Kastal'ski, foreword and notes by the author, Orenberg, 1925, lvii+402 p. [DLC; NN]

End of section on SONGS

Souvtchinsky, Pierre, ed., *Musique russe: études réunies*, 2 vols., Paris, Presses universitaires de France, 1953. [DLC]
In Vol. I articles by Léon Algazi, Constantin Brailoiu, Vladimir Fédorov, Antoine Goléa, Charles Koechlin, and Boris de Schloezer; in Vol. II, by Henry Barraud, Yves Baudrier, Pierre Boulez, Gisele Brelet, Vladimir Fédorov, André Schaeffner, and Pierre Souvtchinsky.

[*Soyuz Sovetskikh Kompozitorov* (Union of Soviet Composers)], "Pervyi vsesoyuznyi s"yezd sovetskikh kompozitorov: sodoklady predstavitelei soyuznikh respublik" [First All-Union Congress of Soviet Composers: Reports by Representatives of the Union Republics], *SI*, No. 17(1105), April 24, 1948.
Short title: *Sodoklady*.

——, *Pervyi vsesoyuznyi s"yezd sovetskikh kompozitorov: stenograficheskii otchot* [First All-Union Congress of Soviet Composers: Verbatim Report], M., 1948, 454 p. [DLC]

——, "Vsesoyuznyi s"yezd sovetskikh kompozitorov" [All-Union Congress of Soviet Composers], *Pravda*, April 22, 1948.

Spendiarov, Aleksandr Afanas'yevich (1871-1928). *See* Shaverdyan.

Sposobin, I.V., *Elementarnaya teoriya muzyki* [Elementary Theory of Music], M., 1951, 222 p. [DLC; NN]

___, *Muzykal'naya forma: uchebnik obshchevo kursa analiza* [Musical Form: A Textbook for a General Course of Analysis], M., 1947, 375 p. [DLC]

Staehlin (Shtelin) von Storcksburg, Jacob (1710-1785), *Muzyka i balet v Rossii XVIII veka* [Music and the Ballet in Russia of the Eighteenth Century], tr. from German and introduction by Boris I. Zagurski, ed. and foreword by Boris V. Asaf'yev, L., 1935, 189 p. [NN]

Stalin, Joseph V. (1879-1953), "Doklad po natsional'nomu voprosu" [Report on the National Question], delivered at the Third All-Russian Congress of Soviets, March 1918, reprinted in *Sochineniya* [Works], Moscow, 1947, Vol. IV, pp. 30-32.

___, "Otnositel'no marksizma v yazykoznanii" [On Marxism in Linguistics], *Pravda*, June 20, 1950.

Stal'ski, Suleiman (1869-1937), *Stikhi i pesni* [Poems and Songs], ed. and introduction by effendi Kapiyev, M., 1936, 153 p. [NNC]; M.–L., 1938, 63 p. [NNC]

___, *Suleiman Stal'ski, 1869-1937*, M., 1937, 78 p. [NN]

___. *See* Sidel'nikov; Vishnevskaya.

Stasov, Vladimir Vasil'yevich (1824-1906), *Izbrannye sochineniya* [Selected Works], introduction and notes by S.N. Gol'dshtein, 2 vols., M., 1937. [DLC]

___, *Izbrannye sochineniya: zhivopis', skul'ptura, muzyka* [Selected Works: Painting, Sculpture, Music], joint eds., Yelena D. Stasova, *et al.*, 3 vols., M., 1952. [DLC]

___, *Izbrannye stat'i o M.P. Musorgskom* [Selected Articles on M.P. Musorgsky], ed. with introduction and notes by Aleksei S. Ogolevets, M., 1952, 234 p. [DLC; NNC]

___, *Izbrannye stat'i o muzyke* [Selected Articles on Music], L., 1949, 325 p. [DLC; NNC]

___, *Mikhail Ivanovich Glinka*, ed., and introduction by Vl.

Protopopov, notes by V.A. Kiselyov, M., 1953, 331 p. [CU; NN]

——, *Nasha muzyka* [Our Music], ed., introduction and notes by Aleksei S. Ogolevets, M., 1953, 111 p. [DLC]

——, *Perov i Musorgski* [Perov and Musorgsky], M., 1952, 42 p. [DLC]

——, *Russkaya opera za rubezhom* [Russian Opera Abroad], ed., introduction and notes by Aleksei S. Ogolevets, M., 1953, 42 p. [DLC]

——, *Sobraniye statei V. Stasova o M. Musorgskom i yevo proizvedeniyakh* [Collected Articles by V. Stasov Concerning M. Musorgsky and His Works], M.–P., 1922, 121 p. [DLC]

——. *See* Balakirev; Komarova-Stasova; Musorgsky; Stasova.

Stasov, V.V., *25-letiye besplatnoi muzykal'noi shkoly* [The Twenty-fifth Anniversary of Free Music Schools], M., 1953, 56 p.

Stasova, Yelena Dmitriyevna (1873-), *Vladimir Vasil'yevich Stasov, 1824-1906: k 125-letiyu so dnya rozhdeniya* [Vladimir Vasil'yevich Stasov, 1824-1906: For the One-hundredth Anniversary of His Birth], M., 1949, 94 p. [DLC]

Steshenko-Kuftina, Valentina K., *Drevneishiye instrumental'nye osnovy gruzinskoi narodnoi muzyki* [Ancient Instrumental Bases of Georgian Folk Music], Vol. I, *Fleita Pana* [Pan's Flute], Tbilisi, 1936, 256 p. [DLC]

"Sto dvadtsat' kontsertov v chest' I.V. Stalina" [One Hundred and Twenty Concerts in Honor of J.V. Stalin], *SM*, March 1950, No. 3, p. 100.

Stolpyanski, Pyotr Nikolayevich (1872-), *Staryi Peterburg: muzyka i muzitsirovaniye v starom Peterburge: istoricheskii ocherk* [Old Petersburg: Music and the Playing of Music in Old Petersburg: A Historical Essay], L., 1925, 187 p. [NN]

Stravinsky, Igor Fyodorovich (1882-), *Chronicle of My Life,* tr. from French, London, Gollancz, 1936, 286 p. [NN]; American title, *Stravinsky: An Autobiography,* New York, Simon and Schuster, 1936, 288 p. [DLC; NNC]

___, *Chroniques de ma vie,* 2 vols., Paris, Denoël et Steele, 1935. [DLC]

___, *Poetics of Music: In the Form of Six Lessons,* tr. by Arthur Knodel and Ingolf Dahl, Cambridge, Mass., Harvard University Press, 1947, 142 p. [DLC; MH; NNC]

___, *Poétique musicale sous forme de six leçons,* Cambridge, Mass., Harvard University Press, 1942, 95 p. [DLC]; 4th ed., Dijon, J.B. Janin, 1945, 166 p. [NNC]; 5th ed. [DLC]; new ed., Paris, Plon, 1952, 97 p. [NN]

___. *See* Asaf'yev; Belyayev, V.M.; *Gosudarstvennyi akademicheskii teatr...;* Slonimski, Yu.O.; Vainkop.

Strel'nikov, Nikolai Mikhailovich (1888-), *A.N. Serov: opyt kharakteristiki* [A.N. Serov: An Attempt at a Characterization], M., 1922, 86 p. [DLC]

___, *Glinka: opyt kharakteristiki* [M.I. Glinka: An Attempt at a Characterization] M., 1923, 43 p. [DLC; NN]

___. *See* [*Leningradskaya filarmoniya*].

"Sumbur vmesto muzyki: ob opere 'Ledi Makbet Mtsenskovo uyezda'" [Confusion Instead of Music: On the Opera *Lady Macbeth of Mtsensk District*], *Pravda,* No. 27(6633), January 28, 1936.

†Sviridov, Yuri (Georgi) Vasil'yevich (1915-). *See* [*Leningradskaya filarmoniya*].

†Taktakishvili, Otar Vasil'yevich (1924-), "O narodnosti v muzyke" [Concerning Nationality in Music], *SM,* December 1952, No. 12, pp. 51-53.

Taneyev, Sergei Ivanovich (1856-1915), *Perepiska i vospominaniya* [Correspondence and Recollections], prepared for publication by Boris V. Asaf'yev, ed. by V.A. Kiselyov, *et al.*, M., 1952, 353 p. (*Materialy i dokumenty* [Materials and Documents], Vol. I.) [MH; NN]

——, *Sergei Ivanovich Taneyev: lichnost', tvorchestvo i dokumenty yevo zhizni: k 10-ti letiyu so dnya yevo smerti 1915-1925* [Sergei Ivanovich Taneyev: Personality, Work and Documents of His Life: For the Tenth Anniversary of His Death, 1915-1925], M., 1925, 205 p. [NN]

——, *Ucheniye o kanone* [Study of the Canon], prepared for publication by Viktor M. Belyayev, M., 1929, 195 p. [NN]

——. *See* Belza; Bernandt; Lunacharski; Sabaneyev; Polyak; Protopopov; Tchaikovsky; Yakovlev.

Taranov, Gleb, *Kurs chteniya partitur* [A Course in Score-reading], ed. by Dmitri R. Rogal'-Levitski, M., 1939, 358 p. French summary. [DLC; NN]

Tchaikovsky, Peter Ilyich (1840-1893), *Chaikovski ob opere: izbrannye otryvki iz pisem i statei* [Tchaikovsky on Opera: Selected Fragments from Letters and Articles], ed. and commentary by I.F. Kunin, M., 1952, 192 p. [MH]

——, *Dnevniki P.I. Chaikovskovo* [The Diaries of P.I. Tchaikovsky], prepared for publication by Ip.I. Tchaikovsky, foreword by Sergei M. Chemodanov, notes by Nikolai T. Zhegin, M., 1923, xii+294 p. [DLC; NN]; Eng. tr. with notes by Wladimir W. Lakond, New York, Norton, 1945, 365 p. [DLC; NN; NNC]

——, *Muzykal'no-kriticheskiye stat'i* [Articles of Musical Criticism], introduction and comments by Vasili V. Yakovlev, M., 1953, 436 p. [DLC]

——, *Perepiska s N.F. fon-Mekk* [Correspondence with N.F. von Meck], ed. and notes by Vladimir A. Zhdanov and Nikolai T. Zhegin, introduction by B.S. Pshibyshevski, 3 vols., M., 1934-1936. [NN; DLC: Vols. I-II; NNC: I, III]

——, *Perepiska s P.I. Yurgensonom* [Correspondence with P.I. Yurgenson], introduction by Boris V. Asaf'yev, ed. and notes by Vladimir A. Zhdanov and Nikolai T. Zhegin, M. *1877-1883,* Vol. I, 1938; *1884-1893,* Vol. II, 1952. [NN; NNC; DLC: Vol. I]

___, *P.I. Chaikovski o kompozitorskom masterstve: izbrannye otryvki iz pisem i statei* [P.I. Tchaikovsky on the Art of the Composer: Selected Excerpts from Letters and Articles], M., 1952, 153 p. [DLC; NN]

___, *P.I. Chaikovski o narodnom i natsional'nom elemente v muzyke: izbrannye otryvki iz pisem i statei* [P.I. Tchaikovsky on the Folk and National Element in Music: Selected Excerpts from Letters and Articles], comp., ed. and commentary by I.F. Kunin, M., 1952, 105 p. [DLC]

___, *Vospominaniya i pis'ma* [Recollections and Letters], ed. by Boris V. Asaf'yev, P., 1924.

___. *See* Al'shvang; Asaf'yev; Berlyand-Chernaya; Bogdanov-Berezovski; Danilevich; Findeizen; Khinchyn; Kiselyov, V.A.; Laroche; Nikolayev; Nikolayeva, Nina; Ogolevets; Orlova, Ye.; Pavlov; *Russian Symphony...; Tsentral'nyi muzei imeni Alekseya Bakhrushina;* Vanslov; Vladykina; *Vserossiiskoye teatral'noye obshchestvo;* Yakovlev; Yamshchikova; Yarustovski; Zhitomirski.

___, and Sergei Ivanovich Taneyev (1856-1915), *P.I. Chaikovski - S.I. Taneyev: pis'ma* [P.I. Tchaikovsky and S.I. Taneyev: Letters], M., 1951, 555 p. [DLC; MH; NN; NNC]

Thompson, Virgil, "Composers in Trouble," *New York Herald Tribune,* February 22, 1948.

Tigranov, Nikolai Faddeyevich (1856-). *See* Gumretsi.

Toch, Ernst (1887-), *Melodielehre: Ein Beitrag zur Musiktheorie,* Berlin, M. Hesse, 1923, 182 p. [DLC]

___, *The Shaping Forces in Music: An Inquiry into Harmony, Melody, Counterpoint, Form,* New York, Criterion Music Corp., 1948, 245 p. [DLC; NNC]

Tolstoi, Sergei L'vovich (1863-1947), and Pyotr Nikolayevich

Zimin (1890-), *Sputnik muzykanta-etnografa: sbornik programm i nastavlenii dlya sobiraniya i zapisi produktov narodnoi muzykal'noi kul'tury* [A Guide for the Musician-Ethnographer: A Collection of Programs and Manuals for Collecting and Recording the Products of Folk Music Culture], M., 1929, 86 p. [NN]

Tomilin, Viktor Konstantinovich (1908-). *See* [*Leningradskaya filarmoniya*].

Tsentral'nyi muzei imeni Alekseya Bakhrushina [The Aleksei Bakhrushin Central Museum], Moscow, *Chaikovski na moskovskoi stsene: pervye postanovki v gody yevo zhizni* [Tchaikovsky on the Moscow Stage: First Performances During His Life], M., 1940, 501 p. [NNC]

†Tulebayev, Mukan Tulebayevich (1913-). *See* "Neobkhodim...."

Tumanina, N., *M.P. Musorgski: zhizn' i tvorchestvo: k stoletiyu so dnya rozhdeniya, 1839-1939* [M.P. Musorgsky: Life and Work: For the One-hundredth Anniversary of His Birth, 1839-1939], M., 1939, 237 p. [DLC; NN]

Tyulin, Yuri Nikolayevich (1893-), *Uchenii o garmonii* [Study of Harmony], Vol. I, 2nd ed., L.–M., 1939.

———. *See* [*Leningradskaya filarmoniya*].

Ukraïns'ka narodna pisnya [The Ukrainian Folk Song], 2nd ed., Kiev, 1936, 605 p. [NNC]

Unger, Heinz (1895-), *Hammer, Sickle and Baton: The Soviet Memoirs of a Musician*, in collaboration with Naomi Walford, London, Cresset, 1939, 275 p. [DLC; NN]
Covers the years 1924-1937.

U.S.S.R. *Komitet po delam iskusstv, Glavnoye upravleniye uchebnykh zavedenii* [Committee for Art Affairs, Main Administration of Education Institutions], *Uchebnye programmy dlya detskikh muzykal'nykh shkol* [Syllabi for Children's Music Schools], M., 1945, 221 p. [DLC]

Uspenskaya, S.L., "Bibliografiya muzykal'noi literatury"

[Bibliography of Musical Literature], *Sovetskaya bibliografiya* [Soviet Bibliography], M., 1950, No. 1(30), pp. 71-85.

Uspenski, Viktor Aleksandrovich, *Turkmenskaya muzyka: stat'i i 115 p'yes turkmenskoi muzyki* [Turkmen Music: Articles and One Hundred Fifteen Songs of Turkmen Music], ed. by Viktor M. Belyayev, M., 1928, xv+377 p. [NN]

____. *See* Pekker.

Uspenski, Vsevolod, *Mikhail Ivanovich Glinka, 1804-1857*, notes by A.A. Orlova, L., 1950, 263 p. [DLC]

"V komitete po Stalinskim Premiyam v oblasti literatury i iskusstva" [In the Committee on Stalin Prizes in Literature and the Arts], *Pravda* and *Izvestiya*, May 11, 1951.

"V Sovete Ministrov Soyuza SSSR: O prisuzhdenii Stalinskikh Premii za vydayushchiyesya raboty v oblasti nauki, izobretatel'stva, literatury i iskusstva za 1950 god" [In the U.S.S.R. Council of Ministers: The Awarding of Stalin Prizes for Outstanding Work in the Fields of Science, Invention, Literature, and the Arts for 1950], *Pravda* and *Izvestiya*, March 17, 1951.

"V Sovete Ministrov SSSR" [In the Council of Ministers of the U.S.S.R.], *Pravda* and *Izvestiya*, May 13, 1951.

Vainkop, Yu., *Igor' Stravinski*, L., 1927, 19 p. [NN]

*Valeyev, Masalim Musharapovich (1888-).

Vanslov, V., *"Cherevichki" P. Chaikovskovo* [*Oxana's Caprices* by Tchaikovsky], M., 1949, 40 p. [DLC]

____, *Simfonicheskoye tvorchestvo A.K. Glazunova* [The Symphonic Work of A.K. Glazunov], M., 1950, 85 p. [DLC; NN]

Vartanyan, Z., "Navesti poryadok v rabote Moskovskoi filarmonii" [Introduce Order into the Work of the Moscow

Philharmonic Organization], *Kul'tura i zhizn'* [Culture and Life], M., No. 6(170), February 28, 1951.

* †Vasilenko, Sergei Nikiforovich (1872-), *Stranitsy vospominanii* [Pages of Recollections], M.–L., 1948, 187 p. [DLC]

——. *See* Belyayev, V.M.; [*Leningradskaya filarmoniya*]; Polyanovski; "Protiv formalizma...."

* †Vasil'yev-Buglai, Dmitri Stepanovich (1888-).

"Velikaya sila sovetskovo iskusstva" [The Great Power of Soviet Art], *SI*, No. 17(1105), April 24, 1948. (editorial)

Veprik, Aleksandr Moiseyevich (1899-), *Traktovka instrumentov orkestra* [A Discussion of the Instruments of the Orchestra], M., 1948, 308 p. [DLC]

——. *See* "Protiv formalizma...."

Verikovski, *see* Verykivs'kyi.

* Verstovski, Aleksei Nikolayevich (1799-1862). *See* Dobrokhotov.

Vertkov, K.A., *Russkaya rogovaya muzyka* [Russian Horn Music], ed. by Semyon L. Ginzburg, L., 1948, 115 p. [DLC; NN; NNC]

* Verykivs'kyi, Mykhaylo Ivanovych (1896-).

* †Veryovka, Hryhoriy Hur'ovych (1895-).

Vetlugina, N.A., ed., *Metodika muzykal'novo vospitaniya v detskom sadu* [Methodology of Musical Education in the Kindergarten], M., 1953, 213 p. [DLC]

* Vinogradov, Vasili Ivanovich (1874-1948), *Muzyka Sovetskoi Kirgizii* [Music of Soviet Kirghizia], M., 1939, 136 p. [DLC; NN; NNC]

——, *Toktogul Satylganov i kirgizskiye akyny* [Toktogul Satylganov and Kirghiz Bards], M.–L., 1952, 213 p. [NN]

——, *Uzeir Gadzhibekov i azerbaidzhanskaya muzyka* [Uzeir

Gadzhibekov and Azerbaidzhan Music], M., 1936, 76 p. [NN]; M.–L., 1947.

——. *See* "Protiv formalizma...."

Vishnevskaya, Yelizaveta Davydovna, comp., *Dzhambul: Stal'ski: Lakhuti*, M., 1938, 68 p. [NN]

• Vitachek, Yevgeni Frantsevich (1880-1946), *Ocherki po istorii izgotovleniya smychkovykh instrumentov* [Essays on the History of the Making of Bowed Instruments], ed. by B. Dobrokhotov, M., 1952, 241 p. [DLC; NN]

•Vitol (Wihtol), Yazep Yanovich (Iosif Ivanovich Vitol') (1863-1948).

•Vladimirov, Mikhail Vladimirovich (1870-1932).

Vladykina, Nina, *P.I. Chaikovski (dlya shkol'nikov starshevo vozrasta* [P.I. Tchaikovsky (For Older School Children)], M., 1940, 213 p. [NN]

•Vlasov, Vladimir Aleksandrovich (1902-).

Vodarsky-Shiraeff, Alexandria, *Bibliography of Skryabin*, New York, School of Library Service, Columbia University, 1934, 23 p. [NN]

——, comp., *Russian Composers and Musicians: A Bibliographical Dictionary*, New York, H.W. Wilson, 1940, 158 p. [DLC; NN; NNC]

•Voloshinov, Viktor Vladimirovich (1905-). *See* [*Leningradskaya filarmoniya*].

•Vorob'yov, Gennadi Vasil'yevich (1918-1939).

•Vorob'yov, Vasili Petrovich (1887-).

Vserossiiskoye teatral'noye obshchestvo [All-Russian Theater Society], *Chaikovski i teatr: stat'i i materialy* [Tchaikovsky and the Theater: Articles and Materials], ed. by Aleksandr I. Shaverdyan, M., 1940, lxxi+354 p. [DLC; NN; NNC]

Articles by Yu. Bakhrushin, Izrail' V. Nest'yev, Shaverdyan, Vasili V. Yakovlev, and B.M. Yarustovski.

"Vystupleniya na otkrytom partiinom sobranii v soyuze sovetskikh kompozitorov SSSR, posvyashchonnom obsuzhdeniyu zadach muzykal'noi kritiki i nauki (18, 21 i 22 fevralya 1949 g.)" [Addresses at the Open Party Meeting in the Union of Soviet Composers of the U.S.S.R. Devoted to a Discussion of the Problems of Music Criticism and Science (February 18, 21 and 22, 1949)], *SM*, February 1949, No. 2, pp. 16-36.

Werth, Alexander (1901-), "Is the Soviet Attitude to Music Changing?," *The Listener*, London, Vol. L, No. 1295, December 24, 1953, pp. 1089-1090. [DLC; NN; NNC]

——, *Musical Uproar in Moscow*, London, Turnstile, 1949, 103 p. [DLC; NN; NNC]

——, "The 'Reform' of Soviet Music," *The Nation*, New York, April 10, 1948, p. 393.

Wihtol, *see* Vitol.

Yagolin, Boris Savel'yevich (1888-), *Die Musik in der Sowjetunion*, Berlin, Verlag der Sowjetischen Militärverwaltung in Deutschland, 1946, 51 p. [DLC; NN]

——, *Soviet Music: Musical Education and Music Making*, London, Soviet News, 1946, 71 p. [DLC]

Yakovlev, Vasili Vasil'yevich (1880-), *Aleksandr Fyodorovich Gedike: Alexander Goedicke*, M., 1927, 35 p. Text in Russian and German. [NN]

——, *A.N. Skryabin*, foreword by Aleksandr B. Gol'denveizer, M.–L., 1925, 99 p. [NN]

——, ed., *Dni i gody P.I. Chaikovskovo: letopis' zhizni i tvorchestva* [Days and Years of P.I. Tchaikovsky: Chronicle of His Life and Work], comp. by E. Zaidenshnur, V. Iselyov, A. Orlova, and N. Shemanin, M., 1940, 740 p. [NN; NNC]

——, *N.D. Kashkin*, M.–L., 1950, 59 p. [DLC; NN]

——, *Nikolai Karlovich Metner: Nikolaus Medtner*, M., 1927, 41 p. Text in Russian and German. [NN]

___, *P.A. Khokhlov*, M., 1950, 47 p. [DLC; NN]

___, *Pushkin i muzyka* [Pushkin and Music], M., 1949, 179 p. [DLC; NN; NNC]

___, *Sergei Ivanovich Taneyev: yevo muzykal'naya zhizn'* [Sergei Ivanovich Taneyev: His Musical Life], Tver', 1927, 104 p. [NN]

___. *See* Asaf'yev.

Yakymenko, Fedir Stepanovych (Akymenko, *pseud.*) (1876-1945), *Praktichnyi kurs nauki garmonii* [Practical Course in the Science of Harmony], Prague, 1925, 128 p. [NNC]

Yampol'ski, I.M., *Russkoye skripichnoye iskusstvo: ocherki i materialy* [The Art of the Violin in Russia: Essays and Materials], Vol. I, M., 1951, 515 p. [DLC; NN]

Yamshchikova, Margarita Vladimirovna (Al. Altayev, *pseud.*) (1872-), *Chaikovski v Moskve* [Tchaikovsky in Moscow], M., 1951, 305 p. [DLC; NN; NNC]

___, *M.I. Glinka*, M., 1947, 263 p. [DLC]

Yankovski, Moisei Osipovich (1898-), *Isaak Osipovich Dunayevski*, L., 1940, 47 p. [NN]

___, *Operetta: vozniknoveniye i razvitiye zhanra na Zapade i v SSSR* [Operetta: The Origin and Development of the Genre in the West and in the U.S.S.R.], L., 1937, 456 p. [DLC; NN; NNC]

___, *Rimski-Korsakov i revolyutsiya 1905 goda* [Rimsky-Korsakov and the Revolution of 1905], M., 1950, 130 p. [DLC; NN]

Yarustovski, B.M., *Dramaturgiya russkoi opernoi klassiki: rabota russkikh kompozitorov-klassikov nad operoi* [Dramaturgy of Classical Russian Operas: Works of Russian Classical Composers on Opera], M., 1952, 373 p. [DLC]

___, *Opernaya dramaturgiya Chaikovskovo* [The Operatic Dramaturgy of Tchaikovsky], M., 1947, 240 p. [NN; NNC]

———, *P.I. Chaikovski: lektsiya* [P.I. Tchaikovsky: A Lecture], M., 1951, 34 p. [DLC]

Yegorov, A., *Teoriya i praktika raboty s khorom* [The Theory and Practice of Choral Work], M., 1951, 235 p. [DLC; NN]

Yelagin, Yuri Borisovich, *see* Jelagin.

*Yesipova, Anna Nikolayevna (1851-1914). *See* Berkman.

Yezhegodnik instituta istorii iskusstv Akademii nauk SSSR [Yearbook of the Institute of the History of the Arts of the Academy of Sciences of the U.S.S.R], Vol. II, *Teatr i muzyka* [The Theater and Music], M., 1948, 356 p. [NN]

Yudin, Mikhail Alekseyevich (1893-). *See* [*Leningradskaya filarmoniya*].

Zagurski, Boris Ivanovich, *M.I. Glinka,* 2nd ed. corrected and supplemented, L., 1948, 172 p. [DLC; NN; NNC]

———, *M.I. Glinka: ocherk* [M.I. Glinka: An Essay], L., 1940, 139 p. [DLC]

* †Zakharov, Vladimir Grigor'yevich (1901-). *See* Bryusova.

Zarubezhom: sbornik statei sovetskikh kompozitorov i muzykovedov [Abroad: A Collection of Articles of Soviet Composers and Musicologists], M., 1953, 194 p. [DLC]

*Zhdanov, Andrei Aleksandrovich (1896-1948), *Essays on Literature, Philosophy and Music,* New York, International Publishers, 1950, 96 p. [DLC]

———, *Vstupitel'naya rech' i vystupleniye na soveshchanii deyatelei sovetskoi muzyki v TsK VKP(b) v yanvare 1948 g.* [Introductory Speech and Appearance at the Conference of Persons Active in Soviet Music in the Central Committee of the All-Union Communist Party (Bolsheviks) in January 1948], M., 1952, 29 p. [DLC]

———, *Vystupleniye na diskussii po knige G.F. Aleksandrova "Istoriya zapadnoyevropeiskoi filosofii" 24 iyunya 1947 g.*

[Address in the Discussion on G.F. Aleksandrov's Book *History of West European Philosophy*, June 24, 1947], M., 1947, 44 p. [DLC; NN; NNC]

___, "Vystupleniye tov. A.A. Zhdanova na soveshchanii deyatelei sovetskoi muzyki v TsK VKP(b)" [Speech by Comrade A.A. Zhdanov at the Meeting of Soviet Musicians in the Central Committee of the All-Union Communist Party (Bolsheviks)], *SM*, January-February 1948, No. 1, pp. 14-26.

Zhelobinski, Valeri Viktorovich (1911-). *See Gosudarstvennyi akademicheskii malyi opernyi teatr; [Leningradskaya filarmoniya]*.

*†Zhiganov, Nazib Gayazovich (1911-).

Zhitomirski, Daniil V., *Balety P. Chaikovskovo: Lebedinnoye ozero, Spyashchya krasavitsa, Shchelkunchik* [Ballets of P. Tchaikovsky: *Swan Lake, Sleeping Beauty,* and *Nutcracker Suite*], M., 1950, 152 p. [DLC; NN]

___, "Igor' Glebov kak publitsist" [Igor' Glebov (Boris V. Asaf'yev) As a Publicist], *SM*, December 1940, No. 12, pp. 5-14. [NN]

___. *See* "Protiv formalizma...."

†Zhukovs'kyi, Herman Leontovych (1913-). *See* "Beseda tov. Stalina..."; Kukharski; "Neudachnaya opera..."; "Novaya sovetskaya opera..."; Protopopov.

Zimin, Pyotr Nikolayevich (1890-), "O muzykal'noi promyshlennosti RSFSR" [About the Musical Industry of the R.S.F.S.R.], *SM*, July 1949, No. 7, pp. 86-87.

___. *See* Tolstoi.

Zivel'chinskaya, Liya Yakovlevna (1894-), *Ekspressionizm* [Expressionism], M., 1931, 139 p. [NN]

___, *Opyt marksistskoi kritiki estetiki Kanta* [An Attempt at a Marxist Critique of Kant's Aesthetics], M., 1927, 209 p. [NN]

——, *Opyt marksistskovo analiza istorii estetiki* [An Attempt at a Marxist Analysis of the History of Aesthetics], M., 1928, 362 p. [NN]

Znosko-Borovs'kyi, O., *Andriy Shtoharenko*, Kiev, 1947.

* †Zolotar'ov, Vasyl' Andriyovych (1873-).

II. PERIODICALS

Abbreviations used in this section:

bimo.	bimonthly	mo.	monthly
biwk.	biweekly	qu.	quarterly
exc.	except	w.	weekly
inc.	incomplete	x/yr.	times per year
irr.	irregular		

Bibliografiya muzykal'noi literatury, see Letopis' muzykal'noi literatury.

De musica, L., Vols. I-III, 1925-1927, *Muzykoznaniye* [Musicology], Vol. IV, 1928. [NN]

Publication of the Section on the History and Theory of Music of the State Institute for the History of the Arts. Articles in Vol. I by Boris V. Asaf'yev; Aleksei V. Finagin; Roman I. Gruber; Vyacheslav G. Karatygin; Sergei S. Prokof'yev; Georgi M. Rimsky-Korsakov; in Vol. II by Boris V. Asaf'yev; Sergei A. Dianin; Aleksei V. Finagin; Roman I. Gruber; Antonin V. Preobrazhenski; G.M. Rimsky-Korsakov; in Vol. III by Sergei A. Dianin; Aleksei V. Finagin; Panteleimon V. Grachov; Roman I. Gruber; Yu. Kaufman; S. Kleshchov; V. Kovalenkov; M. Machinski; D. Maggid; L.G. Nemirovski; Yu. Otto; Antonin V. Preobrazhenski; Vs. Prokof'yev; Andrei N. Rimsky-Korsakov; G.M. Rimsky-Korsakov; Vladimir F. Shishmaryov; Yevgeni Sholpo; in Vol. IV by Boris V. Asaf'yev; Yu.K. Belyi; I.A. Braudo; V.E. Fekhner; Semyon L. Ginzburg; Roman I. Gruber; L.G. Nemirovski; G.M. Rimsky-Korsakov. Vols. I and II include Russian music bibliographies for 1925.

Informatsionnyi sbornik [Information Compendium], M., 1945-?. [DLC: 1945: No. 9-10]
Organ of *Soyuz sovetskikh kompozitorov SSSR* [Union of Soviet Composers of the U.S.S.R.].

Izvestiya sovetov deputatov trudyashchikhsya SSSR [News of the Soviets of Workers' Deputies of the U.S.S.R.], M., daily, 1917- .
Official organ of the government of the U.S.S.R. Title varies.

____. *See* "Neudachnaya opera..."; "Novaya sovetskaya opera..."; "V komitete po Stalinskim Premiyam..."; "V Sovete Ministrov Soyuza SSR..."; "V Sovete Ministrov SSSR" in Section I.

K novym beregam [Towards New Shores], M., mo., Nos. 1-3, March-May 1923. [NN]
Edited by Viktor M. Belyayev and Vladimir V. Derzhanovski.

Katalog sovetskoi muzykal'noi literatury [Catalogue of Soviet Musical Literature], February 1952, No. 1, 10 p. [DLC]
Organ of *Internatsional'naya kniga* [International Book].

Khronika sovetskoi muzyki [Chronicle of Soviet Music], M., mo., (no other information).
Publication of VOKS.

Khudozhestvennoye obrazovaniye, see Muzykal'noye obrazovaniye.

Letopis' muzykal'noi literatury [Chronicle of Musical Literature], M., qu., 1931 - June 1941, 1945-. [DLC: 1945- exc. 1945, No. 1, 1947, No. 3; NN: 1931-1939, No. 3, 1940, No. 1]
Title varies: *Notnaya letopis'* [Sheet Music Chronicle], 1931-1938; *Bibliografiya muzykal'noi literatury* [Bibliography of Musical Literature], 1938 - June 1941. Publication of *Vsesoyuznaya knizhnaya palata* [All-Union Book Chamber].

Literatura i iskusstvo [Literature and Art], M., w., Vols. I-III, January 6, 1942 - November 1944. [CSt-H(inc.): 1942, 1944;

CU(inc.): 1942-1944; DLC: 1942(inc.), 1943, 1944(inc.); MH(inc.): 1942; NN: 1942(inc.), 1943-1944]

Published instead of the newspaper *Sovetskoye iskusstvo* (*q.v.*) jointly with *Literaturnaya gazeta* [Literary Gazette]. Organ of *Upravleniye Soyuza sovetskikh pisatelei SSSR* [Board of the Union of Soviet Writers], of *Komitet po delam iskusstv pri Sovnarkome SSSR* [Committee for Art Affairs of the Council of People's Commissars of the U.S.S.R.], and of *Komitet po delam kinematografii pri Sovnarkome SSSR* [Committee for Cinematography of the Council of People's Commissars of the U.S.S.R.].

Music, see Soviet Music Chronicle.

Musical Chronicle, see Soviet Music Chronicle.

Muzyka [Music], Kiev, mo. (in Ukrainian), Nos. 1-5, April-August 1923. [NN]

Muzyka i revolyutsiya [Music and Revolution], M., mo. January 1926-1929, No. 8. [DLC; NN]

Edited by Lev V. Shul'gin.

Muzykal'naya kul'tura [Musical Culture], M., Vol. I, Nos. 1-3, 1924. [DLC; NN]

Muzykal'naya letopis': statei i materialy [Musical Chronicle: Articles and Materials], L., Vols. I-III, 1922-1926. [NN; DLC: Vols. I-II; MH: Vol. I]

Edited by Andrei N. Rimsky-Korsakov.

Muzykal'naya nov' [Musical Virgin Soil], M., Vols. I-II, Nos. 1-2, October 20, 1923-1924. [DLC; NN]

Through Vol. II, No. 5, edited by A.A. Sergeyev, *et al.;* with No. 6-7, 1924 became the official organ of *Vserossiiskaya assotsiatsiya proletarskikh muzykantov* [All-Russian Association of Proletarian Musicians].

Muzykal'naya samodeyatel'nost' [Musical Amateur Activity], M., Vols. I-II, January 1933 - July 1934, No. 7. [NN]

Muzykal'noye obrazovaniye [Music Education], later *Khudozhestvennoye obrazovaniye* [Art Education], M., Vols.

I-V, bimo., 1926-1928, 8x/yr., 1929-1930. Summaries in German. [NN; DLC: Vols. II(inc.)-V]

Muzykoznaniye, see *De musica.*

Notnaya letopis', see *Letopis' muzykal'noi literatury.*

Novaya muzyka [New Music], L., Vol. I, Nos. 1-4 - Vol. II, Nos. 1-2, January 1927-1928. [NN]
German title: *Neue musik.* Publication of *Leningradskaya assotsiatsiya sovremennoi muzyki* [Leningrad Association of Contemporary Music].

Orfei: knigi o muzyke [Orpheus: Books on Music], P., Book I, 1922. [DLC; NN; NNC]
Edited by Aleksandr V. Ossovski.

Pravda [Truth], M., daily, 1917-.
Organ of the Central Committee of the Communist Party of the Soviet Union.

___. *See* "Baletnaya fal'sh'..."; "Beseda tov. Stalina..."; "Neudachnaya opera..."; "Ob opere 'Bogdan..."; [*Soyuz Sovetskikh Kompozitorov*]; "Sumbur vmesto muzyki..."; "V komitete po Stalinskim Premiyam..."; "V Sovete Ministrov Soyuza SSR..."; "V Sovete Ministrov SSSR" in Section I.

Proletarskii muzykant [Proletarian Musician], M., Vols. I-IV, January 1929 - February 1932, No. 3. [DLC; NN: Vols. II, III-IV(inc.)]
Publication of *Vserossiiskaya assotsiatsiya proletarskikh muzykantov* [All-Russian Association of Proletarian Musicians].

Radyans'ka muzyka [Soviet Music], Kharkov, bimo., 1935 - March-April 1941, No. 2-?. [DLC and NN: 1941, No. 2]
Organ of *Soyuz sovetskikh kompozitorov Ukrainy* [Union of Soviet Composers of the Ukraine].

Sbornik trudov nauchno-issledovatel'skovo instituta muzykal'noi promyshlennosti [A Collection of Works of the Research Institute of the Music Industry], M., pre-1941.

Sovetskaya muzyka [Soviet Music], M., irr. mo., Vols. I-IX, 1933-1941, No. 5, Vol. X-, 1946-. [DLC: Vols. I-IX, No. 3, No. 5, Vol. X-; NN: almost complete; material at CLU, CSt-U, CU,

CtY, ICU, MH, NNC]

Organ of *Soyuz sovetskikh kompozitorov* [Union of Soviet Composers]. For the years 1942-1946 see *Sovetskaya muzyka: sbornik statei.*

——. *See* "K novomu pod''yomu..."; "Novye uspekhi sovetskoi muzyki"; "Sto dvadtsat' kontsertov v chest' I.V. Stalina"; "Vystupleniya na otkrytom partiinam sobranii..." in Section I.

Sovetskaya muzyka: notnoye prilozheniye [Soviet Music: Sheet Music Supplement], M., mo.?, 1950?-?. [DLC: 1950: Nos. 2-9, 11-12, 1951, Nos. 1-3-?].

Sovetskaya muzyka: sbornik statei [Soviet Music: A Collection of Articles], M., Vols. I-IV, 1942-1945. [DLC; NN: Vols. I, III-IV]

Issued instead of *Sovetskaya muzyka.*

Sovetskii fol'klor [Soviet Folklore], M.–L., Vols. I-VII, 1934-1941. [DLC; material at CU, CaTU, DSI-M, InU, MH, NIC, NN, NNM, OCI, WaU]

Organ of *Institut etnografii Akademicheskikh nauk SSSR* [Institute of Ethnography of the Academy of Sciences of the U.S.S.R.].

Sovetskoye iskusstvo, M., irr. newspaper, 1930(or 1931)-1941; 1944 - July 1953. [CLU: 1940 and 1947 (inc.), 1948-; CSt-H: 1945 (inc.); CU: 1933-1934, 1936-1941, 1945-1948 (all inc.), 1950-; DLC: 1934-1936, 1939-1941, 1944 (all inc.), 1945-; DS: 1949- (inc.); ICU: 1946-1949 (all inc.), 1950-; InU: 1945-; MH: 1946-1947 (all inc.), 1948-1950, 1951- (inc.); MiDW: 1948-1949, 1950-1951 (all inc.), 1952-; NIC: 1948 (inc.), 1949-; NN: February-December 1938, Nos. 15-173 (inc.), January-December 1939, Nos. 8-86 (inc.), March-July, November-December 1940, Nos. 19-65 (inc.), January-May 1941, Nos. 1-20 (inc.), November 4 - December 26, 1944, Nos. 2-8, January 9 - April 12, May 1, June 8 - September 14, December 28, 1945, Nos. 2-15, 18, 23-37, 39, 52, May 31 - June 21, October 25 - December 20, 1946, Nos. 23-26, 44-52, January-December 1949 (exc. No. 28); NhD: 1953-; PU: 1945-1949 (all inc.); WaU: 1949 (inc.), 1950-]

Organ of *Komitet po delam iskusstv pri Sovnarkome SSSR* [Committee for Art Affairs of the Council of People's Commissars of the U.S.S.R.], and from June 1938 of the Central Committee of *Profsoyuz rabotnikov iskusstva* [Trade Union of Persons Active in Art]; later of *Ministerstvo Kul'tury SSSR* [Ministry of Culture of the U.S.S.R.]; during World War II published as *Literatura i iskusstvo (q.v.)*; superseded by *Sovetskaya kul'tura* [Soviet Culture], July 4, 1953.

——, *See* "Bol'she vnimaniya..."; "Novaya sovetskaya opera..."; "Prekrasnye traditsii"; "Puti sovetskoi operetty"; [*Soyuz Sovetskikh Kompozitorov*]; "Velikaya sila sovetskovo iskusstva" in Section I.

Sovetskoye iskusstvo [Soviet Art], M., mo., Vols. I-V, No. 8, 1925 - August 1929. [DLC: Vols. II (inc.)-IV; NN: Vols. II, Nos. 1, 3-7, III, Nos. 1-8, IV, Nos. 1-7]
Organ of VOKS (All-Union Organization for Cultural Ties with Foreign Countries). Title varies: *Music; Musical Chronicle.*

Soviet Music Chronicle, M., mo., 1944-1946, No. 8-?. [DLC: 1944, Nos. 8-11, 1945, Nos. 1, 3-8, 10-12, 1944, Nos. 1-2, 5-8]
Organ of VOKS. Title varies: *Music; Musical Chronicle.*

Sovremennaya muzyka [Contemporary Music], M., irr. mo., Nos. 1-32, April 1924 - March 1929. [NN]
Journal of *Assotsiatsiya sovremennoi muzyki pri Rossiiskoi Akademii Khudozhestvennykh Nauk* [Association of Contemporary Music of the All-Russian Academy of Art Sciences], ed. by Viktor M. Belyayev, Vladimir V. Derzhanovski and Leonid L. Sabaneyev.

Za proletarskuyu muzyku [For Proletarian Music], M., biwk., 1930 - March 1932. [NN: 1931, January, October-December, Nos. 1, 20-24, 1932, January-March, Nos. 1-5; NNC: inc.]
Organ of *Vserossiiskaya assotsiatsiya proletarskikh muzykantov* [All-Russian Association of Proletarian Musicians].

INDEX OF COMPOSERS AND COMPOSITIONS

Note: Names and bibliographical references for a number of composers not mentioned in the text or annexes (and consequently not listed here) will be found in the bibliography. See, for example, Bernandt, G.B., comp., *Sovetskiye kompozitory....*

A. Composers of Prerevolutionary Russia and the U.S.S.R., and Russian-born composers living abroad

---

*Zhukovs'kyi's first initial will sometimes be found in Soviet sources as Ye.

B. Western Composers

GENERAL INDEX